SPELLCASTERS

SPELLCASTERS

MARKED BY MAGIC™
BOOK ONE

RIVER TATUM

MICHAEL ANDERLE

DON'T MISS OUR NEW RELEASES

Join the Florid Romance email list to be notified of new releases and special promotions (which happen often) by following this link:

https://floridromance.lmbpn.com/about/sign-up-for-our-newsletter/

Published by Florid Romance
an imprint of LMBPN Publishing
2375 E. Tropicana Avenue, Suite 8-305
Las Vegas, Nevada 89119 USA

Version 1.00, September 2025
eBook ISBN: 979-8-89354-939-3
Print ISBN: 979-8-89354-940-9

ONE

MISHAP 101

Alysia exhaled slowly as she swept a trembling hand through the wax drippings pooled on the marble floor, her heart thrumming with an anticipation she could not deny. The Hall of Echoes was nearly silent at this late hour. The only sounds came from the soft sputter of blue-tipped memory candles that illuminated the hidden alcoves of the library wing. Their glow triggered old rumors that each candle held an echo of a past spell or the presence of the caster's lingering will. Whether that legend was true or not, she found it difficult to ignore the sense of watchful silence lingering on every polished surface.

She could not afford fear tonight. One more misstep in her charm studies and the head instructors would shuffle her off to the Remedial Finesse Lab. And the Lab was a death sentence. Not just for her future, but for her family's name. Another Thorne failing. Her mother's memory deserved better.

Pausing in her preparations, Alysia glanced at the nearest row of shelves. The books seemed to watch her as well; courtesy of illusions cast centuries ago by students who specialized in ocular wards. Tiny motes of light traced the spines, or so she imagined. Countless volumes filled this restricted wing, collectively named the Hall of Echoes for its storied history of magical experimentation. According to whispered lore, the stones remembered every incantation performed here. Those lingering energies thrummed in the floor beneath her knees and slid across the columns in faint, shimmering ribbons that only the keenest eyes could catch.

She had chosen this spot behind a towering stack of archaic texts so no patrolling librarian or late-night insomniac could stumble upon her. Velgrace Academy frowned upon unsupervised practices in advanced charm magic, especially at night when wards across campus were set to minimum coverage. Yet no professor had offered her special guidance when she'd timidly inquired about Level Six incantations, which was the threshold where magic no longer just enchanted objects, but altered the very resonance between them.

Mastering that threshold of complexity required an official license or a recommendation from a senior instructor. Her empty pockets owned neither. She had nothing but determination and an illicitly borrowed runic manual.

She stroked the chalk pattern on the marble, making certain the lines remained unbroken. The glyph was a tight spiral design with a half-moon crest. She had scoured half the library for references until she stumbled on a worn side volume containing diagrams for a Reinforcement Summon. Summon was too strong a word, the text had said. The incantation would harness an external spark of magical energy and temporarily bond it with her own. With luck, she could replicate the effect in front of the examiners next week and impress them enough to let her skip remedial labs. That was the hope.

A drip of melted wax slid perilously close to her drawn circle. Her breath caught as she inched a piece of cloth forward to mop the molten candle remains before it touched the chalk line. If the perimeter of the glyph was ruined, the entire incantation might fail. Worse, an imperfect circle could invite unknown magical consequences—like illusions, wards, or something not yet documented. She repressed a shiver, recalling cautionary tales of illusions running wild and wards turning on their casters at the slightest flinch.

With careful precision, she placed four memory candles around the circle's edge, tapping them once to spark a faint, intangible essence. Then she gently reached for the worn manual. Its binding barely held together, forcing her to treat each page like fragile glass. She turned to the relevant crumbly parchment, scanning the lines under her breath: incantation, a recommended stance, the final sigil flourish. She repeated the words until they no longer stumbled off her tongue.

The quiet of the Hall of Echoes played with her awareness. A brush of cold air near her shoulder nearly made her leap. This wing was known for strange drafts, yet she could not banish the sense that something reached out to watch her. She steadied herself. She had come here for solitude and secrecy. No warden or library official would look kindly on an undertrained student dabbling with a Level Six incantation, especially not one as tenuous as a Reinforcement Summon. But she had no choice. Time was short, and desperation had already carried her this far.

Taking position just inside the chalk ring, Alysia inhaled the aroma of dust, candle wax, and old ink. She angled her right hand above the central glyph. A familiar ache spread through her fingers, a phantom pain that always came when she touched the edges of powerful magic. It felt less like a warning and more like an echo, as if the runes recognized a hollow space inside her they longed to fill.

The manual had stressed the importance of a calm mind, something she rarely possessed when stress gnawed her to the bone.

"Focus," she whispered, then closed her eyes to summon an image of her best intentions: passing the exam, raising her family's standing, fulfilling the promise she had once made to herself by the cliffs to never settle for mediocrity. With each exhale, she steadied her heart. When her eyes reopened, the circle's edges glimmered with a sheen the color of bruised twilight, humming with a low, dissonant chord that vibrated through the marble floor.

She broke into a shy, relieved smile. It was working. At least, so far.

In a soft voice, she chanted the runic phrases.

"Administra...viribus...exaudite..."

The words felt awkward on her tongue, as if they belonged to an older tradition that Velgrace rarely taught in normal classes. She pressed forward, ignoring the goosebumps rising along her arms. The candle flames danced higher, stretching in delicate arcs until the blue tips brightened, casting wandering shadows across the ancient stone shelves. Beneath her boots, she swore the floor shifted. Energy rippled outward from the center of the circle. She gripped the worn manual with her trembling left hand, pulse roaring in her ears.

An odd silence fell over her, so absolute that she heard her own breathing more than anything else. The corners of the library turned hazy, as if the entire Hall of Echoes shrank to the size of the summoning circle. Then a faint hum rose from the chalk lines.

She repeated the last line of the incantation.

Nothing happened for a moment. The lines sputtered as if uncertain. A spark jittered at the edge of the circle. Her mind raced. Had she twisted the second glyph incorrectly? Sweat formed along her hairline. She cursed softly under her breath, feeling the second wave of tension coil around her spine.

Then the circle's violet glow collapsed inward, followed by a thunderous crack, like glass shattering in reverse. The memory candles dimmed all at once, suffocating the wing in near-darkness. Raw energy streaked through the air in a bright flash she could not shield her eyes from in time.

A harsh gust flung open a row of library windows at the far end, sending manuscripts flying in a flurry of parchment. Shelves rocked precariously. A few tomes slid from their resting places and crashed to the floor. The acrid scent of singed pages crept through the gloom. Alysia cried out, staggering as the entire room rattled. She raised her arms over her face to shield herself from whatever force emanated from the circle.

Everything exploded in a burst of violet light. For an instant, she felt weightless, or possibly caught in an unmoored dream. Her vision swam. She stumbled backward, nearly tripping on a pile of fallen books. Behind her, a towering shelf toppled with a deafening crash, scattering old volumes across the floor. Sparks flew around her surging circle, this time laced with the crackle of discharge.

When her breathing finally caught up with the shock, she eased her arms down. Her eyes adjusted, blinking furiously. Several memory candles had blown out, leaving only smoky wisps where they once stood. The chalk circle was half-smudged, though the center still retained a faint glow like embers on the brink of dying. Her ears rang from the violent pulse that had rippled through the library.

Then she saw him.

He lay sprawled in the soot-stained ring, face partially obscured by a cloud of dust. A teenage boy, maybe close to her age, though it was hard to be sure from the angle of his collapsed form. His hair was dark, cut close on the sides but longer toward the front. The strangest part was his attire, not the structured uniform of a Velgrace student. He wore a practical shirt in a charcoal hue and a pair of well-worn trousers tucked into scuffed boots. The left sleeve was torn near the cuff. Nothing about him suggested a typical Academy presence.

Her heart hammered so loudly she barely remembered how to breathe. She blinked once, then again, to confirm he was real. This was impossible. The Reinforcement Summon was meant to harness a stray spark of energy, not conjure a living, breathing person from thin air. The manual had been explicit: an echo, a presence, an illusion. Not flesh and bone.

She crawled closer, ignoring the debris and dust. She had to see if he was breathing.

"A-are you..." She swallowed, her voice echoing unnaturally in the devastated library wing. "Can you hear me?"

He did not respond. A small tuft of dust fluttered off his shirt with each shallow inhale. She checked his neck for a pulse. Warmth met her fingertips. Relief flooded her, though confusion threaded her thoughts. Did she truly summon him? Or was this some bizarre byproduct of a miscast incantation? She fumbled for the old manual, flipping pages to see if there had been any mention of a living form that might transpire. Scanning the cramped lines of text, she saw references to "external energies," to "void-fused illusions," but no direct mention of a person, physically manifested.

A deep unease pressed into her. The soot around him was tinted violet, a marking that sizzled faintly with left-over magic. Her circle had clearly drawn power from somewhere, but from where, or whom?

A dusty cough escaped his lips. His body tensed, and a tremor rippled through his lean frame. Then he fell still once more. She peered at the faint lines of his face, angled cheekbones, the edges of long lashes resting against his cheeks. He certainly seemed older than the younger students at Velgrace, though not by much. The way tension wrapped his fists suggested someone who had known conflict. A trickle of dread slipped through her. Conflict with who? Where had he come from?

A haunted silence remained for several heartbeats. Then the overhead lanterns, which the violet shock wave had snuffed out, sputtered back to lazy life. Their glow fell in wavering circles across the scattered shelves, revealing the full scope of the accident. A worn row of tomes had collapsed behind them, covering the floor in jumbled knowledge from arcane treatises to bestiaries. Broken quills and ink bottles lay smashed, their contents forming dark puddles. The scene felt utterly alien.

Alysia pressed her quivering lips together, trying to gather her courage. She knew she had to do something. She couldn't leave this stranger unconscious on the library floor, but carrying him to the infirmary demanded a story she didn't have. If she admitted she'd been tampering with an advanced incantation in a restricted wing, the consequences would be devastating.

Still, guilt gnawed at her. He looked so vulnerable. The dust settled across his prone figure, every slow breath giving impetus to her sense of responsibility. She had brought him here, after all. Though the how of it remained a mystery.

At last, Alysia placed a careful hand on his shoulder. "Please," she repeated, more urgency in her tone. Leaving him might protect her from immediate suspicion, but it felt wrong in every possible way. She inhaled slowly, fighting tears of frustration. The night's tension and her own fear of failure weighed heavily on her mind.

After another long moment, something in him stirred again. His eyelids fluttered, a shadow crossing his brow, as though he dreamt of something he could not yet name. The library lanterns cast a wavering silhouette across his features, pale but resolute. The sight tugged at Alysia's heart. She might not have known who he was, but she wanted answers and a chance to fix whatever mistake she had made.

Outside, the wind buffeted the open windows, sending a shrill whistle through the cracks in the ancient stone. She steadied her breathing. If the guards or librarians noticed that this section was in chaos, they would come.

The time to act was now. She had never felt more unprepared.

With one last fearful glance at the worn incantation manual, she slid it into her leather satchel. Then she let out a gasp when the unconscious figure's arm twitched, pressing closer to the library floor. Violet sparks rattled, dying out in a final fizz of energy around the circle's center. Her heartbeat pounded at the base of her throat, and she leaned in, voice tight but gentle.

"Wake up," she whispered. "I need to know who—who you are."

He did not answer. He remained still, breathing in shallow puffs. Alysia had no illusions. Tonight's mishap had changed everything. She stared at him, half-terrified of what came next, half-willing him to open his eyes. She was no longer alone in the Hall of Echoes. That single fact pounded through her mind. And if he survive, if he woke, he would have questions. So would she. But for now, in the dusty wrecked library, the only words that formed in her mind were the solemn truth: a stranger had appeared in her miscast circle, and nothing would ever be the same.

CHAPTER

TWO

MEET THE DISASTER

Alysia scrambled backward as the body on the floor began to stir. The boy—no, not quite a boy, she realized, but certainly no older than she—he braced himself on his elbows and groaned, pushing to his knees. A slight breeze wafted in from the open windows, carrying the damp scent of the Sea of Echoes.

His eyes opened. Steel-gray in color, startling and bright, they swept the wreckage of the library's alcove before settling on her. For an instant, neither spoke.

He inhaled a sharp breath and wobbled to his feet, unsteady as he clutched a tilted bookcase for support. For a split second, before the confidence settled over him, Alysia saw it. A hint of raw disorientation in his steel-gray eyes, a shadow of pain that he blinked away almost instantly. He seemed to be putting a mask in place, piece by piece.

In the quiet, the faint squeak of his boots against the polished marble echoed off the tall shelves. A raven lock of

11

hair fell over his forehead as he brushed it aside with agile fingers. Then, with a half-smirk that seemed entirely out of place in the chaos, he spoke.

"Well," he said, his tone dry. "That was dramatic. Is this how Velgrace greets all its visitors?"

Alysia's mind blanked for a moment. He should not know the name of the Academy, and he definitely should not have awakened so casually from a conjuring that no text ever said would pull in a living person. Yet here he stood, whole and apparently uninjured. She tried to swallow her confusion and form a coherent sentence. "I...uh..Velgrace doesn't... You're not supposed to be here," she finally managed.

He gave a lazy shrug, then glanced around as if unconcerned that he had just crashed through a summoning glyph. "I suppose I'm not," he murmured. The accent in his voice struck her as strange, archaic yet precise, shaped by a syntax she recognized from older manuscripts. Most students at the Academy did not speak like that.

Steeling her spine, Alysia tried to regain control of the situation. She snatched up the worn runic manual, pages dangerously bent from the collision. Her entire plan had been to practice a Level Six incantation in secret, just enough to harness a temporary surge of external power for her upcoming exam. Summoning a person, especially one who obviously understood magic, was never part of the instructions. Even if it had been, the text offered no mention of conjuring a living, breathing individual.

"I can fix this," she murmured. "There's a reversal phrase." She located a line of runic text and forced her voice steady. "Okay, stand still. I'm going to send you back or… or unravel the spell. Something."

He glanced over, his eyes amused. "Send me back?"

"That's the idea," she snapped. "Unless you want to remain an unlicensed

presence in the Hall of Echoes. That's a serious offense."

"Is it?" he asked, not sounding particularly worried. He leaned casually against the bookshelf, crossing his arms over a shirt that looked distinctly non-Academy in style, charcoal-gray, well-worn, with faint rips near one shoulder. "By all means, continue."

She gritted her teeth and read the reversal incantation under her breath. The words felt clunky and ill-fitting, as though the vowels stuck in the wrong places. Still, she managed to speak to them in one continuous attempt. Faint magic rose from her, then fizzled in the musty air before dying away.

The stranger cocked his head. "That's not correct."

With a flush of frustration, she scowled up at him. "Excuse me?"

He uncrossed his arms, took a step forward, and tapped the page in her manual.

The book's fragile spine threatened to crinkle under his touch. "See here," he said, pointing at one of the runic glyphs that spiraled across the text. "You're closing the resonance on the final syllable," he said, his voice maddeningly calm.

"It needs to taper, not snap shut. You're commanding

the energy to disperse instead of inviting it to unravel. This kind of magic doesn't obey orders."

She recoiled in disbelief. His nonchalant tone stripped away any attempt she had at maintaining authority. Speechless, she began again, chanting the runic words with a slight adjustment to the middle vowel. Yet the magic's aura sputtered out again, leaving behind only static tension in the air. No swirl, no flash. Her attempt was a hopeless failure.

"Perhaps you should—"

"You do not get to correct me!" she hissed, shutting the book with a trembling hand. "I don't even know your name."

He paused. "Kael." A faint smile touched his lips, both confident and guarded.

"Kael Meridan."

Alysia's eyes narrowed. The name Meridan teased her memory, but she had no time to investigate the thought. Her panic skyrocketed when footsteps and voices echoed at the far end of the library. The clamor of scattered books and the unmistakable dull glow of a staff's crystal tip signaled the approach of faculty members or, worse, security wardens.

She placed a finger to her lips, mouthing a frantic "Quiet." Kael simply raised an eyebrow, unperturbed by the possibility of getting caught.

Within moments, Headmistress Imara Quen appeared with two librarians who carried half-lit orbs. The Headmistress stood tall in subdued slate-blue robes embroidered with subtle lines of gold that gleamed when her magic stirred. Her gaze found Alysia kneeling near the chalk circle's remains, and then she noticed Kael leaning on the toppled shelf. The look in her eyes changed to alarm.

"Alysia Thorne," Quen said, her normally calm voice taut with disapproval.

"Explain what happened here." The two librarians behind her lifted their orbs to cast more light on the chaos. Fragments of singed parchment, scattered volumes, and upended stands all surrounded them. A choir of dust motes spiraled in the lamplight.

Alysia's face heated. She tried to stand but found her knees unwilling to steady. "Headmistress, I... I was practicing a containment incantation from an older reference. It—"

"She was trying to cast a Level Six Reinforcement Summon," Kael supplied almost cheerfully. "But the circle seems to have collapsed in on itself. Unstable wards, I suspect."

Quen's stern gaze shifted to him. "And you are?"

He straightened, dipping into a slight bow. "Kael Meridan, visiting scholar. Pleased to meet you, Headmistress." He said her title with unnerving ease. Where Alysia stammered to find each word, Kael spoke with the confidence of someone who clearly believed he belonged.

The librarians exchanged looks of confusion, while Quen narrowed her eyes. A flare of magic glinted on her fingertips. "Visiting scholar? We were not notified of any such arrival."

Kael spread his hands. "I apologize if the formalities

were overlooked." His accent, antique and refined, rolled so smoothly off his tongue that it nearly calmed the tension in the air. "However, I believe your Founding Rite states that any caster demonstrating sanctioned speech and active charm is to be heard before forced removal."

The Founding Rite. Alysia had read about the sacred vow that was tied to the Academy's own foundational wards. To break it was to invite magical decay into the very stones of Velgrace. No Headmistress would risk that. He was reciting it from memory.

"Sanctioned speech?" Quen repeated. Her posture remained taut, but Alysia saw the subtle hint of curiosity in her eyes. "Prove it."

Kael did not hesitate. He closed his eyes. Soft, lyrical syllables flowed from his mouth in a dialect so archaic that Alysia only grasped fragments. The faint glow of illusions curled through the air, weaving shimmering patterns above his open palms. They spun, weaving ephemeral shapes that layered themselves into the shape of Velgrace's crest, a sigil that represented the Academy's earliest founders.

The librarians inhaled sharply. Alysia felt an odd pulse vibrate in her own chest, as though her wards recognized the signature of older magic. There was no question now. Kael commanded an illusion style with an ancient, official stamp. And by the Academy's oldest laws, that entitled him to safe haven.

At that realization, Quen's sternness shifted to measured acceptance. "Meridan, you said," the Headmistress repeated, her voice carefully neutral, but Alysia saw a spark of something in her eyes—not recognition, precisely, but a deep, old suspicion, as if she were hearing a name long thought buried.

"I cannot verify your lineage or your introduction, but the Rite remains. Our Academy's founders mandated courtesy to any mage wielding recognized illusions. For the moment, you have my attention."

Alysia blinked, her confusion mounting by the second. How had he learned that? Why was he so well-versed in archaic illusions?

Quen's critical stare landed on her again. "Alysia, you obviously initiated a spell beyond your clearance. There will be disciplinary consequences, but focusing on that can wait until I'm certain we are not in immediate danger." She motioned the librarians to disperse. "Summon the night watch. Let's confirm there's no larger threat hidden in the Hall of Echoes."

"Yes, Headmistress," they murmured, stepping carefully over toppled books to exit. Their orbs bobbed ghost-like through the darkness until they disappeared around a corner, leaving only Quen, Kael, and Alysia in the circle's wreckage.

Kael shifted from foot to foot. "I promise I mean no harm." His expression softened, lacking the earlier cocky edge. "My arrival was... unexpected." He offered Alysia a single, pointed glance. She felt her cheeks burn, but she could not parse whether her emotions were due to embarrassment or residual adrenaline.

Quen did not respond immediately. The slightest crease appeared between her brows, and Alysia realized the Headmistress was analyzing Kael's aura, testing for signs of deception. Quen's inherent skill lay in reading magical signatures. If Kael hid something monstrous, she would sense hostility or corruption.

At length, Quen exhaled, though wariness still lined her face. "You are not an immediate threat." Her words carried a grudging acceptance. Then, in a voice brimming with authority, she spoke the tradition known to all senior staff.

"Hospitality must be granted to any bearer of sanctioned speech and active charm."

Something in Alysia's mind reeled. The line was as old as Velgrace itself, rarely used in modern times. It outranked the usual protocols. She remembered reading a footnote about it. Once invoked, the Academy must offer lodging, resources, and basic protections until the visitor's identity was confirmed or proven false. Breaking that vow would defy the earliest laws set by Velgrace's founders.

Kael bowed his head in gratitude. The faint glimmer of illusions around him vanished, leaving no sign of the vibrant crest he had conjured. Alysia stared at him, part of her wishing for a chance to speak privately, to demand an explanation for how he came through her circle. She could practically hear the voices of ancient instructors scolding her rashness.

Headmistress Quen turned to Alysia with an air of finality. "Since you initiated this mishap, it falls on you to remedy it. You will supervise this... visiting scholar until further notice. You have a spare bunk in your dorm, I trust?"

Alysia's stomach lurched. "Spare bunk? Headmistress, I—"

"I will not debate this," Quen said curtly. "You invited him, whether intentionally or not. The Rite demands hospitality, and you shall ensure his compliance with Academy rules. If there is any further disruption, I will hold you personally accountable. Understood, Miss Thorne?"

She dipped her head, blood pounding in her ears. This had to be a nightmare. "Understood," she forced out.

"Very well." Quen offered one more cool glance at Kael, her disposition betraying a hint of annoyance. "Report to me tomorrow morning in my office for a full debrief. No exceptions." Then she pivoted on her heel and strode away, presumably to dismiss the night watch and quell any rumors of intruders. Her footsteps faded, and soon, silence enveloped them again.

Alysia's mouth felt painfully dry. She slowly closed the runic manual, trying not to damage it further. Shattered fragments of chalk and wax stuck to her palms.

"So," she began, half to herself and half to Kael. "You're... assigned to me."

He chuckled lightly, not unkindly. "I suppose so. Think of me as your new study partner, though I'm not certain that's how your Headmistress intended it." His grin turned wry.

She pulled in a shaky breath, uncertain whether to apologize or demand answers. Everything about this was too sudden. "Stop smiling like that," she blurted, setting the manual aside. "And pick up some of these books. We can't leave the Hall of Echoes looking like a war zone."

He obliged with an amused shrug, bending to gather scattered volumes. His dark hair fell forward again, casting shadows across his angular features. In the stillness, Alysia noticed a faint power in the air around him, reminiscent of the illusions he conjured earlier.

She swallowed a rush of nerves. "Kael, was it? You claim to be a scholar, but your illusions. No one uses that archaic dialect. Where did you learn it?"

He stacked the books neatly in his arms, then regarded her with an unreadable expression. "Let's just say my family taught me a few things. And you? You're quite the risk-taker for a mere student." The way he said mere held more curiosity than insult. "Practicing Level Six incantations in secret?"

Her shoulders tensed. "That's none of your business."

He inclined his head, conceding the point. "Perhaps not."

Fresh guilt rippled through her. For all her caution in the summoning, her circle had obviously malfunctioned. She had no illusions about how the faculty would react once the dust settled. Expulsion or remedial labs felt inevitable. But at the moment, the bigger shock was the arrival of Kael himself. She didn't even know if he was telling the truth about his name, let alone the rest of his story. Still, the Headmistress had effectively placed him under her responsibility. Now, she had to watch his every move to ensure he didn't plunge Velgrace further into chaos.

Once they returned the worst of the scattered books to the worn shelf, Kael brushed off his hands. The candlelight played across his features, highlighting the faint lines of weariness beneath his eyes. However self-assured he seemed, he looked as though traveling between realms, if that was what happened, took its toll.

Alysia shifted her weight, feeling the scuff of dust against her boots. "All right," she said quietly, trying to muster some authority. "We're done here. We need to get out before the librarians change their minds or some guard decides to question you more thoroughly. My dorm is in Aurum Spire, top level." She paused, scanning the library's perimeter for any watchers. "Follow me, but do it quietly."

Kael's eyes glimmered with silent amusement before he nodded. Without further argument, he fell into step a few paces behind her. They slipped away from the scene, leaving the Hall of Echoes with half-extinguished candles and scattered debris. Alysia led him through shadowed corridors, heart pounding faster than she cared to admit, until they reached the tower stairs that spiraled toward the dormitories.

She couldn't think too hard about the repercussions. With each footstep, she braced herself for someone to leap out and demand an explanation. Nobody did. At least, not yet. The Academy's wards seemed subdued, as though recovering from the summoning's violent shock. The scuff of Kael's boots echoing behind her reminded her of the impossibility of the situation. She convinced herself to focus on placing one foot in front of the other. This needed to be sorted out in the morning, under the Headmistress's scrutiny. In the meantime, all she could do was carry out the Founding Rite's conditions.

When they entered the quieter hall leading to Alysia's dorm, Kael exhaled softly. "Cozy," he commented, glancing at the heavy wooden doors and the narrow windows that overlooked the moonlit sea. She suppressed the urge to glare, feeling a twist in her chest that mingled apprehension with an odd tinge of curiosity. For all the chaos of the night, she felt an undercurrent that she couldn't name.

She stopped at her door, pressing her palm against a small warding glyph etched near the handle. Blue light shimmered for a moment, then dissolved to allow entry. With a quiet click, she opened the door, stepping inside. Kael followed, taking in her cramped yet organized space. Books stacked on the desk, a single bed, and an empty cot in the corner reserved for extra linens.

He placed his hands on his hips, scanning the plain walls. The leftover tension made the silence almost painful. Alysia drew a slow breath, reminding herself that, by morning, the entire faculty would have opinions on this fiasco. She mentally braced for whatever storm brewed next. Right now, at least, she had to follow protocol. The Headmistress's words hovered in her mind, echoing with finality.

"Hospitality must be granted to any bearer of sanctioned speech and active charm."

And just like that, Kael was assigned to Alysia's supervision.

THREE

UNWELCOME GUEST

Alysia pressed her back against the narrow door of her dorm, trying to still the hammering of her heart. Across the tiny room, Kael perched on the corner of her desk, unbothered by the cramped space that barely contained him. He looked aggravatingly at ease there, one ankle hooked over the other. His attention drifted from the scattered runic texts on her shelf to the modest bunk in the corner, as if he intended to map every inch of her private space. She hated how easily he fit in, how he seemed to claim the territory without regard for her mounting anxiety.

He raised an eyebrow when she failed to speak. "Not the friendliest welcome," he remarked. "Should I scoot over so you can come inside, or do you plan to stare at me from the threshold all night?"

She exhaled sharply and stepped forward, letting the door click shut behind her. The ocean wind thrummed against her window, carrying the brine of the Sea of

Echoes. She often found that scent comforting, but today it set her nerves on edge. She would have no peace until she figured out what she had truly summoned.

"I do not plan to keep you here longer than necessary," she said, attempting a firm tone. "But the Headmistress insisted, so...make yourself at home, I guess." The words felt awkward, especially since this was her refuge, now invaded by a boy who arrived under the strangest circumstances imaginable.

Kael's lips curved in a grin. "Oh, trust me, I already am quite comfortable."

Alysia stalked across the floor and brushed aside a stack of parchment on her desk. She tried to ignore how close he was. The desk had barely enough space for her notebooks, let alone a smirking "visiting scholar." Yet he seemed determined to cling there, arms folded, posture entirely languid, except for the fine tremor in his left hand, which he quickly stilled by pressing it against the desk's edge. Alysia caught the motion, a brief sign of strain before his mask of nonchalance was perfectly back in place.

She could imagine how scandalized the other students would be if they found him in such a casual pose in her room.

She inhaled through her nose and began collecting stray evidence of her late-night fiasco: chalk residue smeared on a rag, a half-burned memory candle, and the worn manual she had borrowed without permission. Each piece felt like an accusation. If a faculty member saw this evidence, she might be summoned to an immediate disciplinary hearing.

"You look like you are sweeping up a crime scene," Kael observed. His eyes gleamed with curiosity. "Hiding something?"

"Obviously," she said under her breath, pressing the rag to a stubborn patch of chalk on the floor. She did not want to broadcast how dangerous her unsuccessful incantation was, nor how close she had come to losing control of the wards in the Hall of Echoes. Worst of all, she had no idea how she managed to yank Kael across realms, if that was even what happened. Velgrace had no standard procedure for dealing with random conjured classmates. "You could help," she muttered, glaring up at him.

He shrugged as if to say that cleaning was beneath him. Then he scooted a bit aside, revealing a scrap of parchment with runic scrawls. The same lines she had chanted the night before. His expression shifted, a shadow of something dark and ancient in his eyes as he stared at a specific spiral. He looked less at a spell and more at a cage. A wave of chills coursed through her as she remembered the glow of the circle, the crash of magic, and his unconscious form sprawled on the marble floor.

She snatched the parchment, shoving it into a desk drawer. "You should not just sit there," she insisted, her voice rising with her frustration. "At least pretend you are concerned about how this looks."

"Concerned?" Kael tilted his head, letting a stray lock of dark hair fall across his face. "Are you worried about your suitemates? Or about the entire academy gawking at the fact that I am here under your supervision?"

"I am worried," Alysia said, gritting her teeth,

"Because everyone is staring. You found a way to make them stare harder by being so cavalier the moment you walked into the dining hall this morning. Do you realize how suspicious you look?"

He touched the coral amulet resting against his shirt. "Suspicious is preferable to helpless," he said softly. "But you need not fret about me. I already charmed two of your suitemates in the hallway. They seem quite enthralled by my stories of lesser-known academies."

Alysia felt her mouth fall open. She had glimpsed him earlier, speaking with Celeste and Daro, neighbors from across the hall, who were known to gossip. Apparently, he had spun them a yarn about traveling the continent to study illusions in remote hamlets. She had heard snatches of it as she walked up, along with squeals of fascination from Celeste. It all sounded ridiculous. So many improbable mentions of lost spell circuits and "ancient roads that shimmered under a double moon." Yet the suitemates devoured every word.

"Charm is craft cloaked in courtesy," Kael quoted, tracing the words on her desk with a fingertip. "Another motto from Velgrace, right? The original, if I recall."

Her spine tensed. That was indeed the oldest creed taught to incoming first-years, though modern instructors rarely emphasized the phrase. Hearing him speak it with such casual fluency stirred an uncomfortable sense of recognition. "Yes, that is our oldest official saying," she answered. "Where did you learn it?"

He lifted one shoulder. "I read. I have my sources." His

lips quirked at the edges, revealing that half-smirk she was quickly growing to despise.

She studied him carefully. It was not unusual for a learned sorcerer to know Velgrace's motto. Yet his accent, the intricate illusions he had displayed in the Hall of Echoes, and his knowledge of archaic runes all hinted at something deeper. The question that loomed in her mind was simple but daunting: who exactly was Kael Meridan?

Turning away, she forced herself to focus on stashing anything that hinted at illicit spellcasting. She reached under her bed, retrieving an empty satchel that she hoped to fill with the runic manual and leftover chalk supplies. When she tried to push the worn manual inside, Kael's voice broke the silence.

"You still have that," he said, glancing down at the manual's cracked spine. The sight of it appeared to amuse him, judging by the curve of his mouth.

"Of course I do. I do not want the librarians to connect it to me." She shoved the manual deeper into the satchel and tied it off with trembling fingers. "As far as they know, it is still on the shelf. I cannot afford to be caught with advanced incantation references."

Kael slid off the desk and took a careful step toward her. "And you are certain that is the book that summoned me? Sometimes, illusions and wards merge unpredictably. Are you sure there was not another factor?"

She clamped her jaw. Truthfully, no. She was not certain. The incantation had been a lesser-known Reinforcement Summon, meant to draw an external spark of energy for personal augmentation, not a living, breathing mage. But she had little else to blame for that disastrous arrival. The ancient manual had been the only reference she used. If something else triggered the event, she did not know what it was.

She stood, dusting the chalk from her palms onto the rag. Kael's nearness prompted an unsettling flutter in her chest. She stepped sideways to create a bit of space, pretending she needed to organize the top of her trunk. Her eyes snapped to the door, then to the single window overlooking the courtyard. She had half a mind to fling the window open and let the wind carry away her worries.

Kael's voice pulled her focus back. "You are quiet. Nervous about the professors?"

She brushed her hair from her face and forced herself to remain calm. "Yes," she admitted. "They keep shooting me sideways glances everywhere I go. Some are bound to question how you arrived here. There is no official record of your enrollment until last night, when the Headmistress declared you a visiting scholar. And you do not even pretend to keep a low profile. You march around the halls, reciting obscure illusions and rewriting my carefully concocted excuses."

"If I walked around meekly, they would suspect I was hiding something," he countered. He took another step toward her, close enough now for her to sense a faint current of magic pulsing in the air around him. It prickled against her arms, raising goosebumps. "Besides, no one truly believes you. Not the story you gave them, not your forced version of how I got here. They know you are covering up the details."

She swallowed, blinking at him. He was far too direct. "You could have helped reinforce my version," she said, her voice low. "I told them you were invited for a short demonstration exchange. But you told them you came at Velgrace's request, that you have old ties here. Why say that?"

"Some ties aren't chosen," he replied, his gaze distant. "They're inherited. Like a debt."

His vagueness set her teeth on edge. She dared to look him in the eye. In the gentle candlelight she had kindled for the evening, his irises gleamed storm-gray, recalling the tempests that periodically pounded the cliffs. Those eyes seemed to hold secrets. She realized, with some discomfort, that he did not wear a typical Velgrace uniform. He wore his own tunic, belted at the waist, dark in color, practical for traveling or for blending in somewhere else. It gave him a displaced appearance, like he was caught between worlds yet belonged nowhere fully.

The thought that he might be as unsettled as she felt offered little consolation.

She cleared her throat. "You mentioned you recognized the older illusions in the Hall of Echoes. Velgrace has a complete registry of past illusions, including the signature of every graduate or expelled student. For centuries, the Academy has kept a magical record. That is standard procedure."

He nodded. "I am aware. They track frequencies, aura patterns, and so on."

She hesitated, then pressed on. "Your magic. It feels... oddly familiar. That is what another professor hinted to me this morning, something about your magic resonating with a sealed archive." She frowned. "If the Academy has not given you a pass before, how could you have a signature in the archive?"

He met her gaze, and the smirk was entirely gone, replaced by a chilling stillness. "Maybe," he said, his voice barely a whisper, "it's not my signature in that archive. Maybe it's my cage."

FOUR

CHARMS CLASS SHOWDOWN

Alysia woke with her pulse already racing. Morning light threaded through the narrow dorm window, illuminating her scattered pages of runic notes. This was supposed to be an ordinary day, just another Charms class. Yet dread bobbed heavily in her gut.

Headmistress Quen's instructions were fresh in her mind: keep Kael out of trouble, do not let him break any Academy rules, and definitely avoid more magical disasters.

She slung her satchel over her shoulder. On instinct, she patted the small silver bracelet etched with the Thorne sigil, the cherished keepsake from her grandmother. The metal felt cool against her fingertips. Renewed resolve waved through her chest. She would handle whatever Charms class threw at her today. She was, after all, working to prove she was a capable student, not a reckless conjurer of uninvited guests.

Outside in the hallway, she nearly collided with Robin,

who juggled a stack of parchment and a half-eaten apple. Her cousin's short, tousled hair fell across her eyes, and the faint trace of an illusion glimmered around her fingertips.

"Easy," Robin said, pressing the apple into Alysia's free hand. "You look like you need breakfast more than I do. Here, take it."

Alysia brightened slightly. "Thanks. I skipped dinner last night."

"Really? Didn't see you at the dining hall. Did you hide away in your dorm? You realize that Kael was teaching half the lounge how to conjure illusions of miniature dragons. The gossip is wild."

Alysia made a face. She had not even realized Kael left the dorm at some point.

"I was cleaning up my mess of notes," she fibbed, refusing to admit she was also trying not to be sucked into Kael's orbit again. "You know how it is."

Robin smirked. "I do. But watch out, people are going to ask questions about him. Everyone's curious. Including some professors."

Alysia exhaled. "Well, if they ask me, I will remind them that the Headmistress authorized him to be here. I cannot do much else." She took a bite of the apple, feeling the sweet-tart taste invigorate her. "I have Charms class. You?"

"Obscura Wing for illusions practice. Maybe I will pick up some real illusions from that traveling 'scholar' your new friend." Robin wiggled her eyebrows mischievously. When Alysia scowled, Robin only gave a playful sigh. "I was kidding. Relax."

But Alysia could not relax, not when every step toward the Aurum Spire lecture hall churned her anxiety. She parted ways with Robin near a corridor lined with gilded sconces. The distinct hum of magical wards thrummed in the air, proof that advanced classes were in session. Hoping to be the first inside, Alysia hurried, her footsteps echoing in the stone hallway.

The wide lecture space for Charms class was already lit by bright orbs overhead. Rows of students' desks curved in a semicircle around an open demonstration floor. Tall, arched windows revealed a glimpse of the sea, whitecaps cresting beyond the cliffs. On any other day, the view might have soothed Alysia. Today, the cheerful sunshine only reminded her how unsettled she felt.

"Good morning, Miss Thorne," said her instructor, Professor Latham, from the front of the room. Professor Latham was a broad-shouldered man with meticulously combed hair and an ever-present glint of curiosity in his gaze. The brass emblem pinned to his robe displayed a single stylized swirl that symbolized the Founders' Trials, a method of combining students with distinct magical approaches in order to push their boundaries.

Alysia returned his greeting politely and took her usual seat near the front row. She expected her partner, Daro, to slide in next to her as always. He was a respectful, unhurried student with steady hands that balanced her sometimes over-precise style. They did fairly well in these sessions. While not best friends, they cooperated smoothly, never letting minor friction undermine their lessons.

One by one, classmates trickled in. Celeste, wearing a bright yellow sash, settled behind Alysia. Min, a timid second-year, busied himself with rummaging through a stack of borrowed wands. Daro finally ambled in, offering a small nod. He plopped down on the other side of the semicircle, scanning the front of the hall.

Odd, Alysia thought. He never changed seats unless told.

Professor Latham cleared his throat, calling the class to attention. The gentle buzz of chatter died into silence. "Today," he began, his voice ringing with enthusiasm, "we start the official selection process for your Final Charm Performance. This is a culminating project for advanced-level students, a chance to immerse yourselves in synergy and produce the highest form of collaborative enchantment."

Alysia glanced around. The final project was rumored to be a demonstration of layering complex wards with illusions, each pair expected to produce a new or specialized effect. She had expected to do precisely that with Daro over the next several weeks.

But something in Professor Latham's posture put her on edge. He was smiling with more vigor than usual, his eyes darting to the door at the side of the classroom. "Before we finalize partnerships, I would like to introduce someone," Latham said. "It appears we have a new exchange student who will be joining us for the remainder of the term."

The door creaked open. Kael Meridan stepped in, looking every bit too casual for an official academic space. He wore the Academy's uniform cloak parted at the front, revealing his own charcoal tunic underneath, and a leather cord around his neck from which the coral amulet hung. Subdued gasps and murmurs rippled through the rows of students.

Alysia felt her stomach dip, as if she had leaped off the highest tower. She gripped the edge of her desk, her eyes flicking to Daro. Daro's eyebrows shot upward in silent surprise, but he offered no explanation. This was apparently news to him as well.

"Kael Meridan," the professor continued grandly, "is a visiting apprentice from outside the standard enrollment. We have agreed upon a special arrangement so that he can participate in certain advanced Charms modules."

More whispers broke out. Celeste leaned forward, whispering just loud enough that Alysia could catch, "Is that the guy from Obscura Wing last night?" Another student muttered something about illusions. Alysia's pulse sped up. She expected trouble, but not this soon.

Kael offered a slight bow, looking nowhere near as anxious as Alysia felt. His gaze slid around the semicircle, pausing momentarily when it landed on her. He did not smile, but Alysia sensed a quiet amusement in his eyes. It was the same look he wore whenever he corrected her incantation or teased her about her scrupulous approach to magic.

"Welcome, Kael," the professor said. "I trust you are ready to meld illusions with standard charm-casting?"

Kael nodded politely. "Absolutely. Thank you for allowing me to join."

The professor clasped his hands. "I trust you and the rest of our class will learn from one another, especially with the upcoming Final Charm Performance. Now, speaking of that performance. The Founders once said, 'Velgrace endures by pairing opposites with purpose.' We carry that tradition by assigning partners with complementary and at times contrasting strengths. It fosters true synergy and spurs excellence in ways self-chosen pairs rarely achieve."

A nervous flutter coursed through Alysia's limbs. She could already sense something shifting in the air. She glanced at Daro again, hoping to see the professor direct him to her. Instead, Professor Latham beckoned Daro and Celeste to stand together at the center of the demonstration floor.

"Daro. Celeste. You will pair for the Final Charm Performance," he pronounced.

A shock of confusion rippled through Alysia. Her seat prickled. Did that mean she would be paired with Min? Or maybe they were rearranging the entire class. But the professor was not done.

"Min," the professor continued, calling the timid second-year, "you will work with Faris." Two more students stood, exchanging uneasy looks. Everyone seemed puzzled by this reshuffling.

Alysia's chest felt tight, dreading the moment she would hear her own name. Sure enough, Professor Latham's eyes roamed to her. "Alysia Thorne," he said, gesturing for her to join him at the front. Her legs felt like lead as she pushed to her feet. She clasped her cloak shut, determined to look composed. This can't be happening. She forced each step to remain steady.

"And Kael Meridan," the professor announced. "I am assigning you two."

Students gasped more openly now. Kael stepped onto the demonstration floor, adjusting the cuff of his cloak. A flash of challenge gleamed in his gray eyes. To everyone else in the room, he might have looked nonchalantly confident. Alysia felt it more like an intrusion, an unveiling of something she had hoped to keep confined to the secrecy of the dorm or fleeting corridor encounters.

"Sir," she began quietly, already feeling heat creep up her neck. She cleared her throat and tried again. "Professor Latham, might I request we keep the partners consistent with prior assignments? Daro and I have established synergy. Perhaps we—"

He cut her off gently with a raised hand. "Miss Thorne, synergy is exactly what I aim to cultivate, but from a different angle. You and Mr. Meridan possess distinct magical styles. You are a careful ward weaver. He is an illusionist who works with spontaneity. The Founders' Trials were built upon the concept of forging harmony from contrast."

Alysia remembered reading about the original Trials, infamous for pairing volatile illusionists with rigid ward weavers, often with explosive results. It was a tradition rooted in the belief that true power was born from friction.

Alysia opened her mouth to argue but stopped herself. Kael was hardly a typical student. He was half under probation, half unconfirmed in the official rosters. She had never seen him cast a standard charm, only illusions. Vague illusions, at that. He had admitted he had questionable lineage. This arrangement felt disastrous.

But Professor Latham looked at her kindly, as if sensing her hesitation. "The Final Charm Performance tests advanced synergy, yes. It also demands trust and adaptability. We will not keep you locked in the safe zone of prior partnerships. Instead, we push you to explore the outer edges of your capability. You could be unstoppable if you learn to blend your wards with illusions."

Kael murmured a soft, "Thank you, Professor," and turned that cool gaze on Alysia. A small, provoking grin tugged at his lips.

She swallowed. She had no way out. The entire class was watching. She ground her teeth, glimpsing the phrase inscribed above the hall: Velgrace endures by pairing opposites with purpose. Some old line leftover from the Academy's founding mages, a line she had recited in her first-year orientation but never believed would directly shape her own work.

"Very well," Alysia said, trying hard not to flinch. "If this is what the curriculum requires."

Her classmates' eyes oscillated between her and Kael, glimmering with excitement at the potential drama. A few, like Celeste, appeared openly thrilled to see those two forced to collaborate. Others, like Daro, seemed uneasy. He offered Alysia a small, apologetic smile from across the room.

Professor Latham nodded. "Excellent. Each pair will spend the next two weeks experimenting with synergy spells. You will present your final demonstration of advanced charm in front of the class and a panel of instructors. Embrace the creative possibilities." He clapped his hands as a signal for them to return to their seats. "Now, I expect the focus today will be on preliminary exercises. You have time to discuss with your partner how you will approach this project."

With that, the professor dismissed them to open discussion. The class erupted in a wave of chatter and desk shuffling. Alysia found herself standing awkwardly at the front, face hot, while Kael drifted closer. He parted from the professor's side, casual, self-assured, making a few illusions, fluttering shapes of gold wisp, vanish in his palm.

"Congratulations, partner," Kael said softly, his voice low so only she could hear. He flashed the grin again, the grin that suggested he found all of this amusing.

She set her jaw, ignoring the tightening of annoyance. "This is not my idea of a good time."

"Why not?" he asked, glancing at her hands, which she had balled into fists. "It might be fun. You practice your wards, I test illusions, and maybe we discover something worthwhile." His tone contained confidence that made the muscles in her neck taut.

Her heart pounded as she tried to maintain composure. "You have no idea what is at stake. I cannot afford any mistakes with this exam. And your illusions might be beyond the standard Academy approach."

He lifted one shoulder in a shrug. "Then teach me the standard approach. I am not here to sabotage you, Alysia."

She stiffened at the use of her name. She was used to hearing Miss Thorne or just Thorne from classmates. The way Kael said it triggered a flutter in her stomach that she did not want to acknowledge.

"Tch," she muttered, stepping away to gather her satchel from the front-row seat.

"We will figure something out. Let's not stand here giving the entire class a show.

They are already busy forming new gossip."

"Lead the way." He gestured gallantly, which annoyed her even more.

They chose a quiet corner near the tall windows. She busied herself by pretending to search her notes. The smell of salt wafted in on a stray breeze, reminding her of the windy dorm tower and Kael's intrusion into her daily life.

"All right," she began, forcibly calm. "We have two weeks to produce a demonstration. Typically, that involves weaving a multi-layer charm with a partner. One provides the base incantation, the other modifies it for advanced interaction. The synergy score depends on how smoothly we merge. That means no random illusions that blow up the classroom." She shot him a pointed look.

Kael watched her with brows raised. "I promise not to blow up anything without your permission." The teasing glint in his eyes burned her patience.

She inhaled a steady breath. "You do not have to joke. This is serious. If we fail, we risk setting ourselves back academically an entire year, or worse, we might both end up in remedial labs. Not to mention the rumor storm that will risel if your illusions run wild."

He folded his arms, leaning against the windowsill. "Understood. I can be serious when needed. Show me the incantation outlines. We can start with your recommended approach, then I can see where illusions fit."

She found herself momentarily speechless, surprised at his willingness to cooperate so directly. She slid her stack of notes from a side pocket in her satchel, careful not to reveal the borrowed advanced manual. They were only sketches of the standard layering approach: a stable ward circle that could host illusions built from within. She pointed to a small glyph. "This is the anchor point. Typically, I would feed the circle's perimeter with enough energy to form a boundary. My partner would cast illusions from inside that boundary, letting them outward in a controlled wave."

Kael studied the diagram. He tapped a spot near the runic vertex. "That glyph can be inverted to strengthen illusions. You see? If you push the vowel shift, illusions last longer. Then you would not need so much raw power fueling them. Less strain on you."

Her lips parted in reluctant admiration. He was not incorrect. In fact, he had discovered a structural improvement within seconds. "Right," she said, swallowing. "I see your point."

Before she could say more, the professor cleared his

throat from across the lecture hall. "Pardon the interruption," he called, lifting a small staff shaped like a baton.

"I want each pair to run a simple synergy test. Please step to the demonstration floor in pairs. Cast your basic, combined charm in front of the class so we can measure your initial alignment. Daro and Celeste will go first."

Alysia watched Daro and Celeste step forward, each raising a wand toward the center. They chanted simultaneously, producing a bright pastel light. The demonstration looked shaky in corners, but not terrible. Professor Latham offered them encouraging remarks.

A few minutes later, Min and Faris tried a jittery series of illusions and wards that fizzled after a single breath. The professor calmly guided them back to their seats, urging more practice.

Alysia's stomach coiled as she realized they were next. Her pulse leaped. She looked at Kael, who was already pushing away from the windowsill. He gave her a small, confident nod, as if to say, Let's show them.

She forced her feet to move. They strode to the center of the room, aware of every eye on them. Rumor had it that Kael was a rogue or a warlock with illusions tethered to a forbidden lineage. She worried students might expect an explosion.

"Whenever you are ready," Professor Latham said. The measuring staff in his hand glowed faintly, prepared to gauge their synergy.

Alysia raised one trembling hand, drawing on the incantation for a basic ward. Her voice wavered, but she fought to keep it steady. She traced a circle in the air with her fingertips, letting the runes bloom in soft, golden lines.

Kael began chanting a delicate illusion. She could not decipher the words, but silver light gathered inside her circle. Her wards bent around it, giving the illusion shape. For a moment, it hung in the air. A small wave of watery color emerged, similar to a sea ripple.

Her heart hammered in surprise. His illusions felt gentle, more refined than she had anticipated.

A shockwave of energy, ozone-scented and violet, crackled along the edges of her ward. It did not feel like it was fracturing. It felt like it was stretching, trying to reshape itself around a power it both recognized and fought. The synergy was a living thing, and it was trying to claw its way out.

"Don't fight it. Anchor it," Kael whispered, his voice a low hum against the magical roar. She realized he was telling her to fortify the circle. She grounded her stance, feeding just enough energy to stabilize. Their combined magic fused, with a wave of silver-blue illusions rolling gently inside her golden ring.

The class murmured in amazement at the shimmering effect. She caught sight of Celeste's wide eyes, Daro's polite nod, and Min's parted lips. Even the professor pressed his measuring staff closer, eyebrows lifting at the unexpected cohesion.

Then, just as quickly, the illusions trembled. A final aftershock of Kael's energy spiked outward. Alysia tried to hold the ward. The wave of illusions burst upward, scattering bright droplets of color that rained harmlessly around them. The demonstration ended in a decorative splash, leaving the dais shimmering with leftover arcs of gold and silver.

Alysia exhaled in a rush. Students burst into soft applause at the display, though a few in the back wore expressions of disbelief. Professor Latham lowered his staff, a grin tugging at his mouth. "That was impressive for a first synergy attempt. Good job containing the final burst."

Heat burned Alysia's cheeks. She scanned Kael's face. His eyes glowed with excitement, though he offered no triumphant cheer. He merely inclined his head in thanks before guiding Alysia away from the center.

A handful of curious students stepped forward with quick, congratulatory remarks, but the professor asked for silence and motioned for them all to sit again. Adjusting his robes, Latham addressed the class. "This is the type of synergy we hope to see refined over the next two weeks, but with even more control. Now that you have your partner assignments, use the remainder of this session to discuss integrative strategies."

All around them, bright voices erupted. Alysia sank into her seat, cheeks still warm. She avoided meeting Kael's gaze. She did not want him to see the flush that warmed her face. The synergy had been stronger than she expected. And it left her feeling strangely breathless, as though she had glimpsed a side of him she had never anticipated.

She pretended to shuffle her notes again. Her mind churned with thoughts. Was she going to endure constant

sparks of that dangerous closeness every time they practiced? Could she keep their precarious magic from
spiraling out of control?

Did Kael know how rattled she felt?

When class time neared its end, Professor Latham
clapped again, summarizing that each duo must schedule
extra practice sessions to refine their synergy. He
reminded them that success meant a flawless, stable
demonstration, one that might even be showcased to a
visiting faculty panel. The stakes were enormous.

Alysia slid her notes into her satchel. Her attention
drifted to Kael. He hovered near one of the window
alcoves, collecting stray illusions into ephemeral shapes
before letting them dissolve. She noticed the faint ward
energy still lingering around him, pulsating like an echo of
their combined power.

Sighing, she got up, preparing to approach. She
wanted to avoid any more stares from classmates. Yet
when she turned, she found him already in her path. He
moved silently, blocking her route in a way that felt
unthreatening yet charged with intensity.

"Looks like we will be spending more time together,"
he said, his voice low. "We cannot pass this final project
without balancing each other out."

She squared her shoulders, refusing to show how his
proximity made her nerves quiver. "We will do the assignment and do it well," she said. "Nothing more."

An amused spark danced across his face. "Of course,"
he answered. "Only the assignment."

She opened her mouth to snap a frustrated retort, but

the students bustled past, jostling them. She pressed her lips together. She refused to be flustered in front of the entire class.

Before either of them could speak again, Professor Latham announced that session was dismissed. Chairs screeched, and classmates poured out, some offering Alysia a knowing grin or a flurry of questions about illusions. She struggled to keep her expression neutral. She felt acutely aware of Kael's presence at her elbow, as if he found every moment an opportunity to unsettle her.

Amid the departing students, he offered her a casual nod. "See you soon," he said. "We should hold our first practice tonight, yes?"

She hesitated, flipping through her mental schedule. Robin wanted her help with a comedic illusions experiment, but perhaps that would have to wait. This final charm performance carried too many consequences if they failed. "Yes," she said quietly. "Tonight. But keep your illusions in check."

He grinned. "I promise. Consider me on my best behavior."

She scoffed, unable to decide if she believed him. With no further comment, she exited the lecture hall, hugging her satchel tighter than before. Frustration warred with a strange spark of excitement in her chest. The synergy they achieved was more than she had expected, which frightened and intrigued her in equal measure. She wanted to maintain control, to keep her wards disciplined and unyielding, but Kael's illusions seemed to carry a life of their own. A quiet voice in her mind whispered that she might discover spells beyond her initial scope if she leaned into his dynamic style. Yet the idea of trusting that unpredictability sent prickles of caution up her spine.

Outside the hall, she pushed through the chaos of students in the corridor. She could almost feel the residual magic from their synergy woven around her. Each step away from the lecture room made her wonder if the entire fiasco was just a dream. But no, her classmates' excitement confirmed that Kael truly was the new exchange apprentice, and he truly was her assigned partner.

As she walked, half her mind churned through all the potential pitfalls, illusions that might run wild, wards that might collapse, disapproving glances from faculty who still doubted Kael's presence. The other half tried to anchor her in the practical steps they would need to take. She would show him the standard layering approach in more detail, perhaps in a deserted classroom, then they could test illusions within a sealed circle. If all went well, they would build an inventive synergy. If it did not... well, she refused to think too hard about the humiliation that might result.

Nevertheless, the truth stood as plainly as the phrase etched in the lecture hall. Velgrace endures by pairing opposites with purpose. She no longer had a safe partner or the routine she relied on. She now had Kael, whose complicated illusions, unpredictable nature, and unnerving smirks might upend everything she thought she knew about how to succeed in Charms.

She caught a glimpse of Kael through the crowd as he moved toward the far hallway. Perhaps he sensed her attention, for he glanced back over his shoulder, meeting her gaze with that familiar half-smile. He lifted a hand in casual farewell, almost mocking. Then he slipped away, leaving her to the students in the corridor.

Alysia's heart thudded. She did not want to admit that part of her was already braced for the intrigue, and even the possibility that, with him, she might craft something more potent than any standard ward circle. But those thoughts brought vivid memories of the near-chaotic surge in the demonstration and the uncertain throb of synergy brimming under her wards.

She clenched her satchel strap and forced herself to keep walking. This was not a game. The final performance demanded perfection, and she could not afford to let Kael's roguish illusions overshadow her control. No matter how much his smirk stirred up both her temper and a gleam of wonder.

When she finally caught up with Robin near the tower staircase, Robin's eyebrows leaped in amusement. "So, new partner," Robin said, crossing her arms. "Word spread fast. I take it you are thrilled?"

Alysia muttered a short, exasperated noise. "Thrilled is not exactly the word. Do me a favor. If I start complaining too much, remind me that I have no choice."

Robin grinned. "I will. You will be fine, Lyss. You still outrank half the people in that class with your warding skill. Plus, maybe Kael can teach you illusions that will blow everyone's minds."

Alysia grumbled. "No illusions are worth the headache."

Robin offered a good-natured pat on her shoulder. "I have to run to Obscura Wing. Catch you later." With that, she hurried down the corridor, leaving Alysia alone in the bustle of passing students.

Alysia stared after her cousin, then let out a subdued breath. As exasperating as the situation was, she had to steel herself for what came next. She would do everything in her power to finish this final project successfully and keep Kael on a tight leash, illusions or not. She refused to be undone by flamboyant magic and a reckless grin.

But as she climbed the winding steps toward her next class, the memory of that synergy fluttered faintly in her mind. She recalled the shimmering reflection of watery illusions dancing within her golden wards, the intangible thrill that spiked in her blood when they merged. Kael had glanced at her with a look that said, we can do this. The possibility of harnessing that potential both frightened and intrigued her.

She resolved to approach the Final Charm Performance with discipline. She would not let Kael see her second-guessing each moment. She would set rigid practice times, shape a precise incantation plan, and keep everything controlled. By the time of the demonstration, they would show the Academy a polished synergy. That was the only way she would preserve her academic standing and keep her dignity intact.

Still, lingering questions gnawed at her. Who was Kael Meridan, really? Why did he adapt illusions so fluidly without standard training? Could she trust him to help her succeed and not ruin her reputation? The quiet murmur of doubt stayed lodged in her mind, but she pressed on fiercely. With or without Kael's playful grin, she had no choice but to see this through.

Soon enough, she reached the upper landing, parted from the flow of classmates, and found a small alcove to catch her breath. Beyond the arched windows, the sea spread out, bright and glimmering, as if its wide horizon promised infinite possibilities. For a moment, she stood quietly, letting the cool air brush against her cheeks.

Yes, she thought, an advanced project with Kael might unlock something extraordinary, or it could unravel in disaster. Whether she liked it or not, the professor's arrangement was final.

She wrung her hands once more, recalling his grin in the lecture hall. Kael acted as if this entire ordeal was some kind of enjoyable pastime. As for her, the humiliating potential weighed heavily. This was indeed a test, not just of magical skill but of endurance. She had no intention of failing it.

CHAPTER

FIVE

MAGICAL SPARRING

Alysia inhaled the crisp morning air and tried to calm the tightness in her chest. She stood in a deserted practice room within Velgrace Academy, tall windows letting in golden light that glinted off the dust motes in the air. The faint clang of distant charms practice echoed from the hallway. She usually preferred the neat structure of Bastion Hall for training ward spells, but Headmistress Quen had encouraged each student pair to find private spaces to "grow synergy."

Not that synergy came easily with Kael Meridan.

He waltzed into the room moments later, hands tucked behind his back, his dark hair in a slight disarray. He had a knack for entering as though he held all the answers. She forced a neutral expression and lifted the worn compendium from her satchel. "We need to coordinate," she said firmly, trying to set the tone. "It's best if we start small with illusions."

He flashed a crooked grin. "I thought we were going

for impressive, not small." His gray eyes glimmered with teasing amusement. He took a step closer, rolling his shoulders to loosen them. "But I can manage if it keeps you from looking so tense."

Alysia's jaw tightened. She was not sure what unsettled her more, his arrogance or the subtle twinge of excitement she felt whenever they practiced together. She opened the compendium to a section on basic illusions that could be layered over wards. With a quick glance at Kael, she pointed to the first incantation. "We use a simple conjuration wave. I'll keep the ward stable."

She placed a chalk circle on the floor, and Kael gave a bored nod. He drew a symbol in the air, releasing shimmering motes that gathered in the middle of the circle. At first, everything glowed in a calm spiral. She exhaled in cautious relief. Maybe this time, they would manage the exercise without fireworks.

But Kael's illusions flared unexpectedly, as though something in the compendium's instructions clashed with his own style. Sparks erupted at the circle's edge, sending a sharp crack through the chalk lines. Alysia gasped, scrambling to repair her ward. She muttered a quick stabilizing chant, focusing on weaving the gold filaments of her magic around the illusions. The attempt lasted three heartbeats before the entire circle burst with a small explosion of amber light.

A plume of pale smoke lingered in the air as Alysia coughed. Kael's illusions faded, leaving a singed patch on the floor. He rubbed the back of his neck.

"That was unexpected. I would guess there is a resonance conflict in that text."

Resonance conflict. She remembered the term from an advanced theory text: a rare phenomenon where two distinct magical signatures, instead of layering, actively fought to cancel each other out. It was mostly theoretical. Mostly.

"You keep improvising," she accused, affronted. "My wards cannot hold if you are constantly changing the flow."

"I am not," he replied, gesturing at the scorched floor. "The illusions are reacting to something. Your circle is too rigid, it is like trying to pour a river into a glass box."

She dusted her uniform cloak and faced him again. "Let us slow down," she managed through clenched teeth. "We will attempt the base pattern again. Only do what we agreed, no fancy flourishes."

He shrugged casually. "As you wish."

They resumed positions. Alysia channeled her focus into the chalk lines, letting a steady glow awaken from her fingertips. She layered each glyph with careful intention, reciting the incantation at half volume this time. Meanwhile, Kael formed illusions in a measured sequence, shaping them into subtle glimmers of light instead of fireworks. For a fleeting moment, they seemed in sync. The illusions danced in a steady pattern within her ward, small orbs of silver drifting like glowing petals.

Alysia suppressed a smile. This was progress. She increased the wards just enough to let the illusions expand. Kael's orbs brightened.

Then the orbs collided in the center, fusing into a single globe that wavered from bright silver to lavender. A startled prickle raced up her spine. The shift felt off-balance. "Kael, adjust it," she whispered.

He tried. Something in the illusions snapped, sending a surge of raw magic outward. She tossed up a hasty barrier. The energy rebounded across the room, ricocheted off one of the old desks near the corner, and ignited it with a wreath of purple sparks.

Alysia watched in mounting horror as the desk transformed, wood groaning and reshaping itself. The grain twisted until it resembled a large cat's face. A splintered drawer yawned like a mouth and let out a whale-like moan. Then, as if offended by its own voice, it spat out small confections that looked suspiciously like frosted cupcakes.

Kael stared at the spectacle in disbelief. Alysia covered her mouth, her eyes wide. The desk waddled forward on newly sprouted legs, continuing to yowl. Each step produced another hail of cupcakes, landing with soft plops that scattered icing everywhere. Pink frosting splattered against the chalk lines on the floor.

"Oh no," she muttered, stepping back. "That's my desk from the dorm. I brought it here last night for notes."

Kael choked back a laugh. "We can fix it," he said quickly. "Probably."

She aimed a scowl at him. "You'd better fix it. I can't sit at a desk that howls and spits pastries."

The desk groaned again, lurching in their direction. A bright-green cupcake sailed past Alysia's ear, spattering icing across her cloak's collar. She felt sticky frosting melt against her skin. Her annoyance flared, but she forced herself to remain calm. She tapped the compendium's pages, scanning for a dispelling formula that might reverse partial illusions. Each second, the desk advanced with unnatural steps, squeaking and moaning.

"Hold it off," she said, her voice taut. "I need to see if there's a quick reversal."

Kael gave a half grin, stepping between her and the lumbering piece of furniture. He extended his arm, conjuring faint illusions around the desk's new legs. For a brief moment, it froze. Then it let out a bellowing croak and spat out another series of cupcakes with alarming speed.

Not wanting to be pelted again, Alysia ducked behind Kael's shoulder. The desk slammed one of its drawers against the floor, sending more dessert projectiles across the rubble of chalk marks.

Alysia skimmed the compendium by the frantic light of illusions. She found a line referencing an "Emergency Nullification" for minor object transformations. With a determined breath, she pressed her free hand against Kael's back, feeling the hum of his illusion magic. "Distract it," she hissed into his ear. "I'll cast the nullification."

He nodded and concentrated. She glimpsed a soft glow around his eyes as he spoke a sequence of illusionary commands. The desk paused, as though perplexed. Its yowling quieted to a whimper. Alysia seized the moment. She knelt, ignoring the sticky frosting at her feet, and carefully traced three overlapping runes from the compendium's instructions. Her voice quivered from the tension, but she pushed through. "Revert, quell, become as you were."

A last wave of purple light shimmered around the desk. With a rattling complaint, it collapsed back into a mundane piece of furniture, though covered in stray icing. An entire platter's worth of cupcakes fell to the floor, deflated lumps of sugary dough that no longer hurled themselves across the room.

Alysia slumped in relief, brushing frosting off her cloak. Kael let out a breath and closed the distance between them. He peered at the desk as if half expecting it to launch another pastry attack. "That was creative," he remarked, his voice laced with dry amusement. "But I was hoping for scones, at least."

She cast him a weary glare. "I'm cleaning it up later," she said, wiping a sticky smear from her hand. The faint sweetness of vanilla drifted in the air. She tried not to notice how close Kael stood, tracing a curious finger across the half-melted icing on his sleeve. Their eyes met, and a subtle glimmer of humor passed between them.

Before she could think better of it, laughter bubbled up in her throat. She put a hand over her mouth to stifle the sound, but it escaped anyway.

Kael broke into a low chuckle, but the sound faded faster than it should have. As he wiped a smear of icing from his sleeve, his smile vanished. A fleeting shadow of weariness replaced it. Alysia saw it, the weight of his true burdens returning now that the distraction was over. The sight made her own laughter catch in her throat.

The tension between them lightened for an instant, replaced by mutual exasperation and something else: an unspoken acknowledgment that they formed a precarious team, forging bizarre but memorable magic.

"This is ridiculous," Alysia said after regaining her breath. "We look like we lost a duel with a bakery."

"You wore the icing far better than I did," Kael teased, pointing at the pink smear on her collar. She shot him a mock glare, then tugged at the cloak's fabric to wipe off the worst of it.

Their voices stayed soft, as though neither wanted to shatter the fragile comradery that had emerged from the fiasco. Alysia's mind, however, churned just beneath the surface. Every time their hands brushed or their eyes met, she felt her pulse lurch, unbidden. Velgrace lore claimed that the strongest magic was woven between hearts, not hands. She had always dismissed that notion as romantic fluff. Yet as Kael offered a small, genuine smile over the remains of smashed cupcakes, something in her chest fluttered with hesitant curiosity.

CHAPTER

SIX

THE WHISPER EFFECT

Alysia pressed a hand against the tall shelves of the nearly deserted library annex, trying to steady the flutter in her chest. Outside the high windows, twilight sank into the stark silhouette of Velgrace Academy's towers, painting the horizon with soft shades of orange and purple. She edged through the aisle of dusty tomes until she spotted Kael, who sat cross-legged in a recessed corner dubbed their "study nook." Books and papers lay scattered around him, their pages glinting in the glow of a single, enchanted lantern.

He leafed intently through a cluster of her notes, his brows slightly drawn. Alysia's heart gave a quick leap at the sight. Getting used to having him immersed in her personal research felt like writing her secrets on a billboard. Yet this collaboration was part of the fragile balance at the heart of their synergy. They needed each other if they stood any chance of mastering the advanced illusions and wards the professors kept assigning. Even if the memory of their most recent fiasco, where illusions had spontaneously transformed her desk into a pastry-hurling menace, still made her cringe, she could not deny Kael's talent or their combined potential.

He did not glance up when she approached, so she slid onto a cushion beside him and cleared her throat softly. The leather of his compendium creaked as it rested near his elbow. Every time she saw that old grimoire, a tiny thread of unease tugged at her. Its archaic runes hinted at knowledge that might be more expansive and dangerous than either of them realized.

"You found something interesting?" she asked, her voice low. The library annex felt fragile, like a bubble she did not want to burst with too much noise.

Kael lifted his gaze, locking eyes with her. An edge of concern darkened his stormy-gray irises. "I was scanning through your runic sequences for layering illusions over wards..." He paused, tapping a single page in her note-book. "This symbol."

Alysia leaned closer to see where his finger rested. Her notes were tight and methodical, lines of runic script, accompanied by small sketches of glyph circles.

She recognized the standard incantations she had studied over the weekend. Then her gaze caught the single spiral near the margin. It curved inward, then outward, she squinted in confusion. "I don't remember drawing that," she said, her voice dropping. As she brushed a finger over the ink, a jolt of unnatural recognition shot up her arm. It was not a memory but an echo, a tune her bones knew from a song she had never heard.

She carefully brushed her finger across the spiral's thin lines, feeling the faint grooves of ink. "Where was this supposed to go in our synergy plan?"

Kael shook his head. "You tell me. I've seen almost every runic shape in your notes, but this one is...unusual. It feels out of place. Maybe it came from that advanced compendium you keep stashed?" He nodded toward a broader stack of reference texts at her side.

A flustered twinge tightened Alysia's stomach. She had borrowed more than one advanced manual from less-than-official corners of the library, determined to refine her wards. But she could not recall any specific mention of this spiral. "It might be from something I skimmed. Or maybe I scribbled it subconsciously." She tried to dismiss it with a shrug, but his eyes remained intent.

"Alysia," he said softly, "I watched you practice illusions for hours. You're thorough, borderline obsessive with details." There was no malice in his tone, only an earnest concern. "I doubt you'd copy a new symbol without understanding it. Consider that maybe it wasn't part of your standard research."

She wanted to refute him. The notion that a random glyph appeared in her notes sent her mind spiraling. Her instincts told her that every accent in runic text carried meaning, rarely harmless, often potent. A chill swept over her arms as she recalled warnings from older students. Certain glyphs were older than the Academy, rumored to belong to a hidden class of illusions that defied standard technique.

She forced a tight laugh. "You're making a fuss. It's probably just a doodle I forgot. Let's not get distracted. We came here to refine the synergy incantation for class."

Kael studied her face for another second, as though debating whether to push the point. His posture relaxed marginally, and he flipped past that page, returning to the standard notes. "Fine." He relented. "But keep an eye on it. Strange runes turn up for a reason."

She nodded, though her pulse still fluttered. She fidgeted with the silver bracelet at her wrist, feeling the cool metal press into her skin. "I'll keep track," she said, hoping that was enough to settle the unease threading through her.

They spent the next hour murmuring over illusions and ward placements, trying to design a stable charm that would neither explode nor take on a life of its own. It should have felt routine by now, but every time their arms brushed or he pointed out a modification with that low, resonant voice of his, Alysia's concentration frayed. She told herself it was just the closeness, the forced proximity that came with working in such a cramped space.

The illusions he conjured were equally distracting. He created drifting motes of light that sparkled in the corners, or illusions of runic shapes that hovered above the parchment. She admired his skill, even if she hesitated to tell him so. Better to keep a cool composure.

When the finishing bell struck from somewhere across

the Academy halls, Kael gathered the notes. He handed them back, and she caught a faint tremor in his expression as he glanced at the page containing the odd spiral. But he said nothing more about it.

They cleaned up in companionable silence. Outside, the corridors rustled with a handful of late-studying students. Their footsteps echoed against the stone floors, creating a soft, rhythmic echo. Alysia parted ways with Kael near the library's exit, offering him a small, polite nod.

"Try not to summon any pastry-launching illusions on your way back," she teased, her voice subdued. Her nerves were still on edge, but jokes came naturally when tension hovered between them.

He smirked slightly. "I'll do my best. Sleep well, Alysia."

She tried not to think too hard about the strange warmth that blossomed whenever he said her name. She let him slip away, disappearing into one of the side staircases. Then, with a slow exhale, she headed for the dorms.

That night, the dorm felt unusually quiet. Robin, who would normally be bounding in with stories or illusions, had some late-arranged project in Obscura Wing. Alysia had the room to herself. She set her satchel down, ignoring her mild hunger. Her mind spun with ideas for tomorrow's synergy practice. If all went well, she and Kael would perfect the layered illusions that day. She kicked off her shoes and reached for her wand, intending to do a short warm-up chant to steady her thoughts.

She froze. A beam of light caught her eye. On the

smooth wooden shaft of her wand, a faint spiral glimmered, the same spiral she had seen in her notes earlier. There, near the handle where her thumb rested, the shape curved and mirrored itself exactly, etched as though by an expert craftsperson.

Her heartbeat thudded in her ears as she raised the wand closer to examine it. She slid her fingertips around the design, feeling a subtle groove as though the wand's surface had literally changed. That was impossible. She had used this wand for weeks, and it had no such decoration. Even more startling, when she angled it toward the candle on her desk, the symbol glowed softly, feeding off the wand's core magic.

"What...?" she whispered to no one. A cold sense of apprehension coiled in her gut. Her mind flashed back to the spiral in her notebook, the one she could not recall writing. Had she unconsciously carved it here too? No, it was too precise, too deeply etched.

She breathed in slowly, trying not to let panic take over. She had studied enough advanced wards to know that runic symbols rarely appeared spontaneously. Yet this design showed no sign of tampering. It felt organic, as if the wand had grown that spiral from within. That notion rattled her more than any tapestry of illusions. It made her feel like she stood on the edge of a deeper well of magic than the Academy taught.

Soft candlelight bathed the dorm in gold, but she felt chilled, as though an unseen presence hovered. Unable to tear her gaze away from the wand, she traced the spiral gently with her index finger. A pulse responded, not just warmth, but a whisper. A silent question directed at the very core of her own magic, asking for a piece of her in return. The sensation was a coiling heat that surged up her arm, feeling less like an invasion and more like a homecoming.

SEVEN

LIBRARY AFTER DARK

Alysia had not planned to return to the restricted wing of the library at such an hour. Most sane people would be asleep beneath patched quilts, lulled by the rhythms of Velgrace's nighttime ocean wind. She, however, stood tucked in the shadows of an arched doorway, heart thrumming with a nervous excitement she struggled to hide. The corridor smelled of old parchment and the faint tang of salt that wafted in through the high windows, remnants of the coastal breeze that never fully left the Academy's halls.

Despite her better judgment, she had agreed to Kael's whispered plan. His insistence had been quiet but relentless: one intense glance across the library during study hours, a surreptitious note slipped under her door after dinner, and a firm reminder of the odd spiral that had mysteriously appeared in her notes and, more disturbingly, on her wand. She still felt the shape's presence whenever she used that wand, as if it were watching her decisions. And Kael, with his restless illusions, had made it clear that ignoring this enigma was no longer an option.

The lights in this part of the library glowed dimly thanks to a handful of enchanted lanterns. They wavered at the edges of her vision, distorting her own silhouette on the marble floors. She felt trapped between these shifting shapes and the quiet of rooms that Velgrace had deemed off-limits to most. A small sign, partially hidden by dust, warned students away from the restricted collection. She swallowed hard.

She spotted movement near one of the tall shelves. Kael stepped from behind a dusty display of archaic tomes. His dark hair partially obscured his face until he bowed his head and peered at her with those storm-colored eyes. A single, slender beam of lantern light fell across his features, highlighting the tension in the set of his jaw. The worn compendium he always carried pressed against his hip, its corners frayed from years of wear. He gave a silent nod to beckon her closer.

She entered the narrow aisle, careful not to let her boots scuff the polished floor. A scattering of old volumes lay undone on a nearby bench, spines splayed as if a harried researcher had abandoned them. A faint mustiness clung to the air, and Alysia caught herself cataloging the scents: aged leather, candle wax, and the subtle spice she now associated with Kael's presence.

"Any trouble?" he murmured.

She shook her head. "No patrols this late. But if the caretaker finds us..."

His lips curved in a wry half-smile. "We'll deal with that if it happens." There was a quiet confidence in his tone, one that stirred a bittersweet awareness inside her. She wondered how he could manage such composure while navigating ground so precarious.

Together, they moved past tall, carved shelves that soared to the ceiling. She occasionally glanced toward the deeper recesses where restricted tomes were rumored to amplify even the smallest illusions if one lacked control. Her own ward magic hummed under her skin, a cautionary signal that the environment was charged with ancient, unsettled spells. Beneath her gloves, her palms dampened with anticipation. She thought of the spiral, that shape she had not recognized from any standard runic text. The specter of its mystery loomed at the edge of her mind.

"We should be quiet," she whispered, pressing close to him. She felt the warmth radiating from his arm. He wore his usual boots and a slightly disheveled uniform cloak, as though he had rushed to meet her. His breath stirred a faint strand of her hair. Her pulse fluttered, strangled by nerves and something more dangerous than fear. The memory of his illusions welding her desk to a living creature still flashed through her mind and so did the exhilaration she had felt at his side.

He nodded and set off at a measured pace, every step deliberate. Occasionally, his magic trembled at his fingertips, a faint shimmer that lit the spines of passing books. It seemed he resisted a stronger conjuration. Perhaps even he realized the precariousness of weaving illusions here, in the heart of wards meant to contain centuries of knowledge.

They navigated a corridor thick with shadows. No staff roamed these parts after curfew, as far as she could tell. Still, the silence carried weight. Each footstep thumped too loudly in her ears, and each shift of cloth felt magnified. At last, they reached a gated archway that demarcated the final boundary into the restricted wing. The gate was sealed by a filigreed lock and an embossed sign in old Velgrace script. She had heard rumors of it requiring a specialized faculty key, but tonight, they lacked any official pass.

Kael paused at the gate. He ran one palm over it, and a subdued glimmer sparkled along the iron bars. "It's warded," he observed quietly. "You can sense it...see how the metal almost vibrates with a barrier?"

Alysia angled her head. Indeed, a faint gold haze glimmered across the bars. She exhaled, carefully channeling her wards. She recognized the style: an older locking ward that responded to incantations, not brute force. A standard student might never break it, but she prided herself on her mastery of ward-breaking and layering. Her family's legacy, for all its taint, taught her a thing or two about unraveling locked spells.

She pulled off her right glove. "Stand guard." Pressing her fingers to the hinge, she closed her eyes, not searching for a flaw in the ward, but for its emotional signature. This was old magic, her grandmother had taught her, woven with intent and feeling. It wouldn't yield to brute force. She hummed a low, pacifying tone, a counter-resonance to soothe the ward's anxiety. Under her breath, she shaped a single, elegant rune of release. The ward shuddered, its defensive heat softening into acceptance, and then the lock clicked open. The gold shimmer blinked out.

Kael let out a soft breath. "Impressive," he murmured, his lips curving into that crooked grin. He grasped the gate handle and tugged. It opened inward with a slight squeal, revealing an unlit corridor beyond.

Before they entered, Alysia replaced her glove and whispered a brief ward behind them so any unwanted observers might dismiss this corridor as empty. The tension in her belly only tightened. She had never broken a ward placed by the Academy. Guilt pricked at her conscience. Yet the spiral symbol on her wand had rattled her too deeply, and Kael's urgent sense of unraveling that very secret overshadowed every cautionary warning.

Darkness reigned in the corridor. A single luminous orb, cracked from age, hung overhead. It cast watery light that left the edges of the passage soaked in gloom. Alysia summoned a minor illumination spell in her palm. Carefully, she let the glow spread across the walls. She spied dusty paintings of old Velgrace librarians, their eyes solemn as if condemning their intrusion.

"This way," Kael whispered, pointing at a massive door at the end of the hall. Arcane designs were etched across it, lines entwined with glyphs older than any standard seal. A worn inscription above the door read, "Archive 8-L." The door's center displayed a circular pattern that made Alysia's heart stutter. It looked eerily similar to the spiral in her notes.

She forced a steady exhale and stepped forward. Each footfall sent echoes bouncing off the stone. Her wards tremored. Kael joined her, his illusions appearing in the gloom. She caught a faint silver gathering around his fingers for an instant. He clenched his fist, and the silver vanished.

The door loomed taller the closer they came. The spiral pattern dominated the middle, with fine lines radiating outward like spokes from a wheel, each inlaid with glyphs reminiscent of old incantations. Despite the dust and the silence, Alysia sensed a vibrant power behind the wood, waiting, as if it had been locked for centuries but never truly dormant.

"I looked up older volumes," Kael murmured, turning his gaze to her. "There's no direct mention of a spiral exactly like this, but references in the compendium hint at deeper archives that house illusions predating the Academy's current code."

Her throat felt tight. "So, you think my wand's symbol could be connected to illusions from that era?"

He nodded. "Something that doesn't follow the typical illusions we know. A few lines in the compendium mention a synergy of wards and illusions that can warp objects permanently...or awaken them."

She repressed a shiver. Awaken them. The memory of her desk's transformation into a cupcake-spewing menace jolted her. That fiasco had been comedic at best, but if the spiral had triggered something else, perhaps on a deeper scale, the consequences could be terrifying.

Ignoring her apprehension, she placed her hand

against the door's spiral design. A faint vibration buzzed against her palm, making her pulse leap. Without warning, a faint light emanated from the grooves, as though the door recognized her. She heard Kael's breath catch at her side.

He laid his own hand next to hers. The etched lines flared with sudden brilliance, gold and silver traveling along the door's pattern. She felt a subtle tug in her core, as if her wards and his illusions resonated. Her heartbeat thundered. In that breathless moment, she tasted the raw synergy that sometimes sparked between them, fascinating and lethal, all at once.

The door responded. The carved spiral started rotating. The lines shifted, circling outward, each glyph flashing white-hot for a heartbeat before dimming. A faint grinding noise came from somewhere deep in the walls. Alysia caught Kael's wide-eyed glance, her own racing thoughts reflected in his stare. They could not turn back now. This was precisely what they had come for, though she had not expected it to be so...alive.

A portion of the door near the base illuminated with a ring of runes as if awaiting instruction. She trembled, recalling how her mother had once told her that certain wards thrived on cooperative magic, a lesson she had never been allowed to practice fully. She had always considered it too dangerous. Yet here she was, hand pressed to a door that demanded she channel synergy with Kael. The air grew thick, amplifying her ragged breathing.

"Ready?" Kael's voice was absently quiet, his focus on

the lines. She gave a small nod, pressing her other hand over his. His warm skin through his glove made her flush involuntarily. She whispered the first set of runic phrases that surfaced in her mind: gentle unravelings mixed with a binding element.

Kael closed his eyes, and the cool, chaotic silver of his illusions met the steady, structured gold of her wards. She felt the magic intertwine not just on the door but inside her chest, a dizzying vortex where his wildness found shape within her control. It was terrifying and exquisite. A single, perfect chord of power formed between them, a harmony she had only dreamed of. The door recognized this unity, this impossible balance it had been built for.

Then the door's center gave a low click and rotated. Suddenly, an ancient latch slid open with a thump. The whine of metal gears filled the corridor. The heavy door cracked ajar, the spiral design parting down the middle. A rush of stale air brushed against her cheeks, smelling of centuries-old parchment and something darker, a whiff of latent magic that had been left to stew.

Dim light spilled out from the gap, illuminating a yawning space beyond. Alysia peered through the crack. She glimpsed tall shelves, crumbling scrolls, and corners that shimmered with drifting, dust-laden motes of magic. Her ward sense vibrated with a deep and unfamiliar energy, one that made her skin prickle. This was no ordinary archive. She could almost hear a distant hum, a low drone as if the air itself carried remnants of centuries-old enchantments.

Kael tore his gaze from the door and looked at her. His

earlier confidence dimmed, replaced by sober awe. The worn compendium at his side rattled slightly, as though reacting to the power emanating from inside.

She let out a quiet exhalation. "I've never felt anything like this."

He gave a tight nod. "Neither have I."

Their combined magic had unlocked something that should have remained sealed by powerful wards. Yet the pull of curiosity, and that relentless spiral lodged in her wand's core, compelled her feet forward. She felt Kael's presence at her side, both comforting and unnerving. They had blundered into synergy so many times, mostly by accident, but tonight, it seemed the library itself waited for them to step deeper, as if predestined.

She grasped the door, pushing gently until it swung wide on ancient hinges. The stale air intensified, carrying a sharper sense of power that stung the back of her throat. Dust motes hovered like spectral lights. The silence deepened. A chill crawled along her arms, no matter that her wards thrummed with readiness.

Kael raised an orb of pale illusionary light, letting some of its glow spill across the threshold. Scrolls rested on high shelves, some bound by chains, others half-rotted from apparent neglect. Strange inscriptions on the floor coiled around a large desk. This was a place legend might have whispered about, where knowledge too dangerous for common study had been buried away.

As Alysia stepped forward, the hum grew louder, as if the archive recognized her presence. A thousand questions crowded her mind. Had her searching awakened the symbol on her wand, or had the symbol come here to beckon her toward secrets the Academy had hidden? She felt a prickle of unease, but she could not turn back. Not after crossing so many thresholds of caution. Her curiosity mingled with the ragged beat of her heart, dragging her onward.

They paused just inside the entrance, shoulders nearly touching. She inhaled slowly and glanced at Kael. In the soft light, his face showed apprehension, but his eyes glittered with quiet determination. Neither of them spoke. Words felt too small for what surrounded them.

Then, in a single motion, they placed their hands on a glyph-lined seal that flanked the interior wall. Sigils flared like awakened serpents, lines of magic coiling up the stone. With an audible crack, the seal broke apart to their combined power. A second door, a vault hidden behind thick glass, revealed itself. The mechanism slid back, revealing a dark interior row of additional shelves and stone pedestals.

Only when that final layer opened did Alysia realize how far they had gone. The air rushing out felt older than the Academy's known libraries, older, perhaps, than the entire institution. A low hum pulsed around them, resonating in her bones. She could almost taste the power on her tongue, a metallic tang that reminded her of lightning storms.

She and Kael exchanged a final look brimming with unspoken questions. Alarm bells rang in her mind, warning of what might happen if they tampered with hidden illusions or wards lost to time. Yet a powerful curiosity eclipsed that fear. The symbol on her wand had drawn her here, and she could not abandon the trail. She squeezed Kael's hand. He gave a reassuring squeeze in return, and together, they edged forward.

They were stepping into the past. And possibly rewriting it.

CHAPTER

EIGHT

THE VOICE IN THE SEAL

Alysia stepped inside the vault, her pulse pounding in her ears. The door sealed behind her and Kael. They had come this far only by combining their magic, and the lingering aftershock of that synergy crackled at the edges of her awareness. Dim light from several hanging lanterns revealed the vaulted ceiling overhead. Ancient shelves lined the walls and curved in a half-circle around the center of the space. A layer of dust blanketed the floor, thick enough to record every footprint.

"This place has been sealed for ages," she murmured. She drew in a breath and tasted stale air tinged with the faint tang of old magic. Her wards, coiled in her mind and ready to protect, twitched with caution as her gaze flitted to Kael.

He nodded. His illusions still glimmered around his hands, a nervous reflex he had developed since they started working together. Whenever he felt uncertain, his

76

illusions crept out in small motes of silver light. They drifted near his fingertips, as if waiting for a command.

Alysia noticed an enormous symbol etched into the floor ahead, a disc-like seal, faintly glowing with lines that curved and spiraled inwards. The runes reminded her of the strange glyph in her notes, the spiral that had first appeared without explanation. It thrummed with energy, responding to their presence as though awakened from a long slumber.

"How do you want to approach that?" she asked quietly. Her breath formed a soft cloud in the cold air. She tried to keep her composure, but the wariness in her chest only grew. Every sense told her they had stumbled on a piece of forbidden knowledge that the Academy had locked away.

Kael's eyes snapped toward the runic designs. He took a few measured steps forward. "Carefully," he said in a clipped tone. The intensity in his voice made the hair on Alysia's arms lift. There was nothing playful about him now. He kept a hand near the worn compendium at his side, as though seeking reassurance from that old text.

The spiral flared brighter beneath their feet, responding to each step. A soft humming grew, filling the vault with a low vibration that tremored through the walls. Alysia tensed. She layered a ward around them both, muttering a quick incantation under her breath. She felt Kael's illusions shimmer in response, weaving along the edges of her protective barrier. The synergy surprised her yet again. His illusions did not clash with her wards this time. They slid into place as though governed by the same rhythm.

They reached the center of the chamber where the largest rune glowed. Alysia tentatively placed a gloved hand near the lines, feeling the temperature shift from cold to a brittle heat. She paused, heart hammering. Tiny sparks of light began to rise from the design, darting into the air like fireflies.

"Look," Kael said, his voice a breath. Sparks scattered across the vault, illuminating the dark corners that shelves and old crates had once claimed. Dust motes rose like small ghosts, dancing in the brightness.

Without warning, the floor seal burst into full brilliance, forcing Alysia to shield her eyes. She could only make out Kael's silhouette behind a haze of gold and silver. Then a tremor rocked the chamber. It felt like a heartbeat, heavy and resonant, echoing from beneath the floor.

A hollow voice reverberated through the vault. "Recorded in bone and shadow. Bound by ambition and lost to time."

Alysia's stomach lurched. She blinked, trying to locate the source of that voice. It sounded neither alive nor purely magical, more like an echo from many centuries ago. She swallowed hard.

Kael turned in a slow circle. The tension in his shoulders told her he was searching for illusions, perhaps trying to see if this was real or something conjured by the seal. She steadied her breathing, pressing one foot back for better balance. Her wards hummed, responding to her rapid heartbeat.

Then a shape materialized in front of them. At first, it shimmered like a thin veil of smoke. Gradually, it solidified not into a ghost, but into a figure woven from threads of fading light and captured time. His form wavered at the edges, as if memory itself were fighting to reclaim him. He was tall and gaunt, his features etched with lines of age or stress. In his right hand, he held a long staff crafted from what looked like bleached bone fused with bright shards of crystal. The staff radiated pale light that turned the dust motes to shimmering flecks.

Alysia's mouth felt dry. She had only read about memory-traps in archaic texts: illusions so powerful they recorded a caster's image and words, leaving warnings or instructions behind. This figure was an example brought to life by whatever was sealed in the floor. She forced herself to keep her posture firm, ignoring the urge to back away.

"Hear these words," the specter intoned. His voice resounded as if from the bottom of a deep well. "You who seek the knowledge of forging identities or breaking them. Beware the price. Memory itself can be reshaped, and those who meddle in such spells risk losing their truths."

Alysia's heart fluttered. She recognized the caution about memory-forging spells. Warnings about them existed in the Academy's restricted sections, always accompanied by unsettling rumors of participants forgetting their own names under misguided illusions.

The ghostly figure lifted his staff. Twin arcs of light

spread from the tip, illuminating more of his face. Creases lined his brow. Beneath his left eye, a faint series of runes glowed. He looked like a scholar worn down by decades of forbidden research. A cruel determination pulled at his thin lips.

Next to her, Kael went rigid. The playful illusions at his fingertips didn't just vanish, they snapped out of existence with a faint, sharp crackle. A wave of cold shock radiated from him, a magical feedback so intense that Alysia felt it wash over her own wards. The illusions on his fingertips vanished, leaving only the ward that Alysia had cast.

The specter continued, oblivious to their reactions. "Memory-forging erodes a man's identity before destiny can claim him" He paused, as if waiting for the words to sink in. "Guard your mind's boundaries, for if your ambitions grow too deep, your reflection may become a stranger."

His staff pulsed once, and the light radiating from it nearly blinded Alysia. She hissed under her breath, arms up to shield her eyes. Then the radiance ebbed. When her vision cleared, the specter had shifted his stance, as though glancing over a shoulder at an unseen apprentice.

Kael's breathing sounded shallow. Then, in a shaky voice, he spoke two words that sent a jolt through Alysia's core. "Master Sorren."

She glanced at him again. His hand trembled at his side. The specter gave no response, but Alysia realized Kael recognized the person, or at least the image preserved here. She wanted to press him, but the phantom started speaking again, forcing her to wait.

"Seek the rightful path," the specter said, his eyes staring sightlessly ahead. The staff glowed brighter with each syllable. "Beware the illusions that tamper with your sense of self. Identity lost cannot always be reclaimed without sacrifice."

A muted crackling spread through the vault. The figure began to waver, strands of light bleeding from his robe's hem as though the memory-trap was nearing its end. Alysia felt a sudden spike of apprehension. Whatever message or warning remained, it would only last a moment longer.

The old charm master's voice dropped to a rasp. "To any who find this place, I have paid my price. I have sown the seeds of my ambition."

The staff of bone and crystal flared with a final surge of brightness. A soft blast of air rippled outward, lifting the dust into eddies. Alysia clung to her ward, feeling the shield shudder around them as the memory-trap winked out in a flash. In less than a heartbeat, the chamber went still, with only faint motes drifting down like glowing snow.

When the last fleck of light vanished, the vault returned as it was. The circular seal on the floor no longer glowed, but the runic designs remained etched into the stone as an unspoken threat. Alysia forced herself to exhale and lower her arm. Her heart pounded so hard that it felt like it would bruise her ribs.

She turned to Kael. "You recognized him?" Her voice came out rough, laced with adrenaline.

Kael's eyes were fixed on the spot where the phantom

had stood. His jaw tensed before he nodded once. "That's him." He spoke quietly, as if not wanting to stir any lingering energies in the vault. "I know that staff. I know his face. I never thought I'd see it again, at least, not here."

Alysia stepped closer, gently touching his elbow. "Who was he?" She could see the conflict in his expression. Kael looked torn between secrets and the trust he had begun to show her.

For a moment, silence filled the vault except for the soft dripping of condensation against stone. Then he let out a shuddering breath. "Master Sorren was the enchanter who taught me most of what I know about illusions. Not in the Academy. He traveled. He collected knowledge and...well, he pulled me out of more than one situation I couldn't handle when I was younger." Kael's gaze dropped to his hands. "But everyone said he disappeared decades ago. Some claimed he died on a rogue expedition into these vaults. Others claimed he suffered a magical accident beyond the borders."

Alysia's mind reeled. "That's impossible. You aren't—" She caught herself. He was only eighteen. If this mentor had vanished decades ago, how could he have tutored Kael in illusions so recently?

Kael took a step back, paced in a short, agitated line, and pressed a hand against his temple. "I can't explain it, but I recognized every line on his face. His staff. His voice." He muttered an oath under his breath. "He was always... older than he looked. He said illusions can mask your age if you handle them well. But I never guessed he had ties to the Academy's forbidden archives."

Alysia felt a knot in her chest. Questions and fears threatened to overwhelm her. If this Master Sorren had indeed recorded that memory-trap, it implied he had dabbled in dark illusions that manipulated identity itself. Fear crept along her spine as she recalled the phantom's warning about losing oneself to ambition.

She rubbed the heel of her hand against her chest, as if to quell the anxious flutter. "Can you think of any reason why he'd leave a message here? That sounded more like a final warning than a normal lesson."

Kael's expression tightened. "No," he said. His voice held an undercurrent of frustration. "He taught me illusions, but never said anything about memory-forging or identity spells. Maybe he never trusted me enough to mention that part. Or maybe if he did, I forgot." He swallowed hard and stared at the spiral on the floor. "He always hinted there were lines no one should cross."

Alysia's wards pulsed in recognition of the residual energies through the chamber. She could not deny the sinister caution in the old charm master's recorded words. Memory forging. Identity lost to illusions. It all sounded too close to the rumors that had circulated about Kael's lineage and the twisted illusions lurking in old Meridan lore.

She felt Kael's eyes on her. His voice dropped to a near whisper. "If Master Sorren left that message... how can he be the same mentor I had only a few years ago? I should have realized he was older than he claimed. But decades?" He took a shaky breath.

Alysia reached for Kael's hand without thinking. His

fingers twitched before curling around hers. She felt the rapid beat of his pulse through that brief contact, a testament to the fear he usually hid behind smirks and illusions.

"Maybe he found a way to sustain himself," she said softly. She tried to keep her tone steady for Kael's sake. "He must have discovered a method to cheat the timeline. That might explain how people thought he vanished decades ago."

Kael's mouth curved into a grim line. He did not answer. Instead, he stared at their joined hands as though uncertain he deserved that comfort. Alysia squeezed his palm, letting him know she was present, if nothing else.

She wanted to reassure him, but the uncertainty gnawed at her heart. The memory-trap's projection circled in her mind, repeating the old charm master's ominous caution: illusions could devour a person's identity until they forgot who they were. She wondered if Kael's mentor had succumbed to that fate.

Finally, Kael let go of her hand with a ragged exhale. He stepped away and ran a hand through his dark hair. "We need to figure out how this empty vault connects to Sorren's disappearance. If he recorded that warning, it may hint at a more dangerous form of illusion research. He used to say illusions were not always false. They could imprint themselves like brandings on the soul if you let them."

Alysia recalled the ghostly shape, the staff of bone and light blazing with twisted runes. "Did he ever mention forging illusions so strongly they affected memories? Because that's exactly what this memory-trap described."

Kael shook his head. "Not in words. But he had a fascination with illusions that were... layered. Multiple illusions stacked over each other until the line between real and unreal blurred. He always insisted I learn to distinguish repeated illusions from living ones." He pressed his lips together, glancing at the worn compendium in his belt, as if suspecting it of hiding more secrets.

Standing in that dark vault, Alysia felt her chest tighten. Sorren's cosmic-level illusions might have extended far beyond normal spells. If Kael had unwittingly trained under a man who practiced memory-forging arts, then the tangled mysteries behind Kael's illusions, and the suspicious spiral glyph that had appeared in her own notes, could be connected to an older, darker magic stored here. She recalled the phantom's parting words: illusions turn truth into a plaything.

She looked at Kael, her throat tight with worry. "We need answers," she said. "If your mentor dabbled in memory forging, then we should find any logs or records he left behind. Something that explains how you knew him when he was... presumably gone."

Kael nodded, though the tension in his shoulders remained. Silence settled around them again, pressing from every corner of the vault. They stood amid the dust and old runes, overshadowed by the knowledge that they had just uncovered a puzzle bridging Kael's personal history and the Academy's most ancient secrets.

He brushed a hand across his face, then sank his

fingers into his hair. "I keep telling myself I left my old life behind, but it looks like it followed me to Velgrace," he whispered, his voice trembling. "I thought Master Sorren had died or moved on. Now it feels like he never left at all."

Alysia hesitated, reaching for the words that might ground him. "We will find the truth," she said, her voice low. "The Academy might have tried to suppress his research, but we know enough to start unraveling it." She bit down on her lip, shaken by the memory-trap's dire warnings. "No matter what we discover, we do it together."

Kael's expression softened for a moment. The illusions around his fingertips glimmered like faint sparks, revealing his lingering agitation. Then he squared his shoulders and tried to bring back a semblance of calm. "Right," he replied, though his voice was quiet. "Together."

They stood side by side, hearts racing. The dust settled, leaving only the faint outlines of old shelves, broken boxes, and the ominous spiral on the floor. The entire vault seemed to watch them, anticipating whatever step they took next.

Alysia swallowed. Her thoughts whirled with the same question. How could Kael be tied to a master enchanter presumed dead for decades?

She felt the weight of that mystery settle on her shoulders, and she knew it would not let them go easily.

CHAPTER

NINE

BREAKING THE LOCK

Alysia's breath shook as she stared at the ancient door they had just managed to wedge open. Everything she had discovered in these hidden vaults churned inside her mind, glimpses of Master Sorren's memory projection, the warnings etched in the runic floors, and Kael's stunned expression when he recognized that ghostly enchanter. The weight of it pressed upon her like a storm brewing behind her eyes.

She pressed a trembling palm against the carved threshold, trying to steady her thoughts. "I can't—" she began, but her voice trembled and died. She hardly recognized the rawness in her tone.

Kael moved to her side, close enough that she sensed the faint crackle of his illusions lingering in the air. He had not spoken much since Master Sorren's phantom dissipated. His silence only magnified her own anxiety. She looked at him, noting how the argent flickers still lingered at his fingertips and realized he was just as shaken. That knowledge pulled at a deep, barely acknowledged sympathy in her chest.

She swallowed, tasting dust and old magic on her tongue. "Kael," she whispered, her voice echoed. "That message, your mentor... t's all connected to illusions that can rewrite memories. I don't know how to handle that." Her throat felt tight.

He met her gaze. A hint of regret lined his features, as though he carried secrets he had yet to share. "I don't know either," he said quietly. "But we can't stay here."

She nodded and forced her feet forward. The next chamber gaped ahead with a heavy lock shaped like interlocking spirals. Runes glimmered on the edges, streaked with age as if centuries had passed since anyone last trespassed here. Alysia could feel her wards stirring, drawn by old power. She felt the corridor tugging at her, an odd, haunting beckoning no rational mind would follow. Yet her heart insisted on pressing on, as though the answers she sought lay just one locked door beyond.

They navigated the debris of broken shelves and toppled stands, stepping carefully around the sharp splinters. One misstep might trigger a trap or draw the caretaker's attention. Every nerve in her body felt wound tight. Their only light came from the faint aura around Kael's illusions and Alysia's own ward-lamp, a small orb of pale gold hovering near her shoulder. The combined glow cast merging shadows around them.

At the far end of the chamber, they found the second warded door. The filigreed lock was more elaborate than any she had encountered in her standard training sessions. Symbols and jagged glyphs scrolled across the metal, layered so densely that her head throbbed at the mere sight.

She paused to study it. Her wards rippled in her mind, warning her that breaching this lock would require far more than a nimble incantation. She recognized the same archaic style as the illusions Master Sorren had left behind. The memory of that haunting projection made her shudder.

"It's definitely bound by older wards," she murmured, running gloved fingers lightly over the etchings. "This is more advanced than the gate outside. I'm not sure if I can break it, and if I do…"

Kael's expression hardened with a determination that lit an uneasy glow in his eyes. "Whatever's beyond it might hold answers about Sorren. Or about the symbol on your wand." His voice lowered with frustration at the secrets that hovered just out of reach. "I hate not knowing."

His honesty prodded a wild emotion in her chest. She also hated the sense of helplessness. She laid her palms flat against the metal, letting her ward-sight probe the glyphs in subtle pulses of power. She whispered a short incantation to coax the wards into revealing their layers. Her tone trembled, reflecting how precarious she felt inside.

At first, the lock refused. Its runic lines remained mute, glimmering only in stubborn refusal. Alysia's frustration built. She was so tired of half-truths, of stumbling in the dark while something bigger orchestrated their fates. Her fury flooding the incantation, she stopped coaxing the ward and instead slammed her magic against it. The runes on the lock flared with a defiant heat, sending a psychic shriek through her own wards that felt like scraping metal against her soul. The door groaned under the assault.

A sharp jolt lanced through her fingertips. The metal flared white-hot. Alysia gasped but did not pull away. If the door responded to power, she would give it everything. She poured her warding magic into the lock, pushing past the usual caution she clung to. Heat crackled along her arms, intensifying the energy that built inside her chest.

Kael stepped behind her, his eyes wide. "Alysia, wait. This feels wrong." His illusions brightened, silver shimmer that danced over her shoulders. She sensed him trying to restrain her, but she could not stop now. Her frustration propelled her onward.

The lock whined in protest. A crack of shifting stone echoed off the vault walls.

She bit down on her lip, channeling more force than she had ever dared. She murmured half-lost incantations, words her grandmother once whispered during practice sessions, words that had never failed her before. A sense of raw power surged out of her, fueled by long-simmering anger at being left in the shadows.

The wards screamed in her mind, and then abruptly, they broke. A deafening crack made the vault tremble beneath their feet. The door's intricate spiral design glowed, then shattered outward in a burst of pale magic. Wind-laced energy slammed into Alysia's chest, hurling her back against Kael. She would have hit the floor if he had not caught her around the waist.

In that same heartbeat, something else, a secondary lock behind the door, flared to life. She felt the jolt, sensed the raw magic yawning open, and she realized too late that the lock she broke had only been a barrier to protect everything else inside. The second ward awakened with a vengeance, fed by her emotional outburst.

A shockwave of light erupted. She screamed as it hit her wards, stinging sparks across her vision. Kael toppled backward, the illusions around his hands flashing chaotically. She tried to reach him, but runic lines uncoiled from the door, snapping like serpents of energy around his right arm. Her eyes widened in horror.

"Kael!" she cried, her voice cracking. She scrambled over fallen crates and reached out, but the coil of magic slithered faster. It shot up his arm and latched onto his palm, forging a luminous glyph on his skin. He gasped and dropped to one knee. The lines seared into him, flaring a brilliant turquoise. His mouth twisted in pain.

Alysia grasped for a dispel incantation. She had no idea how to counter ancient illusions that bound themselves like brands. She tried anyway, pressing trembling fingers over his wrist and muttering a frantic chant. Her wards sparked, but the spirals refused to recede. She felt them pulse, as if answering to a deeper presence.

"I... can't..." Kael rasped. His eyes squeezed shut. The glow on his palm tightened around his flesh, weaving shapes that reminded her of the same spiral etched on the vault door.

A rush of footsteps, or rather, a scraping of ward-driven constructs, echoed from somewhere behind them. Alarm jolted her. The caretaker wards had awakened. The corridor had gone from silent gloom to trembling energies. She heard metallic clangs, beep-like pulses of detection. Heart pounding, she pulled Kael to his feet. She recognized the hum of official security wards on the prowl, perhaps summoned by the door's catastrophic breach.

"We have to run," she managed to say.

He nodded, pain etched across his face, his right palm still glowing. Together, they stumblingly retreated from the door. Their footsteps echoed off the twisted pillars. A sudden voice, cool and disembodied, emanated from the vaulted ceiling. "Intrusion detected. Remain where you are." It repeated in a monotone threat, accompanied by the scraping of something heavy stirring in the darkness.

Alysia's pulse raced. She flung a hurried ward behind them, quick, protective runes that might confuse the caretaker wards or slow them. Kael coughed, pitting illusions against the trailing sparks overhead. The hallway twisted in twinkling shapes, illusions clashing with ward constructs in a dance of clashing light.

They plunged into the preceding chamber, the one lined with old, half-buried scrolls and dusty pedestals. She scanned frantically for an exit. The caretaker wards had sealed the path they came through with a translucent barrier. The hall leading to the library's main corridor remained open, though faint arcs of raw magic crackled around the archway. If they could just make it there, maybe they could outrun the alarms.

Then the shape of a book rose from a toppled desk. It hovered, drifting toward them with strange, methodical slowness. Its covers were worn as if centuries old. Thin cords of light spiraled around its spine. Alysia's breath caught in her throat. She had seen floating books in illusions or advanced study rooms, but none had a presence quite like this one. It pulsed with the same energy that inhabited the second ward.

A whispery voice emerged from the book's pages. "Kael Meridan." The words were so soft that Alysia almost doubted she had heard them. But the shock on Kael's face confirmed it. The book's pages rustled, breathing out more syllables.

"We don't have time for this—"

The caretaker wards' echoing steps closed in, accompanied by a faint glow that threatened to swallow them. Kael let out a ragged breath, staring warily at the hovering tome. The brand on his palm flared again, as though pulling him toward it.

He clenched his teeth. "That thing...it knows me. We can't leave it." He said it like a confession and a curse rolled into one.

"Are you out of your mind?" The abnormal pull of the brand, combined with the book's eerie whisper, told her this was no random text. If they abandoned it, it might only hunt them later. Or worse, it might lead the caretaker wards to them both.

She lunged forward, casting a half-formed snare

around the floating volume, hoping to restrain it. The book merely slowed, as though more curious than threatened, continuing to drift forward. Its pages flipped, releasing faint puffs of archaic spells. She could not sense immediate hostility, but the noise of the approaching wards told her they had seconds at best.

"No choice," Alysia panted, grabbing Kael's good arm. "We run."

The caretaker wards' presence flared bright at the far side of the chamber. She spun, flinging a dispersal ward in that direction. The flash of her magic lit the shadows. A hiss of energy cut across her line of sight. She felt heat sear the edge of her cloak. That was too close. Kael conjured illusions to distract them, a kaleidoscope of decoy shapes that burst like shimmering confetti. The caretaker wards froze, momentarily confused by glistening illusions overlaying the real corridor.

Alysia used that moment to dash toward the nearest corridor exit. Kael kept pace, his breath ragged. The brand still glowed beneath his glove, though the pain on his face had receded to tense concentration. She glimpsed the floating book drifting after them. It dogged their every step, unaffected by illusions or wards as though it had become invisible to pursuit.

They entered the old hallway leading to the main library. Alarm bells chimed faintly from somewhere upstairs. Footfalls, real ones, perhaps staff or other arcane guardians, echoed overhead. Alysia's heart hammered. If caught, they would face immediate interrogation, possibly expulsion. She pushed that terror aside. Right now, escape was all that mattered.

Lighting a small orb to lead the way, she struggled to slow her breathing as they navigated the gloom. Her wards wavered from the draining exertion. When they reached a side staircase, she motioned for Kael to follow. They had used these winding steps before when sneaking into restricted sections. The caretaker wards, large and lumbering, typically did not maneuver well in narrower passages.

They forced themselves up the steps, Kael leaning a hand against the curving stone for balance. Alysia kept a frantic watch on the corridor below. The caretaker wards roamed there in stuttering patrols of magical energy. Her heart pounded with every rung of the spiral staircase. She sensed the brand pulsing beneath Kael's glove, and the trailing presence of that half-sentient book, flapping its pages with a quiet hiss.

At the top, they emerged behind a locked gate that marked the boundary of the restricted wing. Alysia repeated her earlier technique, fumbling to undo the warded latch as quickly as possible. Her pulse thundered in her ears. For a horrifying second, the latch refused to budge, but then she felt the runes yield under her skill. The gate slid open. She and Kael tumbled through.

They did not stop. She recast a ward behind them, weaving illusions and sealing magic to hide any trace of their flight. The corridor ahead led to the standard library shelves, which were dim but not deserted. She heard the faraway rustle of pages, the quiet hum of lanterns. Students might still be reading in the main section.

Kael said nothing. He merely squeezed her hand once, as if to confirm he could still stand, then let go. She noticed how pale his face looked in the corridor's scattered light. Her worry flared again. A blasted brand on his palm that glowed with ancient runes, the half-sentient book whispering his name, he must be in agony or at least wracked with questions.

They hastened down the library's main aisle. Faint arcs of ward-lights blinked near the ceiling, but no caretaker patrolled this far out. Through a narrow side exit, they burst into the open air of an external walkway. Moonlight fell across the high arches overhead, painting the campus nightly silhouette in silver. The cold breeze slapped Alysia's cheeks, jarring her from the suffocating tension of the vault.

She braced herself against a column, her chest heaving from exertion. Kael stood beside her, pressing his gloved hand to his chest and wincing. They had made it out, though not unscathed. The ominous night pressed in around them, but her heart still pounded with the memory of that second ward's explosive power.

"We need to hide," she murmured, searching the walkway for any sign of roving professors or patrol wards. The roof overhang shielded them from direct view. It might not hold if the caretaker wards tracked them outside. "Follow me."

They paced along the open walkway, hugging columns until they reached the shadow of a disused corridor leading toward the lesser-traveled side of Aurum Spire. A few leftover crates and stacked chairs cluttered the corner, offering a cramped hiding spot. Alysia crouched behind them, pulling Kael down with her. The night air felt unbearably cold against her sweat-damp uniform.

He winced and lifted his right hand. Even through his glove, she saw faint turquoise light leaking from the seam between his wrist and the fabric. An involuntary shiver ran through him.

"It's still burning," he said, his voice a low rasp. "It feels... hungry." Alysia swallowed hard. She placed her hand gently over his. A subdued warmth met her touch, a strange counterpoint to the scorching brightness inside the brand.

"Let me see," she whispered.

He tugged off the glove, though his fingers trembled. The glyph that had latched onto him looked like a spiral pattern coiled within an outer circle. It glowed in slow pulses, tracing luminescent outlines along his veins. She felt her wards awaken instinctively, reacting to an unknown threat.

She tried not to recoil. "I'm sorry," she said, her voice cracking. "My power broke that ward, and...I never meant for you to be—"

He breathed, "Stop. This isn't your fault alone." He looked up, and for a moment, tenderness shone there under the layer of pain. "I could have stopped you. I should have realized the illusions inside that vault were never meant to be breached with raw force."

Before she could answer, a faint flutter drew their

attention. The floating book sidled around the corner, its covers quivering. It drifted closer, ignoring the wards Alysia tried to cast as barriers. Her illusions wavered, but the tome passed through them without slowing, as if charmed by Kael's brand. It whispered again, though the words remained indistinct. A spark of pity and fear pooled in Alysia's chest at the sight of it. Whatever presence animated this text seemed lost and hungry, drawn to Kael like a moth to a candle flame.

She gently put a hand on Kael's shoulder. "We can't let that thing float around the campus calling your name. It might draw every patrol to us."

He closed his eyes, steadying his breathing. "I know," he said. "But I sense something in it, something that... recognizes me. For now, it's following us on its own. We'll have to deal with it...once we catch our breath."

Alysia swallowed the urge to panic. They were hidden for the moment. The caretaker wards were still searching the vault. The chill wind rustled the crates. She leaned back, letting her body sink into exhaustion. Kael's face was so close to hers that she found herself counting the flecks of silver in his eyes. Anxiety thrummed in her veins, but the heat of his presence stirred another sensation entirely. She tried to quell it, focusing on the immediate crisis.

Her lungs burned from running. She kept one hand over his brand, hoping that calming her wards might soothe him. He exhaled and let his forehead rest on her shoulder for an instant, as though surrendering to the closeness. They did not speak. Words felt too fragile after what had just happened.

After a minute, Kael pulled away. He studied the floating book, which hovered patiently at eye level, its blank cover turned in silent invitation. Somewhere in the distance, another burst of magical alarms echoed, but it sounded distant now. The caretaker wards must have lost their trail. Perhaps illusions and wards had done their job enough to buy them time.

Alysia's heart pounded as she brushed a shaky hand through her hair, dislodging a stray scrap of cobweb. She forced a steady breath. "We got out," she said softly. "But we awakened something. And... Kael, that brand on your palm—"

"It's tied to the illusions locked behind that door," he said, letting his gaze wander to his glowing skin. "And apparently, it's tied to me."

Before she could respond, the book drifted forward. A thin page lifted, as if beckoning them to read. Alysia reached out with trembling fingers, but she hesitated inches from the text. She sensed no immediate hostility, only that strange, half-sentient curiosity. When she did not move, the book fluttered, repeating Kael's name in a murmur.

"Ignore it for now," Alysia whispered. "We're both exhausted."

He nodded once, his eyes dark. Against her better judgment, she rested her forehead against his unmarked hand, absorbing the adrenaline that still coursed through them. Despite the fear that rattled her bones, she sensed the same underlying synergy she had felt when their magic first fused. Only now, it felt tainted by dangerous relics and half-unraveled illusions.

Neither of them spoke. Somewhere under the weight of night and of newly awakened enchantments, they had crossed a line. A part of Alysia could feel it in every shaky breath. There would be no returning to the simple caution they once clung to.

After what felt like an eternity, she lifted her head. Kael's expression had hardened with resolve, though a quiet tremor marred his usual confidence. She suspected that brand would be a constant reminder of how easily illusions could mark them. Even so, relief mingled with regret. They had escaped. They were alive.

But the floating book remained, turning its pages in slow, methodical swishes. No barrier or incantation would keep it away. It had chosen to follow them, and it refused to be shaken. A chill raced over Alysia's spine. Something had been awakened in those catacombs, something that would not rest. They had learned so many partial truths in the vault, yet more questions rose with every passing moment.

TEN

FAMILY INVASION

Alysia woke to the smell of burnt candlewax and the distant caws of gulls swooping along the cliffs outside her tower window. She stirred under the thin blankets, blinking to clear the haze in her mind. The events of the previous night returned in fragments: the buzzing caretaker wards, the clang of a magical alarm in the library, and the searing light of that brand coiling across Kael's palm. Exhaustion tugged at her limbs, but the faint morning light meant one truth: day had finally broken.

She pushed herself upright, heart pounding with something close to dread. On the small table by the door, a shuttered lamp flickered with the last vestiges of its flame. Her dorm room looked painfully cramped, scattered with half-rolled scrolls and the remains of a hurriedly consumed meal from the night before. The air inside felt stale, as though it had not refreshed since her last frantic sprint back to the dorm.

A gentle flutter broke the silence. She half expected to see that floating book from last night, the one that insisted on following Kael around. Instead, a worn compendium lay open at the foot of Kael's makeshift cot. He sat beside it, still in the clothes he had worn the night before. He had not changed or slept. His right hand was tucked protectively under his left arm, hiding the brand that still pulsed with faint turquoise light.

"Morning," she said, her voice raspy.

He angled his head, offering a half-nod. "Couldn't sleep. Figured I would try to read, but this text is about as comforting as a lecture." He gestured to the worn compendium with a wry smile. Dark circles lined his eyes. "No caretaker wards barged in, at least."

She exhaled, the tension in her shoulders refusing to ease. Guilt rose as she remembered how the brand had latched onto him when she forced the vault door's ward. "Does your hand still hurt?" she asked softly.

He nodded once, his expression guarded. "A bit. I covered it with a quick barrier bandage. The glow's weak enough that maybe no one else will notice."

She frowned at him. "We need to figure out how to remove it."

"Agreed," he said, flipping his hand palm-up. A faint shimmer seeped through the bandage. "But not right now. We have classes soon, and after last night's fiasco, the last thing we need is more attention."

Before she could respond, her dorm door burst open with a clatter. She jolted, nearly tumbling off the bed. A figure stumbled inside, arms overloaded with two large canvas bags, a traveling cloak draped haphazardly over one shoulder.

Alysia's heart leaped into her throat. Then recognition set in.

"Robin?" she blurted, staring at her cousin. "What are you—"

"Oh, don't you 'Robin' me," said the newcomer in a sing-song voice. Robin was the same age as Alysia, though her posture radiated the confidence of someone who walked into any space as though it were a stage. Her short, tousled hair framed a wicked grin. "I find out you blow up some restricted ritual, cause half the caretaker wards in the library to go berserk, and you think I'll stay away? Absolutely not."

Heat rushed up Alysia's cheeks. Robin's presence filled the cramped dorm with immediate mischief. "It was not a blow-up. It was more like a forced door." She cleared her throat. "Why are you here?"

Robin made a theatrical show of dropping her bags onto the narrow rug. They landed with a muffled thump that sent up a cloud of dust motes. "Because you need me. Obviously. And I was bored with my current lodging in the Obscura Wing." She nudged a worn trunk aside to make room. "Heard rumors. Decided to move in for a bit."

Alysia exchanged a wide-eyed glance with Kael. He slouched on the cot, arms folded, watching them with dispassionate amusement. It was the first time she had seen him relax at all. If anything, Robin's dramatic entrance at least diverted attention from the brand on his palm.

Robin pivoted, noticing Kael. She raised an eyebrow, scanning him from head to toe. "Well, you must be the reason behind all the fuss." She set her hands on her hips. "So, you're Kael Meridan, yes? The near-legendary fiasco magnet."

Kael looked at Alysia. His lips twitched, but he said nothing right away. Alysia stepped between them, arms up in a placating gesture. "Robin, be nice. Kael's a student. We're working together right now."

Robin's eyes narrowed knowingly. "Interesting. And you pulled him out of some ritual? That's the story going around?" She gave Kael a smile that resembled a fox scenting a mouse. "Then let me congratulate you properly. I'm the brilliant cousin who cleans up after Alysia's many accidents."

Kael's tone remained cool. "Don't worry. I've got a track record of cleaning up my own mistakes." He kept his voice low, but a faint spark of challenge flashed in his eyes. Alysia recognized that sarcasm.

Robin snorted, dropping to sit cross-legged on Alysia's bed without invitation. "And are you the reason she nearly triggered caretaker wards again last night?" She spun to Alysia. "I got the news from three different classmates. They're all whispering about how the wards flared up in the restricted wing, searching for intruders. Meanwhile, you vanish into your dorm and lock the door. Suspicious."

Alysia felt a headache forming. She rubbed her temples. This was exactly the last thing she needed. "Yes, apparently we triggered a library alarm. But can we not discuss it here? We just need a minute to breathe."

Robin's grin softened. She saw the genuine anxiety in Alysia's eyes and gave a slow nod. "Fine. You'll fill me in later." She glanced around, her gaze catching on the small trunk and Kael's compendium. "I need a corner for my stuff. I'll sleep on the floor if I have to."

Alysia tried not to groan. Her dorm was barely large enough for her and Kael, who had been placed here on the Headmistress's orders to "contain the potential risk." Now jam in Robin's irrepressible energy, and it felt like the walls crept closer.

"Stay if you want," Alysia conceded. "But keep your voice down and do not go rummaging through my notes."

Robin put a hand on her heart in feigned offense. "Me? Invade your precious scroll trove? Of course not." Then she shot Kael a look. "So, do you usually watch people from the corner, or do you talk?"

"I can talk," he replied evenly. "But Alysia asked for quiet. I respect that."

Robin's eyes narrowed again, though not in anger. It was more like curiosity. She seemed ready to poke him with more questions, but she held back. The dorm fell into a brief, tense silence, broken only by the distant calls of gulls beyond the windows.

Alysia felt a wave of gratitude that Kael was restraining himself. She knew all too well that if he wanted, he could fire back with illusions and sarcasm. Instead, he just studied Robin with a calm that verged on polite detachment.

"All right," Robin said, sliding off the bed. "I might head to the lounge and scrounge up some breakfast. One of us needs to keep an ear out for gossip anyway. If caretaker wards start asking questions, better that I'm somewhere else."

She snagged a small bag from her pile, rummaging until she found a velvet coin pouch. With a final grin at Alysia, she beamed. "Don't think you'll escape explaining yourself."

When the door closed behind her, Alysia exhaled, all tension momentarily draining from her body. "That is Robin," she said, gesturing vaguely at the now-empty space. "She shocks your system, but she means well."

"She's entertaining," Kael said, though his tone suggested he remained on guard. "Does she always intrude like that?"

Alysia shook her head. "Not always. She just has a knack for arriving when I least expect it. Usually, it's because she's worried."

Silence settled again. Alysia cleared some books off the single chair and lowered herself onto it. She tried not to stare at Kael's bandaged hand. "We should do something about that brand soon," she murmured. "But not in front of a hundred prying eyes."

He nodded, shutting the compendium's cover. "For now, I'll keep it hidden. I can try illusions if needed, though that might strain me."

Footsteps echoed in the corridor again. Alysia tensed, expecting that Robin had forgotten something, but the sound drifted away. She felt the pounding in her chest. The dorm door was locked now, giving them a semblance of privacy.

Kael seemed about to speak, but he paused. A small shape drifted near the foot of his cot, moving in and out of sight. Alysia stiffened, recognizing the half-sentient book that had refused to leave Kael's side the previous night. It must have been invisible or disguised behind some illusion until now. It bobbed gently in the air.

She eyed it warily. "Does it always just... float?" she asked.

Kael shrugged, though his expression was tense. "Seems so. It has barely spoken since we returned. Maybe it's waiting."

"For what?" she asked, goosebumps running up her arms. She doubted there was an easy answer.

Kael opened his mouth, but a loud knocking on the door startled them both. Alysia's heart jumped. Who now?

She crossed the room, stepping over Robin's bags, and cracked open the door. A red-faced second-year student panted on the threshold. "Alysia." He glanced at Kael behind her, then jerked his head toward the corridor. "Headmistress Quen wants to see you both after midday meal. Something about your unusual library check-in log. She wants an explanation."

Alysia's stomach dropped. She forced a calm nod and thanked the messenger. His eyes snapped warily at Kael before he hurried away. She shut the door and placed her forehead against it. Every muscle felt ready to snap.

Kael's voice was quiet. "We'll deal with it." He slipped the floating book into a canvas satchel, burying it beneath extra papers. Then he put on a new shirt from his trunk and re-tied his hair, as if preparing for a battle that never really ended. "Maybe we can navigate Quen's interrogation if we stick to a partial truth."

Alysia turned, her shoulders slumped. "We have to. She already suspects we're hiding something." She rubbed her temple. "I just hope we can keep the brand out of it."

They spent the next few hours tidying the dorm, as well as searching for any leftover evidence from the night's escapade. Alysia's guilt built with each moment. She noticed that Kael avoided mentioning the caretaker wards or the painful shock he had endured. He refused to show any sign of weakness, and she felt a pang of concern.

By midday, Robin still had not returned. The smell of fresh bread and vegetable soup wafted from the corridor as students bustled to and from the dining halls. Alysia's stomach rumbled, but the looming meeting with the Headmistress left her appetite strangely absent.

She was about to suggest that they look for Robin when a sharp rap on the wooden door startled them. Robin's voice carried through. "I'm not alone, so open up carefully."

Alysia threw a glance at Kael, her pulse speeding. She turned the knob, opening the door just enough to see Robin's face. Moonlight poured through the small corridor window behind her cousin. Beside Robin stood a figure in a hooded cloak, shoulders squared with a poised sort of confidence.

Robin nudged the hooded figure forward. "I told her it might not be the best time, but she insisted. Sorry in advance."

The moment the hooded figure stepped over the

threshold, the small warding glyph Alysia had etched near the handle of her door pulsed with a silent, pained light before fizzling out completely. Alysia's breath caught. Only a mage of immense, unsanctioned power could nullify a dorm ward so casually.

The hood slid back, revealing a woman who shared Kael's sharp features and midnight hair. Her eyes held a speck of gold in the low light, an echo of illusions that felt oddly familiar. She crossed her arms, smirking as though the entire moment entertained her. Alysia did not need an introduction. She remembered the name Kael had once whispered, the sister he had unwittingly harmed when illusions first manifested. Lyric Meridan.

"Miss me, little brother?" Lyric asked, her voice smooth as polished glass. "Or did you hope I vanished for good?"

Kael went still. Beside his cot, the half-sentient book they had recovered from the vaults, the one that whispered his name, fluttered its pages once in a frantic, agitated motion before falling silent as if in fear. Kael's expression hardened, his gaze locking onto Lyric not as a sister but as a storm he had long been waiting for.

"Of course you would show up now," he said, his voice low. "You always show up when everything is about to collapse."

Lyric grinned, leaning a shoulder against the corridor wall as though she had all the time in the world. "Don't look so grim. I heard about your misadventures with caretaker wards. You always had a flair for drama, Kael."

Robin cleared her throat. "Should we, can we go in? The corridor is not exactly private."

Alysia stepped aside, letting them enter. Her dorm, tight with only Kael and her inside, felt impossibly smaller now with four people compressed into the space. Robin hovered near the door, arms folded. Lyric remained near the threshold, scanning the cramped room with a critical eye. Kael rose from his cot and squared his shoulders, but he did not approach Lyric.

"I'm not here to fight," Lyric said, though her smirk suggested she enjoyed the tension. "I came to see what trouble you managed to stir this time... Did you realize that brand is visible through your glove?" Lyric's voice was soft, but the words were sharp as glass. "You never could hide your mistakes."

Alysia saw Kael instinctively clench his right hand, a faint turquoise light pulsing through the leather as if in answer to the jibe. He didn't flinch, but the effort it took to remain still was a testament to the wound she'd just reopened.

A shadow crossed Kael's face, and Alysia felt him bristle. She wanted to intervene but sensed it would do nothing to ease the spark between them. Lyric's gaze swept over Kael's right arm before turning her attention to Alysia.

"You're the one who conjured him in the first place," Lyric said, addressing Alysia. "So, is this your method? Summon trouble and hope it sorts itself out?"

Alysia's cheeks reddened. She refused to step back. "He's free to leave anytime.

But maybe you should ask him why he prefers to stay."

Lyric cocked her head, an unreadable emotion in her eyes. "Ah, protective as well. How interesting."

Robin coughed, trying to draw everyone's focus away from the brewing storm. "Lyric, you said you were investigating some old illusions leftover from your own time in the Bastion Hall, right? That is what you told me when we bumped into each other."

Lyric lifted a shoulder. "Investigating. Visiting. Call it what you will."

Alysia looked to Kael. The usual confidence in his posture had turned rigid. His jaw was set, illusions glimmering faintly around his fingertips. She feared a confrontation would erupt at any second. Meanwhile, Robin's eyes darted from face to face, as if calculating how to diffuse whatever bomb was about to go off.

Lyric took another step closer, the tension between her and Kael thick enough that the dorm's wards seemed to hum. Kael's illusions sparked in the stale air, a silver shimmer at the edges of his glove. For a moment, Alysia wondered if she needed to raise her own ward to keep them from throwing themselves into a magical duel right then and there.

"You don't get to barge in like this," Kael said quietly, his voice laden with an anger he barely hid. "Not after what happened."

Lyric shrugged. "I do as I please. I learned from the best."

Robin set a hand on Lyric's elbow. "We can talk this through. No need to—"

Lyric brushed Robin's touch away, though not violently. Her eyes remained on Kael, measuring him. Then she turned that sharp gaze toward Alysia. "When you tire of stoking his illusions, let me know. Perhaps I can clean up the mess before it becomes a catastrophe."

Alysia could not help the surge of indignation in her chest. She pulled herself upright, ignoring her hammering heart. "I don't know what you think you know about him, or about us, but you're not going to waltz in and claim the moral high ground. He's done nothing to deserve that."

Lyric's smirk deepened, though a trace of genuine pain touched her eyes. "I see his enchantment on you is strong. That's fine. I will stay close in case you want the truth of our dear Kael's talents."

Kael's shoulders tensed as though he might fling an illusion at her. Alysia prayed he would not. Robin swore under her breath, casting an apologetic glance at Alysia.

The crackle in the air was tangible. Alysia forced a steady breath. Two visitors from two different pasts had entered her life in the span of a single morning, one cousin brandishing wit and the other a sister brimming with old wounds. Already, the dorm felt like a battlefield, full of haunted grudges and unspoken alliances.

Outside the window, a gull's cry sliced the coastal breeze. Lyric crossed her arms again, that confident posture letting everyone know she had no intention of leaving. Robin hovered behind her, half amused and half worried, while Kael looked ready to dart from the room or ignite his illusions just to shatter the tension.

Alysia tried to hold herself firm. Everything was

unraveling, layered with secrets and unresolved histories. She swallowed, feeling the dull thud of her heartbeat in her throat. They had no space for additional conflict, yet conflict had come anyway.

Lyric took a single step into the room, and the air seemed to thin, the ambient magic in the walls recoiling from her presence. She ignored Alysia and Robin, her eyes fixed solely on Kael.

"I heard you had been collecting strays," Lyric said, her voice a silken threat that cut through the cramped silence. "I did not realize one of them had managed to get you branded."

Kael's illusions, which had been dormant, sparked to life around his fists. They were not the playful silver Alysia knew but a jagged, angry violet that hissed in the air. The two siblings stared at each other, and in the suffocating quiet, Alysia felt the fragile peace of her world fracture. This was not a family reunion. It was a declaration of war.

CHAPTER

ELEVEN

SPELLS AND SIBLINGS

Alysia pushed aside a stack of spell scrolls on the narrow desk and rubbed her temples. The tight space of her dorm suddenly felt like it had shrunk by half. She had grown used to Kael's presence. He spent many evenings studying illusions or nursing the brand on his palm. Their uneasy dance of near-confessions and unspoken tension had become familiar, almost comforting in its own tumultuous way. Now, though, Robin had returned with a flourish of canvas bags, and Lyric, Kael's sister, had swept in behind her. The result was a living arrangement that bordered on complete chaos.

Late morning light peeked through the high dormitory window, casting elongated shadows across the cramped floor. Alysia had never pegged herself as someone easily flustered, but with Robin perched on the edge of her bed and Lyric hovering in the doorway with her arms crossed, she felt her composure fray. Kael stood by the small wardrobe, gloved right hand pressed against his side as if ready to defend that glowing brand. He kept his eyes on Lyric, whose stance suggested a challenge as potent as any outlaw's.

Robin, oblivious to the tension or simply thriving on it, grinned. "I swear, Alysia, if you had told me you were planning this circus, I'd have brought more pillows. The floor is going to murder my back."

"Then you can move your things to the lounge," Lyric said, her tone cool. She offered a thin smile that could have been mocking or polite. It was hard to tell.

"Your comfort is no concern of mine."

Robin's eyebrows shot up. "Awfully generous of you."

Alysia stepped in, hoping to defuse them before the bickering heated further. "We need to figure out a way to share this space. We cannot let the caretaker wards start investigating if they hear shouting. They already notice everything." That last part slipped out with more desperation than she intended.

She moved to the foot of the bed, carefully shifting a worn compendium out of the way. Kael watched her in silence. His silver-flecked gaze moved between the two newcomers. The tension in his shoulders betrayed an internal battle, but he stayed quiet. Alysia sensed he had no desire to reveal anything personal about his relationship to Lyric while Robin stood ready to pounce on any scrap of drama.

Lyric drummed her fingertips on the doorframe. "I did not come here for living arrangements. I came for Kael."

"You came for trouble," Robin retorted, crossing her legs. "Same difference."

A faint ripple of magical energy pulsed along the dorm walls. Alysia's wards recognized discord as easily as they recognized illusions. She inhaled and attempted a calming technique her grandmother had taught her years ago. Perhaps it was easier to handle active spells than clashing egos.

Gently, she reached for Lyric's arm and nudged her inside. "Just come in so we can talk. You're letting half the hallway overhear this conversation."

Lyric hesitated, then entered, making the space feel even tighter. She stood near the smallest writing table Alysia owned, her posture rigid and regal in a plain black cloak. From the corner, Robin gave a smug smirk. Neither spoke, but the tension rolled off them like heat waves.

Kael cleared his throat. "Why are you both picking a fight?"

Robin hopped up, her arms sprawling wide in mock innocence. "Me? I am not the one who breezed in talking about worthless floors and expecting everyone to kneel." She offered Lyric a pointed look. "You talk like you own the place."

Lyric's lips curved into something that might have been a smile if it did not feel so cold. "I own my choices, illusions included. If you have an issue with my brother, you have an issue with me."

Robin set her hands on her hips. "Fantastic. Then we have plenty of issues to go around."

Alysia pressed her palms together, ignoring the tickle

of ward energy that pricked at her fingertips. "Stop. We are not here to tear each other apart. We have bigger problems."

She thought about the caretaker wards that still patrolled the library. They had been quiet that morning, but her nerves remained on high alert since that catastrophic run-in the night before last. If any more disruptions flared around her dorm, the caretaker wards would swarm this hallway too. The notion of all four of them getting caught after their recent escapades made her stomach twist.

Kael, looking thoroughly exasperated, let out a long breath. "We do have bigger problems. Lyric, tell me exactly why you came. I doubt you came solely to mock our living situation."

Lyric shrugged. "I need to research something in the Obscura Wing. You can help me if you like."

Robin snorted. "Oh, how gracious of you, summoning your brother to be your sidekick."

"Would you prefer I keep him out of the loop and let him stumble into real danger?" Lyric asked, her voice clipped. A moment of tension passed before she added, more quietly, "He is still my brother."

Something in her tone softened, just for an instant. Alysia caught it, that trace of genuine concern beneath the spiky exterior. She doubted Robin missed it either. Her cousin's snark fell silent for a heartbeat, and an odd look crossed Robin's face, equal parts curiosity and caution.

Kael turned away, frowning at the small trunk by the wardrobe. "So, you want to poke around illusions in the

Obscura Wing. Are you looking for something to do with the caretaker wards or something else?"

Lyric studied him. "It concerns illusions and the leftover spells from certain past instructors. I have a lead on who might have been meddling with rogue illusions in the academy's name."

The mention of rogue illusions made the back of Alysia's neck prickle. So many secrets lurked in the academy's halls, each with the potential to shatter their fragile facade. She recalled the illusions that had ambushed them in the restricted vault, illusions so strong that Kael bore a permanent mark on his hand. If Lyric carried a clue about the infiltration or the illusions that threatened them, they needed to hear it.

Robin tucked a short lock of hair behind her ear. "Of course she's got a lead. She probably stumbled across it while rummaging in places no one invited her."

Lyric's smirk returned. "Maybe I did. Or maybe it found me."

Alysia closed her eyes for a brief second. She wanted both of them to get along, if only to reduce the headache pounding behind her skull. She straightened, lifting her chin. "If you do have information about illusions that could be a threat, we should hear it. This concerns all of us. But I am not going anywhere if you two keep sniping every five seconds."

Lyric's eyes glinted in challenge. "I will behave if your cousin does."

Robin rolled her eyes but held up her hands in a show of surrender. "Fine. I will be civil. For Alysia."

Some of the tension in the small room eased. Kael reached for Alysia's writing chair and gently pulled it out, offering her a seat. She accepted with a grateful nod and tried to hide how the simple gesture warmed something deep in her chest.

She cleared her throat. "We have enough trouble as it is. Headmistress Quen is still suspicious after that alarm in the library. If we want to investigate illusions, we should do it quietly."

At that, Robin scoffed. "Good luck with that. Lyric's about as subtle as a thunderclap."

Before Lyric could retort, Kael stepped between them. "I will go with Lyric to check the Obscura Wing. Alysia can handle the wards if anything goes wrong." He paused, glancing at Alysia. "But only if you agree."

She thought about the caretaker constructs that roamed the halls, still in a heightened state of alert. She also thought about the brand on Kael's palm, half-hidden by his glove. Part of her disliked the idea of him confronting illusions or rummaging through old secrets with Lyric while that brand burned beneath the surface. Yet she understood he had to do something, especially if it offered answers about rogue infiltration.

"I understand," she said softly, "but be careful. You do not want to trigger another wave of caretaker wards."

Robin folded her arms across her chest. "Then what am I supposed to do? Twiddle my thumbs here while you all run off?"

Lyric gave a smooth shrug. "You could come. If you try to sabotage me, though, expect retaliation."

"Wonderful," Robin muttered, rolling her eyes. "Sign me up."

Despite the lingering surge of annoyance, Alysia realized having both Robin and Lyric along might be beneficial. Robin's illusions, while not at Kael's level, were cunning enough to distract any random observer. Lyric had knowledge that none of them possessed. Perhaps, with enough caution, they could avoid a full-blown conflict.

She stood and gestured for everyone to calm down. "If we are doing this, we should do it together. But not right away. The Obscura Wing will have classes for a while. We can slip in between scheduled lessons."

"We have a few hours to kill," Kael said, rubbing the back of his neck. "I have some illusions to refine, anyway."

Robin hopped nimbly onto Alysia's bed, ignoring the pointed look from Lyric.

"Perfect. We can do more than illusions. I have an idea for a group ward practice considering we are all stuck in here."

Alysia opened her mouth to protest that her dorm was not suited to boisterous spell testing, but Robin was already rummaging in her bag. She pulled out a handful of colored chalk sticks, each laced with small runic etchings that glowed faintly. A grin lit her face. "I all but perfected a quick-cast ward circle. Let's try it out so we do not lose our edge."

"Here?" Alysia's eyes widened. "I do not want caretaker wards hearing a magical scuffle if we slip up. It is too risky."

"We will keep it small," Robin promised. She leaped off the bed and knelt on the floor, clearing a space amid their clutter. "I will draw the circle. You just contribute your runic knowledge when it is time to lock it."

Lyric watched them with a faint curve to her lips. Her expression was difficult to interpret, alternating between mild interest and guarded aloofness. "If you accidentally set the dorm on fire, I will watch from the hall."

"Like you would pass up a chance to show off your illusions," Kael murmured. A hint of a teasing spark touched his voice. Lyric narrowed her eyes, and for a moment, the old sibling tension flared again.

Alysia nearly pointed out that the floors in this dorm might not handle intense illusions, but she realized that a simple ward circle might actually distract Robin and Lyric from sniping. She fetched her own small supply of chalk from a drawer.

She took a seat on the floor across from Robin, heart thrumming at the thought of spells in such a tight space.

Robin's chalk lines glowed a vibrant pink, humming with a chaotic energy that smelled of ozone and summer storms.

"Alysia, the containment glyphs," she prompted.

Alysia nodded, looking forward. Her own magic was the complete opposite, cool, precise, and silent. She drew two triangular symbols, and they settled into the floor with the steady, golden hum of a perfectly tuned instrument.

"Not bad," Lyric commented, moving forward. "But it lacks finesse." Without asking, she extended a hand.

Threads of shadow and silver bled from her fingertips, weaving into the chalk lines. It wasn't an addition; it was a fusion. The entire circle's hum deepened, its light sharpening from a playful glow to the hard gleam of forged steel. Alysia had never seen illusions so controlled, so exact.

Kael joined in, but his illusions were different from his sister's. Where hers were controlled and cold, his were wild and alive, tendrils of pure silver that danced alongside Lyric's, not blending but harmonizing, like two competing melodies that created a beautiful, heartbreaking song.

Robin completed the circle's outer ring with a flourish. "Time to test it. I will conjure a small decoy, and you two can see if the circle holds it."

She tapped her chalk, and a faint coppery spark danced over the lines. An image of a small, winged serpent coalesced at the center of the circle. The shimmering decoy flapped its ethereal wings, testing for an escape route. The magical boundary held firm.

Lyric angled her head. "Surprisingly successful. You did not blow us up."

"Thanks for the vote of confidence," Robin said dryly. "I could do the same with bigger illusions if we had more space, but I am not trying to tear down the dorm walls."

Alysia exhaled in relief. She touched the runic lines with careful reverence, then used a gentle dispersal incantation. The illusions and chalk glimmers dissolved, leaving only the faint chalk outlines. "All right, so the synergy works. Good. Maybe that helps us if we run into illusions in the Obscura Wing."

Kael's illusions faded, and he flinched, pulling his gloved hand back as if burned. Alysia caught the sharp intake of breath, seeing his knuckles whiten under the leather. The synergy, for all its beauty, had clearly taken a toll on his brand, a cost he was determined to hide.

Alysia noticed and set her hand lightly on his arm. He gave her a tense nod, as if to say he could handle it. Lyric's eyes looked over the motion, her lips thinning. A hint of something crossed her face, maybe guilt, maybe disapproval. Alysia could not tell.

Robin folded her arms. "So. Truce on the bickering? Because we will need to be at our best if we are sneaking around illusions. I do not want caretaker wards chasing us again."

Lyric's scoff was soft. "I will not promise perfection, but I see your point." She looked from Alysia to Kael. "Give me a short while to gather more details about what I suspect. Then we can all head to the Obscura Wing. No crossfire, minimal hexes. Clear?"

Robin rolled her eyes. "Crystal clear."

The faint pink outline of the ward circle remained on the floor, proof that they could work together. Their volatile magic, Alysia's precision, Robin's chaos, Lyric's cold finesse, and Kael's wild heart, could be woven into a single, powerful spell.

As Alysia watched Robin and Lyric trade another pair of sharp, challenging glances, she realized the truth. They were two sides of the same fiercely protective coin, each brandishing sarcasm like a shield to hide the loyalty that burned underneath.

Their greatest strength was this impossible synergy, and it was also their greatest weakness. As they prepared to venture into the Obscura Wing, Alysia felt a fresh wave of dread. It wasn't the rogue illusions she feared most but the possibility that the four of them would tear each other apart long before the enemy ever had the chance.

CHAPTER

TWELVE

THE FOUR SPELLCASTERS

Alysia felt the charged air before she even stepped into the sunlight of the common yard. The day had started with the usual gossip and rumors, but by midday, it had ignited into a spectacle. Someone near the courtyard gate whispered about a duel. Others ran to find vantage points. Curious tension pulled Alysia forward, and her pulse spiked. She threaded past clusters of onlookers until the crowd thinned enough that she could see who stood at the center.

Robin and Lyric circled each other on the flagstones, arms raised defensively. Neither spoke. Even at a distance, Alysia recognized the faint shimmer of illusions trailing around Lyric's fingertips and the prepared wards in Robin's stance. Alysia's stomach lurched. This was not friendly sparring.

She edged closer, slipping between two wide-eyed classmates who were pointing excitedly at the conjured illusions around Lyric's shoulders. Moth-eaten newspa-

125

pers and leaves spun in the air, evidence of an illusory wind stirring from someone's incantation. The sunlight glinted off Lyric's dark hair as she tilted her head, openly assessing Robin. Her quiet smirk dared Robin to make the first move.

Robin brushed a strand of her short, tousled hair off her forehead. She wore a satisfied grin, though her eyes glinted with razor focus. In her left hand, a piece of chalk glowed faintly, runes half-etched along its tip. Alysia knew that chalk. Robin had used it in their cramped dorm the previous night for a ward circle. That small piece contained enough stored illusions to fill an entire corridor with chaos.

"What in all the seas are they doing?" Alysia muttered, half to herself. She expected Kael to answer, but he was not at her side. Instead, she spotted him across the courtyard, pressing through the crowd. He looked as tense as she felt. Already, a handful of watchers had begun shouting encouragement. Some cried, "Come on, make it big!" Others just stared at the spectacle in awe.

Lyric's smooth voice rose above the murmurs. "If you want a demonstration of skill, you need only ask." She made a short motion with her right hand. Illusions shimmered at the edge of her cloak. A phantom swirl of violet light materialized, shaped like a coiling serpent that dripped ephemeral sparks onto the courtyard stones.

Robin held her ground. She gave a mocking bow. "You want me to ask nicely, oh wise illusionist? Because your illusions are lovely, but I do not kneel to other people's fancy lights." She underscored her words with a snort and lunged forward in a half-step, chalk scraping briefly against the ground.

A ripple of shouting broke out from the onlookers. Someone in the back whistled. Another hissed in excitement. This was not a controlled demonstration, not a class activity. It was pure, unfiltered posturing with spells that were far too aggressive for a casual duel. She tensed as she saw Kael push closer to the ring. He looked ready to intervene, illusions stirring around his gloved hand. His gaze shifted from Lyric to Robin, then landed on Alysia's face for a brief moment. She read the warning there. This is about to get out of control.

Alysia inhaled sharply and forced a path through the throng. She nudged aside a couple of wide-eyed younger students. They shuffled back without protest, more interested in the possibility of watching a spectacular meltdown. She reached Kael's side just as Robin made her first real attack.

The fraction of a second's stillness cracked into sudden motion. Robin flung out her arm, releasing illusions shaped into playful, floating orbs. At first, they resembled harmless glass spheres. Then the orbs sparked with greenish lightning, zigzagging across open air and leaving scorched patterns in their wake.

The lightning carved a twisting line on the courtyard floor, dangerously close to Lyric's feet.

Lyric countered by snapping her fingers. A wave of mirrored illusions blossomed at her command. Sparkling shards formed an arc of reflective shapes around her body that deflected the green sparks, scattering them upward like shooting stars. The collision hissed and spat, sending half-real flames skittering toward the nearest wall. Students screamed, choosing either to duck or to scramble behind stone benches.

Alysia flinched, cursing under her breath. This was worse than she thought. The illusions were showy and laced with real power. If either lost control, caretaker wards would appear any second. She darted a glance at Kael. He was already stepping forward, illusions at his fingertips. She shook her head and urgently grabbed his forearm.

"Not yet," she whispered. "If we jump in while they are both charged, they might turn their spells on us."

Kael's jaw tensed, but he stayed in place. His illusion glimmer faded slightly.

Nearby, Robin's illusions collided with Lyric's again. The crowd yelled in alarm when a stray spark sizzled along the top of a decorative arch. Several older students started to form a containment ward around the courtyard, but it was incomplete. A portion of the ward lines glimmered, leaving a glaring gap. Alysia swallowed hard. One misfire could send masonry tumbling.

She looked back at the duel. Both Robin and Lyric circled each other like dancers: graceful, furious, and unwilling to yield. Lyric shot a cluster of illusory shards forward. Robin created a hasty barrier with her chalk. The illusions sparked, sending a wash of tinted dust across the courtyard. Through the haze, Alysia saw Robin's grin fade, replaced by a fierce concentration. For all her casual banter, Robin was clearly not holding back.

"Enough!" Alysia shouted, stepping forward. The spectators parted a fraction so she could see better. Lyric hissed something, too low for Alysia to catch, and raised her arms high. A swirl of illusions shaped itself into a shimmering blade of light that hovered overhead. Robin tensed, dropping her chalk into her other hand. She sketched runes in the air, possibly to conjure a ward circle.

Before the illusions could clash again, Kael stepped forward beside Alysia. He lifted his gloved hand, illusions sparking at his fingertips, and called, "Stop this or I will stop it for you!" The echo of his voice carried across the yard. That was no idle threat. Alysia felt the crackling aura around him, and her heart hammered at the potential collision of illusions if he intervened. She grabbed Kael's wrist, though not to restrain him, more to remind him that they needed caution.

Both Robin and Lyric glanced at Kael, momentarily acknowledging his presence. Fire glimmered in Lyric's eyes as if to say she welcomed the challenge. Her illusions still pulsed overhead, trailing glints of violet. Robin unleashed a fresh flurry of illusions in response, creating butterfly-shaped projectiles. The illusions crashed into each other with a blast of color.

A shard of the conjured blade disguised as a large, fiery wing veered off course. It slammed against the high wall of the courtyard's outer perimeter. Stone groaned under the impact, cracks spreading upward. One chunk of masonry dislodged and fell, missing a cluster of students by a matter of inches. Panic rippled through the onlookers.

Several scattered. Others called for the caretaker wards. The tension soared toward calamity.

She willed her own wards to the surface, her arms curling to shape a protective line across the damaged section of stone. The effort throbbed with tension as she poured her magic into a quick, improvised fix. She was no skilled mason, but her ward might buy enough time for the caretaker wards to reinforce the structure.

Kael stepped into the illusions, his right arm raised. Light flared from his palm, illusions meeting illusions in a fierce clash that sent sparks raining over the courtyard. The brightness seared Alysia's eyes for a moment. When she blinked away the afterimages, she saw Kael forcibly redirecting Lyric's conjured blade into harmless embers. He twisted illusions around Robin's leftover shards, dissolving them into flecks of harmless light.

Robin staggered. Her illusions flickered out. Lyric let out a sharp hiss, her shoulders stiff. For a tense heartbeat, the entire courtyard seemed to hold its breath, waiting to see if either woman would lash out again.

Then it happened. A commanding voice tore through the crowd. Headmistress Quen stomped into the yard, flanked by two caretaker wards shaped like tall, armor-clad figures. Her robes glinted with gold thread as she surveyed the near destruction: the cracked wall, the scorched stone at the courtyard's center, the illusions still fading into the air.

While the caretaker wards set about reinforcing the courtyard's stability, Headmistress Quen's furious gaze swept from Lyric to Robin and then to Kael. Her expression hardened when it fell on Alysia. Alysia lowered her arms, her own wards fizzing out in a ring of faint light. Anxiety sank cold in her stomach.

"Explain this," Headmistress Quen said, her eyes blazing. She gestured at the crumbling wall, the scorched flags, and the frightened students who had pressed themselves against the courtyard's outer edges.

Robin opened her mouth, but Lyric beat her to it. "We had... a friendly disagreement," Lyric said in a cool tone that implied no regret. "A demonstration that got a bit heated."

"Friendly?" Robin repeated, rolling her eyes. "I did not see you holding back, Meridan."

The caretaker wards silently patrolled the perimeter, their metal hands raised to bolster the cracked wall. Their presence alone was a reminder of the Academy's strict regulations about public duels. Headmistress Quen exhaled in exasperation.

"We do not permit unregistered fights on these grounds," Quen said in a measured voice. "That was not a demonstration of academically approved sparring. It was an uncontrolled display of illusions that endangered your fellow students. This is unacceptable."

Robin stiffened. Lyric's face remained impassive, though Alysia noticed a twitch in her jaw. Kael's illusions simmered down as he let his arm fall to his side. Alysia could sense the tension shaping into something that might lead to disciplinary action. The entire courtyard was silent, waiting for Quen's verdict. Whispers about possible expulsions rippled through the crowd.

Quen's gaze scanned the four of them. "You will all face consequences," she said, her voice resonating across the courtyard. "This chaos nearly brought down a wall of Velgrace Academy. If I had arrived seconds later...you could have caused serious harm."

Robin cleared her throat. "It was not all her fault," she said, flicking a glance at Lyric. "I might have been the one to escalate it."

Lyric raised an eyebrow. "Oh, you want to take the blame?"

"Stop," Kael said, stepping forward. "They did not do this alone. This entire fiasco is tied to the illusions we were practicing. Alysia and I contributed. We are a single study team preparing advanced illusions...and we have been training together. Their duel was a...misapplication of that work."

It was a lie, but it was a clever one. He was creating a narrative. A single, unified project gone wrong. It was their only way out of this without Quen making an example of Robin and Lyric. He was giving them all cover. She had to anchor his story, just as she anchored his illusions. A pinprick of gratitude and dread flashed through her.

She opened her mouth, her voice wavering only slightly. "Yes. We...we are all at fault. Our illusions have grown more intricate, and we tested them improperly. Kael and I did not step in soon enough to stop Robin and Lyric. We apologize."

Silence followed her words. Lyric looked as though she might argue, but then she saw how Quen's glare swept around them. Robin bowed her head in resigned acceptance.

The Headmistress's fury was palpable. She eyed Kael and Alysia suspiciously.

"So, you are claiming this was a unified project gone awry? A unified study team?"

Alysia's mouth felt parched. She forced a nod. "Yes."

Robin gave a stiff shrug. "All of us. One team, I guess."

Lyric hesitated, scanning Kael's face. He met her gaze for a split second, something like an unspoken apology hanging there. Finally, Lyric inclined her head. "Fine," she said in a low voice.

Several students gathered near the courtyard's edges exchanged surprised glances.

A unified front from these four was news indeed. Alysia saw a wave of relief cross Robin's features, though she tried to mask it with a look of feigned annoyance. Lyric maintained a regal calm, as if this turn of events amused her more than alarmed her.

Kael brushed dust from his sleeve, meeting Quen's stare. "We take responsibility," he said, his voice steady.

Headmistress Quen pressed her lips into a thin line. She looked as though she wanted to give them all a week of detention or possibly banish them from the academy entirely. But she was nothing if not strategic. A public fiasco in front of half the school demanded immediate consequences, but also a path to prevent further damage. Her eyes looked to the caretaker wards shoring up the cracked wall, then back to her four students.

"Very well," she said. "I will hear the full account of

your illusions and wards. For now, all four of you are to remain under close supervision. If I so much as sense a whiff of unapproved dueling, you will not simply be disciplined. You will be removed from this academy. Am I clear?"

"Yes, Headmistress," Alysia managed. Kael and Robin voiced similar assent. Lyric only dipped her chin in the slightest show of compliance.

Quen pursed her lips, then gestured for the caretaker wards to handle the rest of the damaged courtyard. "The rest of you, back to your schedules," she announced to the onlookers. "This spectacle is over."

A slow exodus began, students murmuring among themselves about the unexpected face-off. Alysia felt the tension still throbbing in the air. She stepped closer to Robin, lowering her voice. "Why in the realm did you challenge her in the first place?"

Robin shrugged, though her bravado barely masked the lingering adrenaline. "She taunted me. I do not back down. Besides, I might have wanted to see what illusions she really had up her sleeve."

"You found out," Alysia said sharply, though her anger toward her cousin was already fading into exhaustion. "You nearly took down a wall."

"And that is why we are doing this again," Lyric said flatly, hooking a thumb toward the caretaker wards. "Repairing damage because we could not collaborate like sensible spellcasters."

Kael passed a glance between them. The courtyard was emptying. "We will figure out how to manage this," he said. He sounded weary but also determined. "No more splitting off on our own. If Quen is forcing us to be responsible together, we do it properly."

Alysia gave a slow nod. She felt an odd unity in that moment, as if they stood on a shared battlefield, bruised from the first round of conflict. Robin and Lyric each possessed a pride that burned hot, too hot, at times. Kael carried illusions that could crush or save them, depending on his focus. Alysia harbored wards that might protect them all if she learned how to apply them under pressure.

They had declared themselves a single study team in front of the entire academy. Now they would actually have to behave like one. As the caretaker wards hammered reinforcements into the stone, and Headmistress Quen stalked off to file her scathing report, the four of them remained behind in the sunlight.

As the last of the crowd dispersed, the four of them were left in the wreckage. No one spoke. Lyric met Robin's gaze with grudging respect. Robin offered a stiff, almost imperceptible nod in return. Alysia looked at Kael, whose own eyes told her he knew exactly what they had just done. They hadn't chosen this. But by declaring themselves a team in front of the entire academy, their fates were now bound. The duel was over, but the real battle had just begun.

THIRTEEN

CHARM DUEL DAY

Alysia stood at the edge of the bustling courtyard, her hands clenched around the thin ridges of her charm-stitched gloves. She could feel the excited hum of energy across Velgrace Academy, a collective anticipation that pressed upon her like a tangible thing. Charm Duel Day had arrived at last. Banners of shimmering silk hung from the stone arches, spelled illusions moved across every column, and students milled about in bright knots, discussing who might triumph this year.

Large, carefully inscribed sigils decorated the central dueling grounds, reflecting sunlight in precise angles.

Despite her nerves, she marveled at the Academy's transformation. For weeks, everyone had whispered about the legendary "final exhibition," a spectacle in which the top contenders faced off in carefully scored charm duels. Professors gave students the day off from regular lessons, focusing all attention on the scheduled roster of illusions, wards, and elaborate enchantments. Vibrant illusions danced in the air, forming winged shapes that soared past the towers. From far off, Alysia heard exclamations as an upperclassman conjured a flying tapestry in front of a delighted crowd.

She inhaled and took inventory of her composure. Robin had teased her early that morning, pinning a glittery paper star onto Alysia's shoulder and insisting it would bring luck. Now, that star flickered in the sunlight, its illusions subtle yet steady. As the breeze lifted the edges of her cloak, Alysia forced herself to breathe deeply.

She scanned the courtyard for any sign of Kael. When her eyes finally found him, her heart gave an uneasy thump. He stood across the courtyard, adjusting one of the illusions on his gloved palm. His raven-dark hair shifted with each movement, but his posture looked strangely tense. Normally, Kael thrived on showing off. He would flash a smirk and conjure illusions that spiraled across the courtyard, delighting onlookers or unnerving them, depending on his mood. Today, though, the illusions that constantly danced at his fingertips were gone. His hands were still, his posture rigid. It was the stark absence of his usual magic that signaled to Alysia how deeply unsettled he was. Alysia stepped around a group of younger students who were busy chattering about the day's line-up. They bragged about illusions they wanted to try but lacked the seniority to participate in the final rounds. As Alysia made her way toward Kael, she passed a table covered with small cups of celebratory punch. The tang of citrus hung in the air, drifting alongside the smell of chalk dust and incanted smoke.

"Hey," she said softly as she reached Kael's side.

He turned, illusions sliding across his fingertips in a chaotic silver sparks. "Hey."

She tilted her head, eyeing how his illusions flickered in uneven arcs. "You good?"

His mouth tugged into a half-smile, no teasing grin, no sly remark. "I'm fine," he answered automatically, but his tone lacked its usual confidence.

Alysia would have pressed him further if Headmistress Quen's voice had not suddenly cut through the courtyard. "Attention, everyone," Quen called, magic amplifying her voice without needing a shout. "We will now proceed with our final bracket of Charm Duel Day. The top remaining contenders, please come forward."

A murmur spread through the assembled crowd. Spectators hurried to find the best vantage points near the ring, cramming onto benches or leaning against tall columns. Students of all years peered eagerly at the main dais, which had been spelled to glow in a ring of pale light. The dais itself was modest, barely elevated from the courtyard floor, but illusions made it appear encircled by shimmering curtains of color.

Alysia glanced at Kael again, lowering her voice. "Let's do our best," she said, letting a note of encouragement seep into her words.

He inhaled slowly and nodded. "Right. Best."

They walked side by side to the dais. A series of duels had already taken place that morning, each one whittling down the top pairs. Now, Alysia and Kael stood among the remaining final teams. Their opponents stepped forward:

a fifth-year duo known for complicated illusions combined with barrier wards. The older pair nodded stiffly in greeting.

Headmistress Quen gestured over the crowd. She explained that each pair would have a brief window to deliver a combined spell demonstration, intricate illusions or wards, or a synergy of both. Points would be awarded for creativity, control, and unity of magic. The score tallies from earlier duels counted toward the final result.

Alysia's pulse pounded. She stepped into the ring, taking her place near Kael. From the corner of her eye, she noticed how his gloved hand trembled once. He quickly pressed it against his side, as though trying to hide the tremor.

They launched into the demonstration. The plan had been outlined in detail: Alysia would open with a blossom of wards shaped like filigree lines, forming a protective lattice. Kael was to weave illusions around that lattice, transforming them into dancing shapes of light and color. They had practiced the exact sequence.

But the moment she traced her first runic lines in the air, she sensed his illusions faltering. Usually, his illusions glided smoothly into place. Now, they fractured in mid air, dissolving into a gray, joyless smoke before they could touch her wards. The crowd's murmuring grew louder. A wave of uncertain energy rippled through the wards and jostled her focus. She tried to compensate and layered an extra stabilizing glyph. Kael aimed to send fractal illusions across the dais, but they fizzled into scattered sparks.

Alysia's heart lurched. The crowd remained politely

silent, though she could sense confusion as watchers traded glances. The older pair of opponents waited on their side of the dais, arms crossed, expecting a spectacular unveiling. Instead, all seemed offbeat.

Her wards formed stunted arcs, more blocky than elegant. She pushed more power into them, but that only produced arcs of energy straining to keep shape. Kael's illusions fluttered in harsh bursts. She stole a glance at him, noticing sweat along his temple.

The crowd began to murmur in earnest now. Alysia heard a student somewhere in the back call, "Are they messing up?" She swallowed, pushing away a sting of humiliation. This was heartbreakingly far from the synergy they used to share, however brief it had been. She remembered a recent practice session when their combined illusions had blazed with brilliance, only to fade once Kael pulled back. He was pulling back again. She could feel it in the jagged tension of the air.

She heard a faint, encouraging whoop from Robin's direction. That sparked a thread of determination in her gut. She was not going to watch everything unravel.

Then Kael's illusions abruptly sputtered out. She half expected him to continue forcing the plan. Instead, he froze.

She realized with startling clarity that the plan, their meticulous, practiced structure, was suffocating his magic. It needed a foundation, not a cage. In that split second, she abandoned the routine. Trusting an instinct that felt more real than any textbook, she hooked three wards into the air and shaped them not as a static lattice but as a dynamic, rotating ring.

He blinked, his gaze flicking to her spinning wards. She spoke softly, so only he could hear, "Let me anchor. You find your own rhythm." Her voice sounded calmer than she felt.

For a heartbeat, he did not move. Then a small, uncertain flutter of light glowed at his fingertips. He curled it into a shape that shimmered in watery arcs.

Alysia anchored the wards in a slow rotation, fueling them with gentle pulses of magic. An audible murmur came from the crowd, intrigued by the improvised ring. She felt Kael's illusions brush against it. In that moment, she realized he found his footing, as though an invisible lock clicked.

He conjured illusions that formed ribbons of silver, each floating across the rotating wards. They twisted with the ring's motion, propelled by the protective lines Alysia offered. This was not the delicate swirl they had practiced. It was something rawer, more emotional, like Kael was baring his own pulse in the illusions. The ribbons flared brilliantly.

Warmth rushed into Alysia's chest. She responded with wards forging new patterns around his illusions. The ring expanded, arcs bending outward to meet the illusions that soared like fish in a luminous tide. Surprise sparked across Kael's eyes, and together they guided those illusions in an ever-widening dance.

Her heart pounded. She could tell no one had expected such a display. Chatter swelled in the courtyard, low at first, then roaring with excitement. A few illusions soared overhead, reflecting rainbow glimmers across the watchers. A sense of awe fell in the front rows.

Alysia's limbs tingled with adrenaline. She had never conjured wards in such a flowing style before. She told herself to keep calm, to keep the rotation stable, but she could not stop the grin that tugged at her lips as she watched their combined magic paint the air in shimmering arcs.

The illusions pulsed in vibrant synergy, the wards stepping in to cradle them whenever they went astray. For his part, Kael conjured shapes she had never seen, shapes that shifted from geometric fractals into fleeting images of sea creatures, shell-like whorls morphing into graceful wings. It was mesmerizing and oddly tender, as though each illusion was a piece of himself offered to her wards for safe-keeping.

She realized she was sweating too, but now it felt exhilarating rather than terrifying. He shot her a look that held something simmering under the surface: gratitude, longing, maybe even reassurance that he was letting his walls down at last. Their magic collided and grew. The ring of wards expanded overhead into an luminescent canopy.

When the final wave of illusions burst in shining arcs that cascaded like a waterfall of light, the courtyard erupted into applause. The dais was flooded with the afterglow of silver sparks. Alysia stood there, heart pounding, breath coming fast, illusions dissolving around her in a haze of color.

Next to her, Kael lowered his hand, illusions shimmering faintly away. She saw relief in his eyes, along with something deeper that made her pulse spike. For a single beat, the rest of the Academy seemed to vanish, and all she knew was the steady weight of his presence.

Then the crowd's roar intensified. Students leaped up from their seats, cheering, clapping, whistling. The ring of wards cracked apart in a final, showy flourish. She shuddered out a breath, dazed by the roar of approval. It felt unreal.

CHAPTER

FOURTEEN

AFTER THE APPLAUSE

Alysia stepped through the crowd gathered just inside the Academy's main corridor, her skin still humming with leftover adrenaline from the duel. The rowdy applause outside on the dueling grounds had become softer now, changed into scattered pockets of cheers and echoing congratulations. Still, she felt the buzz of excitement clinging to the air like traces of sparks. This was the aftermath of victory, an energy so intense she could almost taste it.

Robin was at Alysia's side, half-laughing and half-gasping, her bright eyes darting around the corridor for anyone interested in swapping stories. "I swear," Robin said between huffs of breath, "if we could bottle the look on that one fifth-year's face when you and Kael did those illusions, we'd be the richest pair in Velgrace." She tucked a lock of hair behind her ear, grinning.

Alysia tried to match Robin's enthusiasm, but her own heartbeat hammered in a tight, conflicting rhythm. She had seen Kael slip away moments before the circle of admirers had a chance to close in. He had lingered on the edge of the courtyard long enough to exchange a nod with one of the professors, then walked briskly in the opposite direction of the applause. Now, for reasons she could not quite name, an uneasy feeling kept her from fully celebrating.

She forced a small smile. "It wasn't just me," she replied quietly, thinking of Kael's illusions that had danced across her wards with such vivid synergy. "He made it possible."

Robin's grin softened. "Yeah, but you're the one who anchored those illusions. You both looked unstoppable out there." Then, catching the shift in Alysia's expression, Robin's eyebrows tilted. "Where'd he go, anyway?"

Alysia looked over the heads of a small group of cheering first-year students. Professors from Obscura Wing were milling near the hallway ends, exchanging subtle glances. She realized they were noticing Kael's absence as well. "Not sure," Alysia admitted. "He was... right beside me, and then he seemed to see something in the crowd. He turned pale and just walked off."

Robin blew out an exasperated breath. "That boy's mood changes faster than the tide." She tapped Alysia's forearm, then nodded toward the exit. "Go find him. I can keep your fan club occupied."

Alysia blinked, about to protest. She could just imagine how awkward it would be, chasing after Kael moments after a major performance. Yet a surge of concern spurred her on. Something had unsettled him, and if she knew Kael, it did not bode well to leave him alone with that unsettling thought.

She slipped past a couple of older students congratulating her with polite bows. The corridor opened into one of the interior courtyards where a handful of watchers remained. Most were still buzzing about the demonstration. As Alysia entered, she glimpsed bright banners flapping from the upper balconies, each shimmering with illusions from the day's festivities. The sunlight filtering down made the flags glow like trapped rainbows.

At the far edge of the courtyard, she finally spotted Kael. He had paused against a column, standing oddly rigid. A man in a plain instructor's robe had just passed him by, leaving lingering conversation in his wake. Alysia recognized the older man only vaguely, someone who had been at the final bracket but seldom taught first- or second-level wards. He was adjusting a small pendant around his neck as he wove through the crowd. Something about that pendant flashed with an ominous resonance.

Alysia's pulse quickened. She hurried to close the distance between herself and Kael. "Hey," she said softly, touching his elbow. "Are you all right?"

He startled at her voice, illusions sparking at his fingertips for an instant. Then, with obvious effort, he dismissed the wave of magic. He inhaled slowly, not meeting her eyes. "I'm fine," he answered curtly.

The tenseness in his shoulders contradicted the words. She could sense the agitated energy around him. They had just shared a victory, one that everyone seemed determined to celebrate, so what could possibly end his triumph so abruptly?

Alysia pressed her lips together, searching for the right approach. "You disappeared right after we finished," she said. "You didn't want to stay for the applause?"

His jaw twitched. "Applause means nothing if our entire demonstration might have been shadowed by a threat."

She paused, the weight of his statement settling between them. "Threat?" She glanced at the robed instructor who had disappeared into the corridor. "What do you mean?"

Kael's gaze moved toward where that man had gone. "Did you notice his pendant?" His tone was barely above a whisper. "It bore a symbol I recognize from old rumor, an insignia some rogue charm practitioners have used for years. I've heard it referred to as an 'echo brand.' But I never thought I'd see it here, in broad daylight."

"The brand is a key," he added, his voice dropping lower. "Its bearers can see the echoes of powerful magic, feeding on its resonance. Our synergy in the duel would have been like a lighthouse beacon to them."

Alysia's eyes widened. She tried to recall illusions or emblems she had studied in the library, but the hallways around them erupted in a sudden burst of cheering. A group of second-year illusions students trotted past, calling Kael's name and showering him with illusions shaped like tiny confetti bits. Kael nodded stiffly in acknowledgment, but his jaw remained clenched. Alysia followed his line of sight again, but the instructor was already gone.

She stepped closer to him, speaking low. "Are you sure it was that mark?"

Kael let out a soft, humorless laugh. "My father once told me that rogue illusions often hide out in plain sight. They look innocuous until you see the brand that ties them together. I've seen sketches of that symbol, stylized lines crossing an eye. I recognized it instantly."

Alysia shivered. She had never heard Kael reference his father much. He rarely spoke about his family unless pressed. The significance of him sharing this now hinted at just how disturbed he was. "And you think that person is... what? Part of a faction?"

"I don't know," Kael said through tight lips. "But it's no coincidence. Our illusions today drew a massive crowd, including watchers not from our Academy. If the rogue faction has an informant or ally here, we might have just performed for them without realizing it."

Her mind whirled. Professors had grumbled for weeks about infiltration, though no one had concrete proof. She recalled that moment during the final duel when the illusions had soared overhead, mesmerizing everyone. If a rogue agent was present, they would have observed the synergy between wards and illusions in perfect detail.

"Kael," she said softly, "they didn't see everything. We never revealed how we formed the synergy, just the outcome."

He exhaled, black hair shifting around his temples. "It

might still be enough. That demonstration was too public."

She reached for his hand, hesitating only briefly. When her fingers brushed his, she felt him tremble. "Let's talk in a quieter place. Standing here in the corridor with all these people…we can't think straight."

He cast a grim glance at the bustle around them. "Fine," he said, his shoulders sagging. "Lead the way."

Alysia guided him to a narrow side staircase that wound toward a deserted classroom. The day's events had almost emptied the rooms, since everyone was still celebrating outside or moving between halls. Her footsteps echoed on the stone steps, that felt strangely ominous. She felt the burn of her own tension seeping into the soles of her feet. A victorious day had spiraled into an uneasy puzzle, and she could hardly keep her thoughts in order.

Once they reached the small classroom, Alysia slid the door shut behind them. Dust motes floated in the slivers of light from the high windows. A chalkboard and a few pushed-aside desks provided the only furnishings. It smelled of old books and stale enchantments. She forced a steady breath.

Kael leaned against the wall, arms folded. The coral amulet against his chest glinted faintly. "Sorry," he muttered, blinking as if to clear his head. "I don't mean to ruin the moment."

"It's not ruined," she insisted, stepping closer. "We just need to understand what we saw."

He looked down, illusions dancing at the edges of his fingertips before vanishing again. "I recognized the symbol. That's enough to put me on edge. I'm not sure if that instructor was wearing it knowingly, but the brand is never random."

Alysia tried to recall anything from the Academy database about suspicious symbols, but her own knowledge came up short. "We can talk to Headmistress Quen," she offered, though her voice lacked conviction. The Headmistress might not take kindly to a direct accusation without solid proof. "Or maybe we ask Robin to gather more information. She's good at gleaning rumors fast."

Kael's lips curved into the slightest grimace. "Any approach is dangerous if we tip off the wrong person. Quen might already have suspicions. This infiltration could be bigger than an individual wearing a cryptic pendant."

She exhaled, pressing her hand against the nearest desk to steady her thoughts.

"Why do you think they want to watch us?" she asked. Her words rang hollow even as she said them. She knew full well that the illusions she and Kael shaped were far from ordinary. Their synergy stood out, attracting both admirers and possible enemies. If a rogue faction wanted to harness that, they'd be watching very closely.

"We might be valuable," Kael said quietly. "Your wards and my illusions. That combination could be… extremely powerful in the wrong hands." He gripped the amulet at his throat. "I don't want to hand them anything they could exploit."

Alysia listened to the echo of each word, recalling the fleeting sense of dread she had felt earlier. She felt torn between the pride of what they had accomplished and a sudden fear that they'd drawn someone dangerous right to them. Her mind turned to Robin, who would have a hundred opinions about secrets, infiltration, and the abrupt shift in Kael's mood.

She stepped within arm's length of him, noticing how tense his posture remained. Her voice gentled. "You don't need to bear this by yourself." Her words carried conviction. "We can keep an eye out. We'll figure out if that pendant truly signals a rogue affiliation. But shutting down or shrinking away from your success won't help."

For a moment, Kael kept his gaze fixed on the floor. Then, as if summoned by her sincerity, he finally lifted his eyes to hers. "It's never been easy for me to trust. Everyone at this Academy questioned whether I was the threat. Now I see the real threat might be right here, walking the same halls."

Alysia's breath caught in her throat. She remembered the illusions he had conjured on the dais, how the final burst had shimmered with an exhilarating harmony. That memory felt warm against her chest, a reminder that just hours ago, they had soared together. Now, shadows threatened to taint it.

She placed a hand on his arm. "We'll stay watchful," she said firmly. "But we can't let fear steal what we fought for. You earned that applause. We both did."

A reluctant spark of a smile flitted across his face, though it did not reach his eyes. He angled his head, perhaps wanting to say more. Then footsteps squeaked in the corridor, announcing someone's approach. Kael took a quick step back, illusions scattering at his fingertips in reflex.

Robin's voice filtered through the door. "Alysia? Kael? If you're in there, don't be all weird. We have admirers waiting to fawn over you both, and I can't stall them forever."

Alysia exchanged a brief glance with Kael, noticing how his charismatic mask slid into place. He swallowed, squared his shoulders, and nodded for her to open the door. She obeyed, revealing Robin leaning against the doorway, arms crossed in feigned impatience.

Robin's eyes fitted between them. "Enjoying the solitary corners while everyone else is in the mood for a hero's welcome?" Her tone was light, but the slight pinch in her brow showed her concern.

"We needed a moment," Alysia said. She kept her voice calm, trying to hide the tension in her mind. "It's been a long day."

Robin gazed at Kael, then at Alysia, and pursed her lips. She did not push. Instead, she let out a dramatic sigh. "Fine. Well, I've managed to direct your more enthusiastic fans back to the main courtyard. Professors Dain and Morn applauded your technique." She paused, her gaze lingering on Kael. "But people are noticing your absence, and your face, Kael. Everybody's talking about your illusions. They'll want to see you look proud of them, not gloomier than a storm cloud."

Kael cleared his throat. "Right. Perhaps I should—"

"What happened?" Robin interrupted gently. "You

look spooked." She locked eyes with Alysia, who tensed at the question.

Alysia answered before Kael had to. "We saw something that felt out of place. We're worried it could be a sign of trouble."

Robin narrowed her eyes, scanning their faces. She spun a finger as though reeling them in. "You two can't do anything halfway. Fine. We'll talk about it after the excitement dies down. We do not want rumors spreading. The last thing we need is more speculation." She took a half-step back, beckoning them to follow. "Let's return to the others and at least act like we're enjoying the applause, yes?"

Alysia glanced at Kael. He dipped his head almost imperceptibly, consenting to Robin's plan. The three of them left the quiet classroom in silence. They stepped into the corridor again, where the proud chatter of students and faculty eddied in a constant hum. Someone yelled, "Alysia, Kael, there you are!" A new wave of illusions lit the air, forming shimmering shapes that resembled bright phoenix birds flapping overhead. Applause rippled from all sides.

Alysia tried to let the positivity soak into her skin, tried to recall the surge of triumph she had felt during the final duel. She forced a small smile, giving short nods to admirers who approached them. Yet the memory of Kael's sudden alarm in the courtyard blunted her enthusiasm. She could sense Kael also wearing a polite, distant expression that never quite relaxed.

One of the professors, a tall, slender figure who

specialized in advanced illusions, congratulated them on creating a combined spell effect unlike any she had witnessed in recent years. Her words echoed the general awe drifting through the Academy: that synergy was so seamless, so vibrant. Alysia offered a grateful bow, swallowing a lump of uncertainty. She heard Robin laughing with a younger student who complimented the glimmering arcs that had formed around Alysia's wards.

In the midst of all this praise, Alysia felt like a lantern glimpsed through fog. She could shine and respond with gracious words, but just behind that glow, she sensed a shadow creeping closer. Glancing at Kael, she saw the same tension in his eyes. He offered the bare minimum of polite acknowledgments to those who congratulated him. Every so often, his gaze moved around them, scanning for that robed instructor or the disturbing pendant.

Students lined the corridors, a testament to how widely the news had spread. A couple of them shouted, "Incredible show, Alysia!" She mustered a smile. Another group of watchers bowed their heads to Kael, exclaiming, "Teach us some illusions next time!" He gave a nod, but the corners of his mouth barely quirked.

Robin hung back a step, observing the way Kael's posture stayed guarded. Alysia felt Robin's stare, knew her cousin was noticing exactly how forced Kael's responses were. But Robin, for once, stayed quiet. If, in that moment, she had teased him, it might have triggered a scene, and nobody wanted that. The students were too elated to comprehend the undercurrent of fear slicing through the three of them.

Eventually, however, the crowd thinned. People meandered away to grab refreshments or to find friends who had also dueled. Some teachers strolled off in small groups, discussing the day's results. The corridor quieted to a low murmur of voices and distant clapping from some other corner of the Academy. The entire atmosphere seemed to shift into a subdued calm.

Kael slipped a hand into one of his cloak's hidden pockets, his face drawn. "I think," he said slowly, addressing Alysia and Robin both, "I'm going to get some air, maybe along the bluff behind Bastion Hall. I just...can't be around all this right now."

Robin started to speak, but Alysia shook her head gently. She suspected that pressing Kael to stay would do more harm than good. "All right," she said, her voice soft. "Just be careful. We don't know who else is watching."

Kael's mouth twitched into a grim half-smile. "I know." He hesitated, glancing at Alysia. His gray eyes softened for a moment, as if he wanted to say something to reassure her. Instead, he gave the smallest of nods, turned, and walked away. Soon, the shadows and flickering torchlight swallowed him, leaving only the memory of his tense posture.

Robin released a slow breath. "That's that, I guess," she murmured. Around them, the corridor still rang with faraway applause and a celebration that had lost its luster. Alysia noticed the sting in her own chest, an odd mix of triumph and dread. She had wanted her success with Kael to feel like the start of something bright and unburdened. Instead, it dangled under a cloud of suspicion.

She and Robin began to walk down the corridor toward the main lounge, navigating between the last few students lingering in conversation. A scraping sound came from a caretaker ward patrolling the hall, shifting the left-over illusions clinging to the stone walls. Robin turned to her cousin, her voice subdued. "This isn't the reaction I expected from him after winning the final duel. Did something else happen out on that dais?"

Alysia shook her head. "No. It was perfect, up until we saw that pendant. Then his mood vanished." She hesitated, then added, "If the rogue faction has truly found a way inside, we might be in greater danger than we thought." The words tasted bitter.

Robin set a consoling hand on Alysia's arm. "We'll figure this out. Right now, there isn't much we can do besides keep our eyes open. We should focus on the rest of the day, at least look like we're celebrating, or people will ask questions."

Alysia nodded, resisting the urge to chase after Kael again. While the applause might not sound so sweet anymore, ignoring the recognition would only draw more unwanted attention. She and Robin, side by side, turned toward the lounge where pockets of cheering students beckoned them with enthusiastic waves.

But inwardly, Alysia's thoughts spun. She could not stop picturing Kael's stricken expression, could not forget the gleam of that strange pendant or the ominous brand it carried. She remembered how, earlier, she had felt almost invincible next to him, yet now the cracks of uncertainty gaped wide. She told herself she would unravel this puzzle soon, discover if that symbol indeed belonged to the rogue charm faction. All that stood between them and a new threat was vigilance, caution, and the fragile trust they had painstakingly built.

Another burst of applause rose nearby as she and Robin stepped into the lounge. This time, it rained down on them in bright illusions of stars and shimmering ribbons, courtesy of excited classmates. Alysia raised her hand in a halfhearted wave. She saw Robin attempt a grin, trying to dispel the awkward tension. Yet the corridor's dull hum lingered in Alysia's ears, reminding her that danger lurked even in celebration.

She plastered a polite smile on her face, graciously accepting the many praises, but her mind drifted back to Kael and the sudden darkness in his eyes. The day had promised triumph. Instead, a chill settled in her stomach, a silent warning that sometimes the biggest threats wore unassuming robes and carried inconspicuous pendants. The voices around her mingled into an incoherent chorus of bravado and cheer, and she forced herself to respond in kind, all the while questioning who might be an ally and who might be an enemy in disguise.

Robin caught her eye during another round of cheers and offered a faint, knowing nod, confirming that she felt it too, the edge of danger creeping into the corners of this celebration. Alysia gripped her cousin's arm briefly, and they moved deeper into the lounge, stepping through illusions that fluttered around their feet. A wave of laughter rippled toward them, but the sound did little to ease the tension bristling under Alysia's skin.

For the rest of the evening, she carried that silent disquiet like a cloak she could not remove. No matter what the Academy had planned for this victory, no matter how the professors applauded or how valiantly the students admired them, one fact remained painfully clear: not everyone in these halls was safe to trust. And if a rogue presence truly existed within Velgrace, then what came next might place them all in peril.

At the lounge's far side, pennants still soared in a mesmerizing display of illusion-crafted finery, each banner shimmering with heartfelt admiration for the day's winners. Alysia forced herself to nod politely while offering thanks to those who congratulated her. Her chest felt tight as she mustered every bit of composure. When she and Robin finally found a quiet corner, Robin squeezed her arm again.

"It'll be fine," Robin repeated so it might conjure reassurance. She gestured at the corridor beyond the lounge, where more applause drifted in an echoing wave. The Academy thrived on triumphs, but tonight's triumph felt tarnished by secrets.

Alysia exhaled and closed her eyes for a moment, listening to the cautious tempo of her own heartbeat. "We'll watch, we'll wait," she murmured, "and if something is truly wrong, we'll face it."

Robin nodded. "Absolutely."

But as they stepped back into the bustle of watchers and well-wishers, Alysia could not shake the hollow ache in her arms and legs. The applause struck her ears like distant thunder, and every burst of light from the illusions sparked a prickle of caution. The Academy around her glowed with the remnants of celebration, but her gut whispered that those who clapped the loudest might well be hiding the sharpest blades.

In that moment, the reality sank in. Their victory had drawn attention, both welcome and unwelcome. And Kael, somewhere along the cliffside, was likely wrestling with the implications of what he had seen. Alysia knew she would have to find him again soon, if only to remind him that neither of them was alone in this confusion.

Until then, she waded through the crowd, forcing small smiles to those who sounded her name, ignoring the knots of dread that coiled inside her. The hallway lights dimmed as evening approached, turning the illusions more vibrant against the shadows. At any other time, she might have relaxed under the lamplight glow. Now, though, caution pricked at her every step.

Cheers jolted through the corridor once more, but she sensed the emptiness behind them: an echo of glory that felt borrowed rather than fully claimed. As more students recognized her passing by, the warmth of congratulations enveloped her, yet she found little comfort in it. She glanced where Kael had gone earlier. He was nowhere in sight.

Robin sighed softly at her side. "Well," she said under her breath, "maybe it's better we left official victory speeches to the older students. You look like you've seen a ghost."

Alysia shook her head. "Not a ghost," she murmured. "But something just as disturbing."

Kael's jaw tightened, and without another word he turned toward the western arch, cloak snapping behind him like a severed banner. Alysia moved to follow, but Robin's hand closed around her wrist. "Give him breathing room," her cousin murmured. "Whatever he saw in that pendant rattled him more than the duel itself."

Students drifted past in uneasy silence. The air smelled of burnt sigils and unasked questions. When the corridor finally emptied, Alysia bent to retrieve her cloak and found a scroll tucked beneath it. Kael's precise script lined the first half. The second was a ring of unfamiliar copper-ink runes that pulsed faintly, as if aware of her touch. *Kael never abandons half-finished work*, she thought, unease prickling her skin.

She slipped the parchment into her satchel.

"Trouble?" Robin asked quietly.

"Or a warning," Alysia answered. "Either way, I'm not letting him face it alone."

Together they turned toward the dormitory stairs, determination drawing their shoulders square while illusions grew faint behind them.

FIFTEEN

A SPELL TOO FAR

Long after curfew, Alysia sat cross-legged at her desk, the scroll Kael had "forgotten" unfurled beneath a single ward-light. Exhaustion weighed on her eyelids, but fascination and fear kept her spine straight. The outer margin was pure Kael, crisp notes on illusion synergies. The inner ring of sigils, however, throbbed with an energy she had felt only once before when the rogue pendant flashed during the duel.

Every pulse seemed to ask the same question: Will you follow him into this danger or stand aside? She traced the first copper rune with a fingertip, and the glyph shimmered like an opening eye. A quiet shuffle of movement sounded behind her. She turned and saw Robin peeking around the doorframe, her left arm draped in a casual sling of pillows, as if she had dragged them from her own room. She wore an air of mischievous curiosity.

"You still up, Lyss?" Robin whispered. "I figured you'd have passed out by now."

"I tried," Alysia replied. She lifted the scroll so Robin could see it. "Kael left this in the lounge earlier. There are notes on illusions, but not the usual ones."

Robin stepped inside, carefully clicking the door shut. She leaned over Alysia's shoulder to eye the parchment. The lamp's glow danced across odd, splintered glyphs. Robin's brow creased, and she whispered. "Why does it look like it's half-burned? Did Kael say what these runes are?"

Alysia shook her head. "He never mentioned them. I found it under some of my notebooks when I came back."

"Strange," Robin muttered. "He's usually careful with half-finished illusions. This almost looks abandoned." A wry smile curved Robin's lips. "Bet he's embarrassed if it's a failed experiment."

Alysia sighed. "I'm not sure. He's been so distant since the duel, especially after... well, after he thought he recognized that rogue pendant in the courtyard. I haven't seen him smile like he used to." She traced a fingernail across Kael's scrawl. "I guess I can ask him when he returns from wherever he went tonight."

Robin raised a skeptical eyebrow. She whispered, "Or you can ask him why he left you something so suspicious."

"Suspicious?" Alysia forced a laugh. "This might just be notes, Robin. Don't go conjuring drama."

"I conjure illusions, not drama," her cousin shot back, though her gaze stayed fixed on the scrawled lines. She shook her head. "I'm telling you, that looks more than odd."

Alysia felt a twinge of defensiveness but let it pass. She

refused to join in the chorus of doubt that had followed Kael ever since rumors pointed to his dangerous lineage. Instead, she closed her textbook and slid the scroll to a clear spot on the desk. "I'll figure it out," she said. "He'd tell me if something was truly wrong."

Robin sighed in exasperation. "You're a better person than me."

Before Alysia could respond, the parchment responded for her. It shifted with a sudden ripple of energy. The edges gave a twitch, as if invisible fingers tugged the corners. Alysia gasped and snatched her hand away. A surge of magic coursed through the air, setting the tiny flame in her lantern dancing wildly across the walls.

The ink on the parchment seemed to bleed and re-form, the lines writhing like living things before coiling into the final shape. It did not just glow but pulsed with a cold, malevolent intelligence. The air grew thin and smelled of dust and ozone. Alysia felt the glyph's wrongness in her teeth, a low hum that vibrated up from the floorboards. Hot and cold fear mingled in her chest. She felt Robin grab her arm and pull her a step back, away from the desk and the unsettling glow.

"Lyss," Robin whispered, "tell me that is just your imagination."

Alysia swallowed a knot of panic. "No," she said. "It's… real. It's a rogue marking."

Robin released a shaky breath. Her gaze darted between the scroll and Alysia's face. "I knew something gave me a bad feeling from that weird script. I thought it might be incomplete illusions, but that is definitely not incomplete anything."

The rogue sigil's glow built, then receded to the faintest flicker. Slowly, the scroll settled down onto the desk with a sad rustle. Alysia clutched the edges of her chair, trying to steady her breathing. The entire event lasted only a few seconds, but each second stretched with dreadful intensity.

Robin's voice came out thin but firm. "All right. This is a sign that Kael's not telling us everything. You saw how involuntary that was. Rogue magic is forbidden for a reason. I can't believe he would just leave something like that lying around unless he wanted you to see it."

Alysia bristled, though a quiet dread coiled in her stomach. "He wouldn't set me up," she said. "He's never shown any interest in rogue magic, and he's been the most vocal about infiltration. He warned me about that pendant, remember?"

Robin crossed her arms. "Sure. But maybe he recognized the pendant because he's seen these sigils before. You can't ignore that possibility. He might know more about the faction than he's letting on."

Alysia's thoughts spiraled. She pictured Kael's face earlier that evening, tight with worry, his eyes flicking over every shadow. Was he afraid, or was he hiding something? He had pulled away from the crowd the moment he spotted that suspicious observer. He had avoided giving a clear explanation, mumbling only that it might be a threat to their illusions. That memory sparked her frustration. If he had any real knowledge of a rogue's presence, why not share it?

"You know Kael better than I do," Robin said gently, "but we can't pretend we didn't see this. That sigil is trouble."

Alysia tried to swallow the building tension in her throat. She was too exhausted

to fully trust her own interpretations, yet she despised how quickly suspicion had invaded the dorm. It reminded her of the day Kael first arrived, when everyone whispered behind his back. She had defended him then, insisting that he was more complicated than the rumors said.

But this scroll was no rumor.

"Maybe he found it," Alysia whispered. She forced herself to consider other explanations. "He might have been studying this mark to try and expose the faction, or to figure out how they create illusions. He's good at deciphering runes. He could have recognized something crucial."

Robin exhaled slowly. "That's still not exactly comforting. If Kael is messing with rogue symbols alone, that's reckless. If an infiltration is behind this, you need to be safe, Lyss."

Alysia let her gaze shift from the glowing sigil to the gentle shadows cast by the lantern on the dorm walls. The dorm that once felt so secure, lined with neat wards and small personal touches, now felt crowded by an unwanted presence. She could almost taste the electric tang of leftover magic in the air.

She remembered how Kael's illusions mingled with

her wards in the courtyard earlier, how everyone applauded their synergy. She had never felt so attuned to another caster's magic. Yet doubt nudged at her. That synergy relied on trust. Her mind flashed to the duel, to the feeling of their magic weaving together in perfect harmony. How could a person capable of creating something so beautiful and pure also be connected to a sigil that felt so corrupt? The two realities warred within her, a dissonance that was more painful than simple suspicion.

Robin touched her shoulder. "Look, I'm not telling you to confront him with torches and pitchforks, but you can't ignore that he left something like this behind. It's shady."

Despite her panic, Alysia tried to keep her voice calm. "I won't jump to conclusions. I'll talk to him, find out what this is about." She fought to steady her trembling hands. "Kael's been through enough. Everyone expects him to crack under pressure. I refuse to be one more person piling on false accusations."

Robin hesitated. Then she nodded, though skepticism lingered in her eyes. "Be careful. Your big heart is one of your best traits, but sometimes it blinds you. Never forget how dangerous illusions can be in the wrong hands."

A whispered knock echoed on the door. Both girls froze. For a heartbeat, Alysia wondered if Kael had returned. She felt a burst of wild hope, followed by a surge of apprehension. She rose and opened the door a crack, only to find a sleepless first-year holding a sealed envelope from a professor. The younger student apologized for the interruption and shuffled away. Alysia shut the door with a sigh, her heart still pounding.

Robin gave a nervous laugh. "I think you might be too jumpy to get any real sleep tonight."

Alysia could not deny that. She glanced at the scroll, now resting still on the desk, its rogue symbol dark and silent. The specter of that earlier glow lingered in her memory, like a brand she could not ignore.

"I'll store it," she said, her voice low. "I'll lock it in my trunk until I can question Kael."

Robin eyed the parchment warily. "Keep a ward around it, if you can. I don't trust that... thing."

Nodding, Alysia reached into a side drawer and lifted out a small warding box used for quarantining volatile spell components. She placed the scroll inside with extreme caution, her hands trembling. She secured a basic containment spell that glowed faintly around the edges of the box, confirming the seal.

Robin grabbed the pillows she had dropped and tucked them under one arm. "I'll let you try to rest," she said softly. "But if you need me, you know where to find me. Don't stay up all night obsessing."

Alysia mustered a grateful smile and watched Robin slip out of the dorm. As the latch clicked shut, the silence pressed heavier. She sank onto her narrow bed, her eyes drifting to the sealed ward box on the desk. Her mind churned with half-formed worries.

She wanted to believe in Kael. It was easier to recall the warmth in his eyes whenever he managed to forget his burdens and share a rare grin. That side of him, playful, almost hopeful, felt genuine, and it clashed sharply against the possibility of him hiding something dangerous. Confusion gnawed at her. She thought back to the illusions they created together. She could still feel the phantom hum of their combined power. He had faltered at first, but together they soared. Would someone truly compromised by rogue magic produce something so beautiful?

She fetched a soft blanket from the foot of her bed and wrapped it around her shoulders. The dorm's small window was beside her desk, and through it she glimpsed the moonlit academy spires. The Sea of Echoes beyond glimmered with pale starlight, its restless waves a constant reminder that dark secrets might lurk beneath calm surfaces.

Sleep refused to come. She lit a small candle on her bedside table and stared at her grandmother's old notations pinned to the wall. Those scribbled runes whispered of all the complexities wards could hold, how easily magic could flip from protective to destructive if misaligned. The parallels to Kael's illusions weighed on her. If a single misunderstood rune could unravel a delicate synergy, how much risk did they both face if rogue spells wormed their way into his illusions?

She sat up straighter, gripping the edges of her blanket. The memory of the sigil's glow formed a dull ache behind her eyes, as though reminding her that she could not ignore it. She had pinned her faith to Kael more than once, had believed in his loyalty even when others harbored doubts. Would that faith be enough now?

A soft breeze ruffled the pages on her desk. The lantern flame bobbed as if hungry for more oil. Alysia traced her finger over the faint ward lines on her dorm door, ensuring the spells held firm for the night. She breathed in slow. She wanted answers, and only Kael could give them. But after seeing that sinister mark, she knew she could no longer dismiss Robin's caution. The seed of doubt had been planted, and she hated how it spread through her thoughts like a persistent weed.

The dorm felt colder than usual. A thousand questions beckoned, each one demanding an explanation she did not have. She told herself Kael deserved the benefit of a direct conversation, something face to face, without accusations or panic. Still, her heart pounded. His secrecy, his sudden disappearances, the scribbled glyphs...

A knot formed in her throat. The quiet pressed in. She closed her eyes and rubbed her temples, fighting a rise of anxiety. She thought of the look in Kael's eyes after their illusions dazzled the entire courtyard, the unspoken vulnerability he revealed for only a fraction of a moment. That vulnerability convinced her he could not be the traitor people feared. Yet the scroll argued otherwise, shimmering in her memory with its rogue symbol.

She slid off her bed and paced the short length of her dorm, ignoring how the boards creaked beneath her bare feet. Doubts pummeled every corner of her mind. She resolved to speak to Kael tomorrow if he returned or chase him down if he tried to avoid her. She refused to hide from the truth.

As she eased back onto her bed, the lantern began to sputter. She cupped the flame gently, guiding it into darkness. Her arms slid into the folds of the blanket, and tension lined every muscle in her shoulders. The night felt far from over.

In the silence, the ward box remained sealed on the desk, harboring that wicked sigil. A single question throbbed in her chest. What if Kael did know more than he let on?

Alysia inhaled shakily and let her head fall against her thin pillow. She still wanted to defend him, to hold faith in the synergy they shared. But the image of that rogue mark kept breaching the edges of her thoughts, refusing to let her rest fully. She could almost hear Robin's warning echo across the quiet dorm. "He's not telling you everything."

She tried to believe otherwise. She tried to remember their final performance as proof he would never harm her, or the academy. Yet fear and concern twisted together, planting uncertainty in her core. Kael's silence, his avoidance, his history, it was all too much to ignore.

CHAPTER

SIXTEEN

FACULTY FIRESTORM

Alysia stepped off the last stair leading to Headmistress Imara Quen's office, her pulse echoing with each thump of her boots on the polished stone. The corridor was unusually quiet this afternoon. Torchlight cast long shadows across the high-arched ceiling, and every time she passed one of the tall windows, tendrils of ocean wind made the flames sputter. She inhaled, wishing that a single breath could steady her nerves. It did not.

The summons had arrived only a quarter hour ago. A frazzled first-year in Aurum Spire colors had approached her in the courtyard, stammering that the Headmistress wanted her in the office "immediately." No reason offered, only an unmistakable note of urgency in the first-year's voice. Alysia's stomach had dropped, because she knew. She had been expecting something like this ever since unsanctioned magic, her unsanctioned magic, according to the rumors, was spotted near the vaults. And after that suspicious night in her dorm room, where she and Robin had discovered Kael's rogue sigil scroll, she could feel the academy's watchful eyes land heavily on her.

She reached the oak doors. They loomed taller than some of the archways around the Great Hall, polished to a shine that reflected her silhouette. A spiral motif of carved runes circled the handle, faintly glowing if the occupant inside had wards active. Right now, that glow shone with an ominous intensity, confirming that the wards were fully engaged.

Beyond these doors, Headmistress Quen would be waiting, and possibly other faculty members. Alysia swallowed. On good days, she felt only mild intimidation at the Headmistress's presence. The woman commanded unwavering respect but often showed glimpses of genuine concern for her students. On difficult days, Quen could be stern, unrelenting, and determined to root out any threat to Velgrace. Today, Alysia sensed, would be a very difficult day.

She steeled herself and knocked. Her knuckles met the wood with a hollow echo. On the other side, the faint hum of conversation ceased. A pause followed, and then a clipped voice called out, "Enter."

She pushed the door open. At once, she felt the heightened press of wards around her. The Headmistress's office was a spacious chamber dominated by a wide desk carved from driftwood. Various scrolls lined the walls, and a tall bookshelf behind Quen's chair bore a phoenix carving that shimmered even in the subdued light. Quen sat in her high-backed seat, hands clasped. Along the left side of the office stood two familiar figures. Warden Evara Morn, whose severe gaze felt like a physical weight, a defense ward pressing in, and Magister Belros Dain. The shadows in his black cloak seemed to deepen, and Alysia had the unnerving sense they would shift if she dared to tell a lie. Their combined presence told her this was indeed official and serious.

"Alysia Thorne," the Headmistress said. She spoke softly, yet the measured tone carried authority. "Close the door."

Alysia obeyed, pressing it shut until the latch clicked. She tried to calm the skittering in her chest. She focused on the routine: stand straight, greet them respectfully, maintain eye contact. But the tension in the room made the air feel heavy, like a presence that refused to disperse.

"Headmistress," Alysia acknowledged quietly, forcing her voice to remain steady. She inclined her head toward the other faculty as well. "Warden Morn. Magister Dain."

Warden Morn's eyes narrowed. She offered no greeting, only crossed her arms tighter. Magister Dain, by contrast, gave a single pointed nod. An illusion shimmered at his cloak's edge as though responding to his internal mood.

Quen laced her fingers together on the desk. "Alysia, do you know why you've been called here?"

Ticking off her possible transgressions, Alysia swallowed again. "I suspect it concerns the vault incident, ma'am. And perhaps... rumors about certain spell usage."

The Headmistress's gaze shifted to the side. A slightly ironic twist curved her lips. "Your 'suspicions' are correct.

Let us be frank. There was a breach in one of the lower vault wards last night. My watchers detected faint traces of advanced charm-layering. We also received multiple reports that you, Alysia Thorne, have exhibited a sudden leap in charm proficiency, well beyond your usual capacity. This aligns with suspicious magical signatures from the corridor near the restricted vaults."

Alysia's cheeks flared. "Headmistress Quen, I was not—"

Warden Morn's voice cut in. "We want the truth, Miss Thorne." The warden's arms remained crossed, her glare unwavering. "You've been seen with Kael Meridan repeatedly in areas off-limits after hours. We have reason to believe you accessed wards below Bastion Hall that even seasoned instructors approach with caution. Some suspect you of..." She paused, the corners of her mouth tightening. "Conspiring, intentionally or not, with rogue influences."

That last phrase lodged in Alysia's gut like a barbed hook. "Rogue influences," she repeated in a trembling voice. She wanted to refute it violently, to proclaim that she had no link to any infiltration. But the memory of Kael's scroll, the rogue sigil that shimmered to life.

Magister Dain, stepping forward, let his illusions coil around his fingertips in small flickers of shadow and light. "We're well aware of the complexities you and Kael face. However, the presence of advanced illusions led by rogue practitioners has grown more pronounced. The faculty is duty-bound to investigate any anomalies, especially those that might compromise Velgrace's defenses."

Alysia glanced between them. She wanted to summon the calm logic she relied upon when analyzing wards, but her mind buzzed too loudly. "I didn't break into the vaults," she said. A twist of guilt gnawed at her, recalling that her involvement was more complicated than that. "I… I studied in the library earlier. I used some advanced synergy spells in class last week, so maybe that's the leap they're referring to. But I haven't participated in infiltration or sabotage." She forced the words out, determined to maintain her composure.

Headmistress Quen lifted one eyebrow. "Yet you've displayed proficiency with wards that some third-year students would struggle to replicate. That is concerning. The question is how you acquired this skill. Did you or did you not attempt an unsupervised experiment to refine illusions in the restricted floors?"

Alysia recognized how precarious her position was. She recalled that scalding moment in the desert classroom with Kael and the quiet of her dorm room when the rogue symbol appeared. Telling the truth might endanger him, but lying outright could earn her immediate expulsion. She took a careful breath. "I studied runic layering from old Thorne family notes," she answered, picking words as if each were a delicate chord. "Some of those notations are advanced, yes, but they're not stolen from the vault." She lifted her chin. "I only wanted to improve so I wouldn't be a liability if the infiltration worsened."

Warden Morn's jaw remained set. She looked unconvinced. Quen's expression, though stern, showed faint traces of consideration. Outside, the sky rumbled with distant thunder, as though the Sea of Echoes itself had opinions about this confrontation.

Then the door behind Alysia opened without warning. She spun, her heart stuttering. Kael Meridan stood on the threshold, one hand braced on the handle. His hair was half-damp from either the misty air outside or a rushed attempt at rinsing away sweat. As always, the coral amulet around his neck pulsed faintly with illusions, like a second heartbeat.

He scanned the room. His gaze settled on Alysia for a split second, then darted to Headmistress Quen. "Apologies for the interruption, Headmistress. I heard about this meeting."

Warden Morn frowned. "This is an inquest for Alysia Thorne, not you."

Kael let the door drift shut behind him, ignoring Morn's pointed tone. A glow of illusions coiled at his fingertips, then vanished as he squared his shoulders. "But it concerns me," he said. "Because I was the one who pulled Alysia into my experiments."

Alysia's pulse jumped. Pulled her in? He was the one with the suspicious scroll. Why was he claiming it was all his idea?

He stepped closer to the desk. Headmistress Quen regarded him with cool interest. Belros Dain observed quietly, illusions dancing in his gaze.

Kael continued, his voice measured. "I overstepped, Headmistress. I put Alysia in a position where she had no choice but to push her wards further than normal, beyond the authorized curriculum. In short, if there was an unsanctioned demonstration or vault tampering, it was because I tested illusions that I wanted to perfect." He lowered his head in a gesture that could have been contrition, but the tension in his jaw belied the bravado. "She bears no blame."

Alysia felt coldness seep into the room, a subtle shift in the magical resonance. It was Kael. He was actively suppressing his own aura, cloaking his immense power to appear less threatening, more contrite. The effort it took was immense. She could feel it in the air, a vacuum where his vibrant energy should have been. He was not just confessing but magically crippling himself for her.

Alysia's throat constricted. "Wait," she blurted, stepping forward. "That isn't—"

He shot her a sidelong glance, one that silenced her protest. Beneath it, she saw a hint of quiet resolve. It rattled her more. Why was he taking responsibility for something that lay at both their feet?

"You claim you were involved in potential advanced illusions near the vault area?" Quen asked, her voice calm. "When exactly did this occur?"

Kael exhaled. "Over the past few nights, I was testing illusions to see if I could replicate a synergy with Alysia's wards. Curiosity led us deeper into the academy's lower corridors, but it was never her intention to break rules. I took advantage of her interest in refining wards. If you must punish someone, punish me. Alysia didn't deserve to be called here."

Silence settled like dust motes. Alysia's heart pounded so loudly she thought the entire room could hear it. She despised the half-truth in Kael's confession. He was omitting details, like the rogue sigil or that suspicious instructor's pendant, everything that had spurred her to investigate further. But the faculty did not know what she and Kael had witnessed. They only saw in front of them a student apparently admitting to wrongdoing.

Warden Morn's stare roved over Kael, suspicion etched across her stern features. "And why, Meridan, should we believe this is not simply a ploy to shield Alysia?"

Kael squared his shoulders. "I'm telling you the truth. If you track the leftover illusions from those corridors, you'll find my signature, not hers." At the last words, a faint tension showed in his neck, as if bracing for a blow.

Headmistress Quen leaned back in her chair, an unreadable expression in her dark eyes. "This is irregular, Meridan. You're aware of your precarious standing at Velgrace. If these claims are proven, you face not just expulsion but closer scrutiny by the Council. Are you willing to risk that?"

His hand lifted to his amulet. "Yes," he said.

Quen turned her gaze to Alysia. Her expression softened by the faintest margin. "Alysia, do you corroborate Kael's account?"

Alysia hesitated, torn between revealing the entire truth and letting Kael shoulder more than his share of blame. She inhaled, searching Kael's face for some sign that this was a ruse he could handle.

"Kael didn't force me into anything," she managed carefully. "But... he's telling the truth that the illusions were his. He was the one pushing that research. I only stepped in to help stabilize it." She had to grit her teeth at how easily that explanation rolled from her tongue, half-truth though it was.

Warden Morn let out a dismissive grunt. Magister Dain tilted his head, illusions dancing around his pupils like faint starlight. Headmistress Quen's gaze shifted between the two students.

"Then Alysia is free to go," Quen said at last. "Kael, you will meet with me again soon to account for these experiments. Once we verify the wards remain uncompromised, we will decide if further disciplinary action is required." She paused, pressing her palms flat on the table. "This fiasco does not inspire trust. You both must tread carefully." Her tone made it clear that she had not yet forgiven anything.

Morn gave a curt nod but said nothing more. Dain's expression remained opaque, shadows dancing at the edge of his cloak. With a sharp gesture, Quen indicated that Alysia and Kael were dismissed.

Alysia exhaled, tension loosening in her chest, though a coil of resentment lingered. She and Kael exited the office in silence, stepping into the corridor. Only when the heavy door closed behind them did Alysia find her voice, low and raw.

They walked some paces from the office, each footstep echoing dully. A pair of younger students scurried by, their eyes wide at the tension that practically radiated from Alysia's posture. When the corridor emptied to a quiet turn, she wheeled on Kael, her heart pounding with anger and relief and confusion.

"Why did you do that?" she asked, her voice shaking. "You all but told them you're guilty of infiltration."

He shrugged one shoulder, clearly more exhausted than triumphant. "They're suspicious anyway. If someone has to take the blame, better me. You've worked too hard to earn your place here to have it snatched away by one slip."

Her anger thundered. "So that's it? You don't think I can handle the consequences of my own actions?"

"That isn't what I said." He rubbed his temples, the illusions at his fingertips shimmering briefly before fading again. "It's easier for me to stand under scrutiny than watch you lose everything." His tone was layered with frustration and an edge she could not quite decipher.

Alysia clenched her fists at her sides. Down the corridor, the scenic windows overlooked the Sea of Echoes. The waves outside looked calmer than she felt. The ripple of leftover tension made her entire body buzz. "I don't need saving, Kael. I need honesty. Why do you keep taking the brunt of this, when we both—"

"You think honesty is safe right now?" He lowered his voice, stepping closer. She saw the strain in his eyes, the seed of guilt that apparently weighed on him. "If I laid out everything we suspected, from rogue sigils to suspicious instructors, they'd suspend us both before we had proof. Morn is already itching for an excuse to lock me up, maybe banish me from Velgrace. You, I won't let you share that fate."

Conflicted emotion roiled in her gut. Outside, lightning flashed over the sea, illuminating the corridor in a brief, bright glare. Then thunder rumbled in the distance.

"That doesn't answer the question, Kael," she said, stepping forward until she was near enough to sense the faint aura of illusions around him. "Why? Why put yourself in the crosshairs for me?"

His gaze moved down the hall, checking if anyone lingered behind corners. Satisfied they were alone, he lowered his voice. "Because someone has to."

SEVENTEEN

TRUTHS AND TENSIONS

Alysia left Headmistress Quen's office feeling as though the entire corridor had shrunk. The high-arched ceiling pressed down from above, and even the flickering torches along the walls seemed to twist in accusing shapes. She drew in a shallow breath, trying to gather her scattered thoughts. Moments before, Kael had all but offered himself up as the academy's scapegoat, taking blame for their unsanctioned spell-work near the vault. Freed of immediate punishment, Alysia should have felt relief. Instead, she felt only the reminder of a deeper uncertainty gnawing at her.

She caught sight of Kael leaning against the wall opposite the door, arms folded, his hooded eyes fixed on a spot near his boots. His posture looked casual, but tension tightened the corners of his mouth. Faint illusions sparkled at his fingertips before fading away into the corridor's shadows. The rest of the hall stood empty. The younger students, who had lingered earlier for a glimpse of the inquisition, had departed once it was clear no dramatic expulsion was taking place.

When he finally glanced up, the muted lamplight illuminated his storm-colored eyes. She opened her mouth to speak, but words tangled at the back of her throat. She was still furious and confused by how quickly he had claimed the blame, robbing her of a chance to speak for herself. Even so, she could not entirely ignore the wave of concern rising inside her. He looked exhausted, as if he had spent all his energy erecting illusions that disguised his real turmoil.

"We can't keep doing this," she said at last, keeping her voice low for fear of the echoing arches.

He let out a slow breath. "You're right."

She did not expect his ready agreement. Gathering her courage, she stepped closer so she could speak without raising her voice. She noticed a faint bruise on his forearm, just beneath where the coral amulet hung around his neck. The sight made her breath hitch. She fought the urge to lift her hand and check it.

"Why did you lie?" She swallowed, grateful the corridor was empty. "I was ready to tell them the truth, but you jumped in with that half-baked confession."

His eyes darkened with a cold frustration she rarely saw. "Because they would have questioned you for hours, demanded you give up answers you don't have. If I had stayed silent, you would have tried explaining everything, eventually revealing...too much." He paused and took a measured breath. "I can handle the consequences. You shouldn't have to."

She bristled. "Stop deciding for me. I can bear the consequences just as well."

His gaze shifted away, but he did not deny her statement. Instead, he gestured for them to leave the corridor altogether. "Not here," he said quietly. "Walls have ears."

She suppressed a shiver and nodded. Together, they walked through a narrower passage leading out into one of the academy's open courtyards. The moonlight offered feeble illumination, bathing the stone benches in silver-blue. Alysia could smell salt drifting in from the Sea of Echoes, cool and insistent against her skin. She glanced at Kael, who studied the deserted courtyard with caution.

They took seats on a low bench near a leafless ivy trellis. This felt eerily intimate, like a place between worlds. She tucked her hands beneath her cloak for warmth and willed her heart to calm its frantic pace.

"By taking the blame," she said softly, "you left me with even more questions."

He gave a short laugh under his breath. "That was unavoidable."

She shook her head. "I still deserve an explanation." Her voice quavered slightly. "What are you so desperate to hide?"

For a moment, he did not speak. Wind ruffled a cluster of loose gravel near their feet, scattering pebbles across the flagstones. Alysia wondered if he might simply get up and walk away. Her stomach tightened at the thought. She wanted answers, but she also inexplicably wanted him to stay.

He slipped a hand to the coral amulet at his neckline,

his fingertips grazing its smooth surface. "It's not about being desperate to hide something for the fun of it," he said, his voice thick with pent-up frustration. "It's about keeping something locked away so it doesn't consume everything."

She drew a shaky breath. "The rogue sigil you left in my dorm, how does it tie into all this? That was no ordinary illusion, Kael. It was powerful, dangerous."

He bowed his head slightly, letting the silence stretch. Finally, he lifted his gaze to meet hers, his storm-gray eyes filled with reluctance. "There's a reason I recognized the rogue glyph. It's part of a legacy that's bigger than me, bigger than any single mage. My bloodline is tied to illusions that are forbidden for a reason." His jaw tensed, as if wrestling with what to say next. "The sigil you saw is one fragment of it. It connects with certain spells that," he made a small, helpless motion with his hand, "might call me whether I am willing or not."

"Call you?" she echoed. "Like a summons?"

He nodded. His finger tapped against the amulet, and she saw a faint glow twist around its coral edges like a subdued thread of light. "You remember the day we met, when you tried that advanced charm? You said it was an accident... that you only wanted to avoid failing a test." A faint smirk crossed his lips, though no humor touched his eyes. "It wasn't random chance that I appeared. Your magic tapped into something old. Something that recognized my...lineage. My name."

"So," she said, her voice unsteady, "you mean you

weren't just traveling near the academy and got pulled in by a misfired incantation?"

"I wasn't anywhere near this realm," he said, his voice raw. "Your spell latched onto me from a distance, like a beacon. My family's illusions respond to certain wards or charms that align with ancient runes. You triggered them."

Her world tilted. It felt like the stone floor of the courtyard had dropped out from under her, leaving her in a dizzying freefall. Every casual touch, every shared glance, every moment their magic had hummed in harmony was now recast in the light of this terrible, inescapable fate. She hadn't just summoned him. She had activated a lock to his cage.

She gripped the bench edge for support as she studied his face. He looked tired, weighed down by something invisible. "When you found that scroll in your dorm," he continued, "it wasn't ready. I left it behind by accident, scattered among your notes. I knew it might react if you or your cousin tried to interpret the runes. Some rogue illusions can anchor themselves to unsuspecting casters. That's what you saw that night. The symbol recognized your ward magic, saw the same pattern that reached out across realms to pull me here."

She closed her eyes, images flashing through her mind: the night sky, the new wards she had tested, and the moment Kael had appeared in her botched charm circle. She had never questioned the possibility that something deeper had guided that mishap. Her chest tightened. "If that symbol recognized me... then it recognized you, too."

"Yes," he said softly. "Like a lock and key."

Her stomach gave a queasy roll. "So, everything, your arrival, your illusions, even the dangerous spells that keep appearing, none of it is coincidence?"

"No coincidence," he confirmed, his voice barely above a whisper. "You see, the Meridan lineage has always been rumored to connect illusions to living souls. My ancestors discovered ways to bind illusions to blood. That scroll was just one piece of a larger puzzle. My presence at Velgrace… that is another. The same force that made me come here is stirring, and it's going to put anyone close to me at risk." He exhaled in a trembling rush. "You especially."

She studied him intently, searching for any wisp of deception. She found only honesty. Yet that honesty was scarier than any lie could have been. "What am I supposed to do with that knowledge? Pretend I didn't hear it and go on crocheting wards as if nothing is amiss? We have infiltration rumors everywhere. Suspicion is at an all-time high. This just makes it clearer that—"

"Alysia," he interjected, pressing his palm lightly over her hands. The warmth of his skin flowed through her gloves, sending a distracting flutter across her chest. His illusions sparked faintly around his fingertips, painting ghostly shapes on the bench before fading. "That is exactly why I begged you not to keep pressing. I'm telling you, the bloodline aspect is…lethal. It has toppled entire families. It turned my ancestors' illusions from art into weapons."

She pulled her hands free, ignoring how her skin tingled where he touched her. "I can't just walk away. I'm already in danger, aren't I? Or do you think the rogues will avoid me just because I'm clueless?"

He hung his head. "They will target you precisely because you share synergy with my illusions. We discovered that synergy in front of everyone during the courtyard demonstrations. Now they know."

Her mouth felt too dry. She recalled how the crowd had cheered when they cast illusions together. She remembered how it fell the moment Kael spotted that strange onlooker wearing a forbidden pendant. The memory clashed with her hopes for an innocent explanation. Betrayal, fear, and a rush of protectiveness darted through her. "You still haven't told me everything."

A ghost of a smile touched his lips. "If I told you everything, you would run."

"Try me," she challenged, though her heart pounded.

He lifted a shoulder in defeat. "Fine. I wasn't just traveling for relics. I had been searching for a way to...free myself from my ancestor's hold on illusions. Then I felt your magic, like a jolt through my amulet, and I found myself pulled across wards, across realms, landing right here. Every attempt I made to break free from the Meridan curse has led nowhere. And now you, with your wards and your unwitting summons, have locked me in place."

She swallowed. "But the sigil that showed up in my dorm... it looked like pure rogue magic. Are you telling me your entire family line is entangled with that?"

"Yes," he answered, his voice tight. "The Meridan illusions were corrupted centuries ago," he said, his voice tight. "The magic is parasitic. It feeds on the caster's life force, growing wilder and more sentient over time unless it's anchored to a balancing power. That's the real curse."

Lightning flared overhead, silent and distant, but bright enough to momentarily illuminate the courtyard. Alysia noticed how it cast sharp shadows across Kael's face. He was not triumphant in revealing his secrets. He looked as though every word weighed him down more.

She toyed with her bracelet; the Thorne crest cool beneath her fingertips. "If someone is searching for you, believing you can harness these illusions, then I need to know how to defend myself...how to defend you if it comes to that."

His eyes flickered with something close to admiration. He forced out a soft chuckle. "You are too good for your own safety, you know that? Most people would have exiled me the moment they read half of what my family did. But you insist on stepping into the crossfire."

She offered a fragile smile. "No one else is going to do it."

He reached for her hand again, this time slower, as though granting her permission to pull away if she wished. She did not move. Their fingers interlaced, and she felt the faint hum of illusions dancing between them. It felt oddly comforting and equally terrifying.

"I don't want you caught in this fight," he said, his thumb brushing over her knuckles. "I've seen how twisted illusions become when fueled by old curses. And if we delve deeper, it might trigger something we can't stop."

She lifted her chin, meeting his gaze with steady insistence. "But they're coming for us anyway," she said. "I can't stay ignorant."

His reluctance was clear. He tightened his hold on her hand, then let go, leaving behind a warm impression in her palm. "Alright. But if we do this, we do it carefully. No grand confessions to the Headmistress, no rummaging in forbidden vaults alone. One step at a time."

She swallowed, unnerved but resolved. "Tell me one truth right now, then. Something solid to keep me from feeling like I'm wandering blind."

He glanced at the sky, then closed his eyes as if resigned to fate. "You did not summon me by accident. Your wards and my illusions were fated to collide. The sigil is part of my family's inheritance, and it binds me to certain spells. Once you cast that advanced charm, the sigil found me. That is why I was pulled here."

A cold wave washed through her. "So, we're bound by that magic?"

He nodded. "In a way. And old illusions rarely let their chosen vessels go." He stood, scraping a hand through his dark hair. The courtyard's shadows skewed around him, illusions rippling with his agitation. "Which means there are secrets better left buried. I'm warning you not to go chasing them. Some truths, if unleashed, could destroy us both."

Alysia's pulse slammed in her ears. She looked up at him, this roguish illusionist who wore guilt and defiance in equal measure. She wanted to demand more answers, yet her instinct whispered caution. She remembered how fiercely he had tried to shield her from the Headmistress's questions, as though determined to spare her from something bigger and darker. That protective instinct both confused and tugged at her heart, no matter how furious she was at him for withholding information.

She stood as well, her arms pressed to her sides. Wind combed through her hair, carrying the brine of the nearby sea. "Then why mention any of it?" she asked quietly. "If you think I'm safer not knowing, you could have kept me in the dark."

He folded his arms, his expression troubled. "Because you deserve the chance to walk away or stand and fight with full understanding of the stakes. If I lied to you, or kept you ignorant, I wouldn't be much better than the rogues who manipulate illusions behind closed doors."

She stepped closer, trying to read him in the silver-blue moonlight. The tension between them tightened, coiling in her chest as her eyes drifted to his amulet. She felt that familiar flutter, the one that surfaced whenever he let his guard down even slightly.

"And if I choose to stay?" she asked, her voice trembling. "What then?"

He hesitated, illusions dancing over his fingertips like small pale flames. "Then everything changes."

Fear prickled along her spine, yet determination flared. "Good," she whispered.

They stood in fragile silence. Overhead, clouds skimmed across the moon, casting the courtyard in shifting patterns of light and shadow. Alysia's mind spun in circles. Kael had finally answered part of the riddle that plagued her, yet it only spawned more questions. The sigil was a familial mark, not some random quirk of dangerous illusions. Her magic had somehow been the catalyst. The revelation left her shaken, uncertain where to turn. Still, she could not deny the strange sense of closeness she felt now, or the flood of worry that walked hand in hand with it.

Kael glanced at her again, regret etched into his features. "I know it's not fair to you," he said. "If I could break this connection, I would. I'd keep you safe from every threat in the world if it meant you'd never have to face the darker side of my lineage." He lifted a hand, then let it drop, as though he longed to touch her cheek but could not bring himself to do so. "But I can't. The best I can do is warn you. Knowing more might put a target on your back. There are people who would kill to harness what we've stumbled upon."

Alysia managed a small nod. The night air felt heavier than before. "Then tell me I'm not imagining the danger... or the possibility that we might find a way out of it."

He swallowed, his gaze steady on hers. "No, you're not imagining it. And yes...I believe we can find a way. If we trust each other enough."

She heard the unspoken question in that statement. Could they really trust one another? She thought of the academy's suspicion, the gossip swirling in the corridors, the cold stares from certain instructors. She thought of her cousin Robin's worried eyes each time she caught Alysia poring over cryptic runes. Now Kael stood before her, caught in a web of illusions he never asked for, tied to a rogue mark that threatened them both.

She inhaled shakily, stepping back so she could see his face fully. "You said unearthing these truths could destroy us. Yet, I can't walk away. You must know that. I need to understand."

His expression grew pained. "Then promise me you'll be careful. Don't go delving into old vault records, or rummaging where you think you can handle it, without telling me first. We do this together or not at all."

She nodded, ignoring how her heart fluttered at the implicit vow to stay by her side. "Agreed."

His shoulders relaxed a fraction, though she could see tension still thrummed inside him. He held her gaze a moment longer. "That's all I can offer tonight. Please, be safe."

She watched him turn toward the exit, illusions melting away from his shape until he looked just like any other student walking out of the courtyard. She remained behind, hugging herself against the chill. Part of her longed to call him back, to demand more clarity, but caution knotted her throat.

In the moonlit stillness, she heard her own pulse thudding in her ears. The new information rushed through her mind, and every emotion twisted into an uneasy knot. She recalled the look of dread in Kael's eyes when he confessed that her magic had summoned him, that the sigil was anchored to his bloodline, that they faced dangers beyond anything taught in the standard curriculum.

He had urged her not to delve deeper, insisting that there were secrets better left buried, warning it would put them in jeopardy. Yet the framework of her entire life at

Velgrace, her relentless thirst for understanding wards, illusions, and everything in between, would never let her rest on a partial truth. She needed all of it, no matter the cost. That necessity fueled a creeping sense of fear but also an undeniable, unsettling yearning to trust him.

She tried to calm herself. The sky above churned with faint clouds, and the Sea of Echoes sighed in the distance. Her world had changed so quickly that it felt ready to tilt beneath her feet. She shut her eyes, picturing how Kael had looked when he explained his haunted bloodline. There had been such defeat in his voice, as though he suspected he would lose her if she truly knew everything. Instead, she was confronting a pull toward him that she could not entirely resist, a pull that terrified her far more than any direct question Headmistress Quen could have posed.

He had told her just enough to leave her reeling. She sensed countless hidden layers behind every confession. In that moment, though, she understood one truth clearly: he was bound by illusions he had never invited, and her magic had opened the door for them to collide. The more she unraveled these threads, the more she risked tangling her own future with his. Despite the danger, she could not ignore how deeply her heart ached to believe him.

Her chest tightened painfully. Was this genuine trust, or reckless desperation? Was it foolish to cling to the possibility that their synergy might lead to salvation instead of tragic ruin? She breathed in the salt-tinged air until her trembling subsided. With slow steps, she turned to leave the courtyard, stirred by both dread and an inexplicable warmth.

He had told her not to go too far, not to chase truths that could unravel them both. Yet she knew herself too well. She would never back down when mysteries beckoned, especially mysteries that were now entwined with her own ward magic. If she hesitated, she might lose any chance to steer this fate before it devoured them.

Her steps echoed along the empty walkway as she headed to her dorm. Halfway down the corridor, she paused near a tarnished window that overlooked the dark sea. She pressed a hand against the cold glass. In her reflection, a faint aura of tension shadowed her features.

Everything had changed in the span of one confession. Kael's revelation, about her spell calling him, about the sigil binding them, about the potential havoc that lurked in his family's illusions, lodged inside her thoughts like a jagged shard she could not remove. He had tried to shield her again by telling her just enough to frighten her away. It was too late. She was already too deep under the spell of questions and undeniable sparks.

He had warned her not to delve further, claiming that unearthing the truth would put them both in danger. Alysia felt torn. She stood between curiosity, fear, and something far more dangerous: how much she wanted to trust him.

CHAPTER

EIGHTEEN

MARK OF THE ROGUE

Alysia stood at the edge of the overgrown Academy gardens, absently tugging the collar of her cloak against the afternoon breeze. The once-neat rows of lily shrubs and dew-speckled vines had yielded to tall weeds and drifting petals. Rumors claimed that maintenance had been neglected after recent chaos on campus, but Alysia suspected the real reason was that the faculty's attention lay elsewhere. So many wards had frayed in the last few weeks that everyone scrambled to fortify crucial defenses, leaving places like this garden to wither.

She had only come here for a moment of quiet, a chance to breathe before heading back to the ceaseless illusions and half-rumors about infiltration. But the sight before her was anything but calming. Robin stood knee-deep in sprawling vines, prying a muddy book from the dirt with a triumphant grin. Lyric, perched on a low stone bench, watched with narrowed eyes.

Alysia's pulse kicked up. She drew closer, stepping

196

around brittle stems and uneven stones in the garden path. From afar, she saw that the book's edges were ragged and soaked, pages stuck together by dampness and algae. She asked, "What did you find?"

Robin straightened, wiping mud from her cheek. "An old journal. It was half-buried under these vines. Look at this." She tapped the cover, which seemed ready to crumble under her fingertips. "We only got a glimpse, but it might be about a—"

"Charm Gate," Lyric cut in, her voice cool. She stood with elegant composure, her arms crossed. A few strands of her dark hair blew across her face, but she ignored them as if determined not to show even slight discomfort. "I have no record of it in Bastion Hall's library and neither does the standard course reading. The diagram in those pages looks like an ancient glyph-lattice for illusions and wards."

That word, Charm Gate, sent a soft shiver through Alysia. She had encountered the phrase once in a half-forgotten note penned by her grandmother. Nothing concrete, only a mention that certain gates harnessed synergy between illusions and more structured wards. If the rumor was true, such an artifact could be both miraculous and perilous. She tried to keep her tone neutral. "Are you sure that's what it is?"

Robin carefully pried the journal open, flipping through waterlogged pages until she stopped at a large, faded diagram. The ink was smeared, but Alysia recognized half-formed glyphs around a central circle. Her breath caught. Despite discoloration, the scrawls resembled wards layered with illusion-based lines. Where the arcs overlapped, she saw something that looked like a stylized crest or anchor.

Robin held the journal out toward Alysia. "That anchor is labeled 'Meridan.' We also saw the name 'Kael' scribbled in the margins." Her lips pressed in a thin line. "Couldn't make out the rest. The text mentions a protective anchor in some old rite, but the details are half-blurred. It's like whoever wrote it was in a hurry or got interrupted."

Alysia's stomach twisted. She leaned forward, studying the spiraled lines that framed the diagram. Even with the water damage, she could see they formed a focal point around that single anchor symbol. The name Kael was scrawled on the page, faint but still legible. A chill brushed over her skin, and she reached out with unsteady fingers, tracing the ghost of his name in the soaked parchment.

Lyric cleared her throat. "We found it near the statue of the first Headmistress. No idea how it got there or why it calls Kael a protective anchor, but I suspect it ties to old illusions from the academy's earliest days. Possibly connected to the original Meridan lineage."

Alysia's mind raced. She had learned enough of Kael's family line to know it brimmed with dangerous illusions. Part of her still reeled from the revelation that her own ward magic had somehow pulled him here. Now this document labeled him as a protective anchor in a presumably ancient construct known as the Charm Gate. It felt contradictory. Every rumor she had heard cast the Meridan line as a threat, not a safeguard.

"That can't be right," she murmured. "Kael's illusions aren't exactly famous for keeping the peace. They're often described as...destructive or manipulative." Her voice faltered. She hated speaking about him in that manner, especially after everything he had done to protect her. But the uneasy feeling refused to subside.

Robin brushed caked dirt from the journal's spine. "We're not sure. The writing is messy, as if the author was frantic. Maybe they intended to harness or redirect illusions through the gate. This anchor reference could mean anything, but it's definitely spelled out here."

Holding back a quiet exhale, Alysia flipped another page. Most of the text had smeared into oblivion, but a few lines remained: "The Meridan blood serves as a living anchor," she read aloud, her voice barely a whisper. "It must remain stable, or the Gate will fracture the conduit. True synergy depends on—" The rest was lost to a dark, watery blotch. She scanned the edges, hoping for more clues, but the water damage had claimed nearly every section.

Lyric gently plucked a stray leaf from her sleeve and tossed it aside. "If Kael truly is some protective figure within this design, it contests the rumors that his illusions only ever bring havoc. We might be missing a key part—" She paused, her expression tightening. "Or maybe the old illusions feed on him in ways that can be twisted."

The possibility left Alysia feeling hollow. She closed the journal carefully and tucked it under her arm. The vines crackled beneath her boots when she turned to face the old fountain at the garden's center. Twisted statue shards emerged from the water's surface. Petals drifted around them, saturating the air with a faintly sweet, decaying smell.

She glanced at Robin, then at Lyric. "Thank you for risking your kneecaps in the weeds to find this. If there's a hidden meaning, I'll figure it out. I need to talk to Kael, see if he's seen or heard anything about this gate or that anchor role." She tried to project composure, but inside, her heart hammered. Kael's name in an ancient manual felt like a harbinger. The words protective anchor conjured images of elaborate illusions that might tear the campus apart if unleashed improperly.

She and Robin started back toward the main path of the academy, leaving Lyric behind. Lyric seemed in no hurry to join them, her gaze lingering on a cracked cherub statue near the fountain. Perhaps she wanted a moment alone to mull over what they had discovered.

Robin sidestepped a briar patch, balancing the worn journal in her hands. "Alysia, are you sure about involving Kael so soon? After everything that's happened, you don't want the faculty swooping in if they suspect him of being tied to more secret rites."

Alysia shook her head. "He needs to know. He deserves honesty, not half-kept truths that only feed more rumors. Plus," she added softly, "I can't hide something like this from him. Not anymore."

Robin nodded. She said nothing else as they wove past the orchard's edge, where neglected fruit trees drooped under their own weight. Alysia had time to think about how drastically things had changed. Only days ago, she and Kael had endured a tense inquest with Headmistress Quen. Yet they had ended up forging a fragile understanding. Now, she was about to drop this new revelation in his lap.

A few minutes later, they reached the main courtyard. Clusters of students practiced minor illusions under the watchful eye of a tutor, while others scurried to late-afternoon classes. Furtive glances landed on Alysia and Robin as they walked. Whispers circulated about Kael's past, whispers that seldom carried the full truth.

Overhead, the sky rolled with a dull haze, threatening rain. Alysia clutched the journal, mindful that further water damage would erase what little remained in those pages. Quiet dread gnawed at her ribcage. Kael was no stranger to entanglements with ancient illusions, but reading his name in a near-forgotten grimoire threatened to unravel her composure.

She passed the wide archway leading inside the academy's central hall. Lamps blinked overhead, their mage-light dancing along polished floors. She found Kael standing near a corner, arms folded, his brows drawn tight. The coral amulet around his neck glowed with faint illusions that coiled around his fingertips.

His gaze found her instantly, and a subtle warmth glimmered in his storm-grey eyes. "You look worried," he noted, stepping away from the wall.

Robin, always quick to read the mood, patted Alysia's shoulder. "I'll give you two some space. Meet me in the lounge afterward," she said. With that, she left, her footsteps echoing down the corridor.

The hallway emptied, leaving only Kael and Alysia. She offered him a shaky smile. "You have a knack for reading my expressions."

His mouth curved slightly. "Your eyes get that pinched look whenever you're bracing for bad news. Tell me."

She inhaled, summoning her courage. Then she held out the journal. "Robin and Lyric dug this out of the overgrown gardens. It mentions something called the Charm Gate, an ancient construct. And...it references you. By name. See for yourself." She opened to the diagram, tilting it so he could read the text.

His interest grew, and he gently took the journal from her hands. His illusions shifted around the coral amulet, brightening as if searching for a clue in the water-damaged pages. He ran his thumb over his own name, written in blotchy ink. An uneasy exhale told her enough before he even spoke.

"What does protective anchor mean?" he asked quietly, his eyes scanning the fragments of text. "And why is my name scrawled here like some prophecy?"

Her lips parted, but dread coiled in her throat. "I'm not entirely sure. Something about synergy with illusions and wards. Maybe it's a blueprint for a deeper ritual that needed someone from your lineage. Or maybe it's an older reference tying the Meridan bloodline to a gate used here at Velgrace."

Kael carefully turned another page. Damp sections tore in places, and he winced. "This is basically unreadable. But…" His gaze moved to a faint word near the bottom, something that might have read "rogue," though the letters had bled into the paper. "Do you see that? Mark of the rogue? Could that be what it says?"

Alysia leaned in. Though the ink was too smudged to be certain, the shape of the half-faded letters suggested it might well say Mark of the Rogue. Her pulse gave a nervous jump. The mention of that ominous phrase repeated the same cautionary rumor that traced back to Kael's ancestry. Some still called him a living echo of the rogue illusions that once plagued the Academy.

He pressed his lips together. "This is worse than a half-finished prophecy. Why would someone bury it in that garden, and how did they know my name?"

She shook her head. "I don't have answers yet." Her voice dropped. "But I do know that it's not a coincidence. None of this is. The infiltration, the illusions, your arrival. I think it all ties back to something bigger than we realized."

For a moment, they stood in silence. The corridor's lamp cast shifting shadows across Kael's features. He looked older than usual, weighed down by a new layer of worry. As if he sensed her scrutiny, he lowered the journal and gave a short, humorless laugh. "Every time I think I have a handle on my family's curses, something else leaps out of the shadows."

Alysia stepped closer. She lifted one hand, resting it lightly on his arm. Despite everything around them, a gentle current of warmth passed between their bodies. "We'll figure it out," she said firmly. "You're not alone in this. If that gate or anchor or mark is part of an older design, we'll unravel it together."

He glanced at her hand. A faint smile tugged at his lips, and for a precious second, they shared a tenderness that defied the tension. Then he inhaled, focusing again. "We should show this to someone who can decipher older illusions. Maybe Magister Dain."

Her eyes narrowing, Alysia hesitated. "Yes, but we have to be careful. The last time we brought something suspicious to the faculty, it nearly ended with you getting expelled and me under watch. Dain might know something, but we need to approach him discreetly."

A footstep echoed from behind them. They turned to see Lyric advancing quietly, her expression guarded. She paused a few paces away, glancing from Alysia's hand on Kael's arm to the journal. "So, you showed him," Lyric said, her eyes flicking to Kael's face.

Alysia caught it then, a hint of something that was not surprise in Lyric's eyes, but confirmation. And beneath it, a sliver of fear. She did not just suspect this, she knew what this journal meant.

Kael pressed the book against his side. "You suspected I had ties to an ancient gate?"

Lyric shrugged. "I had no clue if it was accurate. I wanted to see your reaction first." She looked at Alysia, a ripple of sympathy in her gaze. "If that text calls you a protective anchor, maybe it's not a condemnation. It could be a path to harness illusions for defense, not destruction."

The thought offered a slim thread of hope. Alysia

latched onto it. "Yes, or it might be telling us how to block the infiltration. Maybe that gate is the key to shutting rogue illusions out for good."

Kael's expression darkened. "Or it's a blueprint for forcing me into a role I never asked for. This academy has a history of messing with illusions too powerful to control. Being called an anchor might just be a fancy way of saying sacrifice."

His voice cooled, though a flash of hurt shone in his eyes.

Alysia's chest tightened. She remembered how he had risked expulsion to shield her from blame. The idea that he might be manipulated into an even greater danger made her uneasy. Her voice shook slightly. "We won't let that happen to you. One step at a time. We interpret the diagram. We figure out the illusions around this gate before letting the faculty see it."

Lyric nodded, folding her arms. "Let me help. I have some resources in Bastion Hall, including references to old wards that might clarify half these runes."

Kael gave a brisk nod as well, though his posture remained tense. He stared at the partial phrase near the bottom of the page again. Mark of the Rogue? He seemed unable to look away from those smeared letters, as if he recognized them from somewhere.

Alysia forced a calm tone. "We should keep the journal safe until we can examine it properly. Let me ward it tonight, so no more water or scuffs ruin the text."

He exhaled. "Alright. But be careful. Whatever is in

here might draw attention from the infiltration…or from worse."

She reached for the journal, and their fingers brushed. That small contact sent a shiver through her. She was reminded that no matter what the text claimed about Kael, this was still the person who had fought illusions by her side and taken blame that should have fallen on them both. Fear stirred under her ribs, fear that she might lose him if his ancestry kept hurling new threats into their path.

The corridor seemed to close around them. Lamps hissed overhead, and somewhere distant, a door slammed. That hollow echo made Alysia want to run to a quiet corner, to share her worries with him face to face. Yet the moment was too fragile. Lyric lingered, the campus wards hummed, and the worn journal felt heavier than any tome she had ever carried.

She clutched it to her chest. "I'll pass by your dorm tonight," she told Kael, "and we can see if the text reveals anything under certain illusions. Sometimes runes hidden by water damage respond to glyph-lights." She glanced at Lyric. "You too. If you have references in Bastion Hall, bring them."

Lyric gave a quick nod. "We have limited time. The infiltration might sense we're onto something. The rogue faction always seems to smell secrets in the air."

Alysia swallowed hard. With the journal pressed against her, she turned to leave, her mind buzzing with possibilities that refused to form a coherent plan. Behind her, Kael took a half-step forward, as if to say something more. She glanced over her shoulder. Their eyes met. That unspoken trust passed between them again, and he gave a faint nod.

Even so, his stance remained rigid, as though he could already feel the noose tightening around him. Alysia's heart clenched at the sight. She pivoted down the corridor, forcing her feet to move. She needed to confirm what hidden knowledge the pages held, to clarify whether this Charm Gate was a saving grace or another dangerous snare. One thing was certain: Kael's name scrawled in an ancient volume meant the stakes were higher than she had imagined.

She exited the building, heading into the open court-yard. The sky overhead had grown darker, clouds roiling with the threat of rain. She caught glimpses of other students hurrying indoors. Each step prompted new ques-tions, spinning inside her mind like restless gusts. She did not know if the phrase Mark of the Rogue spelled doom or if the idea of a protective anchor implied a path to redemption. But she could sense that the answers would change everything.

She thought of Kael's resolute face when he saw his name in the journal. She recalled the illusions around him, the shape of his protective wards during their last brush with infiltration. And she felt a pang of dread. He had always insisted his illusions could be used for good, if only he could break free of the darkness in his bloodline. Now, this Charm Gate threatened to confirm or destroy that belief.

Lightning flashed in the distance, illuminating the

towers of Velgrace with a sudden glare. Alysia tucked the journal beneath her cloak, shielding it from the first warm droplets of rain. Then she hurried onward, her mind spinning with runes, anchors, and a name half-lost to watery ink. Every step pounded home the same realization. She had only scratched the surface of Kael's involvement, and what lay beneath might be far more terrifying than any infiltration scheme they had faced so far.

Her questions multiplied, but so did her dread.

NINETEEN

THE HIDDEN CHAMBER

Alysia lay awake in her small dorm room, watching the faint glow of ward-lights dance across her ceiling. Her thoughts raced with new questions, all tied to Kael's name scrawled in that half-buried journal Robin and Lyric had uncovered. She recalled how the blurred words had linked him to a forgotten construct called the Charm Gate, suggesting he was some form of protective anchor. She could not sleep when so many uncertainties pressed on her. Protecting Kael was imperative, yet everything hinted that his lineage ran deeper than even he realized. She knew the answers lurked in the vault, buried beneath layers of wards and illusions.

She threw aside her blankets, dressed quietly, and slipped into the corridor. The hour was late, though Velgrace Academy at night never offered her true comfort. Instead, it amplified her anxieties. The passageway's torches had been turned down to narrow flames, revealing patches of shifting shadows along the walls. She walked with careful steps, hugging her cloak to her body and listening for any sign of patrolling instructors or restless students.

Kael spotted her before she saw him. He stood at the far end of the corridor, leaning casually against a stone pillar with the hood of his cloak drawn low. She halted, her heart thudding, unsure if she should speak. He gave a slight tilt of his head, beckoning her forward. His presence eased her nerves somewhat, though tension still roiled in the space between them.

"Couldn't sleep?" His voice was soft, so as not to echo in the quiet corridor.

She shook her head, realizing that admitting her anxiety to him felt oddly comforting. "I kept thinking about that journal," she said, "about the references to you and the Charm Gate. I need more clarity. The vault is the only place that might yield answers."

He nodded, his gaze showing understanding. "I thought you might try going there tonight. And if you did," he added, letting a gentle shrug move his shoulders, "I planned to go with you." The corner of his mouth curved in a faint smile, though it did not chase away the worry in his eyes.

They moved in silence through winding halls, closer to the vault's entrance under Aurum Spire. A set of protective wards shimmered above the threshold, faint runic lines shining whenever the vault's powerful locks sensed movement. Officially, the area was restricted to certain faculty or advanced wardsmiths, yet Alysia and Kael had long since proved the wards could be bypassed by combining their unique talents. The infiltration rumors within Velgrace meant that not even the most restricted corners were truly safe, but she and Kael had always faced those dangers together.

Near the vault door, Alysia paused. The large iron gate looked more imposing than usual, as though it wanted to warn them away. Rows of carved glyphs formed a protective circle on the floor. She set her palm against the largest one, inhaling to steady her thoughts, and then let her magic flow into the lines. She felt Kael's presence at her shoulder, drawn by her wards. His illusions soon melded with her energy, weaving a shimmering outline across the runes. A moment later, the vault recognized their combined signature and unlocked with a low, resonant clang.

Inside, stale air pressed against them, carrying the scent of old spell residue and damp stone. Their footsteps echoed in the darkness until Kael conjured a faint orb of light in his palm. Shadows leaped across the walls, revealing dusty shelves and sealed compartments. Alysia steeled her resolve and led the way deeper. She remembered the many relics stored here, the books that whispered secrets when opened, and the wards that had tried to repel them on earlier visits. Tonight, she expected a new layer of hidden knowledge, something that might connect to that worn journal's puzzle.

They reached the far side of the main vault corridor, where a series of carved steps descended into gloom. These steps were rarely traveled, even by the faculty. Alysia recalled that only a handful of archivists kept any knowledge of what lay below. She thought again of the infiltration. If certain conspirators had found a route here, they might have harnessed even more dangerous relics. That possibility made her stomach clench. She glanced at Kael, who watched her with a protective light in his eyes.

"We should stay alert," she whispered. "Who knows if we're alone."

He nodded and stepped close enough that she felt the soft brush of his cloak against her arm. Together, they swept their gazes across the rows of silent alcoves. Each alcove displayed a thick iron door emblazoned with ward sigils. Some of those wards glowed faintly, as though only half-active. The infiltration had strained the academy's defenses, leaving pockets of vulnerability behind. She felt her chest tighten at the sight of the weakened wards, aware that anything sealed away might be able to stir with far less provocation.

At the very end of the corridor, she noticed a new pattern she had never seen before. It was a cluster of runes shaped in concentric rings, carved into the floor. She crouched, training her lamp-like illusions from Kael's conjured light across the pattern. The lines seemed to spiral inward, each ring hosting smaller glyphs that inter-locked like puzzle pieces. Curious, she ran her fingertips across the cold stone, feeling a muted vibration.

"This is new," she said, her voice tense with excitement. "Or maybe we never looked closely enough before."

Kael knelt beside her, letting his orb hover in the air above them. With both hands free, he traced the outer ring. The lines responded to his illusions, shining gently before dimming again. "I sense a partial ward. Could be a door or a hatch. The runes look incomplete, though. Something is missing from the center."

Alysia's mind raced, recalling how their synergy sometimes unlocked hidden pathways. Without overthinking, she laid her palm over the central segment of the carved pattern. She channeled a careful strand of ward magic, letting it flow from her wrist down into her fingertips. The glyphs brightened with a pale glow, reacting to her presence. The stone at her knees rumbled, and an inner portion of the floor sank inward, revealing a staircase that curled into deeper darkness.

Her pulse jumped. She looked back at Kael. He swallowed, his eyes shining with anticipation. "This must be it," he said quietly. "What the infiltration never found, or never quite managed to open."

They exchanged determined looks, then stepped onto the hidden stairwell. The low steps felt damp beneath Alysia's boots, as though water seeped in from the sea beyond the cliff. Their footsteps echoed in a steady rhythm, while Kael's floating light spun shadows along the dripping walls. A sense of unease coiled in her stomach. She reminded herself that no matter what they found, facing it with Kael felt safer than facing it alone.

At the base, they arrived at a curved chamber lined in intricate sigils. The floor, walls, and even the low ceiling were etched with carefully arranged markings that glistened in the light. It was like standing inside the very circulatory system of the academy's magic. The glyphs weren't just patterns; they were arteries, pulsing with a life of their own, and she felt their ancient, rhythmic heartbeat in the soles of her feet. Alysia gasped at the sight. Many of the lines appeared to form constellations that mapped the sky overhead, shifting from one arrangement to another. Yet this was all carved in stone, hidden beneath Velgrace, so old that the builders' names had been lost to time.

Kael walked forward, turning in a slow half-circle to take in every angle. Illusions flickered across his knuckles in fascinated response. "It looks like an ancient cosmic diagram," he said in an awed murmur. "As if they tried to replicate an entire star field down here. Or maybe they anchored illusions to stars for extra power."

Alysia searched for an anchor point. Her eyes drifted across the patterns until she noticed one mark near the center that glowed differently. While the other symbols emitted a cold gleam, this one shimmered with a softer warmth. She was strangely drawn to it, her breath catching as she moved closer. She realized it was shaped like her family's crest when viewed from a particular angle. Or perhaps that was wishful thinking on her part. Either way, something about it felt personal.

She paused a few steps away and pressed both hands to her body, feeling her heart beat. Anxiety mingled with a powerful curiosity. Kael must have sensed her hesitation because he placed a hand gently on her arm, a silent question in his eyes.

"It's calling me," she admitted, her voice trembling. "But I don't know what it wants."

He studied her face. "Do you think it's dangerous?"

She swallowed. The memory of other wards that had tried to repel or ensnare them flitted through her thoughts. Still, this mark did not feel menacing. She felt no sting of ill intent, only a gentle invitation. "I don't sense malice," she answered quietly. "Not the way we did with the rogues' illusions."

He nodded and stepped back, letting her approach. She felt an odd comfort in his trust. Carefully, she stepped into the center of the chamber, watching the shimmering lines on the wall. The soft glow of the central sigil radiated in pulses, faint at first, then brighter in intervals. She sank to her knees, ignoring the cold dampness of the stone, and extended her left hand. Her ward magic tingled in her veins, as though readying itself for something grand.

When her fingers brushed the glowing mark, a wave of warmth surged up her arm, coursing through her entire body. She inhaled sharply, bracing herself for pain, but discovered only a curious sweep of energy that wrapped her like a comforting breeze. It was not gentle or timid, but it carried no sense of harm either. She heard a low thrumming noise, and the constellation of runes on the walls began to shift as if rotating in slow unison, turning the chamber into a living galaxy of light. Part of her mind reeled at the magnitude of it. This was a form of magic she had never experienced.

She closed her eyes, letting the hum flow through her senses. Images drifted through her thoughts more as impressions than visions. She sensed threads of old wards, illusions from a bygone era, and something akin to the heartbeat of the academy itself. A voiceless message pressed at the edge of her mind, but she could not decipher the exact words. The gentle pulses seemed to echo in sync with the beat of her heart.

Kael's voice cut through the haze. "Alysia, look." He sounded cautious, though a note of wonder touched his words.

She opened her eyes and saw that streaks of light had emerged along the floor, connecting her position to smaller runes encircling the room. Like lines of starlight, they wove from the center outward, forming a complex web of magical pathways. Each line glowed with the same gentle warmth as the central mark she touched. The entire chamber felt alive, awakened by her presence.

"Its resonating with your ward magic," Kael observed as he stepped closer. His illusions moved around him and reflected colors off the curved ceiling. "I recognize an echo of your Thorne runes, but also something else. This place is older than the academy's official archives."

Alysia's hand remained on the central mark. She felt her pulse slow, drawn into the calm waves of the chamber's energy. She tried to speak but could not find the right words to express her wonder. Only days ago, she had feared being an outsider at Velgrace. She had worried about rumors, about her reputation as a Thorne with a troubled family past, and about Kael's precarious status. Now, with her hand on this mark, she sensed that the structure beneath Velgrace recognized her and welcomed her. She was not merely a student in its eyes.

"How can a place be so open to me?" she said softly, half to herself. "I am not the most powerful wardsmith here, not an official caretaker of old illusions, and I have no rank that grants me special access."

Kael exhaled, shaking his head in awe. "Titles may not matter to magic this old. Perhaps it only wants a spirit committed to seeking the truth. Your grandmother's notes, your devotion to wards, and your refusal to walk away from what scares you. Maybe that is exactly what calls to you."

Her eyes burned with unshed tears. This place was not merely recognizing her Thorne lineage but answering a call from the core of her own magic. The energy surging from the central glyph felt less like an external force and more like a part of herself she never knew was missing that had finally returned home. It was a profound, aching sense of completion. She lifted her hand away, and the pulse of warmth receded slightly, leaving behind a faint light that hovered on her palm for a moment before fading. The entire chamber still thrummed, but it was calmer now, like a giant heart that had recognized its keeper.

Kael offered her a hand and helped her rise. Their eyes met, and for that moment, it felt as though the distance that usually stood between them had vanished. She could almost feel the echo of his illusions melding with her wards. Despite the mysteries still unsolved, a fragile strand of hope wove between them, reminding her they were not alone.

"This place holds answers," she said. Her voice trembled from the surge of magic still coursing through her. "We can learn more about why the academy was built above these sigils, about the Charm Gate or the references to a protective anchor. And maybe about your name in that journal. The infiltration must tie in here somehow."

Kael gave a resolute nod. "If the rogues have discovered even half of this, they would try to exploit it. We have to get there first."

She stepped away from the center of the diagram, and as she did, the lines on the floor dimmed, returning to a subdued glow. She turned in a slow circle, scanning every inch of the chamber's celestial carvings. Bit by bit, the light receded from the walls, leaving only the faint luminescence around the center mark. She felt an echo of that gentle energy tingling in her limbs, as though it had branded her with a deeper purpose.

Standing beside Kael in the hidden chamber, Alysia recognized how expansive her world had just become. Only a short time earlier, she had believed that excelling in classes and repairing her family's tarnished reputation were the biggest challenges she would face. Now, the living constellation carved beneath Velgrace seemed to whisper that she was part of something far greater. Excitement, dread, and determination knotted in her chest.

"I feel different," she admitted, her voice barely above a whisper. "I can't explain it. Everything about this place... it's telling me that my role here is bigger than passing an exam or proving myself. I am part of a magic that has been waiting."

Kael reached out and tentatively touched her shoulder. "Not everyone would open themselves to it the way you did. You claim you lack rank, but you showed a kind of courage plenty of master enchanters never muster."

She closed her eyes, letting his gentle warmth anchor her. In the darkness behind her eyelids, she could still see the lines of glowing star-runes etched into her memory. She might have stayed there, lost in that boundless sense of possibility, if Kael's illusions had not shimmered, signaling his watchfulness. She stepped back, remembering the infiltration danger. She could not afford to let her guard down for too long.

They exchanged a final glance and then picked their way back toward the staircase. Each step felt oddly reverent, as though she were leaving a temple dedicated to secrets that had chosen her. She remained hyperaware of the gentle vibration beneath the stone, as if the entire network of runes still recognized her presence.

Halfway up, she paused to look over her shoulder. That pulsing mark shone clearly in the center of the dark chamber. Unlike ominous wards or sinister illusions they had encountered before, this radiated warmth and acceptance. She wondered whether the infiltration was a direct threat to the chamber's power, or if the infiltration was a symptom of deeper tensions that the academy's founders had once tried to seal away. Regardless, she knew she could not walk away now.

Kael's close footstep nudged her to keep moving. At the top of the hidden stairs, they silently resealed the floor behind them. The carved pattern on the flagstones shifted back into place, as though no secret path existed. Yet

Alysia knew the path was very real and that it had waited for her to find it.

She walked beside Kael, heart pounding, her mind with more questions than ever. Until now, her primary goal had been to prove herself worthy at Velgrace, to show that a Thorne could excel and maybe even stand on equal footing with the best ward-crafters in the realm. But the discovery of this second chamber hinted at something far greater than academic success. If the lines and runes were any indication, her presence mattered in ways she could barely comprehend.

Kael opened his mouth to speak, then closed it again, as though he, too, struggled to put the moment into words. Finally, they reached the main vault corridor, where his orb cast longer shadows against old crates and sealed relic cases. The exit loomed just ahead. She felt relief to see it, mixed with an ache of reluctance. A part of her longed to follow the path of that hidden chamber until every star-like rune revealed its story.

She paused near the vault doors, turning to face him fully. "We have to figure out how it connects," she said. "That charm diagram is not there by accident. Something or someone made it respond to me. The infiltration might be searching for the same answers. If they discover the link first—"

"They won't," Kael interrupted gently. He lifted one hand as though to rest it on her cheek, then hesitated. She found herself closing the distance to let him, ignoring the dangerous twist of longing in her chest. His palm was warm against her skin, illusions crackling faintly at his fingertips. "We'll protect the secret until we understand it," he said, his voice firm.

She placed her own hand on top of his for a heartbeat, letting that small contact steady her thoughts. Everything about this strange cosmic vault had stirred new possibilities, new responsibilities. She breathed in his scent, a mix of parchment, old sea air, and the faint tang of iron from the wards. She let her fingers curl around his, feeling the synergy again: wards and illusions, weaving together in something neither one could replicate alone.

They exited the vault into the corridor's cool air, locking it quietly behind them so that no trace of their presence remained. Silence claimed the hallway except for their low breathing. She held her cloak tighter around her shoulders. She wanted to speak, but no words came, not even a ripple of the awe she felt at discovering that constellation of sigils beneath the academy's foundation.

Kael finally broke the silence, his voice laced with curiosity. "Are you all right?"

She let out a soft breath, then nodded. "I am," she said. "I just feel...changed, I suppose."

He kept his eyes on her, searching for more explanation. She grappled with how to phrase it, how to convey the impression of cosmic purpose pressing against her soul. At last, she let her gaze shift back toward the sealed vault door. Her words came out in a whisper.

"I'm not just a student trying to scrape by anymore," she said. "I feel connected to something ancient, maybe dangerous, but definitely powerful. I can't pretend it isn't real. That mark proved it to me."

The realization settled over her like the lull before a brewing storm. She squeezed Kael's hand once and tried to calm the restless flutter in her stomach. Deep inside, she understood that returning to ordinary lessons would never feel the same. The corridor lamps blinked, and she imagined the pulse of that hidden chamber still thrumming, calling her forward into a fate she could neither run from nor fully embrace. She took a slow breath, braced her shoulders, and decided there was no turning back now.

TWENTY

BOUND BY GLYPHS

Alysia braced her knees against the cold, damp stone. Her palm settled on the central glyph etched into the floor, and a trembling current of magic surged up her arm. The chamber's torchlight flickered in unison with that rising power, casting wild shadows across the ancient carvings that filled every wall. She had expected a spark, some reaction to her ward magic, but this felt as though the entire chamber had awakened to greet her. No ward training had prepared her for the exhilarating blend of fear and awe now thrumming beneath her skin.

She pressed her hand more firmly against the glyph. At once, the carved lines illuminating the floor ignited in a spiral of light. The geometry spread across the chamber like a constellation reversed, bathing the stone in radiance. Her breath caught in her throat. The shapes reminded her of star arrays or hidden ley paths she had only read about in obscure volumes. Except these designs seemed alive, not just scrawled or carved. They shifted as if they possessed their own quiet heartbeat.

Her cousin Robin was absent, chasing leads in another corridor, and Lyric had vanished not long after showing them glimpses of the journal that referenced Kael's name. Tonight, it was only Kael and Alysia who had dared to descend deeper. She felt him standing behind her, close enough for her to sense the faint hum of his illusions. He was silent as he watched the light around her fingers, letting her take the first step as though he trusted she knew how to harness what they had discovered.

The moment she allowed a single thread of her ward magic to flow into the glyph, a sudden pulse washed over the chamber. Something like a wind, but there was no breeze in this hidden space. The lines on the floor brightened, revealing additional shapes between them. They radiated outward, weaving a shining network all around her. Through it, she glimpsed sigils that resembled forbidden illusions, wards from the earliest ages of Velgrace, and runes that teased ancient sea-bound secrets. She recognized fleeting symbols for protection, entrapment, and synergy alike. Each glowed, then faded, like pieces of a puzzle offering her a glimpse before slipping back into the broader tapestry.

Her breath emerged in shallow bursts, almost overwhelmed by the scale of what she was seeing. She thought of her family's tarnished legacy, of the incomplete wards her mother had perished trying to master. More than once, Alysia had feared she might follow that same tragic path. Now, the energy beneath her fingers seemed to whisper that she was part of something ancient and grander than any single bloodline. She shivered, the weight both comforting and terrifying.

Kael knelt beside her, a hand hovering near her shoulder. He worked illusions instinctively, conjuring a faint halo of light that rippled in response to the glyph's shimmer. She sensed his presence as a steady warmth at her side, a reminder that she was not alone in this. For so long, she had kept her ward experiments private, refusing to let outsiders see her raw vulnerability. Yet Kael had stepped into her life, unasked, chaotic, and mesmerizing. She had never planned to trust him with her secrets. Now their fates tied them together in ways neither fully understood.

He exhaled slowly, his voice soft. "You're all right?"

"Yes." Alysia tried to steady her heartbeat. "It's a lot. I didn't expect it to awaken like this." She pressed a bit more magic into the glyph. The patterns on the floor brightened further, revealing new veins of light that stretched across the curved walls. Above, faint lines ran along the arched ceiling, connecting in a mesmerizing tapestry. It reminded her of star charts, each path forming a chord of energy. She realized this might be a map, but not of any landmass she knew. It was a map of magic, charting illusions, wards, and hidden energies across realms yet untraveled.

Kael let his gaze roam the chamber. "This place...it's responding to you. Can you feel that hum in the stones? Almost like it's calling an answer to your wards."

"I feel it," she whispered. Her hand tingled at the point of contact. Each breath filled her lungs with invisible potency, as if the chamber's power had blended with the air itself. She swallowed, half-frightened by what might happen if she lost control.

He reached out, resting his hand gently over hers. At once, a fresh wave of dazzling color spun across the floor, mingling illusions with wards in a brilliant display that reminded her of a sunrise. She felt Kael's illusions sliding through her wards, not warring with them, but resonating in bright harmony. The effect deepened the chamber's pulses until it felt like standing at the center of an immense cosmic clock.

She closed her eyes and allowed her focus to expand. She sensed the presence of multiple threads. Some were old illusions tinted with malevolent undercurrents, others were wards that might have once protected the Academy from infiltration. She saw glimpses of sigils rumored to be lost to time, including a symbol that mirrored Kael's surname, Meridan. A thousand half-formed runes danced at the edges of her vision, beckoning her closer. Her head felt light, and she fought to keep focus.

Kael's voice reached her as if from a short distance. "Easy. You don't need to absorb it all at once."

She forced her eyes open, grounding herself in the sight of his face. His stormy gaze shone with concern, illusions flickering around him like protective armor. The magic around her subsided ever so slightly, enough for her to catch her breath.

"I can see...so many patterns," she said, almost breathless. "They're wards and illusions woven together. Old spells, maybe from the founding of Velgrace. Some feel... twisted or incomplete." She swallowed hard. "I don't recognize half of them, but I sense them linking to me."

He studied her expression, then nodded. "You're not forcing them. They're responding on their own. Whatever is here, it wants your wards as a catalyst. You saw how they glowed the second you came into contact."

She remembered how the glyph had glimmered beneath her palm like an old friend acknowledging her touch. Usually, wards were static until conjured or anchored by a caster. But this place felt as though it had always been waiting for Thorne magic to reignite it. That realization made her heart pound. She asked herself if this was how her mother had felt in her final moments, on the brink of discovering something too great to tame.

Then the lines across the walls flared. A new array of lights coalesced overhead, creating a circular design that pulsed with every beat of Alysia's heart. Emblems of branching illusions and overlapping wards spanned the chamber's vaulted ceiling. Collectively, the shapes resembled doors. She sensed that a single push of will might open them, unleashing forces she only half-understood.

She glanced at Kael, her voice trembling. "This chamber... it's more than old runes. I think it's a map of every ward or illusion that has ever touched the academy. I see references to infiltration attempts, protective anchors, and even designs that look like sea-bound illusions from the merfolk realm."

He lifted his gaze to the glowing overhead patterns.

"That means it must be tied to the original magic that created Velgrace. The place was built to unify wards and illusions, right? Maybe these lines show us where that unity was once perfect, and where it broke." Lowering his eyes, he added softly, "And if it broke, it can be restored."

She pressed her lips together in a tense line. Could they restore it alone? She thought of the infiltration rumors, the half-buried truths. The worn journal that named Kael a protective anchor. She felt an almost painful urgency to decode every symbol at once, even though she knew that path could destroy her if she rushed. The memory of her mother's failed ward flickered in her thoughts, a warning that power untamed was as dangerous as any rogue faction.

Magic surged anew through her fingertips. The design on the ceiling rippled, shifting to reveal a single, central shape. It resembled a lock or focus glyph. She recognized partial curves that might be from the Thorne family crest, interlaced with the Meridan illusions anchored to Kael's bloodline. They fit together with startling precision. Her heart ached with the weight of it all. This was not a random accumulation of old spells. Someone had built this synergy to rely on a Thorne ward and a Meridan illusion.

She saw Kael's expression shift as he made the same realization. A silent tension hung between them, something that trembled with possibility and dread. For a moment, neither of them spoke. The chamber lit their faces in otherworldly color, and she could almost hear the echoes of ancient voices whispering along the walls. This had been planned by mages long dead, planned perhaps centuries ago, waiting for them to fulfill a design that might end in salvation or calamity.

She rested a hand against Kael's chest, feeling the fast beat of his heart. It matched her own, thrumming with shared adrenaline. He set his fingertips on her cheek, illusions dancing behind his eyes. His voice was soft and unguarded. "You've always thought you were broken, that your wards didn't measure up to your mother's or your grandmother's. What if that was never true? What if you were exactly what this place needed?"

Her throat felt tight, stung by the gravity of that thought. When she had arrived at Velgrace, her main desire was to prove herself worthy, to pass her classes and maybe restore her family name. She had never aimed to stand at the threshold of something so vast it could shake entire realms. The glyphs overhead hinted that they might be able to fix the fraying illusions or harness them in new ways. Yet the cost could be high if they misstepped.

She swallowed. "Kael...why does it have to be me?"

"Because it responds to you," he replied, his voice trembling with intensity. "No one else could have done this. The wards are yours, not just your family's. This place is reacting not to an idea of a Thorne, but to who you are. A conduit for something beyond a single discipline."

The word conduit rang through her like a clear bell. She had been taught that wards required discipline too rigid for illusions, that illusions fed on the intangible forces wards tried to pin down. Yet in this chamber, illusions and wards coexisted in perfect unison. She pictured how the worn journal had labeled Kael a protective anchor. Perhaps it was never solely about him. Perhaps it was about who might unify the illusions with wards to complete what had once been deserted. The thrumming in her hand intensified, as if the glyph recognized her acceptance of this possibility.

She closed her eyes, letting the magic appear behind her eyelids. Colors danced across her mind, bright and mesmerizing. She faintly sensed other illusions fluttering around the edges of her consciousness, echoes of infiltration attempts, the ghosts from prior eras, the sea that ties the Academy to merfolk alliances. She sensed Kael's illusions weaving with her wards in a circuit of raw potential. Could she rewrite lost wards? Could she anchor illusions in a new shape? The thought thrilled and terrified her in equal measure. So many had failed at forging stable synergy. So many had died trying.

Kael's thumb brushed gently across her cheek. "Breathe," he whispered, his voice gentle. "You are not alone. Whatever this place expects, we face it together."

She sighed against his touch, her heart beating so fast it threatened to crack her composure. Her entire life had been defined by caution, by fear of crossing magical boundaries she did not fully understand. Now, those boundaries lay scattered around her feet. A single mistake could unravel wards that protected the Academy from infiltration and illusions that might swallow them all. Yet the alternative was letting the infiltration deepen, letting the rogue faction exploit these pathways first.

A jolt of determination cut through her. She moved her

palm over the glowing glyph again, pressing enough magic to meet it halfway. The conflagration of lights spun faster, and somewhere in the corner of the chamber, a faint melody seemed to emanate from the stone, as though the rock itself was celebrating new life. Her wards tingled in her veins. She felt her Thorne crest on her bracelet vibrate in time with that cosmic hum. Tension and energy fused into a single chord.

Kael watched her with steady awe. "They said your family's wards were incomplete. But maybe they were just waiting for the right illusions to fill the gaps." He paused and exhaled. "They told you your family's wards were broken," he whispered, his voice filled with awe. "They were wrong. They weren't broken. They were waiting. For you."

Her eyes misted. In that moment, she allowed herself to believe his words. Every lash of self-doubt, every memory of her mother's downfall, every fear about repeating those mistakes, she let them all drift from her mind. In the brilliance of the glyph-light, she felt a kernel of hope. The chamber vibrated as if sensing her acceptance.

"I might be the only one," she murmured, her voice trembling. "I don't know if that means I can save what was lost or unleash something worse. But I see it, Kael. Everything is at my fingertips. If I focus in the right way, I could stitch illusions and wards into a new spell. Or I could shatter them beyond repair."

He let silence settle, then gently drew her hand away from the glyph. The glow in the floor lessened, but still glimmered with an echo of life, reflecting the last vestiges of her ward magic. He studied her face. "You decide where this goes next. You are the conduit." His voice dipped low. "And I will stand by your side, no matter what."

Alysia felt her heart twist at the promise threaded through his words. She tilted her head to meet his gaze, inhaling the faint smell of old stone, salt air, and lingering illusions. The resonance in the chamber had not faded. It hovered in the corners like a living presence, urging her to acknowledge that she had become the key to something far larger than she had ever imagined.

She dared not dwell on every possible outcome. If she let panic control her, the synergy around them could crack, or worse, turn destructive. Yet the knowledge brimming in the air filled her with a solemn certainty: her entire life had led to this hidden vault, to these entwined sigils, and to the man before her who anchored illusions in ways no one else ever could. She trembled at the enormity of it all, at the power curling through her fingertips like golden threads waiting for a weaver's hand.

Her exhale quivered. "I might be the only one who can rewrite all this," she repeated. Then her stare roamed over the softly pulsing designs, their glowing lines forming a map of what was possible. "Or I could destroy it."

The last words left her lips in a near-whisper. They held both hope and dread. The chamber's lights flickered around them, wrapping them in a fragile luminescence that felt like standing on the edge of a dawn, uncertain whether it promised daybreak or ruin. The power at her command trembled in the vault's carved stones, and she knew her next steps would define not only her future, but the fate of every ward and illusion bound to Velgrace. She stood beneath the tapestry of glyphs, Kael at her side, her heart poised between creation and devastation. And discovered she could not look away.

CHAPTER

TWENTY-ONE

INTERRUPTED MOMENTS

Alysia inhaled slowly, pressing her fingertips against the cool stone of the vault's inner corridor. Each breath carried the subtle tang of old magic, a dry scent like scorched parchment tinged with a trace of sea air drifting from the academy's coastal cliffs. Although she and Kael had come here before, the silence felt heavier this time, an unspoken promise lurking in every flicker of torchlight.

She let her gaze drift over the intricate glyphs carved along the walls. Dim, pulsing lines trailed across the stones, remnants of ward spells laid by archivists long ago. Twice earlier that evening, the wards had glowed, drawn to the synergy of her ward-magic and Kael's illusions. She was still trying to settle her pounding heart. Moments ago, one of those hidden passages had opened under their combined touch, leading them deeper into the newly discovered chamber. Now the vault's main corridor felt downright intimate, shielded from the rest of Velgrace Academy by layers of thick, seamless rock.

234

"Do you think these wards remember us?" she murmured, brushing a hand along a faintly glowing rune. Its surface quivered with warmth under her fingertips, as though the stone had come alive only for her.

Behind her, Kael's boots scuffed the floor in a slow approach. "They remember you," he said softly, his voice reverberating in the still air. "They haven't shown that level of response to illusions alone."

Alysia turned around, finding him watching her again. Lantern-light caught at his gray eyes, giving them a silver sheen that hinted at the illusions smoldering in his veins. He wore the same travel-worn cloak as always, its hood trailing down his back. She tried not to stare. She tried to focus on the runes. Yet each time she felt his closeness, warmth uncoiled low in her stomach.

"Don't say that," she teased, though her smile held an edge. "I'm sure these wards are equally charmed by your illusions."

"And by equally," Kael replied, stepping nearer, "you mean not at all."

She snorted, though a spark of humor danced in her chest. "Don't be so modest. I saw how you unlocked that hidden door earlier with just a sliver of your illusion magic."

He tilted his head. "You were the one who showed me where to place my hand."

His gaze lingered on her face, and she realized that her adrenaline-laced excitement from uncovering that new chamber was now giving way to a different kind of energy: tension, vibrant and nearly overwhelming.

She swallowed. The presence of infiltration across Velgrace and the knowledge that dangerous secrets lay in these vaults should have made her fearful. Instead, she felt unstoppable when he stood beside her. Their synergy was a power no infiltration rumor could dampen. It was a temptation to get lost in the magic, and in the closeness sparking between them.

"This corridor is stable," she said, clearing her throat. "No ward disruptions that might collapse the place while we're down here."

Kael arched a brow. "I'm more interested in what we might learn from that new seal we found. There could be another passage. You said the lines looked incomplete, right?"

"They did," she answered, letting her hand drop from the rune. "But maybe it isn't about the lines being incomplete. Maybe it's about waiting for the right caster to complete them, or two casters in tandem."

A muscle in his jaw flexed. He nodded in silent agreement, stepping closer. "Could be. This place has been sealed for ages. The infiltration never figured out how to open half these chambers, I bet. You..."

He paused, glancing down at her. She felt a warmth that had nothing to do with corridors or wards. His expression softened, as though he was deciding whether to speak his next words. Her pulse thudded in her ears, and she wondered if he could sense it. Probably. Their synergy was so strong lately that each shift in her wards mirrored a shift in his illusions.

She reached back, pressing her palm against the stone behind her for balance. "What was that?" she asked, her voice coming out more frightened than she intended.

He exhaled a quiet laugh, running one hand through his dark hair. "I was going to say you're brilliant when you're deciphering these old marks. But most of the time, I can't manage that sentence without sounding like I'm issuing a challenge."

"You're always issuing a challenge," she said, unable to stop the tiny smile tugging at her lips. "What changed?"

"Maybe nothing." His voice deepened. "Maybe I'm just noticing how easily we work together."

The tension built, crackling in the narrow space. Alysia felt a heightened awareness of everything around them, the flickering sconces that painted dancing shadows on the walls, the scuff of Kael's boots, the quickening of her own breath. Alarm bells in her mind warned her this was dangerous in more ways than one. They were alone in a restricted space, illusions and wards thrumming like a living pulse. Yet she could not bring herself to back away.

They stepped carefully around a toppled column fragment lying across the floor. The vault had seen centuries of partial collapses and hasty repairs, leaving debris behind. With each shift of rubble, dust rose in the lamplight, drifting between them. She noticed the tiny flecks catching in Kael's hair.

"Do you think someone else might stumble in?" she asked, half-hopeful that no one would.

He shook his head, illusions dancing briefly around his

fingertips in a protective shimmer. "I left a small ward at the entrance. If anyone tries to open the vault without the override, we'll feel it."

"Then it's just us," she said.

"Seems so," he murmured, stopping again just an arm's length away. Somewhere deeper in the vault, a droplet of water echoed in a faint plink, reminding her of the sea. She swallowed again, trying to focus on practicalities, like the infiltration threat or the possibility of hidden constructs. But her gaze stole toward the line of his jaw, the shape of his lips.

A thousand thoughts tumbled through her head: how they'd nearly discovered vital information about the infiltration, how he'd saved her from a misfired ward last week, how she'd begun trusting him in ways she never trusted anyone else. It both thrilled and terrified her. He was no stable figure. He was half legend, half rumor, a conjurer of illusions. Yet he felt achingly real with every breath, every time she glimpsed that flicker of vulnerability in his eyes.

She exhaled shakily. "We should check the next chamber," she said, not moving from where she stood.

His voice lowered, a soft rumble. "We will."

Her heart lurched at how simply he said it, as though he was content to stay in this quiet corner forever. She told herself to gather the courage to slip past him, to continue investigating. Instead, she felt her footsteps still. His closeness shimmered in the dusty air. His illusions stirred, a visible shimmer in the air that answered the faint glow of her own wards. The synergy was like a magnetic tug that pulled them together whether they wanted it or not.

Alysia forced out a breath. "Kael," she began, her tone unsteady. She was not sure what she aimed to say, a warning or an invitation. The tightness in her stomach suggested both.

He took one more step closer. Now his cloak almost brushed her arm. She could smell the faint mixture of salt air and old paper that clung to him, reminders of the academy's windy towers and a lifetime of collecting magical volumes. She stared up at him, her pulse a hammer in her chest. For all her careful study of wards, for all his mastery of illusions, this moment felt like the most potent magic she had ever encountered.

"You can tell me if you want me to back off," he said quietly. "I know we're both...uncertain."

She swallowed. Admitting uncertainty felt like giving infiltration conspirators an advantage, as if vulnerability here might lead to heartbreak later. But she refused to lie. "I don't want you to back off," she whispered.

Her words ignited something in his gaze. He reached up, his hand hovering near her face. His knuckles almost brushed her cheek, illusions flickering across them in a faint glow. Her wards thrummed in response, sending a gentle tingle along her arm. He was close enough that she could make out the faint line of an old scar near his eyebrow, a testament to the dangers he had faced, illusions or otherwise.

"Then I won't," he said simply.

She lowered her lashes, trembling. She was acutely aware of her own breathing, shallow and quick, and the soft catch in his throat whenever he hesitated. Slowly, as if a single sudden movement might break the spell, she lifted her hand to lightly rest on his chest. She felt the rapid beat of his heart through his shirt, a mirror to her own pounding pulse. Luminous sparks danced around their joined point of contact, illusions and wards colliding in a mesmerizing display.

His lips curved into a half-smile, almost disbelieving. Then he leaned in.

She froze for a heartbeat, letting the reality of the moment settle around her, letting the tension coil so tightly she could barely breathe. They were alone, hidden from prying eyes and infiltration threats, bound by the same determination to uncover the vault's secrets. She could have pushed him away, but she did not. Instead, she let her hand slide up toward the nape of his neck, tangling in a lock of his hair.

He dipped his head. Her eyes fluttered closed. She tasted anticipation on her lips. His breath skimmed her cheek. Everything else, the infiltration, the cryptic runes, the screech of old locks, fell away.

A sudden, violent pop shattered the silence.

Alysia jolted, her heart nearly leaping from her chest. Bright, puffy kernels of enchanted popcorn burst through the corridor in every direction, bouncing off the stone floor and walls. She gasped, stumbling back. One piece landed on her shoulder, another ricocheted past Kael's ear. Half-blinded by the flying snacks, she spun, only to see Robin strolling in with a smug expression, a half-open bag of magical popcorn clutched in one hand.

"Wow," Robin drawled, stepping over scattered kernels. They wiggled across the floor, trailing stray sparks of leftover enchantment. "Hope I'm not interrupting anything important."

Alysia's cheeks flamed. Kael stepped away so quickly that she felt the loss of his warmth like a sharp draft. They both turned to Robin, who tossed a kernel into the air and caught it in her mouth, unconcerned by the tension crackling through the vault.

"We were—" Alysia began, her voice hoarse. She pressed her lips together, fighting the urge to glare. The abrupt shift from near-kiss to prying cousin was dizzying. Her heart still hammered. She forced a steady tone. "Robin, what are you doing down here?"

Robin shrugged, strolling forward with a lazy grin. "I could ask you the same." She gestured at the glyphs overhead and the treasure trove of gloom around them. The bag of enchanted popcorn crackled again, but thankfully it did not detonate a second time. "There's plenty to do outside this dusty crypt, you know."

Kael coughed, raking a hand through his hair. Some of the dust from the stone and the faint glow from illusions still lingered on him, but the intimate moment had shattered completely. "We were, uh... investigating," he said pointedly.

Robin mulled this over, popping another piece of popcorn. "Investigating, sure. Looked more like 'getting cozy while ignoring infiltration risks.' But who am I to judge?"

Alysia glared at her cousin in exasperation. "You said the infiltration was quiet for the night. I guess you decided to barge in here instead?"

Robin held up her half-empty snack bag. "When you two vanish, I get worried. I come bearing refreshments, and apparently I have timing that's perfect, as usual."

Kael's lips twitched, but he kept his face turned away, probably to hide the heat in his cheeks. Alysia tried to calm her own racing pulse. Excitement still fluttered in her chest from how close they'd been. The sudden interruption left her simultaneously relieved and painfully disappointed.

Scattered popcorn rolled beneath her heel as she stepped toward the corridor's threshold. "Robin, you nearly gave me a heart attack."

Her cousin just shrugged again, her eyes dancing with mischief. "Better a popcorn scare than letting you two do something you'll regret if the infiltration decides to show up."

Alysia opened her mouth to argue that she would not regret it, but the rush of confusion tied her tongue. Instead, she watched Kael gather himself. His illusions, previously so alive around his hands, faded into a muted glow. That alone made her ache with unspoken longing. Before she could reach for him again, the dim torchlight at the vault door flickered, accompanied by a heavy grinding sound.

"Oh no," Robin said, "The door's resealing."

Alysia whipped around. Indeed, the metal bars across the threshold had begun sliding into place, an automatic mechanism triggered by their earlier tampering with the wards. Groaning metal echoed through the vault. They must have spent too long without re-affirming the security spells, and now the vault's enchantments were closing them in.

TWENTY-TWO

FESTIVAL LIGHTS

The early morning sunlight broke over Velgrace Academy like a fanfare of gold, announcing the day of the Charm Festival. Alysia stood at the top of the main courtyard steps, her gaze wandering across the colorful booths and banners that sprouted overnight. Students and visiting mages bustled around in excited clusters, chatter blending with the hum of conjured music. The air smelled of salted sea breezes mixed with sweet pastries, as if the entire campus had agreed to indulge in a rare day of celebration and mischief.

Alysia touched the silver bracelet at her wrist, reminding herself to breathe. A festival might be exactly what their tired spirits needed, but an undercurrent of unease rippled through her thoughts. The infiltration threat remained unresolved, and every time she noticed an unfamiliar face or of illusions out of place, her pulse spiked. She tried to shake off the tension, rubbing her arms as a mild breeze ruffled her hair. The festival would only last one day, and she promised herself to let go, even if it was only a partial reprieve.

A sudden whoop from below made her glance down. Kael was racing across the courtyard, weaving between the booths with a grin that seemed too bright for him. He waved and called her name in a voice loud enough to make passing first-year students gape. His illusions flickered in silver arcs around his arms, a playful side to him that Alysia rarely saw anywhere else.

She stepped carefully down the stone stairs. "You're early," she said as soon as she reached him.

Kael tapped the worn compendium at his hip. "I have illusions to show off. Wait until you see the levitation races near the Bastion Hall arch. You'll definitely want to join."

Alysia folded her arms. "Are you determined to drag me through every booth in the academy?"

He gave a tilted smile, his eyes gleaming. "Without question." The warmth in his gaze pricked awareness along her spine. An uncertain but undeniable spark hovered in the space between them, as though the day were tinted with possibility. "Let's find Robin and Lyric before they unleash something catastrophic."

She gave a light laugh at that. "Good idea."

The courtyard was filled with charm-lights that bobbed in the air, conjured by students who formed impromptu teams to craft the brightest illusions. A row of tables showcased miniature fireworks that popped into dancing illusions of creatures, phoenixes, unicorns, sea serpents. Children from the nearest village had been allowed in for the festival and now pressed eagerly against the velvet ropes, their eyes wide at the spectacle.

Alysia scanned the crowd, expecting to see Robin's short-cropped hair blazing with some new mischief. Instead, she spotted a brief glint of midnight-blue braids: Lyric Meridan, half-hidden behind a tall booth selling enchanted pastries. The older girl seemed preoccupied with something near a set of stacked crates. Judging by the brief glint of cunning that crossed Lyric's face, Alysia guessed that some manner of trouble was about to begin.

"She's not exactly subtle," Kael said, following her line of sight. "Shall we intervene or watch from a safe distance?"

Alysia considered. "Robin is the expert at equally reckless stunts. If we leave them alone, they might set half the courtyard on fire. But if we stop them, they'll only find another place to cause chaos." Half of her wanted to keep the festival lighthearted, but the other half found herself curious about exactly what the two troublemakers would do.

Kael placed a hand at the small of her back, guiding her toward an arched walkway. The brief contact sent a flutter across her stomach. Each new closeness between them seemed to grow more natural and more dangerous at once. "We'll keep watch," he said softly. "I'm not in the mood to bail them out of a formal scolding on a perfect day like this."

She did not resist as he steered her away from the direct line of mischief. Instead, she let her gaze drift over the vibrant festival. Charms fizzed in the air, in every color of the spectrum. A group of second-year students passed with floating trays of fruit tarts that smelled of honey and cinnamon. Laughter reverberated at every corner. Some part of Alysia's heart relaxed just enough to let in the joy.

They reached a booth decked in ribbons. A sign reading "Levitation Race. One Token to Enter." dangled from a post. A handful of students toyed with small platform charms, waiting for the next race to begin.

Kael rummaged through his belt pouch. "I have tokens. Let's do this."

Alysia wrinkled her nose. "You recall how I did with that levitation assignment last term. My wards anchored me so thoroughly that I crashed like a boulder."

"Then this is your redemption arc," he teased. He handed a token to a bright-eyed student running the booth. "Two participants," he announced.

The student gave Alysia a conspiratorial grin. "Step on the levitation disk, keep your balance, and float to the finish line. First one across wins. Ready when you are."

Kael hopped onto a floating disk with an elegance that made her roll her eyes, but she stepped onto the second disk anyway. It hovered a foot above the ground, wobbling dangerously under her weight. She breathed deeply, trying to focus. The wards in her fingertips twitched with anticipation, struggling against the illusions that kept the disk airborne.

The booth attendant raised her arm. "Go!"

Alysia pushed forward, the disk bobbing along the marked path. She clenched her fists, channeling just enough ward energy to keep the platform stable but not so much that it canceled the illusion entirely. Kael glided ahead in a graceful arc. With a hiss of annoyance, Alysia pressed forward, coaxing the disk to move faster. She felt its illusions strain against her wards, threatening to fizzle if she poured too much power in. A few spectators cheered and pointed, as though they recognized her from advanced wards class.

She caught up to Kael right as he approached the midpoint. He glanced over his shoulder, surprise brightening his eyes. "You learned control, I see."

"Shut up and race," she said through gritted teeth, but a grin tugged at her lips. Adrenaline thrummed in her veins. She whipped her focus from him to the path, each marker shimmering with the faint glow of competition wards. Inch by inch, she gained on him until they were nearly neck-and-neck.

Pink images suddenly burst near Kael, courtesy of a random first-year cheering from the sidelines. He twitched in surprise, letting an unguarded wave of illusions slip into his disk. His platform jolted sideways. Alysia seized the moment, surging ahead and passing the finish line first. Her disk sputtered to the ground at once, leaving her breathless but triumphant.

A crowd of younger students whooped at her victory. Kael landed a second later, rolling his eyes in mock defeat. "I let you have that one," he drawled, though Alysia caught the approving spark in his expression.

"Sure," she said smugly, wiping perspiration from her brow. "But I'll take the win."

They left the booth to a smattering of applause. Kael slipped his arm around her shoulder just briefly, leaning in so only she could hear. "I like seeing you smile." Her heart fluttered at the quiet intimacy in his voice. He was mere inches away, and the rest of the festival seemed to fade. She opened her mouth to respond, a jest or an admission, she was not sure which, when a thunderous boom echoed across the courtyard. They both tensed. Illusions shimmered around Kael's fingers while wards gathered in Alysia's palms.

Glitter exploded from behind a booth near the library steps, showering the entire area in shimmering flecks of gold and silver. Laughter and coughing followed. Through the bright cloud, Alysia saw Robin's silhouette bounding away, followed by Lyric sprinting after her, both howling with delight. Students fled the immediate area, trying to escape the deluge of glitter that stuck to robes, boots, and even hair.

Kael let out a relieved sigh. "And so it begins."

Alysia laughed despite herself, the tension easing from her chest. She jogged closer to assess the situation. The entire stretch of path glimmered under the morning sun, children squealing with delight as they tried to catch falling specks. Robin, obviously the culprit, had managed to conjure illusions that turned into shapes, a flurry of miniature dragons, hearts, and flowers flashing gold before dissolving in midair.

Lyric stood at a safe distance, pressing a hand to her forehead as though not sure whether to be annoyed or impressed. When she spotted Alysia and Kael, her mouth twisted in a half-smirk. "I take no responsibility," she said, brushing stray sparkles from her braids.

Robin, panting and wild-eyed, pointed a finger. "Oh, you are absolutely responsible. You gave me the enchanted powder in the first place."

"Not for that," Lyric retorted, her arms crossed. Her expression was haughty, but her eyes had a proud gleam. "I was saving it for something a little more subtle."

Robin shrugged. "Subtle is overrated. Besides, this is a festival."

"You're both going to be on cleaning duty," Alysia said pointedly, trying not to laugh. She brushed a stray bit of glitter off her cloak, though more clung stubbornly to the fabric. "At least an entire hour, maybe more."

Robin just winked. "As if they could catch me. There are so many corners of this academy to hide in." She then whipped a small pot from a hidden pocket. "But the day is young, and I have bigger illusions planned."

Lyric narrowed her eyes. "Don't think I'll let you top this. I have a plan for a floating dessert stand that might or might not sing show tunes."

Horror and amusement struggled in Alysia's mind. She stepped forward, half-imploring. "Keep the sabotage friendly. The Headmistress will not appreciate campus-wide illusions that explode. Promise me you'll at least avoid setting anything on fire."

Robin grinned and offered a theatrical bow. "Scout's honor. When have I ever broken a promise like that?"

Kael snorted softly. "Too many times."

Alysia smiled at the banter, enjoying how, for a

moment, the infiltration threat felt distant. "I'll hold you to it," she said, letting the two spree-makers dash off. Rising laughter gave her hope that perhaps the day could remain bright.

While the sun climbed higher, Kael and Alysia explored more of the festival booths. One section, tucked near Bastion Hall, featured conjured animals racing around a tiny track. Students bet sweet tokens on everything from miniature illusions shaped like frogs to colorful birds woven from light. A string quartet hovered behind them, courtesy of someone's well-placed illusions, and performed a lilting tune that made the entire courtyard feel like a carefree carnival.

Alysia found herself mesmerized by every gem of color, every magical brilliance glowing above the stands. At one point, she and Kael paused at a pastry booth decorated with flickering illusions of sugar flowers. She used a single token to buy two pastries, the sweet dough drizzled with honey.

Kael took a bite of his pastry and nearly moaned with delight. "That's better than anything I've tasted in weeks," he admitted, leaning against the booth's edge. "You sure you don't want to devour them all?"

Alysia smiled wryly. "I have to leave space for the rest of the day, or I'll be in a sugar coma before noon. But yes, they are fantastic." She licked a sticky drop of honey from her thumb, suddenly conscious of how Kael watched her with a warm, intense gaze. An unexpected pulse of awareness rose between them again, as tempting as the sweet pastry on her lips.

For a moment, she was aware of nothing but the taste of honey and the faint salt of coastal air on Kael's skin. A memory stirred, a near-kiss in a vault, an explosion of popcorn. She felt her cheeks heat. The public courtyard definitely was not the place to repeat any close moments, especially with watchers everywhere.

Swallowing, she forced her attention back to mundane chatter. "You might want to see the illusions in Obscura Wing's exhibition. They set up a hall of trick mirrors. Could be your specialty, right?"

Kael brightened. "I've read about those. Last year's illusions caused mild chaos when the mirrors spontaneously rearranged. Let's see if they improved security."

His excitement was infectious. They meandered toward Obscura Wing, passing game stalls. Between each booth, groups of friends haggled for tokens, tested charm illusions, or simply enjoyed the music. The festival seemed to have coaxed laughter from even the most somber faculty. Headmistress Quen was nowhere to be seen, but a couple of professors watched from afar, sipping cider and eyeing the illusions with cautious acceptance.

They reached the hall set up outside Obscura Wing. Mirrors of all shapes and sizes lined a wide corridor lit by orbs of shimmering ghostlight. A sign invited people to stand in front of each mirror to see how illusions might alter their reflections.

A pair of third-year illusions students explained the premise. "Any reflection might show you as older, younger, or in a different profession. It's all in good fun."

One winked. "Beware the last mirror, though. It's rumored to show your deepest fear."

Kael's eyebrows shot up. "Sounds intriguing."

Flat unease roiled in Alysia's stomach. The idea of confronting illusions about her unspoken worries felt a bit too real. Still, they walked in. The first mirror made Kael look half his height and gave Alysia elongated arms, prompting a burst of laughter. The second mirror conjured them in formal court attire, with Kael wearing a black cloak embroidered in runes. It made her grin fade slightly. He looked far too regal, reminding her of whispered rumors about his bloodline.

The next mirror showed Alysia in an elegant teacher's robe, older and poised at the front of a lecture hall, while Kael's reflection displayed him reading a heavy tome behind her, as if they were academic partners. She tilted her head. The reflection felt comforting somehow, even if it was an impossible scenario.

Kael laid a hand on her shoulder. "You all right?"

She nodded, exhaling. "Yeah, just...interesting illusions."

He moved forward to the final mirror. Oddly, darkness wreathed its frame, as though the illusions inside were more shadow than light. A few festival-goers had gathered to watch from a safe distance, presumably enthralled by the possibility of glimpsing another's fear.

Kael stepped in front of it first. The mirror's surface rippled. A reflection took shape. Instead of Kael's usual form, the glass showed him standing alone in a war-torn courtyard, his illusions out of control, devouring everything in specks of gold and black. The reflection wore an expression of agonizing regret.

He stumbled back from the mirror as if struck, his face ashen. The illusions that constantly surrounded him vanished in an instant, leaving him starkly, terrifyingly unprotected. Alysia reached for him while the cold wave of his despair washed over her through their bond. His shoulders were rigid beneath her hand, his breath catching on a silent, ragged gasp.

He took a shaky breath, his gaze fixed on the floor.

"I'm fine," he murmured.

Her throat felt too tight. She faced the mirror, bracing herself. At first, all she saw was her own reflection in normal form, but then the image wavered. When it cleared, she saw her wards failing, arcs of broken runes falling around her like shattered glass. She was alone in an empty vault, the stone walls dripping with a dark, viscous magic that mocked every charm she tried to conjure. Helpless. The reflection's eyes were wide with terror, brimming with the same panic Alysia had endured in her worst nightmares.

She backed away, willing the illusions to vanish.

Neither of them spoke for a moment. The watchers looked uneasy, murmuring among themselves. The illusions students in charge offered to dispel the mirror's magic, but Alysia shook her head, stepping into the corridor's light again. Her heart hammered with the reminder: a single day of laughter would not erase the threat hovering over them. The infiltration might still overshadow everything if they made one wrong move.

Kael slipped a hand around hers, lacing their fingers together. "Come on," he said quietly, swallowing hard. "I think we've had enough illusions for the moment."

She squeezed his hand, a short, firm pressure. It was a silent acknowledgment: *I see your fear. It mirrors my own. You are not alone in it.* He squeezed back, a fleeting but grateful response that said more than words ever could.

They left Obscura Wing with a heavier mood. The sunshine outside felt abrupt and almost too bright, the festival music clashing with the dread that the mirror had stirred. But as they stood there, adjusting to the warmth, a sudden roar made them spin around. A charmed firework dragon soared overhead, belching plumes of colored smoke that rained down like confetti. Several watchers squealed and clapped, delighting in the spectacle. The gigantic spark-creature looped above the courtyard, then faded away in an eruption of neon sparks.

Alysia fixed her gaze on the fireworks. In that dramatic flash of color, she recognized the handiwork of either Robin or Lyric, probably both. Despite the weight in her chest, a wry smile tugged at her lips. She glanced at Kael, who looked equally torn between anxiety and reluctant amusement.

"Looks like the festival is still going full force," she said softly, inhaling a mix of smoke and sugary air. More illusions shimmered in the distance, layered by giggling students. Confetti dust, tinted silver and gold, drifted across the cobblestones like stardust.

Kael squeezed her hand. "We should let ourselves have something good. Even if it's just for today."

She nodded, lifting her eyes to him. The voices and color surrounded them, and for a moment, the rest of the world stilled. She noticed the faint shadows beneath Kael's eyes, the tension at the corners of his mouth from seeing his own reflection's worst fear. Her heart twisted. Perhaps there was no simple cure for their anxieties, but she could offer him her presence.

"I'm with you," she said. It came out nearly a whisper, but she sensed he heard the promise beneath those words.

Kael's thumb traced a light circle against the back of her hand. "Then let's find the next adventure."

She allowed him to lead her deeper into the festival, the illusions and vibrant laughter washing over them in waves. The day wore on in bright moments: overhearing Robin's dramatic pranks, ducking under confetti storms, sampling more confections than they should have. Every now and then, Alysia caught glimpses of the guarded look in Kael's eyes, or perhaps felt the ripple of wards inside her chest whenever she spotted a suspicious figure. It pressed a quiet tension against the base of her thoughts, reminding her that everything was fleeting.

Still, the Charm Festival had a way of mending small fractures in one's spirit. Even as the initial adrenaline of illusions gave way to a calmer afternoon, the crowd never lost its buoyant cheer. Music drifted from the Great Hall, where a band of upper-year students performed a lively reel. Children dashed through the courtyard with illusions shaped like dancing ribbons. Professors who normally frowned upon rowdy displays smiled at the harmless chaos.

And for once, the infiltration threat did not consume every moment. Alysia allowed herself to laugh. She raced Kael through a charm-juggling match, nearly tripping over her own illusions but catching them at the last second. He teased her for her undone hair, which had come loose from its braid in the breeze, and she teased him for the glitter that still clung to his collar from Robin's earlier explosion.

By sundown, the ephemeral firelight tinted the sky in pale lavender shades, casting the academy's spires in soft silhouettes. Lanterns rose above the courtyard and drifted on illusions, bathing the festival in a dreamy glow. A final wave of fireworks illuminated the sea beyond the cliffs, reflecting on the water's surface in brilliant sparks.

Alysia and Kael stood near a stone railing, gazing at the display. She leaned her forearms on the cool stone, feeling his presence close behind her. When another series of pops lit the sky, she saw his reflection in the faint glimmer on the sea, his gray eyes shining with a mixture of contentment and lingering worry. She understood it well. No matter how beautiful the fireworks, nothing guaranteed tomorrow would be free of danger.

He touched her shoulder gently. "You're thinking about the mirror again, aren't you?"

She exhaled, shaky. "It's hard not to. But the festival helps." She turned to face him, brushing a lock of hair from her cheek. "I wish...we had more days like this. Where everything feels normal, or nearly so."

Kael's lips curved in a careful smile. "We'll take them

where we can get them. And we'll handle whatever comes next."

A pulse of confidence warmed her chest, hearing the way he spoke. Perhaps he was reassuring himself as much as her, but it still mattered. She rested a hand lightly against the front of his cloak, noticing the faint, golden spark of illusions threading between them.

In the distance, the final barrage of festival fireworks began, painting the sky in arcs of vivid color. Students cheered, huddled in groups to watch. Even Robin and Lyric paused their rivalry to stand side by side, albeit with an unspoken agreement not to hurl any more glitter bombs.

Alysia let the brilliance wash over her. For one day, laughter had been stronger than fear, turning the academy into a place of joy. Tomorrow's troubles remained unspoken, but for now, life thrummed with the possibility of hope, fragile though it was.

She glanced up at Kael, and he leaned closer, so near their breath mingled in the

night air. The moment stretched taut, charged with more than fireworks. Alysia's heart beat quickly against her ribs, her pulse as bright as the illuminations overhead. But she did not move. She only searched his eyes, uncertain if she dared close that final distance.

Around them, the fireworks flared in a final burst of color, lighting the courtyard in warm gold. Applause and laughter echoed. She could almost forget the infiltration, almost set aside the dread lurking at the edges. The world was briefly beautiful, and the two of them stood on a threshold between danger and relief.

She swallowed, letting the tension settle inside her. When Kael's fingers grazed hers, she felt heat coil through her veins. Her eyelids fluttered, and she wondered if he might kiss her in plain sight, festival watchers be damned. Yet the moment passed and he merely curved his mouth into a gentle smile.

"Tomorrow," he said simply, as if willing her not to worry about anything more.

Alysia nodded. She turned to watch the sparks fade in the sky, lingering in the afterglow. Her heart felt unsteady, like a charm spell balanced on a fraying thread. But for now, she let the last fading embers of the festival lights guide her into the calm of the night.

TWENTY-THREE

UNLEASHED ILLUSIONS

Alysia tilted her head back, her eyes trained on the shimmering bursts of magic blooming in the night sky. The Charm Festival's lightshow competition had drawn nearly every student and instructor into Velgrace Academy's central courtyard. Streams of prismatic sparks arced high above the stone walls. Spectators gathered in clusters, many perched on the carved oak benches that circled the courtyard's perimeter. She could barely hear the chatter over the whistles and crackles of conjured fireworks dancing against the clouds.

She stood with one hand resting lightly on the curve of her silver bracelet. A gentle breeze carried the scents of roasted chestnuts and sweet confections from nearby booths that had remained from the festival's earlier revelry. Even at this late hour, the courtyard thrummed with excitement. Students huddled around a floating scoreboard that recorded the illusions' complexity and visual impact. From dragon-shaped lights to mesmerizing starbursts, each performance seemed more spectacular than the last.

Alysia exhaled in awe as yet another set of illusions spiraled overhead. The shapes hovered in wide loops, forming intricate glyphs that shimmered in pink, gold, and silver. She felt a hint of envy. The illusions soared with such artistry that even she, devoted to wards, found herself clapping. Across the courtyard, she spotted Kael leaning against a stone pillar. His dark hair brushed his collar, and sparks of reflected color danced across his storm-gray eyes. He watched the aerial performances with an unreadable expression, his arms crossed loosely. She knew him well enough to guess the tension in his stance. He rarely showed excitement in public, but she had caught glimpses of fascination in his gaze tonight.

Robin sidled up to Alysia, her face alight with mischief. "Some of those illusions rank among the best I've seen. Think you can top the spiraling phoenix trick? I heard a group of second-years combined illusions with a voice-echo charm."

Alysia shook her head, keeping her voice low. "Not with wards to handle. My illusions would vanish in a blink. I'm better at containing illusions, not creating them."

Robin shrugged and offered a playful grin. "Suit yourself, Warden Thorne. I'll be off adding my own sparkle to the scoreboard before dawn." She flounced away, leaving Alysia with a smile tugging at her lips.

Next to a marble balustrade, Kael uncrossed his arms. He caught Alysia's eye, prompting her to walk toward him. The clamor grew louder as the crowd erupted when a fiery ribbon draped itself across the sky. Though Kael feigned indifference, she could sense him brimming with an unspoken energy. The day's festivities had largely been a reprieve from the infiltration rumors stalking the academy, and even his subtle wariness had softened enough for him to linger among the cheering students.

She stepped close, lowering her voice to avoid eavesdroppers. "No illusions from you tonight?"

One corner of his mouth curved upward. "We already have enough illusions overhead. Besides, if I meddle, a fair competition will become less fair. That might kill the mood."

Alysia snorted softly. She glanced at his clasped hands. "Sometimes I wonder if you ever let yourself just be part of these events without analyzing how your illusions compare."

He shrugged. "Old habit. I was taught illusions were either tools or weapons. Celebrations were optional."

Her heart twisted. She reached out to rest a hand on his forearm. "There's more than one way to use magic. You know that, right?"

He glanced at her. His eyes seemed caught between gratitude and hidden conflict. "I'm learning."

Before Alysia could reply, a swell of excitement rustled the crowd. Crackles of bright pink and green fireworks lunged skyward, and the cheers doubled in volume. She turned, eager to watch the next round of illusions. As she did, a prickle of unease trickled down the back of her neck.

For a moment, the kaleidoscope of lights overhead seemed to flicker.

Something felt off with the illusions. Many of the conjured shapes trembled, their once-sharp outlines turning blurry. Whispers of confusion rippled among the audience. A scattering of sparks drifted sideways, losing their color. Then a heavy, electric crackle suffused the air.

A gust of wind surged across the courtyard, whipping banners off their stands. Alysia's bracelet throbbed with a pulse in time to her racing heart. Overhead, the illusions that had been so impressive only moments ago began to collapse. Streaks of color splintered and fizzled. The crowd groaned in disappointment, but the sense of something more dangerous took hold when a low thunderclap rumbled in the distance. A shroud of dark clouds gathered above the academy, moving with an unnatural, predatory speed. The wind that swept the courtyard didn't smell of rain or sea salt; it smelled of ozone and old, angry magic. Alysia felt the Academy's wards groan under the pressure, not like a shield holding against a storm, but like a body fighting off a poison.

Alysia tried to focus on the wards woven into the courtyard itself. Usually, the protective shell around Velgrace could funnel rampant magic into safe channels. Tonight the wards felt frayed as though worn by an external force. Her throat constricted.

Kael's eyes narrowed. "A storm." His voice carried an undercurrent of warning.

She cast her gaze to the horizon. Flashes of lightning illuminated the roiling clouds, but the sky should have been clear. Whatever formed above them was no ordinary weather. It advanced with unnatural speed. One moment, the illusions flickered uncertainly. The next, an invisible wave of force slammed into the courtyard.

Shrieks rang out as floating lanterns set for the light-show competition erupted in showers of sparks. Glowing shards peppered the crowd, though the wards glimmered faintly in an attempt to shield the onlookers. The protective barrier faltered, letting a few shards through. Students ducked. Others scrambled away, covering their heads or extinguishing the pieces as they landed.

Alysia flinched but instinctively shaped a ward with her left hand. A faint shimmer of runes encircled her and Kael, deflecting a cluster of falling embers before they could scorch a bystander's robes. Heart pounding, she looked up in time to see one of the academy's older towers groan. It was a slender spire that housed several dorm rooms, built decades ago. The structure trembled under the magical onslaught. Loose bricks slipped, tumbling onto the courtyard in a rattling cascade.

Instructors shouted commands, urging everyone to move away from the tower's vicinity. People rushed to help those who had been struck by debris. Alysia's adrenaline spiked. She twisted around, scanning for an approach. If that tower fully collapsed, it might topple against the adjacent building. That would cause massive damage.

Her breath caught when Kael broke into a sprint. He pushed through the crowd, illusions already flickering around his fingertips. She willed her body into motion, chasing after him. Something in his posture told her he was about to attempt magic well beyond standard illusions. He reached the base of the quivering tower and stared up at the fractured stone near the top.

A group of advanced-year students formed a shaky barrier to keep passersby from wandering under the tower's crumbling edge. Kael ignored them. Alysia rushed to his side, her heart pounding.

He glanced at her, and in his eyes, she saw a flash of raw terror mixed with grim resolve. "This is going to hurt," he said, his voice barely a whisper against the wind. "And it will break every rule about illusions at Velgrace. But I'm not letting that tower fall."

She opened her mouth, intending to caution him, but the words stuck in her throat. Another tremor rippled through the tower, shaking the parapet so violently that decorative gargoyles started to crack. It would only take a gust of hostile magic or another wave from that storm for the entire spire to come crashing down.

Kael raised his hands. He inhaled slowly while illusions danced around him in bright, electric streamers that glowed with a forbidden hue. She had watched him conjure illusions all week, but never like this. The power he channeled felt heavier, ancient, and sorrowful. The silver of his illusions was threaded with veins of deep, mournful violet, the color of a dying star. It was not the magic of a student but the magic of a king in exile. The coral amulet at his chest gleamed with a fierce radiance as it fed or amplified the illusions he aimed at the tower's top.

TWENTY-FOUR

UNMASKING THE SOURCE

Alysia awoke with the lingering taste of dread on her tongue. Dawn's gray light spilled through the slanted window of her dorm, illuminating the small piles of spell scrolls and half-burned candles scattered across every flat surface. She had tried to rest. She had tried to calm her thrumming pulse by diligently reviewing wards in her notebook the night before. But sleep had refused to settle. The memory of the storm, wild illusions cracking overhead and Kael stepping forward to hold the tower upright, still gripped her mind.

She wrapped her fingers around the silver bracelet on her wrist, the Thorne sigil faintly etched along its curve. A ripple of tension fluttered in her chest, and she sucked in a slow breath. Word had traveled fast, as it always did at Velgrace Academy. The storm was not forgotten. Everyone knew it should never have reached the courtyard in such force. Yet the wards, which were supposed to protect students, had buckled under a suspect surge of magic.

Overnight, the rumors gathered power: Kael's illusions, Kael's recklessness, Kael's unstoppable aura.

Alysia forced herself upright, shuffled into her boots, and grabbed a cloak from the back of her chair. She slipped into the corridor, where students bustled in the early light with notes pressed to their chests, exchanging secrets in frantic whispers. Snippets of conversation floated past.

Her stomach twisted. She recognized the path their gossip took. If an orb had recorded Kael's aura, that meant they had proof of his illusions, and if rumors were accurate, it was proof that might paint him as a culprit rather than a savior. She wanted to hold her head high, reassure everyone that Kael had saved them, not doomed them. But an uncomfortable prickle warned her that these rumors would only build. At Velgrace, evidence could either exonerate or condemn.

She nearly bumped into Robin, who stood guard outside the dormitory stairs, arms folded and eyebrows pinched in a scowl. Her cousin's short hair had bright teal streaks running through it, a sign of some new illusion-based prank or an attempt to lighten the gloom. Robin fixed Alysia with a worried expression.

"Finally," Robin whispered. "I've been waiting for you. Have you heard about the orb?"

Alysia listened to the muffled chatter of nearby students, then shook her head. "Only bits and pieces. People said it caught Kael's illusions during the storm. Is that true?"

Robin's lips tightened. "Yes. Apparently a faculty

scrying orb was active in the courtyard, recording the entire fiasco. It picked up Kael's aura with absolute clarity. He's not denying it either. Claims the illusions were part of saving the tower—"

"Which is true," Alysia broke in, heat rushing to her cheeks. "He did save it."

"Exactly," Robin said. "But you know how people twist stories. Some are calling him a show-off who might've conjured the storm himself. Others say they spotted suspicious runes in the sky that prove sabotage."

Alysia's pulse throbbed in her ears. She remembered how the wards had stretched thin, how Kael's illusions had fought to keep the tower from collapsing. She remembered the raw power surging around them. No one could fabricate that kind of fear. "And the orb?" she asked, lowering her voice. "Is it in the Council's possession now?"

Robin glanced at the students passing them. "That's the thing. It vanished from storage this morning. The Council was supposed to review it, but it's gone."

Alysia felt her blood turn cold. "Someone stole it."

"More like smuggled it out, but yes," Robin muttered. "Looks like we have a leak.

Quen's entire staff is reeling. The orb's caretaker swears it was locked behind wards, but we both know those can be bypassed if the traitor knows the Academy's defenses."

Alysia inhaled, trying to steady her racing mind. Kael's illusions were at the heart of rumors, and now the only solid piece of evidence, the orb, had vanished. The words sabotage and infiltration floated in her thoughts, echoed from nights spent searching the lower vaults with Kael. It was all too convenient a coincidence. The disappearance of that orb could remove any chance for Kael to clear his name properly, but it could also hide key evidence about who triggered the storm in the first place. She needed answers.

"Have you seen Kael?" she asked Robin.

"Not since sunrise," Robin replied, running a hand through her teal-streaked hair. "I think Magister Belros Dain wanted to question him. Something about illusions in Obscura Wing. Also, Headmistress Quen is calling for an assembly mid-morning. People are saying she'll demand a formal interrogation."

Alysia swallowed. "Find me if you hear anything else. I'm going to look for Kael."

Robin hesitated, then nodded. "Be careful. A lot of people are on edge."

Alysia turned and wove her way through the crowd of students, her cloak brushing the stone floor. Muted confusion hummed in the corridors, as though too many rumors collided at once. She passed the open courtyard doors and caught a glimpse of the sea beyond the academy's walls: restless gray waves that mirrored her own churn of thoughts.

Crossing into Obscura Wing, she found the halls dimly lit by flickering illusions that reflected from the arched ceiling. Her footsteps echoed. She remembered training here with Kael, his illusions dancing in the air while he half-teased, half-instructed her on harnessing small illusions to complement her wards. Thinking about it now brought a dull ache to her chest.

At last, she spotted him near one of the stone pillars that lined the hallway. He stood facing Magister Belros Dain, who wore a voluminous cloak that melted with the shifting shadows. Kael's posture was rigid, his arms folded, but he seemed calm.

Alysia paused beside a carved mask display. She heard Belros Dain speak, his voice carefully neutral, though the hall's acoustics carried his words clearly. "...and you understand, Kael, this entire matter puts you in a dangerous position. The faculty will not accept another near-disaster. They demand accountability."

Kael's gaze flitted across the hall. For a moment, his storm-gray eyes caught Alysia's. An unspoken tension passed between them, and she could almost feel the question in his look. Would she stand with him?

"I understand," Kael said quietly. His voice had a subdued edge, like a blade sheathed but not at rest. "But the storm was not natural. I've told you. Something or someone conjured it or at least manipulated it to sabotage the wards. My illusions countered it. They did not cause it."

"Your illusions indeed stabilized the tower," Belros Dain replied. "But the orb's footage is missing. We cannot verify your claim to the Council. Circumstances are suspicious."

Alysia stepped forward, unable to linger in the shadows. "He's telling the truth," she said, her tone sharper than she intended. "I was there. Without Kael, the tower would have toppled."

Belros Dain's face remained impassive. Shadows clung to the angles of his cheeks, giving him a cryptic air. "I do not doubt you, Miss Thorne. But the Council requires hard proof. The orb was that proof. It has been stolen."

Alysia clenched her fists at her sides. "So now what?"

The magister's lips pressed into a tight line. "Head-mistress Quen will decide how to proceed. She summoned the faculty for a strategic meeting before the assembly. My suggestion to both of you is to remain calm and cooperative. The truth has a way of shining through illusions, eventually."

He offered a slight nod, then turned down the hallway. His footsteps faded behind him. Kael exhaled a breath and brought one hand up to graze the coral amulet on his chest. In the half-light of Obscura Wing, Alysia saw tension bracket the corners of his mouth.

"You okay?" she asked softly, stepping closer.

He looked at her. "Sure. Being suspected of orches-trating a catastrophic storm is the highlight of my day."

She managed a faint, sympathetic smile. "I'm sorry. I know how frustrated you must feel."

A muscle in his jaw tensed. "It's not just frustration. It's dread. The infiltration threat is real, and someone inside these walls is fueling it. Maybe they're trying to throw blame on me so no one looks their way."

"That is exactly what I am afraid of," she admitted. "If they can weaken your credibility, they can operate freely."

"It is more than that," Kael countered, his voice low

and urgent. "They do not just want me out of the way. They want the Academy to tear itself apart with suspicion. The stolen orb is not just about framing me, it is about making everyone distrust the person next to them. It is a classic rogue tactic, sow chaos, then seize power when everyone is too busy pointing fingers."

"I told Belros Dain that the storm was triggered remotely," Kael went on, leaning one shoulder against the pillar. He lowered his voice, mindful of passing students. "I could sense it was more than ordinary weather. Some illusions or wards were twisted together and aimed at the academy's defenses. When I tried to calm it, the chaos was so thick it nearly shattered my illusions."

Alysia remembered the black clouds overhead. She swallowed. "That means the conspirators know how to manipulate the ward boundaries. Or at least they have enough inside knowledge to cause massive damage. They must have realized that if your illusions were recorded, people might suspect foul play. So they took the orb before the Council could discover the truth."

Kael's throat worked as he swallowed. "Someone with access to storage lined with wards. Only staff or advanced-year students would know how to break in. That's not a random thief."

She nodded slowly. "Which means our infiltration has deeper roots than we realized."

His expression turned grim. "Headmistress Quen will want me to give a full explanation of how I stabilized the tower. She might also ask me to replicate the illusions.

That's dangerous, but I can't refuse if I want to clear my name."

Alysia touched his arm lightly, feeling the tension coiled in his muscles. "We'll find a way to prove you're not the enemy," she said. "And we'll figure out who stole the orb."

He covered her hand with his own, though his touch trembled. "You shouldn't have to defend me every time. I don't want you risking your standing here."

She inhaled, trying to keep her voice steady despite the turmoil in her chest.

"You're my partner in this, whether the rest of the school likes it or not. I'm not backing down."

For a moment, he said nothing. A brief glimmer of warmth crossed his features. A fragile expression that revealed how deeply he needed her reassurance. Then footsteps echoed down the hall, and both of them turned to see a stern-faced professor approach, summoning Kael for a meeting with Quen. He gave Alysia's hand a last squeeze and followed the professor without protest.

She stood alone in the hallway, her heart pounding. Something heavy pressed behind her ribs, the realization that the infiltration ran deep. A short time later, she found herself wandering toward the courtyard, searching for Robin. Word of the assembly began to spread, and anxious students headed in the same direction. By the time Alysia arrived, a throng had gathered.

A dais was set at the courtyard's far end, enough space for the senior faculty to address everyone. The ocean breeze carried the scent of salt. Broken confetti from the festival still littered the flagstones, a bittersweet reminder of how joyful the campus had been just yesterday, before illusions and infiltration overshadowed them again.

She spotted Robin near a cluster of second-year illusions students, all of whom looked ready to explode with questions. The moment Robin noticed her, they shouldered past the group and hurried over.

"I just heard from the older staff," they whispered. "Quen and a handful of professors confronted Kael. He told them everything, how the storm was triggered, how he stabilized the tower. He insisted that the orb would have verified his claim, but..."

Alysia finished the sentence. "But the orb is nowhere to be found." A wave of disquiet washed over her. "Do you think this is enough to convince faculty that Kael isn't behind it?"

Robin shook their head, frustration etched on their face. "Hard to say. Some staff trust him, especially those who saw him hold the tower in place. Others think it's too convenient that the orb disappeared and that his illusions are too powerful for a mere student. Panic makes people paranoid."

Alysia folded her arms, ignoring the coastal wind that whipped her hair across her cheeks. "Then we have to figure out where the orb went. If we could prove that someone stole it to frame Kael, the Council might start believing us about infiltration."

Headmistress Quen stepped onto the dais, flanked by Warden Evara Morn and Magister Belros Dain. Quen's expression was carved from stone, and her gaze swept over the assembled students with stony composure.

"Students of Velgrace," she began, her voice carrying through the courtyard, amplified by a minor charm. "As you are all aware, last night's storm nearly wrought destruction upon our campus. We owe thanks to those who intervened, preventing loss of life. However, new questions have emerged about how such a storm could challenge our wards so profoundly. The academy's wards are designed to stand against natural weather events. Therefore, we suspect foul play, an external or internal force that compromised our defenses."

A subtle gasp moved through the crowd. Alysia's stomach clenched. She already suspected as much, but hearing it stated publicly put a sharper edge to the threat.

Quen continued. "We had hoped to review scrying orb records to shed light on this matter. Regrettably, that orb and its contents are now missing from secured storage. The significance of its disappearance cannot be overstated."

A low rumble of shock rippled across the courtyard. Students exchanged startled glances, and some turned toward Alysia and Robin. More than one onlooker scowled or muttered, the speculation lighting in their eyes. Alysia pressed her lips together, wishing she could speak up to defend Kael on the spot.

"Until further notice," Quen said, "certain corridors and facilities will be restricted. We will hold mandatory interviews with those who witnessed or participated in last night's spells. We ask for your patience and cooperation. If anyone has information regarding the missing orb, you are to come forward immediately. Treachery has found its way into our halls," she said, her voice dropping to a steely, dangerous quiet that was more terrifying than any shout. "It will be found. And it will be purged with fire and iron."

She nodded curtly to the faculty, and Warden Morn gave a swift signal to dismiss the crowd. Students began drifting away in tense clusters, buzzing with speculation. Alysia remained rooted in place, Robin at her side. Within moments, Quen and the professors began dispersing as well, giving no chance for follow-up questions. The court-yard carried a heaviness that felt like a dull ache beneath the bright morning light.

Robin glanced at Alysia. "This is bigger than we thought. Before, it was rumors about infiltration. Now we have public acknowledgment, and no orb to prove Kael's innocence."

Alysia touched the silver bracelet again, breathing slowly to keep her voice steady. "We have to do some-thing. If someone inside the Academy is orchestrating sabotage, they'll keep striking until we're too divided to fight back."

Robin's gaze darted around around warily. "We have no leads on who might've stolen that orb."

An unsettling thought coiled in Alysia's mind. "They had to know exactly how to slip past security wards. That means inside knowledge. It must be an advanced student, staff member, or someone with explicit clearance."

Robin's shoulders tensed. "Which means frequent

contact with the infiltration, someone playing the loyal academic while secretly aiding the rogues."

Alysia exhaled, the weight of her realization sinking in. "Yes. There's no other explanation."

The assembly concluded, leaving behind a storm of uncertainty. As the courtyard emptied, Alysia lingered at the dais, staring at the stone floor that had so recently echoed with laughter and festival music. It felt like the color had seeped out of Velgrace overnight, replaced by fear. She closed her eyes and recalled Kael's face, the tension etched across it when he spoke of sabotage. A pang of anger and protective resolve flared in her chest. She would not stand by while he was blamed for something he had risked himself to stop.

Her mind spun, brimming with half-formed plans: searching restricted wings, questioning older students bordering on suspicious, re-checking the library logs. Yet every approach led to the same conclusion. Whoever had stolen that orb was well-placed within the Academy and well-versed in illusions or wards.

TWENTY-FIVE

SUMMONS AND SECRETS

Alysia stepped into the council chamber, her fingers curled tight around the silver bracelet at her wrist. The chamber felt vast and cold this morning. Tall stained-glass windows threw shards of blue and violet light across the polished floor. She stopped in the center, aware of the semicircle of academy officials looming above her on a raised platform. Headmistress Quen stood at the center, stone-faced and silent, while Warden Evara Morn and Magister Belros Dain flanked her on either side.

The tension in the air felt heavier than any ward Alysia had ever cast. She swallowed, trying to calm her pulse. Moments ago, an attendant had escorted her here, refusing to answer questions. Now she waited, her heart pounding, as the council glared in disapproval. It felt like a trial, though no one had formally named it as such.

"You stand before this council under grave suspicion," Headmistress Quen began. Her dark hair was pinned in a coronet of braids, and her voice carried the weight of authority. "Reports indicate your wards have grown unstable. Moreover, you continue to collaborate with Kael Meridan, whose illusions jeopardized the Academy's reputation and safety."

Warden Morn crossed her arms over her chest. A faint scar on her temple contrasted against neatly pinned silver braids. She spoke with a voice that rumbled like distant thunder. "Students reported that you frequently meet with Kael in hidden corridors at odd hours. This is questionable behavior when we suspect infiltration from within."

Alysia stayed silent, not wanting to defend or deny. Any retort might sound like a childish excuse.

Headmistress Quen fixed Alysia with a sharp gaze. "This council requests your candor. How far have you delved into advanced wards with Kael's illusions?"

Alysia held her chin high. "We studied combined charmwork and illusions. We tried to reinforce the Academy's defenses, not break them." Her voice came out steadier than she felt. "He isn't the threat the rumors claim."

Magister Belros Dain lifted a hand. Shadows seemed to pool in the folds of his cloak. His weathered face showed little emotion, though a ripple of curiosity passed across his gray eyes. "You aided Kael in conjuring illusions powerful enough to recast parts of the Academy's wards. Some might argue this was heroic, but the manner in which he harnessed forbidden elements causes alarm."

Alysia inhaled against the knot twisting in her stomach. "I never saw him use illusions to harm anyone here.

Everything he did was to mitigate damage, especially when that tower almost collapsed."

Warden Morn shook her head. "Your perspective is not the only one. Several of our senior students claim they witnessed you channeling unstable sigils. Some say your wards cracked. Others suspect you and Kael conspired to sabotage the wards so he could display his illusions and gain sympathy." She flexed her hands as though ready to subdue an enemy. "We cannot ignore these allegations."

A flush of anger rose to Alysia's cheeks. "That's untrue," she said, careful not to raise her voice. She needed them to listen. "Kael caught the collapse before it crushed half the courtyard. Yes, the wards buckled, but it wasn't our fault. Something or someone orchestrated that storm."

Headmistress Quen pressed her palms flat on the wooden rail of the platform. "Regardless," she said, her voice taut, "the Academy's highest ranks must safeguard Velgrace. That means we need certainty your wards, and Kael's illusions, won't cause further incidents."

Quen's tone sharpened as she turned pages on a leather-bound ledger. "We have documented sightings of you sneaking around restricted areas. We know you visited the library's sealed sections. You walked the corridors after curfew. You corresponded with Kael during times you should have been in supervised classes. If you insist he poses no danger, then perhaps you can help us monitor him."

Alysia let out a tight breath. She had expected harsh

words, but this felt like a direct blow to her integrity. "Monitor him...how?"

Silence fell. Then Magister Dain spoke again, his voice smooth as if he tested her readiness.

"The council has a proposition," Magister Dain said, his voice smooth as polished stone. "Kael Meridan trusts you. He lets you see a side of his magic he shows no one else. You will become our eyes. You will report on his activities, his moods, the very nature of his illusions. And if you refuse..." He let the silence hang in the air for a heartbeat before Quen finished the thought.

"If you refuse," the Headmistress said, her voice devoid of all warmth, "your legacy ends here. You will be expelled, Alysia Thorne. Your name will be struck from the records, and you will leave Velgrace in disgrace, just as your grandmother did."

The words struck like a physical blow. Alysia's knees locked, forcing her to remain upright. Losing her place at Velgrace would mean losing any chance to redeem her family name. It would unravel everything she had worked for. Her mind raced, with fear, defiance, and worry about how Kael would react if she agreed to this. She remembered the night they saved the tower, the hum of combined magic coursing between them, and how she believed in him even when the Academy turned suspicious.

Yet the threat of expulsion loomed bigger than her own pride. For a moment, she thought about refusing. She thought about flinging the truth in their faces, that infiltration was real, that the orb's disappearance proved a traitor lurked within these walls. Yet she sensed that would do no good. The council wanted a scapegoat or a collaborator. They had chosen her.

She took a trembling breath, her hands clenched at her sides. The bracelet on her wrist felt cold. "I understand," she said softly. "I will...do what you ask."

The quiet that followed was harsher than any scolding. Warden Morn's eyes narrowed, her posture stiff with distrust, but she nodded once. Headmistress Quen's shoulders eased marginally. Magister Belros Dain regarded Alysia with a hint of pity or regret in his guarded expression.

"Then we have an agreement," Quen said. "Our staff will provide you with the details. You will observe Kael, submit weekly reports, and alert us if he shows signs of reckless magic. Should you withhold any such findings, we will not protect you from disciplinary measures."

Alysia forced herself to bow, though every muscle in her body rebelled. Her words felt numb and distant. "Yes, Headmistress. I won't fail."

They dismissed her with no ceremony, leaving her alone in the silent chamber. She stared at the tall stained-glass windows, her heart pounding in her ears. Bitterness burned her throat. Choosing to "monitor" Kael felt too much like betraying him. She knew the council did not trust her either. They simply saw her as a tool to keep Kael close. Resentment mingled with sorrow in her chest.

She swept from the chamber, the corridor's cold air stinging her cheeks. Beyond the arched doorway, she spotted Robin leaning against a pillar. Her cousin straightened, worry etched in her features. "They had you in there like you were a criminal," Robin said quickly. "What happened?"

Alysia tried to speak, but her voice shook. "They gave me a choice. Either watch Kael for them...or get expelled."

Robin's face paled. "That isn't right. They're turning you into their spy."

Alysia rubbed at her eyes, fighting the urge to break down. "I had no other option. I can't lose my place at Velgrace, Robin. My mother's memory is tied to these wards. I've made too many promises to just walk away." Her throat constricted. "And...I want to protect him. It's safer if I stay close, maybe figure out who actually stole that orb."

Robin's mouth opened, but she hesitated. "Does Kael know?"

Alysia lowered her gaze. "Not yet. I'll have to tell him."

The conversation ended when she glimpsed movement farther down the corridor. Kael's dark hair and lean figure appeared, making her stomach flip. He caught sight of her and stopped, his storm-gray eyes immediately narrowing. Students walked past them, oblivious to the tension crackling in the hallway. Alysia's heart rate spiked. She felt the council's ultimatum like an invisible chain around her neck.

She approached him with careful steps. "Kael—"

He raised a hand. "I heard you met with the council. They summoned me earlier, but I refused to go until I knew what they wanted from you first." He glanced around, his voice dropping lower. "What did they say?"

His expression was a mixture of wariness and an odd rush of hope that maybe she brought good news. Alysia forced herself not to choke on her words. "They demanded I...that I keep an eye on you. To report your illusions and everything you do."

Kael's face hardened. "So that's what they're resorting to. They want you, someone I trust, to turn into their perfect informant." His hands curled into fists at his sides.

Alysia tried to speak slowly, to make him understand. "They threatened to expel me if I said no. They left me no choice."

His jaw set. He took a step back, as if her explanation only confirmed his worst fears. "No choice?" he asked quietly. "So, you agreed?"

She glanced aside, ashamed. "I had to. Please, believe me... I'm not doing this because I doubt you. I'm—"

"You're spying on me." His voice cut through her explanation with chilling finality.

Alysia's eyes burned. She tried to keep her composure. "Kael, I can't help you if I'm kicked out. And I believe there's infiltration at work. If I'm still here, I can gather clues. I can—"

He threw up a hand, illusions flickering around his wrist. Even that brief glimmer carried crackling energy. "You should have refused them. You should have trusted that we'd find another way."

Her anger surged. She did not want to snap at him, but the tension was too thick.

"And what would that have solved?" she demanded, her voice trembling. "They made it clear my entire future at Velgrace hung in the balance. If I'd refused, they would have expelled me on the spot. Then I'd be useless to you. I can't clear your name if I'm not allowed within these walls."

He met her gaze, and for a moment she thought he might relent, that maybe he saw the agony in her eyes. Instead, he exhaled in disbelief and looked away. "So you're going to watch me, take notes, and hand them a neat little report. I guess that's loyalty...in some twisted sense."

She pressed a hand to her churning chest, her voice dropping. "I'm not proud of this. But it's the only way I can protect you in the end."

Those words must have struck him wrong, because he let out a bitter laugh. "Protect me? You realize how insulting that sounds? If you truly believed in me, you would have defied them. Instead, you signed up to be a spy."

"That's not fair," she whispered, her chest tight. She saw the pain behind his eyes, yet he acted as though her choice was a betrayal on par with the infiltration itself.

He shook his head. "I spent my whole life trying to avoid people who wanted to monitor me because of my illusions. Now it turns out the one person I thought might stand for me... decided to do exactly that."

Alysia's voice broke. "Kael, wait—"

"I think I've heard enough." He stepped back. The flickers danced at his fingertips, illusions fueled by sorrow or anger, she could not be sure. "You can tell the council that Kael Meridan is on his best behavior." He gave a single, sharp laugh that held no humor, only the sound of something breaking. "Go on then, Alysia," he said, his voice hollow. "Run back to your masters. Tell them their leash fits perfectly."

He pivoted and walked down the corridor. Passing students sensed the tension and moved aside, giving him a wide berth. Alysia could only stare at his retreating form, her mind numb. She tried to follow, but her feet felt rooted to the ground as if the wards themselves refused to let her chase him.

Robin, who had remained close by, walked up slowly. She touched Alysia's shoulder, her expression crestfallen. "He'll come around," she offered gently. "He's hurt. He can't see the bigger picture right now."

Alysia blinked back tears. "He thinks I betrayed him. And maybe he's right in a way. I never wanted to become their informant, but they forced me."

Robin gave her a sympathetic look. "I get it. What else could you do? You're trapped between your own future and the trust you spent so long building with him."

Alysia stared at the corridor where Kael had disappeared. She remembered his voice trembling with anger, the illusions sparking around him. She wanted to run after him, to make him see that she was doing this to protect them both. But the lingering echo of his words froze her.

Robin guided her gently away from the bustling hallway, toward a quieter alcove near a tall window. The salty sea air drifted in, a reminder of the cliffs that guarded Velgrace. Alysia leaned against the cold wall, her entire body heavy with regret.

"He hates me now," she murmured. "I saw it in his eyes."

Robin's features softened. "Kael doesn't hate you. He's lashing out because that's what he does when he feels cornered. He spent his life proving he wasn't a monster, and now he thinks the Academy is tearing away the only person who believed in him."

Alysia closed her eyes. The memory of Kael's illusions weaving gracefully in the courtyard still shimmered in her mind, that raw, brilliant power balanced by everything she admired about him.

"I can't lose him, Robin. Not like this."

Robin sighed. "I know. But you both have secrets. The infiltration, the missing orb, the sabotage...it's all turning into a perfect storm. You're stuck in the middle."

Alysia swallowed, bitterness creeping into her voice. "They basically blackmailed me. Either I keep final-year privileges and maintain my status, or I get thrown out."

"You did what you thought was best," Robin said. "But you should brace yourself. Kael will need time, if he ever forgives you."

Alysia pressed her nails into her palms until they stung. She felt the sting of tears but fought them back. This was not the outcome she wanted. She never asked to become the council's puppet. She simply refused to vanish from Velgrace as another failure. Her mother's memory weighed on her, and the knowledge that infiltration still threatened the Academy told her she needed to remain inside these walls. That did not erase the knot of guilt tangling inside her.

Robin caught her gaze. Her voice dropped to a near-whisper. "They forced your hand. There wasn't really a good choice."

Alysia nodded slowly. "I'll find a way to fix this," she said, though the promise sounded hollow. "I'll show Kael that I only did it to keep us both safe."

Robin exhaled, her expression filled with worry. "You have to understand that this may run deeper than an argument. He might see it as betrayal, even if your intentions were good."

Alysia drew in a shaky breath. She gazed at the window, where sunlight sparkled on the distant sea. Her heart twisted, remembering how she and Kael once practiced illusions together in an empty classroom, how he teased her about her over-cautious ward diagrams. They had trusted each other then. Now a fissure spread between them, carved by suspicion, fear, and the Academy's demands.

She pushed away from the wall, her shoulders tense. "I can't let them push him into a corner. If I do, I'll lose him forever."

Robin placed a comforting hand on her arm. "You might not be able to solve it all at once. The infiltration isn't going away, and the council will keep pressuring you for reports. Kael might resent you for giving them any information at all. That frustration won't vanish overnight."

Alysia's pulse throbbed. "I just want to keep everyone safe... including him."

Robin pursed her lips, then spoke earnestly. "Then

tread carefully. Don't lie to Kael, but remember the council is waiting for any excuse to target you both. And the infiltration, whoever they are, will seize on this rift if they sense it."

Alysia clenched her fists. She wondered if the saboteur within these walls walked freely, enjoying the chaos they had sparked. They might be laughing at the confusion, at how easily the Academy turned on itself.

Robin studied her face and sighed. "Alysia, you know I'm in your corner. Just know that this is not going to end with a simple apology. Kael's humiliation, your sense of duty, the infiltration, it's all tangled."

Alysia attempted a nod, though her chest felt tight with dread. "I know. But I have to try."

A brittle silence settled between them, broken only by distant echoes of conversation from the main hall. Down the corridor, the day's bustle continued as if nothing momentous had occurred, as if the Academy was the same place it had always been. Yet Alysia knew everything had changed. She had walked out of that council chamber with her academic standing intact, but at the cost of Kael's trust. The betrayal cut her deeper than any threat of expulsion.

Robin looked upon her with sympathy, then spoke in a raw, quiet tone. "I really am sorry. But you have to see this from Kael's side too. He's been fighting to prove he isn't the Academy's enemy, only to discover the one person he let close is now assigned to watch him."

Alysia's breath caught. "He did let me in," she conceded, her voice barely above a whisper. She thought of the night they patched up each other's bruises from failed illusions, how close they stood, laughter mingling in shared relief. That bond felt so distant now.

Robin rested a gentle hand on Alysia's shoulder. "Give him space. And if you want to mend this, start by being honest with him whenever you can. Don't let their demands twist your words beyond repair."

Alysia nodded, though worry still chewed at the edge of her thoughts. How would she juggle these weekly reports without losing Kael's friendship entirely? She thought of telling the council the barest facts that kept them satisfied, but she knew even that would feel like betrayal in Kael's eyes.

Robin squeezed her shoulder. "We'll figure something out. But right now, let him be angry if he needs to be. He probably feels trapped."

Alysia glanced at the floor, forcing her tears away. Outside the tall windows, sunlight gleamed, mocking the darkness that coiled in her chest. "He called it spying. I can't blame him."

Robin's voice dipped, solemn and frank. "It isn't just a simple trust issue, Lyss. They threatened your education, but they threatened everything that kept Kael believing he had a partner here. Now that your partnership is tainted by suspicion, he might see you as just the Academy's tool."

Alysia's eyes closed. The last shred of her composure nearly slipped. She heard the council's ultimatum on repeat: Watch Kael or be expelled. She imagined the heartbreak in Kael's face as he walked away from her. She felt the emptiness in the corridor where they once exchanged secrets and half-smiles.

Robin's hand slipped from her shoulder, leaving Alysia with the uncomfortable truth. "Robin..." she started, but her voice wavered into silence.

Her cousin exhaled, her gaze grim. "I'm sorry. I wish I had a better fix. But you need to be ready for what this does to you both. You mentioned infiltration, hidden enemies, stolen evidence. You can't fight that alone, but Kael has every right to feel betrayed. You might both get burned."

Alysia lifted her head and allowed the tears to fall. "I'll make him understand eventually," she whispered. "I have to."

Robin gave a weary nod. She looked down the corridor, where Kael had vanished, and then returned her concerned gaze to Alysia. Her voice dropped to a near whisper as she offered the only warning she could. "Just be careful. I don't think you realize how much deeper this cut is. This isn't a small rift. Everything you built with Kael is on the line."

Alysia could only stand there, her arms pinned to her sides, as if something large was crushing her. She replayed the expression on Kael's face, the anger and betrayal in his gray eyes. She had tried to save them both, but perhaps she had only driven a wedge between them.

Robin spoke with finality, the words echoing through the quiet alcove. "Alysia, this wasn't a simple trust issue. This was a fracture."

TWENTY-SIX

THE CLOAK BETWEEN US

Alysia sat on a low stone bench at the edge of the academy's training grounds with Robin by her side. An early evening chill settled over the open field, the amber glow of sunset spreading across the clouds in fiery streaks. Faint echoes of earlier practice lingered in the air. Charms had been unleashed here only a few hours ago, illusions flaring before dissolving in bright cascades of sparks. Now, the field lay nearly empty, save for a few straggling students hauling practice equipment back indoors.

She pulled her cloak tighter around her shoulders, unable to stave off the cold knot of worry in her chest. Kael had left her side not long after the council demanded she monitor him, a betrayal he refused to accept. He had walked away, illusions sparking at his fingertips, leaving her with the bitter taste of regret. She had not seen him since.

"You're going to wear a path in the grass with all that

pacing," Robin remarked softly. Alysia had not noticed she was tapping her boot in jittery rhythm against the bench. She forced her foot still and clasped her hands in her lap.

For a moment, they sat side by side, quiet except for the rasp of the breeze. Alysia's gaze shifted to Robin's profile. Her cousin's short hair, streaked with teal illusions, caught the last remnants of daylight. Robin always teased about her own illusions, calling them harmless "prank level." But Alysia knew Robin had a sharper mind than she let on, one that understood exactly how fragile the academy's defenses had become since infiltration rumors began. No one felt safe anymore, not even in broad daylight.

"So, which is it?" Robin asked, her voice cutting through the quiet. "Are you in love with him, or just too stubborn to admit you broke his trust?"

Alysia swallowed hard. Hearing those words out loud sent a jolt of heat to her cheeks. She kept her gaze fixed on the horizon, where the sun dipped lower over the ocean's surface. About a dozen gulls swooped near the cliffs, their cries barely audible over the distant rush of the sea. She did not want to answer. Part of her suspected the question cut too close to the truth.

Love, or pride? Did it matter when Kael was gone and she'd all but shattered the trust they had built? She thought of him defending her in front of the faculty, illusions spinning protective walls around them both. She recalled how his quiet smirk could light her pulse on fire, how he tested her wards until they nearly cracked, forcing her to improve. And now she had agreed to watch him for the council's sake, painting herself as their informant. Her throat felt tight.

Robin sighed when Alysia's silence dragged on. "He'll come around," she added in a lower voice. "Eventually, at least. Kael's too stubborn to run forever."

"I wish I knew where he went," Alysia murmured, finally allowing her shoulders to droop. An ache throbbed under her collarbone, something that refused to let her breathe easy. "He always hid in Obscura Wing when he was upset, but it's empty. Magister Dain said he never showed up to the illusions lab. Headmistress Quen claims she didn't see him leave campus."

Robin shrugged, fiddling with a scrap of faintly glowing illusory fabric she'd conjured to amuse her restless fingers. "He might be avoiding everyone on purpose. If I were him, I wouldn't want to face half the academy's stares, either. Especially not after the gossip that erupted once the council pinned suspicion on him again." She sent the illusion aloft, where it drifted like a glowing feather before dissolving.

Alysia glanced at the empty training circle in front of them. Deep grooves in the dirt marked where heavy illusions had once collided with wards. Some training dummies had lost limbs, their cloth torsos torn or burned. A faint, acrid scent of scorched burlap lingered in the breeze. The entire scene mirrored her own fractured sense of stability. She felt torn at the seams, undone by duty and longing.

"He saved me so many times," she said under her breath, her voice so low that Robin had to lean closer to hear. "And I, I could not even stand up for him without risking—" She paused, not wanting to utter the word: expulsion. She had made a choice when threatened with losing her place at Velgrace. She had chosen to comply, to watch him, to file weekly observations. It felt like stepping onto a battlefield in the wrong uniform.

"Do you regret it?" Robin asked, sharper than usual.

Alysia closed her eyes, recalling the council's ultimatum, the sight of Quen's stern gaze, and the memory of her mother's tragic failings that she refused to repeat. "I don't regret staying," she said quietly. "But I regret not having a better plan. I hate that Kael's caught in the middle of my decision." Her hand brushed over the silver bracelet etched with the Thorne sigil. The metal felt too cool against her skin, as though reflecting the chill in her heart.

They sat in silence for another few minutes, watching the sun sink until the sky turned a dusky purple. Crickets began to chirp in the nearby hedges, and muffled chatter from the departing students faded as they headed back into the academy proper.

"How do you think the infiltration ties into all this?" Robin asked, her voice subdued. "We know someone inside these walls is stealing artifacts and records. We know they took that scrying orb that recorded Kael's illusions during the storm. Now, the academy's wards feel as though they're being tested for weaknesses each night. It's not a coincidence."

Alysia nodded, though dread weighed heavily on her chest. "Whoever it is must want Kael out of the way. He's too dangerous if he can prove something bigger is at play.

This isn't just about discrediting him," she went on as the pieces clicked into place with a dreadful certainty. "It's about removing a key player from the board. Kael is the only one who has faced their illusions head-on and survived. If they can make the Academy cast him out, who will be left to stop them when they make their real move?"

She swallowed while a bitter taste flooded her mouth. "I guess forcing him into isolation or turning the council against him achieves exactly that."

Robin's expression darkened, but she kept quiet. The two of them stared at the twilight sky, each lost in thought. Alysia's mind replayed the moment she had admitted to Kael that she would have to submit reports on him. His eyes had held such betrayal that she felt it crushing her. She could still see the flicker of illusions sparking around his hands when he'd turned away. He had looked so alone, as though everything he feared was confirmed.

Eventually, Robin exhaled and stood up, running a hand through her teal-streaked hair. "Let's not wait here all night. People will start wondering if we've turned into statues." She offered Alysia a hand. "We'll keep looking. If he's somewhere on campus, we'll find him. And if not, we can set up a watch in case he comes back."

Alysia accepted the help, pushing herself up off the bench. The stone left a chill on the back of her legs. She brushed grass and dust from her cloak, glanced around the darkening training grounds, then nodded. Together, they walked a slow circuit around the field, checking possible hiding spots, an abandoned gear shed, the supply nook behind the wards hut. All empty. The night descended faster than she liked to admit, and the flickering torches around the perimeter lent a haunted air to the deserted grounds.

They made their way toward the main academy building. Stone archways loomed overhead, carved with the crest of Velgrace, and rows of smaller braziers ignited in response to the approaching darkness. A handful of upper-year students crossed their path, muttering quick greetings. Alysia caught a few stares, though not unkind ones, and she wondered if rumors had spread that Kael vanished somewhere into the corridors. Everyone seemed on edge, as if expecting an attack at any moment. Infiltration thrived on fear, and Velgrace was ripe for it.

In the corridor leading to Aurum Spire's dormitories, Robin paused, absently tapping her cheek. "I'll head toward the mess hall, see if maybe he's skulking around the kitchens." She frowned. "He does skip meals sometimes, but the cooks might have seen him. If I find anything, I'll come straight to your room."

Alysia nodded. "Thank you."

Robin started to turn away, then hesitated. "Lyss," she said softly, using Alysia's old nickname. "Don't beat yourself up too much. You had no good option in that council chamber. Maybe Kael won't understand it right now, but I know you did it to save him from worse consequences."

A heavy ache swelled in Alysia's chest, but she mustered a weak smile. "I appreciate you saying that. I just... I want him to see that I'm still on his side."

Robin's eyes shimmered with empathy. "He will.

Sometimes, people just need time." Then she walked off, her footsteps echoing down the corridor.

Alone now, Alysia felt an unsteady flutter in her chest. The day had worn her thin, and the fear of Kael disappearing for good whispered nasty doubts in her mind. She had already checked Obscura Wing, the library, and the courtyard. She doubted he would hide in the basement vaults alone, too many wards to bypass without drawing attention. But Kael was resourceful, and he had illusions on his side.

She ascended the winding stairs to her floor, her footsteps growing heavier with each step. Her dormitory door was warded with a basic locking spell. She touched two fingertips to the runic latch, whispered the passphrase, and heard the faint click of magic releasing. The hinges gave their usual creak as she pushed the door open.

Inside, her room looked exactly as it had that morning: neat in a functional way, though a messy scatter of scrolls covered her desk. She half expected to see Kael perched on her small wooden chair, rolling his eyes at her cluttered notes or half-smiling in that aggravatingly confident way. But the space was empty. No illusions flickered, no voice teased her from the corner.

She locked the door behind her and set her cloak on a hook, trying not to let the silence suffocate her. Light from a single enchanted lantern glowed softly on the desk. Her reflection in the dorm window looked drawn, like she was holding her breath. With a weary sigh, she went to the small basin near her bed, splashed cool water on her face, and exhaled in a shuddering breath.

She wondered what Kael was feeling now. Anger? Hurt? Maybe both. She imagined him venturing to the tower roof or climbing beyond the academy walls to brood under starlight. If infiltration conspirators lurked in the shadows, would they target him?

The worry churned in her stomach. Kael was powerful, but isolation made him vulnerable to rumors and manipulation. If the infiltration's goal was to keep him off-balance, they had succeeded spectacularly. The missing scrying orb, the sabotage of wards, and now the wedge of distrust driven between him and Alysia, none of it felt like an accident.

Unfastening her boots, she sat on the edge of her narrow bed, letting the wave of exhaustion roll over her. Her thoughts strayed to the council scene, replaying Headmistress Quen's words and the dull shock she felt at the threat of expulsion. Could she have chosen defiance? Would Kael have trusted her more had she refused to monitor him?

She glanced down at her silver bracelet and turned it in the lantern's light. The Thorne sigil etched into the metal glinted faintly. She had taken an oath in her heart to protect people, not betray them. And this decision had felt like a betrayal, even though her intention was to protect Kael from a harsher punishment. Closing her eyes, she pressed her fist to her chest, feeling the rapid beat of her heart.

Minutes passed, or perhaps hours. She changed into her nightshirt, her thoughts spinning in circles. The distant sounds of the academy at night reminded her that, at this hour, some people studied quietly while others snuck out for mischief. And one person, specifically, was avoiding her altogether.

She lit a small memory candle from the corner of her desk, letting its flame flicker azure and cast dancing shapes on the walls. The gentle glow brought her a measure of comfort. She sank into her wooden chair, elbows on the desk, and stared blankly at her open books. She had no focus to read, but leafed through a half-written summary on layered wards. Her pen lines were shaky from earlier that day, a visual record of tension. She let out a breath and tried to steady her nerves.

Her gaze drifted back to the dorm's cramped window. The sky was fully dark now, dotted with glimmering stars. By the angle of the moon, it was close to midnight. Soft footsteps outside her door made her tense, but they faded, and no knock followed. Her heart pounded with disappointment. Was it Kael? Or just another student passing by?

She set the pen aside, rubbing her palms together for warmth. Her mind was too full to find rest, yet too exhausted to do anything productive. She had to make peace with the fact that Kael might not be ready to forgive her. Maybe he just needed to vanish for a night, to let his anger cool somewhere she could not follow.

The emptiness of the room pressed in around her. She stood, paced a few steps, then cracked the window open to let the ocean breeze seep in. The briny scent reminded her of the vantage where she and Kael used to practice illusions that danced in the gusty air. She could almost see

him in her memory, half-smiling as he coaxed bright illusions around her wards.

She lingered by the window until the chill made her
shut it again. At last, with a heavy sigh, she returned to her
bed, pulling the covers up around her shoulders. The
sounds of waves filtered through the stone walls. She
listened, tears stinging her eyes before she blinked them
away. She fought the desire to leap out of bed and comb
every corner of the academy again, to make him understand why she had chosen such a devastating bargain
with the council. But she stayed put. Another search this
late might only draw attention from curious faculty, or
worse, from the unknown traitor who might still be
watching.

Hours passed. The single lantern flame dimmed to a
faint gray glow. She drifted in and out of restless dozing,
her heart thrumming each time her mind conjured an
image of Kael stepping back through her door. She would
snap awake, glance around, and see only the glow on the
desk's worn piles of scrolls.

She clenched her hands in the blanket, pressing a
silent prayer to the wards that draped over the academy.
Please keep him safe. Please.

She was not sure if the wards answered prayers, or if
they even listened. She only knew the night felt painfully
long, and that Kael had walled himself off from her when
she needed him most.

The last of the candle's flame sputtered and died,
plunging the room into darkness. But Alysia did not move.
She stared into the gloom, the ache in her chest hardening

into something else: resolve. She had made a choice to protect the Academy and in doing so had wounded the one person she most wanted to protect. She would not make that mistake again. She would find the real traitor, clear Kael's name, and mend the trust she had broken. Whatever the cost.

TWENTY-SEVEN

THE SIGIL RETURNS

Alysia stirred in her narrow bed, uncertain at first why her eyes flew open or why her heart hammered. A pale light glowed against the dark ceiling, ethereal and wavering, as if painted by invisible fingers. She blinked, then sat up, nearly tangling her legs in the thin blanket. Damp nighttime air drifted in through the cracked window, and a shiver coursed through her.

She squinted at the light, her pulse leaping when she recognized the shape. A sigil marked her ceiling, glowing with a faint, predatory blue. It wasn't projected there, it seemed to be bleeding through the stone from the room above, a stain of corrupt magic that pulsed in time with her own frightened heartbeat. The same rogue emblem she had glimpsed before, the one linked to twisted illusions and infiltration. Though it pulsed softly like a moonlit reflection, it looked ominous, as if something inside it breathed. She reached a trembling hand up, tracing its edges in the air. It flickered in response, a mocking echo of her gesture.

She inhaled slowly, attempting to calm her nerves. After the Academy's council forced her into spying on Kael, tension had run rampant for days. She had tried to sleep, but rest came in fitful scraps that rarely lasted more than an hour. Tonight, insomnia might have saved her from missing whatever sign or warning this was. Yet the question remained: who had conjured that sigil, and why here?

Steadying her breathing, she glanced around the small dorm room. Her books lay stacked crookedly on the desk, half-finished notes on advanced ward theory left unrolled. She had consulted them earlier, searching for ways to unravel illusions quietly without triggering suspicion. No immediate danger filled the darkness, but Kael was nowhere in sight. Her stomach knotted at once. She and Kael had not spoken much since their argument. He had distanced himself, vanishing at odd hours. For him to break in silently and leave a message would be dramatic, even for him, unless he needed her help.

She slipped her feet to the floor, her toes curling against the chill of the stone. The air smelled faintly of sea salt and burned candlewax. With a murmured word, she summoned a soft flicker from the lantern on the desk. Its glow revealed the rest. Her bed was rumpled, the floor free of footprints, and the lone window latched from the inside. Strange. Whoever had conjured that sigil had done so without disturbing the wards on her door. A trickle of unease crawled under her skin.

Rising, she approached the desk. Her gaze fell upon a single sheet of parchment. The letters shimmered in magical ink, shifting from silver to faint gold.

"Come to the Gate. Midnight. Alone."

The scrawling lines resembled no handwriting she recognized. Her heart skipped a beat. She read the message through twice, searching for clues. The invitation might be a trap. It might be from Kael, or from the infiltration ring, or from someone else entirely.

She swallowed hard, pressing her shaking hand against the surface of the desk. The meaning could not be clearer. Someone wanted her at the Gate in the dead of night. A meeting. Possibly an ambush. Or an attempt to share critical information. That rogue sigil on the ceiling hinted at a darker possibility. She closed her eyes, fighting to steady her racing thoughts. Her mind scrolled through every reason not to go: the council's mistrust, the infiltration that lurked around them, the risk of stepping right into the enemy's arms. But she could not ignore the possibility of Kael being involved. Her chest squeezed at the memory of how he had looked when he last walked away, illusions sparking with anger and heartbreak.

Her next breath came out shakily. The note bore no signature. If Kael wanted to contact her, would he choose these symbols? She could not be sure. If it were the rogue conspirators, they might twist the meeting to coerce or threaten her. Yet the fear of doing nothing tore at her more savagely than the fear of confronting them. She felt a tug in her gut that said the time for passive waiting had ended. The infiltration was no longer a rumor. It had become her daily reality. For all she knew, the stolen scrying orb or missing artifacts had led to some new scheme. And the fact that this message appeared now, in her private dorm, meant the conspirators could breech her wards at will if they desired.

She exhaled and steeled herself. No matter the source, she had to uncover the truth. She grabbed her small wooden trunk from under the bed, popping it open with a whispered key-charm that parted the latch. Inside, a plain cloth-wrapped dagger gleamed dully, the blade etched with a protective ward. A "charm dagger," as many called it. She had carved the runes herself, ensuring the weapon could disrupt illusions on contact. Rarely did she carry it, but tonight, it felt essential.

She strapped the dagger to her belt and quietly ran through her mental checklist of spells. She would need concealment if she was to travel unnoticed through the Academy grounds. If whoever left the note truly wanted secrecy, she intended to keep every advantage for herself as well.

Her reflection in the small mirror near the desk caught her eye. She wore a simple nightshirt, so she hastily tugged on a pair of black trousers and a dark academic robe. Her hair, still mussed from sleep, tumbled around her face. She considered twisting it into a quick braid, then decided time was too precious. Instead, she ran fingers through it and braided loosely, not wanting strands to obscure her vision if something happened.

With a soft word, she dismissed the glow from the lantern. The dorm hovered in shadows, illuminated only by the eerie blue of that rogue sigil on the ceiling. Reaching deep for her magic, she murmured an incantation she had tested only once: a layered concealment meant for short distances. The air around her rippled faintly, as if a wave passed through space. Her body blurred at the edges, blending with the darkness. She felt her heartbeat quicken as the spell wove a partial cloak around her presence. Not foolproof, but enough to evade most casual detection.

She unlocked the door, glancing into the silent corridor. Dim light from the sconces cast pale stripes on the floor. No sign of watchers or patrolling staff. She shut her door without a sound, the hinges mercifully well-oiled, then hurried along the hall. Her pulse throbbed in her ears with every step.

Surging tension accompanied her down the winding staircase. She kept her footsteps light and stuck close to the wall, practicing the flattened stance that Warden Morn had taught in stealth drills. She felt a pang recalling that the same warden now mistrusted her, suspecting her part in Kael's illusions. By leaving her dorm at midnight, she risked fueling new suspicions. But the note demanded she move now.

She slipped outside into the Academy's central courtyard. A chilly breeze ruffled her robe. The moonless sky offered little illumination, yet the faint shimmer of wardlights dotted the walls. She paused, scanning for any shapes that might be watchers. Occasionally, a guard made rounds near the gates, checking for intruders. Tonight, the courtyard seemed deserted. Even the usual night-owl students must have gone to bed or hidden themselves in some tucked-away corner.

Her concealment spell crackled softly, straining under the open space. She renewed it with a second whispered phrase, focusing on each glyph in her mind. Across the courtyard stood the grand stone arch leading to the Academy's outer gate. Torch brackets along the arch had been extinguished, leaving a black silhouette against the star-speckled horizon.

She approached slowly, scouring every corner for movement. The quiet pressed around her, broken only by the distant roar of waves against the cliff. Each step amplified her heartbeat. The courtyard stones bore faint burn marks from earlier illusions gone wild. She swallowed the memory, forcing herself to stay alert.

When she reached the tall arch, she noticed no figure waiting. She stood there, concealed. She turned in a slow circle, tension threading her muscles. Nothing. No hidden silhouette, no illusions. Was the note a cruel prank? Or had she arrived too late?

She inhaled again, scanning the gloom. Beyond the gate's threshold lay the open path leading to the Academy's outer walls. A small guardhouse was built into the side, typically manned by older students or staff. Tonight, its windows were dark. The door was shut and latched. She bit her lip, uncertain what she should do. If someone had wanted to meet outside the campus wards, they might expect her to move farther. But wandering beyond Velgrace at night, alone, felt reckless. The infiltration rumors involved sabotage and well-placed illusions that could lure her off a cliff if she was not careful.

Her throat tightened. Another possibility struck her. The message might be from Kael, urging her to slip away from the watchful eyes of the Academy so he could speak without being overheard. He might be testing her willingness to trust him, or to defy the new arrangement that demanded she spy on him. But would he adopt that rogue sigil if it meant scaring her? That question twisted her thoughts.

After one more fruitless search, she eased along the outer walkway, pressing against the cold stone walls of the arch. She lifted her free hand and conjured a small wisp of ward light. The shimmering flame hovered over her palm, bright enough to illuminate a few steps ahead. If there was writing or a clue hidden in the shadows, she wanted to see it. She kept the charm dagger in her other hand, her knuckles white on the worn hilt.

She walked several paces, her breath echoing in her ears. Nothing stirred. The infiltration might be laughing at her right now, or they might be perched just beyond the next corner. She hated the sense of being watched, the prickling on her neck that refused to lessen.

A thought struck her. If some illusory marker guided her, she could attempt a detection ward. She halted, inhaled, and pressed her free palm against the walkway's edge. Slowly, she closed her eyes and whispered the incantation for a reveal spell. The cool stone thrummed beneath her fingertips, as if the wards of Velgrace recognized her.

She poured a trickle of magic forward, coaxing hidden illusions into view.

At first, she perceived no change. Then the air ahead shimmered. The air ahead shimmered. A trail of faint, ghostly footprints, each glowing with the same corrupt blue as the sigil, appeared on the flagstones, leading her directly through the arch and up the path. She tensed. Indeed, it was an illusion. A partial sign that someone had left behind as a beacon or a puzzle. As she watched, the lines flickered in and out, beckoning her forward.

Her mind spun. If she stepped into that half-circle, she risked being snared. Yet if she gave in to fear, she would learn nothing. Gritting her teeth, she pressed her lips together. Trusting her instincts, she raised the charm dagger, braced it near her chest, and stepped forward, crossing the threshold.

A ripple of energy coursed up her legs and across her torso. It felt like walking through a thin veil of water on a windless day. She sucked in a breath. The lines brightened, then receded into the darkness.

She blinked, sweeping her ward light around. Ahead lay the stone walkway that led toward the eastern portion of the campus perimeter. She saw a fleeting flicker near the top of the path, as though someone stood there with a dim lantern. Her heart thundered. She took a step, then paused. A voice within her demanded caution. She was alone. No direct backup, no Kael to shield her with illusions, no Robin to crack jokes and keep her calm. Yet she could not retreat. That flicker could be the only lead she had.

Bracing herself, she followed it, her mind racing with half a dozen possible confrontations. Each echoing footstep resonated with her fear. The minutes stretched long as she climbed the gentle slope. Eventually, the flicker of light winked out. She reached an iron fence that demarcated the campus boundary from the wilder hillside. Grass rustled in the wind, and the starry sky leaned in overhead like a silent observer.

She found no living soul. Only silence. The faint glimmer of wards around Bastion Hall glowed in the distance, a faint ring of protective luminescence. Her concealment spell wore thin, warning her that she had little time before it faded entirely. She bit back a curse, scanning again. If the infiltration group had lured her here, were they going to jump out now? Or was this some trick to confirm that she would defy the Academy's curfew?

Frustration bloomed, mixing with dread. The note said midnight. Alone. She was alone, and it was surely past midnight. She felt the restless magic around her, a tension in the crisp air that promised more than an empty walkway. But no one showed.

A shiver gripped her. Every new second felt like a sly game, as if the infiltration tested her reaction. She pressed a hand to her chest, feeling the quick pound of her heart. Then she remembered the last words she had read: "It was no longer just about Kael. It was about the truth." That line ran through her head exact as she had interpreted it. She had to discover what connected that rogue sigil, Kael's disappearance, and the infiltration's deeper plans.

She looked once more at the quiet horizon. The Gate itself stood behind her, silent and unoccupied. No footsteps approached from either direction. The sheen of the half-circle illusion had fully dissolved. She knew she could not linger indefinitely, not without risking exposure to patrolling staff or worse. She could also not pretend this night had not happened. Something was set in motion.

Her grip tightened on the dagger. For an instant, she considered venturing farther into the darkness, beyond the boundary gates, to search for additional illusions. The notion of stumbling blind into unwarded territory alone sent ice through her veins. The infiltration wanted her isolated, perhaps, or wanted to scare her. She was not so foolish as to let them toy with her life on a whim.

She glanced around for a sign, a written scrap, anything to prove she had not imagined the faint light. Yet the hillside and the path yielded only the moonless night. The Academy's silhouette cut a solemn figure behind her. A pang of disappointment and anxiety threatened to overtake her.

At last, she resolved to return to her dorm, to weigh her next steps carefully. She could not vanish into the darkness with no plan. She had gleaned at least one confirmation tonight. The infiltration had the ability to project illusions within her private space. That alone changed everything. If they could do that, they could orchestrate events far more cunningly. She needed to be ready.

She inhaled, letting her concealing aura fade gently so it would not crack with a flash. Then she pivoted and made her way back toward the main courtyard, her senses on high alert. The desire for answers raged within her, but caution overrode the urge to rush blindly ahead. Each shadow loomed with possible danger, each faint breeze teased at illusions that might emerge again.

Her steps led her through the arch, where she paused one last time. She turned her head, scanning the corridor of darkness that stretched outside the Academy's protective boundary. The rogue sigil in her room had summoned her here, then vanished like a mirage. Perhaps that was the point: to show her that the infiltration moved freely, even into her private sanctuary. Or perhaps it had been Kael, leaving the sigil as a cryptic sign. Yet Kael's illusions rarely carried such sharp edges of menace.

Her throat went dry. She whispered, "You won't scare me away," to no one in particular, a vow that only the night could hear. Then she guided herself across the courtyard, returning to the dorm tower on unsteady legs. Though her limbs trembled, her mind sharpened with a new determination.

She reached her door without encountering a single passerby. After stepping inside, she locked it, reinforced the seal with a fresh ward, and sagged against the wood. The glowing rogue sigil on her ceiling had vanished, leaving a faint afterimage in her vision. When she looked at the desk, the parchment was gone, replaced by a single black ash mark shaped like an obscured glyph. She felt a chill spiral from her spine to her neck.

She pressed her palm to the mark, and it smeared across her skin, leaving sparks of energy that tingled before evaporating. Whoever planted it had ended the message in the same cryptic manner it arrived. Tired and unsettled, she sank onto her bed, hugging her knees to her chest. Nothing about this night made sense, except for the undeniable truth that a new threat had crossed the threshold of her world.

In the quiet, she closed her eyes, focusing on her racing heartbeat. The infiltration had extended its reach, calling her out at midnight. She did not know if they intended to confront her soon or if they meant to toy with her. She did know that she could not rely on anyone else to unravel it for her. The truth now beckoned like a distant light through the gloom, leaving her with only one certainty: she had no choice but to chase it. It was no longer just about Kael. It was about the truth.

CHAPTER
TWENTY-EIGHT
THE BETRAYER'S MARK

Alysia tightened her grip on the charm dagger at her hip as she descended deeper into Velgrace's sprawling catacombs. The air felt heavy with damp chill, and her breath caught whenever she stepped across loose stones or uneven steps. She had slipped away from her dorm unnoticed, spurred by a strange, insistent pull she felt in her own magic. It was an echo of the spiral now etched on her wand, a resonance that guided her forward into the depths. Each pulse guided her forward, deeper into corridors lined with worn carvings of warding glyphs. She recognized some from her grandmother's notes, old runes meant to seal enchantments that were never meant to see daylight again. Now those same runes appeared half-erased or chipped away, leaving the catacombs vulnerable.

Her cloak brushed the rough-hewn walls, and she winced when droplets of condensation ran cold against her fingers. She paused at an arched passage, focusing on the echo of her own breathing. She had never ventured this far below the Academy before tonight. A quiet blanketed everything, disturbed only by the faint hum that her enhanced senses picked up, perhaps vestiges of the wards overhead, or maybe the distant stirrings of forbidden magic. She swallowed, then forced herself to keep going.

She could not forget the note she had found: an unfamiliar script telling her to come to the Gate alone. She had seen scraps of that writing in previous encounters, evidence of infiltration, perhaps. This time, the message had led her to an even more unsettling place. The memory of the rogue sigil burned in her mind, and the spiral on her wand, tucked in her satchel, seemed to thrum with a faint, impatient energy. It had first appeared in her dorm, shimmering on the ceiling. Now, she could feel it feeding off the dense magic of these catacombs, pushing her to discover whatever lay ahead.

Soon, the corridor opened into a massive circular chamber. She froze just inside the threshold, letting her eyes adjust to the gloom. It was an underground Gate chamber, but it felt more like the skeletal remains of a dead god. The air was thin and vibrated with a low, dissonant hum. Runic columns, slick with moisture, ringed a dais where a stone arch stood. The arch didn't just crackle with energy; it seemed to breathe it, inhaling the chamber's magic and exhaling a faint scent of dust and decay. Strange pulses of violet and blue light flickered across the walls, as though the entire place breathed with hidden power.

In the center stood a tall stone arch flanked by two broken pillars. She sensed the undercurrent of illusions around it, an echo of the creation magic used to build old Gates between worlds. The hair on the back of her neck lifted at the knowledge that someone might have been working to reawaken it. She stepped closer, noticing a slender figure leaning casually against one of the pillars.

Lyric Meridan.

Alysia's heart hammered. She had encountered Kael's twin sister before, but she had never grown comfortable around her. Lyric carried a harsh sort of grace in her posture and a constant aura of secrets. Tonight, the glow of illusions cast ill-defined shadows across her face, making it impossible to read her expression.

"Alysia," Lyric said in a calm, almost resigned tone. "You actually came."

Alysia kept her steps measured as she approached, scanning the chamber for traps or lurking figures. "Strange that you're here at such an hour," she said. She tried to control the tremor in her voice. "You left no name on that note."

Lyric shrugged, a slight tilt of her shoulders. "I prefer to let the sigil speak for me. Besides, you and I have never been the type to exchange polite invitations, have we?"

Alysia's chest tightened at the memory of Lyric's ambivalence whenever Kael was mentioned. She recalled the times Lyric had stood on the edges of trouble, offering half-answers that left Alysia uncertain of her role. Tonight, everything felt more precarious. The lights in the Gate chamber sharpened the tension in the air, and the dagger at Alysia's side felt both reassuring and terrifying.

She stopped a few paces away. "What do you want?"

Lyric cast a glance at the arch behind her. Faint arcs of shimmering magic rippled across its surface, suggesting someone had tried to awaken its energies. "I want to show you the game you're losing," Lyric said, her voice echoing slightly in the vast chamber. "You think you're protecting Kael. You're not. You're the council's pawn, and the infiltration is using their paranoia to corner him. He is in more danger now than he ever was during the storm. And you, with your unwavering loyalty to him, might lose him if you keep trusting the wrong people."

Alysia's stomach lurched at the mention of Kael. Even though they had not spoken much lately, she felt the pull of his absence keenly. She inhaled. "What do you mean, danger from the Academy?"

Lyric lifted her chin. Her hair, braided with silver cords, caught the flicker of the illusions overhead. "Think about the council's threats. Think about the infiltration that has everyone paranoid. The Academy is under pressure to find a scapegoat. Kael might become that scapegoat if you don't act soon. They suspect him, again. And there are those on the inside who want nothing more than to see him banished or worse." She paused, letting her words sink in. "He's not safe here, no matter how you try to protect him."

Alysia clenched her fists at her sides, resisting the urge to step closer. "You make it sound like everyone's turned against him." Her voice rose despite her attempts to keep calm. "That implies some deep betrayal within the Academy itself. But we both know there are real traitors too, people sabotaging wards, fueling illusions in secret. Kael has nothing to do with that. We have been trying to expose it."

Lyric's lips pressed thin. "Exactly. And that infiltration is powerful enough to shift suspicion wherever it pleases. The moment Kael stepped out of line, the moment he used illusions that night on the training grounds, he became the perfect target. Rumors are easy to spread, and half the Academy hasn't forgotten his cursed lineage."

For a flicker of a second, Alysia thought back to the tension on campus, the voices whispering that Kael might be behind the stolen ward stone or that he was an agent of some old Meridan plot. She had tried to defend him, but the council had cornered her into monitoring him. That betrayal still tasted bitter in her mouth.

She squared her shoulders. "You claim to warn me, but you haven't told me why.

Tell me plainly: who is behind this infiltration? Where are they hiding? Don't dance around the truth."

Lyric's expression hardened. "If I name them, will you even believe me? You've seen your share of illusions, and loyalties have shifted before. Headmistress Quen does not trust me, and I doubt you do, either." She cast her gaze at the Gate. "But if you truly want to help Kael, you need to step away from the Academy's watchful eyes. They will brand him the culprit. They will brand you as complicit. You'll both be threatened with worse than expulsion."

Alysia's heart drummed a frantic beat. She hated the

ring of possibility in Lyric's words. Stress weighed on her chest, as if the entire underground chamber pressed in on her. The illusions crossing the Gate's arch reflected in Lyric's eyes, making them gleam with an eerie light. She forced a steady tone. "Why should I trust you, then? You've avoided giving me answers before. You show up now, calling me down into the catacombs, telling me Kael's in danger from everyone. That's not enough, Lyric."

For a long moment, Lyric studied her. The silence built, broken by the faint hum of magic from the columns around them. Finally, Lyric pushed off the pillar and stepped forward. A faint dusting of ancient stone crackled under her boots. "Because, like it or not, you and I both need Kael safe. He is...necessary. I have my own reasons to ensure he does not fall into the Academy's clutches or the rogue faction's trap. You want proof of my loyalty? Fine."

Lyric lifted her sleeve, baring her left forearm. At first, Alysia only saw smooth skin. Then Lyric muttered a brief incantation under her breath. The illusions dissipated, revealing a dark spiral etched into her flesh, a mark that glowed with sickly purple light.

Alysia recoiled as if struck. The mark was not just a sigil but a living wound, the skin around it puckered and scarred. The purple light pulsed with a sickly, parasitic energy that made her own brand ache in sympathy.

"That is their mark," she whispered, her voice trembling. "You are one of them. You have been working with them this whole time."

Lyric's eyes flashed. "I infiltrated the infiltrators. I needed to see how they planned to use Kael. They are convinced his illusions will be key to shattering the Academy's wards once and for all. But they also see him as a convenient victim to discredit if something goes wrong." She paused, letting out a sharp breath. "That is the danger you must recognize. Even if you think the faculty might absolve him once they catch the real traitors, the infiltration has ways to tip the blame."

Alysia slowly unclenched her fists, though her pulse refused to slow. She tried to parse Lyric's words for truth. The brand on Lyric's arm told a story of compromised loyalties, and yet Lyric was standing here offering a warning instead of setting a trap.

"You bear a brand of the infiltration, and you stand in this chamber with old illusions at your feet," Alysia said, a brittle edge to her voice.

"Then why summon me alone?" Her gaze moved to the dark corners of the room, searching for accomplices. "Where are the others?"

Lyric's lips curved in the faintest trace of a sad smile. "I am alone tonight because I couldn't risk watchers. And if you noticed, I have cast my own illusions to mask the infiltration's presence. I couldn't speak freely anywhere else. Now, you must decide if you will believe me or walk away."

"Suppose I believe you," Alysia said, swallowing the dryness in her throat. "What do you want me to do? Where is Kael right now?"

Lyric studied her again, this time more carefully. "He's hiding in plain sight, wandering the Academy's deserted halls. He refuses to stay in one place for long, afraid the infiltration or the council will corner him. He's trying to shield you by keeping his distance, but that might only make it easier for enemies to isolate him. They are planning to strike soon, to force him into a public confrontation." She lifted her arm, letting the brand's glow illuminate the arch behind her. "And they plan to use this Gate as part of that trap."

Alysia's eyes locked on the Gate's patterns. She gathered that someone had reawakened it. "This Gate... Is it functional?"

"Barely. Enough to spin illusions or maybe open brief passages," Lyric said. She lowered her sleeve again, covering the brand. "This Gate doesn't just open a passage. It amplifies. If they can channel Kael's unique illusionary signature through it, they can turn a single rogue spell into an army of them inside the Academy's walls. They can rewrite Velgrace's own wards from the inside out. He is the key to their entire plan. Imagine illusions merging with old Gate energy, unstable and unstoppable. But if that fails, they can claim Kael orchestrated it."

Alysia tried to steady her breathing. Anxiety needled at her thoughts. She had always known the infiltration's sabotage ran deep, but the possibility that they would deliberately manipulate Kael's illusions into a cataclysmic breach made her knees tremble. She realized she needed to warn someone, but who could she trust? The council had demanded she spy on Kael, and half the campus feared him. If the infiltration had indeed planted traitors inside the faculty, raising alarms might only deepen their suspicion of Kael and accelerate his downfall.

She pressed a hand to her chest, feeling the steady thump of her heartbeat through her cloak. "If you want me to help, I need proof or at least some direction on how to stop them. Have you learned any names? Any direct evidence that can turn the Academy's eyes away from Kael and toward the real conspirators?"

Lyric hesitated, and for the first time, Alysia saw a flicker of genuine uncertainty in her eyes. "I have bits and pieces. Enough to suspect some senior staff might be in league with the infiltration, but I can't prove who is giving the orders. The infiltration is layered with illusions inside illusions, and the brand prevents me from directly attacking them without causing my own unraveling. I came here tonight to warn you that time is running out. If Kael could be cornered in public within the next few days, the infiltration might pin the stolen ward stone's sabotage on him. The council, under pressure to protect the Academy, might choose to sacrifice him."

Alysia's heart twisted. Her mind replayed every interaction with faculty in recent weeks, the council's stony faces as they interrogated her, Headmistress Quen's careful neutrality, Warden Morn's suspicious glances. She thought of how easily rumors sparked, how illusions could be planted, how a single false note in the logs she submitted on Kael's activities might condemn him. "That's exactly what the infiltration wants," she whispered.

"Yes," Lyric said softly. "And once that happens, the path to activating this Gate will be wide open. No one will question the infiltration's real manipulations until it is too late."

Alysia exhaled, her breath catching in the stale air of the chamber. She felt a flicker of rage that the infiltration had turned trust and caution into such a dangerous weapon. She stared at Lyric, uncertain whether to hate her for the brand on her arm or to cling to her for guidance. Maybe both. "You risk a lot by telling me these things," she said. "You could have tried to stay covert, using me as a pawn."

Lyric's gaze dropped for a fraction of a second. "Perhaps I am using you, in part. But I'm also giving you fair warning. Think of me however you like. I want Kael out of the line of fire. That means telling you enough to protect him. You can decide whatever else you want to do with the information."

Alysia bit her lip, her thoughts churning with frustration and concern. She had to find Kael, make sure he was reminded that she was on his side. She also needed a plan to ferret out the real conspirators without plunging both of them into the infiltration's trap. But hostility toward Lyric still flared in her gut. Lyric was complicit in some way. The brand's presence was proof that she had stepped into the infiltration's circle, no matter what reasons she gave.

At length, Alysia cleared her throat, forcing herself to speak evenly. "Your help comes at a distasteful cost, Lyric. I can't pretend I'm not furious about your silence before now, or about your ties to that mark. But Kael…I can't lose him over something he was never guilty of. If I have to stand against half the Academy, I will."

Lyric's face revealed nothing for a moment, then her tense posture softened slightly. "Good. I hoped you would say that. Then heed my last warning. Do not bring this information straight to Quen or the council without gathering evidence. They are desperate for answers, and even the well-intentioned among them might blame Kael for the infiltration if they lack a clear alternative suspect. Start small. Find out which staff or students have secrets lurking, or who might be forging illusions. Above all, find Kael before they do. The infiltration has networks of illusions that can mislead even him if he's alone."

Alysia nodded, though dread settled heavily on her shoulders. The illusions around the Gate flickered again, and for a moment, she had the uneasy feeling that the entire chamber was listening to their conversation. "All right," she said. "I appreciate the warning, but I need to confirm your story. If it's true, I'll do everything to protect him. If it's a trap..." Her voice trailed off, leaving her threat hanging in the air.

Lyric accepted that statement with a brief dip of her head. Then she turned, glancing at the looming arch. "There is something else. The infiltration may try to exploit Kael's illusions differently than you expect. If that happens, you'll notice a new pattern among the wards. Watch for wards that flicker or warp in a spiral shape. It means they've been tampered with. That's the infiltration's signature. Once you see it, you'll know they're closing in."

Taking a final, cautious step back, Alysia eyed Lyric. The brand along Lyric's arm glowed faintly, revealing the spiral pattern in vivid purple. The parallel to the infiltration's illusions made sense in a sickening way. "I'll keep that in mind," Alysia said grimly.

A faint vibration trembled through the floor, indicating some shift in the magical energies of the catacombs. Lyric's posture grew rigid, and she looked behind one of the columns. "We should leave this chamber," she said. "The infiltration keeps watch. If they sense my illusions masking us, they might send someone."

Alysia felt the sigil on her wrist twinge anew, as if it also perceived approaching danger. She stared at Lyric, uncertain whether to fight her or follow her. But the echo of Kael's name in her mind silenced her doubts. She needed to get out, find Kael, and figure out how to clear his name before a final blow was struck.

She moved toward the exit first, stepping carefully over cracked tiles. One final glance showed Lyric tracing a shimmering line in the air, dispersing illusions that had concealed their discussion from prying eyes. Then Lyric hurried after her. Together, they reached the corridor that wound upward to the Academy's lower levels.

Alysia did not speak until they were halfway to the surface. Her thoughts churned with everything Lyric had revealed. Kael was in danger from the infiltration, from the Academy's paranoia, from accusations that might be pinned on him without recourse. And here was Lyric, the twin sister who bore a mark that bound her to the infiltration, swearing she wanted to protect him. Alysia struggled to separate the truth from deception, aware that illusions curled around them in every shape.

At last, she paused by a worn iron sconce, glancing sideways at Lyric. "This brand you carry, does it guarantee the infiltration trusts you? Or might they suspect you are working against them?"

Lyric's lips tightened. "They doubt everyone, but I keep my role hidden. They believe they can corrode my will with that brand. They don't understand how stubborn I can be."

Alysia almost smiled at the faint note of pride. Stubbornness seemed to run in the Meridan blood, she thought wryly. That same trait fueled Kael's resilience, even when everyone else judged him. Part of her wanted to believe that same fierce spirit in Lyric now served a righteous cause. Another part still quaked with suspicion.

They kept silent the rest of the way up, trailing through corridors with flickering lanterns. Finally, they reached a point where the catacombs' damp chill gave way to the slightly warmer Draft Hall, a lower passage outside Bastion Hall. Lyric halted in the shadows while Alysia scanned for roving watchers or night patrols. The hall seemed deserted, but she knew wards might record passersby at any time.

Lyric inclined her head. "You go first. If anyone sees us together, it will raise questions." Then she added, quieter, "Stay cautious. If the infiltration senses your next moves, or if the council decides Kael is a threat, you will face them alone. Be sure you know who you can trust."

Alysia exhaled shakily. "I'm not sure I trust anyone,

Lyric, not fully. But I will do anything necessary to protect Kael."

Lyric's face remained impassive, though her eyes flickered with something like relief. Then she slipped back into the darkness, illusions cloaking her steps until she vanished from sight.

Alone, Alysia pressed her back against the cold stone wall, her pulse racing. Her hand trembled where she clutched the dagger hilt. Lyric's words replayed in her mind, merging with the hum of old magic that still clung to her skin from the Gate chamber. She thought of how easily illusions could bend perceptions, how quickly suspicion might attach itself to Kael if the infiltration wanted. She felt the tang of betrayal on her tongue, a taste that lingered like bitter metal.

In that crumbling silence, she realized her painful truth: she did not know whom to believe within the Academy's ranks. She had been coerced by the council. She had been manipulated by illusions. She had discovered traitors wearing the faces of mentors. Now Lyric stood at her side with a cursed brand, half-admitting she'd infiltrated the very group they were fighting. And Kael, somewhere in these halls, remained caught between all sides.

Her legs felt weak. She closed her eyes, steadying her breath. The infiltration had gained more ground than she realized, and she was running out of time to prove Kael's innocence before they set the final trap. Danger pressed in from every direction. She had to act, but how could she do so without risking Kael's life? Without trusting the wrong ally?

Slowly, she pushed off the wall and forced her feet toward the narrow stairs leading up to the main floors of Velgrace. Her mind churned through possibilities, each one darker and more uncertain than the last.

The air near the staircase carried the faint smell of old torches, a reminder that these halls were well-traveled in daylight. Right now, no one stood watch, or at least she saw no sign of patrolling staff. Maybe they were posted elsewhere, maybe illusions masked them, or maybe the infiltration had re-posted them to mislead her. She grimaced at each thought, an ache growing behind her ribs. They wanted Kael trapped, singled out. And they had turned her into an unwilling spy with those council-issued reports. Now she wondered if those same reports would be twisted into evidence against him.

The final flicker of the brand on Lyric's arm lingered in her mind's eye. A mark of complicity, or perhaps a sign that Lyric had risked her own freedom for Kael's sake. The lines between friend and foe had blurred to the point of distortion. Would she confront the infiltration head-on? Would she gather quiet proof in the library, or would she corner Quen with her suspicions? The prospect of each path made her insides coil with dread.

Footsteps echoing in the corridor above jolted her to attention. She caught herself flattening against the wall, her heart pounding. When the sound died away, she resumed her climb, one hand tight on the dagger's hilt, the other pressed to the cold stone for balance.

Kael was in danger, Lyric had warned. Or perhaps he had been all along, from the moment the council singled him out. Alysia remembered how Kael's illusions once flared in the training grounds when he felt cornered, how the academy's rumor mill devoured any hint of wrongdoing. Now, with an infiltration that knew how to manipulate illusions from the inside, the threat was a thousand times worse.

Emerging at last into a dim corridor near Bastion Hall, Alysia felt the pressure ease from her chest as the catacomb's weight receded. She paused by a guttering torch bracket, letting the faint warmth wash over her chilled skin. Part of her demanded she run down every corridor searching for Kael. The other part admonished caution. Something in Lyric's eyes had carried genuine desperation, and that haunted Alysia more than she wanted to admit.

She took one last look at the staircase behind her, half-expecting to see shadows with illusions or to glimpse Lyric standing there. But nothing moved. The only sound was the crackle of the torch. She swallowed, tasting that bitter residue of betrayal again, and continued into the hall, her mind already racing with questions. Whom could she trust? Who was an enemy disguised?

She had secured Lyric's warning, but it felt like stepping onto quicksand. The infiltration's brand and illusions around that underground Gate told her there were layers to this conspiracy she had never imagined. The Academy might be as much a threat to Kael as the infiltration itself, if fear trumped reason. She pressed on, uncertain how to shield him from the storm brewing on all sides.

And though her heart pounded with resolve, the sense

of betrayal burned the back of her throat. She did not know which voices whispered truth and which ones spread lies. Every step forward reminded her that she had no choice but to move quickly. But as she slipped deeper into the corridor's shadowed emptiness, one realization chilled her to the core.

She was no longer sure who the real enemy was anymore.

TWENTY-NINE

SPELL OF UNMAKING

Alysia's footsteps echoed in the damp corridor as she clutched her hand against her chest. The burn on her palm throbbed in time with her pulse, each jolt confirming the power she had just unleashed. Drips of moisture slipped down the vaulted stone walls, and every breath of air felt cold against her clammy skin. She recalled how Lyric had pressed that scroll into her fingers with a look that bordered on desperation. A forbidden tracking charm, she had said. A spell to find lost magic. Alysia wondered if forbidden might have been too mild a term.

She had lingered in the catacombs because Lyric insisted they needed privacy, a place where the prying eyes of Velgrace Academy could not interfere. Torches burned low in iron brackets, casting flickering shadows across Lyric's face. Even before Alysia spoke, Lyric seemed to sense her hesitation.

"Take it," Lyric had whispered, holding out an ancient

scrap of parchment. The edges crackled with leftover wards. "Use the incantation exactly as described, or the backlash might be worse than a burn."

Alysia forced herself to meet Lyric's gaze. Night after night, suspicion had grown between them. She still doubted Lyric's motives, but the mention of Kael, of the infiltration pressing in, tugged at her. If Lyric could truly help her locate the illusions or figure out who intended to trap Kael, then Alysia had no choice but to listen.

She remembered swallowing her fear. "You say it can find lost magic. Is it strong enough to track illusions rooted in forbidden relics?"

Lyric looked at the jagged columns overhead. "It can track more than illusions. But there is a cost. You will feel it for days."

Without waiting for a reply, Lyric moved behind Alysia, guiding her free hand to hover over the parchment. The air stirred with electricity. Alysia read the glyph scrawled in trembling ink: a coiled serpent with a circle around its head. She recognized some of the runes as archaic. The others looked like pure invention, and that scared her more than anything.

"Breathe slowly," Lyric murmured. "Concentrate on who or what you want to find. Then speak the words on the scroll."

Alysia closed her eyes, letting the steady drip from a distant corner calm her nerves. She pictured an elusive collection of illusions that might belong to the infiltration, the twisted sigils she had glimpsed in her room. She thought of Kael too, remembering the times his illusions danced unpredictably, revealing heartbreak he attempted to hide. The infiltration wanted him cornered, or so Lyric claimed. Perhaps this spell could show her the path to protect him.

She exhaled and spoke the incantation. The words left a bitter taste on her tongue, as though she had scooped them from a well of rancid water.

The moment she spoke the incantation, the parchment did not simply burn but dissolved into a stream of crimson ash that burrowed directly into her skin. A scream tore from her throat as searing pain shot up her arm. Every vein felt filled with molten glass. When the agony subsided, a jagged spiral was etched into her flesh, glowing like a fresh wound under the torchlight. It was not a mark but a scar, a brand of forbidden power she could never erase.

It hurt, but not as much as she expected. She flexed her fingers, ignoring the dull ache.

"That is your tether," Lyric said, moving to stand at Alysia's side. "It will let you sense illusions or hidden magic nearby. If you focus, it might show you more."

Alysia studied the scarlet lines. "Spell of Unmaking," she read from the last shred of the scroll. The words seemed to leap out in smoky letters before vanishing.

"Why call it that? This is a tracking spell, not a destruction rite."

Lyric's gaze lowered. "Its name is older than the usage. Some believe it unravels illusions from the inside out, revealing glimpses of their original form. In the wrong hands, it can tear unprotected magic apart. Be careful with it, because you carry the burden now."

Alysia shivered, though the catacombs felt swelteringly close all at once. "I'll manage," she whispered. She wanted answers. She wanted to protect Kael. If this was the only way, she would survive the cost.

Without another word, Lyric turned on her heel and left Alysia alone. The final echo of footsteps lingered in the corridor. Alysia realized that Lyric had said nothing about how to remove the spiral, or if it could be removed at all.

She pressed her left hand against the catacomb wall, inhaling shakily. Exhaustion crept through her bones, but the searing brand pulsed with restless energy. With each throb, she felt a subtle tug, as if the spiral wanted to guide her deeper underground. She resisted and began the long climb back to the main halls.

When she emerged from the catacombs at last, midnight had fallen across Velgrace's courtyard. Moonlight streaked across the flagstones. A breeze carried the scent of salt from the Sea of Echoes. Alysia paused near a worn archway behind Bastion Hall, rubbing her palm idly. No illusions laced the air here, but she sensed the hidden tension that pervaded the academy at night. Ever since the infiltration rumors surfaced, the entire campus felt primed for an ambush.

She reached her dorm tower without seeing a single patrol or staff member, which only raised her suspicions. Usually, Warden Evara Morn scheduled rotating sweeps of the grounds. The infiltration must have forced them to shift their tactics. She wanted to question the staff, to confirm if anyone else had glimpsed rogue illusions tonight, but she knew better than to roam the halls with a throbbing forbidden mark. Already, her mind spun with possibilities.

When she slipped into her dorm room and locked the door, she found Robin waiting, her arms folded tight. The lantern on the desk projected a golden glow across Robin's face, highlighting eyes that burned with anger. Alysia knew that look. Robin had been worried.

"You're playing their game," Robin said in a low, furious voice. She took one step forward, pointing a trembling finger. "I saw you sneak out. I heard rumors that you've been meeting with Lyric. And now you come back like... like this?" She jerked her chin toward Alysia's hand.

"How did you—?" Alysia began. She glanced down. She had forgotten to tuck her injured palm out of sight. The glowing spiral had dimmed, but the red mark remained stark against her skin.

Robin's eyes narrowed, frustration rolling off her in waves. "I was half afraid you were caught in some new ward sabotage. Then I realized you let it happen. Is that mark a brand? A cursed relic? You cannot trust Lyric."

Alysia closed the door behind her. She steadied herself with a breath. "It is a tracking charm. She said it can help me find illusions. Or lost magic. Maybe it can lead me to whoever is controlling the infiltration from the shadows."

Her words sounded hollow even to herself. She rubbed the brand, biting back the rush of pain. Robin raked a hand through her short hair, exasperation coloring every gesture.

"Do you have any idea what you've done?" Robin's voice was shaking with a fury Alysia had rarely seen. "That's not a tracking charm, Alysia, that's a soul-brand! It feeds on the user. Lyric didn't give you a tool, she gave you a poison, and you drank it down without a second thought!"

Alysia tasted bitterness, thinking of Quen's distrust and the council's threats. She had already tried to do things the official way. They cornered her into spying on Kael, then cast suspicion on her every action. She saw no easy route. "They would never let me handle this my way," she said softly. "And I cannot wait around until the infiltration gets further ahead. Lyric was the only one offering me a direct method."

Robin approached, her eyes bright with concern that she tried to mask in sarcasm. "A direct method of self-destruction, maybe. That spiral looks carved into your flesh. Gods above, Alysia, you have never been one for impulsive decisions, and now you do this?"

A flush of anger rose in Alysia's chest. "I am not being impulsive. I need to know who is controlling illusions that can slip through locked doors. If the infiltration can walk into my dorm at midnight, we have no safe place left."

She paused, feeling tears threaten to break. She felt the weight of everything. The brand on her hand. The precarious fate of Kael, who roamed the campus alone. The bitter taste of the council's ultimatum, forcing her into an impossible role. She hated crying when she felt cornered, so she swallowed against that lump in her throat.

Centering herself, she looked at Robin. "We cannot

fight illusions we do not understand. This brand can show me where they come from. Maybe it can reveal Kael's location if he vanishes again." Her voice wavered at the mention of him, but she continued. "I know it is dangerous, but sometimes danger is the only path left."

Robin's expression softened slightly. "I do not want you to lose yourself in black magic. If that brand twists your mind, or if it bleeds your life away, is it worth it?"

Alysia hesitated. "I do not know," she admitted. "But I could not do nothing. Besides, I felt something when the spell took hold." She lifted her marked palm, letting the lantern show the ridged lines of the spiral. "It was like a door opened. I glimpsed a corridor lined with illusions, as if each connected to a hidden thread. It, there was a flicker of someone standing in the distance. Someone who looked like—"

She stopped short, shaking her head. She had not let herself dwell on that figure. Tall, cloaked, features blurred by illusions, yet strangely familiar. Impossible.

Robin's gaze sharpened. "Who did you see?"

Alysia pressed her lips together. "It does not matter," she said, her voice rough. "It might have just been the infiltration playing tricks. Everything about this charm is new to me. I will not jump to conclusions."

Robin let out a slow breath, then set a hand on Alysia's shoulder. "I am mad, but I am also your friend. If you are set on using that twisted magic, I am going to help, whether you want me to or not."

Alysia let out a shaky laugh. The tension in the room felt suffocating, but Robin's concern grounded her. "I would not refuse your help," Alysia said. "I just wanted to protect you from dealing with more illusions."

Robin snorted. "You do realize you never were good at handling everything alone, right? That is what I am here for. To remind you that you do not have to carry the entire weight of your name or Kael's fate or the infiltration by yourself."

The knot in her chest loosened, and a small smile curved her lips. She set her bag aside. The brand still throbbed, though. She peered at it in the lamplight. "Lyric called it a burden. It does not seem to be fading. Do you think it will last?"

Robin frowned. "I cannot say. Maybe we can check an advanced healing text in the library tomorrow, or talk to Magister Belros Dain. He might know of illusions that brand themselves into flesh."

Alysia nodded. "You are right. For now, I should put a ward on it to keep it from activating unexpectedly." She moved to her desk, rummaging for a small pot of salve and a piece of chalk. She scrawled a simple warding circle on a scrap of parchment, pressing her palm against it. The spiral warmed, then settled to a dull glow.

She exhaled with relief. At least it would not flare up in the middle of the night or alert the infiltration if they had some way to sense it. She still burned with the memory of the corridor she had glimpsed while the scroll's magic took hold. The sense of impossible recognition had shaken her.

Robin watched in silence, her arms crossed. "We can fix this," she said softly, though her eyes still carried worry. "You have me. You do not have to fight a war on your own."

Alysia was grateful. The day had felt endless. Anxiety coiled around her like a second skin. Even the quiet glow of the desk lantern offered limited comfort. But standing there with Robin, she felt a flicker of hope. The infiltration was dangerous, cunning, and unrelenting... yet Alysia was tired of being the hunted.

She closed her eyes for a moment. The hum of magic in the dorm's wards buzzed at the fringes of her awareness. Her brand tingled again, but this time it did not sting as badly. She remembered Lyric's words: It can track more than illusions. It might show you more. A part of her wanted to seal it away forever, but her desire to uncover the infiltration's secrets felt stronger.

Finally, Robin cleared her throat, her voice quiet. "Get some rest. Tomorrow we can talk about how to use that brand safely, if that is even possible."

Alysia shuddered. "Thank you," she said. She heard Robin's footsteps retreat to the door. Before leaving, her cousin paused.

"Promise me one thing. Do not let your fear or desperation push you too far. Whoever is behind this infiltration I will help you bring them down. Just remember who you are. You are not Lyric, not Kael, not anyone else. You are Alysia Thorne, the most stubborn ward-weaver I know."

A wry smile bent Alysia's mouth. "I promise I will try to remember."

With a final nod, Robin left, lantern light flickering in her wake. Alone, Alysia sank onto the edge of her narrow bed. Her dorm felt suffocatingly tiny tonight. She removed her boots, set them aside, then studied her palm again. The spiral's glow dimmed to a faint pulse, much like a heartbeat under the skin.

She reached for a thin quilt to drape around her shoulders. The night air drifting in from her window carried the tang of sea salt and distant breezes. She wanted to drift off, to let her exhausted mind rest, but every time she closed her eyes, she remembered the corridor of illusions, and that figure in the distance.

All the colors had twisted around them, part of an echo she did not understand.

She had never seen illusions that vivid outside Kael's conjurations, but the presence felt older than him, more ruthless. The moment she tried to focus, the vision vanished, leaving her with a nauseating sense of unreality. The infiltration might be tied to that figure, or it might be something altogether worse.

Lyric claimed the brand could guide her to the infiltration's secrets, but what if it guided her straight into a trap? The possibility weighed on her. Yet the alternative was waiting for Velgrace's wards to fail. She was done waiting.

She picked up a small mirror from her desk, tilting it so she could see her face in the faint light. Shadows circled her hazel eyes. Strands of dark hair fell loose from her braid, an unruly halo around her tired features. She placed her hand against the mirror's glass, letting the brand reflect back in a distorted shape. An uninvited fear crept in. What if this mark changed her?

She set the mirror aside, drawing the quilt closer. The

night felt too loud, the darkness too deep. She inhaled slowly, forcing herself to focus. Lyric had given her a tool, however dangerous. Robin had offered her unwavering loyalty. Somewhere on campus, Kael remained in the crosshairs of illusions that threatened to twist blame onto him.

She touched the spiral brand again, half-hoping it would spark a vision that explained everything. Searing pain jolted her, but with it came a whisper of that corridor. For the briefest second, she saw something else: scorched runes around the silhouette of a figure with eyes like molten silver. She sensed longing, rage, and the intangible echo of powerful illusions.

Then it was gone, leaving her breathless. She sank back, her palm tingling where the brand lay. The edges of the spiral glowed faintly, as though acknowledging her attempt to reach out. Her heart hammered. She had seen illusions before, but never a glimpse of such raw emotion from an unknown presence. This was not simply about infiltration anymore.

She wrapped herself in the quilt and lay back on the bed, letting the tension ride through her limbs. Sleep would be scarce, but she needed to rest if she hoped to function in class tomorrow. Besides, she had to stay alert in case the brand decided to flare unexpectedly.

In that quiet space, she tried to calm her mind by thinking of simpler days, days before Kael's illusions, before the infiltration, before the weight of her family's legacy pressed on her shoulders. She remembered studying the basics of ward-weaving on the cliff's edge near Bastion Hall, letting the sea's roar fill her ears. She felt a pang of nostalgia, then realized how far she had come. She was not the uncertain girl from a year ago. She had learned to stand her ground, to fight for those she cared about, to shape wards capable of shielding entire courtyards.

But tonight, everything felt precarious again. That forbidden charm glowed on her hand, a constant reminder that she was dabbling in a realm of magic the academy would never endorse. Robin's words haunted her. "Do not lose yourself to this."

She turned her face into the pillow, exhaling shakily. The brand's faint hum reverberated in her bones, catching every flicker of her heartbeat. A thousand questions churned in her mind, no answers forthcoming. She let her eyes close for only a moment.

Visions returned at once. This time, she saw watery illusions. A silver-eyed shadow flickered at the center. She sensed a complicated yearning in that silhouette, a push and pull that made her soul quake. The brand seared with an intensity that sent shocks through her entire arm. She tried to will it away, but the image persisted, so clear that it felt more real than any dream.

Then, in an abrupt shimmer, the illusions collapsed into darkness, and she almost thought she heard her name echo in the void. A raw shudder dispelled the vision, leaving her sprawled on the bed, her heart pounding. She pressed her hand together, forcibly clenching her fingers to break the memory.

She whispered to the empty room, "What are you

showing me?" Her voice trembled, lost under the hum of the wards. No reply came. Only the complaint of an old dormitory window rattling in the wind.

She knew one truth. The brand's power was real, and it answered to her call whether she felt ready or not. She dreaded the cost. Yet the lure of discovering who or what lurked behind those illusions pulled at her with a force she could not deny.

Outside, a gull cried overhead, then faded into night. Within, the solitary lantern flickered, and Alysia's palm glowed bright again. She closed her eyes and surrendered to the restless pull, determined to find what stoked it.

In that final stretch of half-sleep, she recalled the corridor of illusions once more. The figure in the distance was not only an illusion. It felt too solid, too tangible, like someone she should recognize but could not name. The brand pulsed, and she saw a flash of impossible recognition in the haze, the glint of silver eyes that were not Kael's but achingly familiar, and a throne made of shadow and regret. It was a memory of a king, ancient and broken, and it felt like it was her own. Her throat tightened with confusion.

Yet amid the fear, a strange possibility buoyed her. If the brand could reveal hidden truths, if it really could track illusions to their source, then maybe she was one crucial step closer to protecting Kael from the infiltration and proving his innocence. She needed only to endure the pain, and trust she would not unravel in the process.

Alysia shivered under her quilt, alone in the dorm, her hand stinging with new life. She could practically hear

Robin's warning in her head, urging her not to give herself over to the game Lyric might be playing. But it was already far too late to turn back. She felt the brand's influence under her skin, beckoning her to push deeper.

Her eyes fluttered shut at last, and the image of that silver-eyed silhouette drifted through her mind, entwined with illusions she could neither name nor dismiss. The brand had pierced her reality, forging a link to lost magic that dwarfed anything she had seen before.

She wanted to deny it, to call it a trick. But the memory clung with haunting clarity, etched as firmly as the spiral on her flesh. She knew, with a sinking certainty, that the charm was not just a path to knowledge. It was a key to something deeper and more dangerous than she had imagined.

And even as fear coiled through her, so did a strange sense of wonder, because the spell had shown her something impossible.

THIRTY

A MEMORY NOT YOURS

Alysia pressed her back against the sturdy door of her dorm room. She had locked it moments ago, but the click of metal did nothing to quiet the churn of thoughts inside her head. Her hand throbbed in time with her heartbeat, the spiraling burn bright against her palm. It was the mark Lyric had pressured her to accept, the forbidden charm that was supposed to lead her to hidden magic. Now, it felt as though the magic had found her first.

She drew in a careful breath. Her sleep shift and dressing gown did little to warm her, and the evening air carried a salty chill through the narrow window. A single lantern flickered on her desk, dancing shadows across the stack of ward manuals she had neglected to tidy. For a moment, she considered snuffing out the lantern and slipping into bed, pretending none of this had ever happened. Yet the violent glow under her skin reminded her there was no escaping the power she had awakened.

She slid down to the floor, resting her back against the wooden frame of her bed. Her legs felt unsteady, half-numb from the run back here after leaving the catacombs. That damp underground corridor had been oppressive, full of twisting illusions, but at least she had not been alone. Now that the door was shut, she had no one left to face the brand except herself.

She swallowed hard as the burn pulsed again. She remembered how Lyric had told her the charm might reveal illusions or forbidden truths. She also remembered how Robin's eyes flashed with anger when she returned, urging her not to lose herself in dark magic. It was too late for regrets and half-measures. The brand had already anchored itself to her.

Her gaze darted toward the small circular mirror propped on her nightstand. She could see the reflection of her hand, faint red lines coiling over her skin like an other-worldly tattoo. When her pulse quickened, the lines brightened, turning the spiral into something alive. Carefully, Alysia traced the pattern with her free fingers. Heat radiated from its center until it seemed to sear straight into her bones.

She gasped softly as a flash of light tore across her vision. She squeezed her eyes shut. The dorm room didn't just fall away; it was violently ripped from her senses. The brand on her palm seized control, forcing images into her mind with a dizzying, nauseating pull. This wasn't her memory. It was an echo, a psychic scar, and it was dragging her into its depths against her will.

Her breath caught. She had experienced illusions

before, especially around Kael, but this was different. The magic seemed to be burrowing into her mind, unsteady yet insistent, prying open a memory that did not belong to her.

She pushed the heel of her free hand against her temple. "Stop," she muttered through clenched teeth, though part of her wanted to let the vision unfold. She had to know what this charm was trying to show her. If it held secrets about Kael, about the infiltration, about the illusions moving through Velgrace, she could not turn away.

Gradually, the blurred shapes sharpened into a scene. She saw a dimly lit chamber with stone walls that seemed older than any she had walked in. A single torch cast flickering light across the floor. In that pool of illumination stood a woman. She wore a simple robe, pale in color, and her dark hair was braided with slender chains. A gentle smile curved her lips. The woman's eyes. Alysia's breath stuttered. They weren't just similar to her own; they were the exact shade of hazel unique to the Thorne line of ward-weavers. And on the woman's wrist, glinting in the torchlight, was a silver bracelet identical to the one Alysia wore now.

It felt impossible. Yet the resemblance was so strong that Alysia's stomach flipped in recognition. She tried to move in the vision, to step closer, but realized with a jolt that she had no body here. She was more an observer than a participant.

Her hated brand flared hot, tearing her attention to the stone altar at the center of the space. A small child, no older than three, stood there. He had rumpled dark hair and wide eyes as grey as a storm. Releasing a tiny, halting breath, he stared at the woman with shy curiosity. A raw ache settled over Alysia's chest. She knew those eyes. Even in miniature, they were Kael's.

The child's thin shoulders shook with a tremor, unsure of his surroundings. The woman bent down and brushed a gentle hand over the boy's head. Her voice, low and soothing, whispered words Alysia could not fully make out. She tried to listen, straining for the sound, but only fragments reached her: illusions... connecting... chosen...

Alysia's heart pounded, her own mouth dry. The child-Kael took a hesitant step forward, confusion filling his gaze. He wore a small leather band around his wrist, similar to a warding bracelet, but it glowed with faint illusions rather than runic wards. The woman placed her palms lightly on his shoulders, guiding him toward the arc of magic behind them. The illusions reminded Alysia of certain archaic creation spells she had once read about in her grandmother's notes, the kind that bridged realms. Except these illusions felt wilder, as if they drew power from a deeper source, perhaps older than the academy's wards.

Then the child turned his head, and Alysia's breath caught. She could see a gentle purple light shimmering behind his eyes, reminiscent of the illusions Kael often summoned. The sense of seeing him so vulnerable made her chest tighten. She realized, with a pang that left her dizzy, this was more than a stray memory. This was a pivotal moment in Kael's life. And somehow, her brand had dragged her inside it.

The woman leaned close to the child's ear and murmured something softly. Though Alysia could not hear the words, she sensed reverence in the woman's tone, as if this moment marked a grand offering. Slowly, almost ceremonially, the little boy was led into the center of the illusions. The presence of that woman, this older figure with Alysia's own shade of eyes, simmered with a quiet power that made Alysia's spine tingle.

A loud clang yanked her back into awareness. In her room, the little mirror on the nightstand toppled off its wooden stand. She blinked, disoriented, cold sweat trickling down her neck. Her dorm walls rushed into clarity. The vision threatened to slip away. She clamped her marked palm more tightly, her nails digging into her skin, desperate to hold onto every detail.

It was too late. The memory receded like a wave withdrawing from shore, leaving her alone once more on the dorm floor. Her breathing felt ragged, her pulse hammering. She lifted her hand to the lantern's light, staring at the brand. It still glowed faintly, as if mocking her.

She whispered, almost accusingly, "What did I just see?"

No reply came. The brand offered no second vision. Outside, the sea wind gusted against the stone tower walls. She heard the distant call of gulls, nocturnal cries echoing far below. Tremors ran through her fingers, and she pressed her palm to her chest, willing her heartbeat to slow.

Kael... as a child. She replayed the glimpses in her mind, his inquisitive grey eyes peering at that robed woman. That woman's features so eerily similar to Alysia's own lineage. The more she thought of it, the more it frightened her. Had it been her mother? Or an ancestor? Her grandmother's notes had never hinted at anything so personal, yet the possibility gnawed at her. And the memory suggested that Kael's presence at Velgrace was no accident.

Her teeth set on edge, she braced her arms on her knees, fighting a sudden swell of guilt. Kael had told her, more than once, that his illusions sometimes felt like they carried an ancient echo. She had always dismissed it as a metaphor, something about his Meridan lineage. Now, she realized there might be more. The brand on her palm was bridging parts of their past that had been kept hidden, by time, by illusions, or by fear.

She forced herself to stand, though her legs wobbled. She paced a slow circle around her cramped room, passing her desk strewn with half-rolled scrolls and a worn ward manual. Her stomach churned. Could everything about Kael's arrival at the academy be bound to a plan older than both of them? The woman's quiet smile in the vision had been tinged with a sadness Alysia could not decipher. She tried to recall the shape of those lips, the angle of that gaze.

The memory implied that Kael had been...offered up? By that woman's own hand? Why would anyone do that to a small child? Even more unsettling was the undeniable sense that Alysia's own magic had triggered the final step in a much older puzzle. If Kael was chosen, it meant someone had set him on this path long before she ever arrived at Velgrace or fumbled that summoning attempt in the library.

Her mind reeled, trying to escape the single, terrifying conclusion. That woman, a Thorne, her ancestor, had not been comforting the child-Kael. She had been preparing him. Offering him to ancient, dangerous magic. The summoning in the library had never been an accident. It was the final, echoing step in a ritual set in motion generations ago. And Alysia, in her desperation to pass an exam, had unknowingly completed it.

She ran a hand over her face. It felt warm and clammy, laced with the residue of the charm's power. A thousand questions buzzed in her skull. She remembered the catacombs earlier, when Lyric hinted that illusions ran deeper than the academy ever guessed. Now, Alysia wondered if Lyric had known about this memory all along. Perhaps even wanted her to discover it. That possibility twisted her gut with anger at being manipulated, but it also sparked curiosity. If Lyric thought that unearthing these hidden truths could keep Kael safe, maybe the brand and the vision were part of a bigger scheme.

She cast a glance at the closed door, half-expecting a knock. Nobody came. Not Robin, not Lyric, not Kael. She was alone with her new knowledge. She returned to the foot of her bed, lowering herself carefully as if the floor might shift beneath her. Her gaze dropped to the brand once again, and she whispered, "Show me more." Silence answered. The spiral glimmered faintly, but no illusions rose to claim her senses.

She clutched a pillow, pressing her face into the fabric.

The pillow smelled faintly of chamomile from the sachet she had placed there, a small comfort against nightmares. This new revelation felt far beyond any typical nightmare. Kael was not just the boy who trespassed into her carefully warded life. If the memory was accurate, he had been singled out, guided by illusions older than the academy itself. Possibly guided by someone tied to her bloodline. The thought twisted alarmingly close to fate, and she hated attributing anything to fate. She preferred to believe that if the brand had forged a bond between them, it was a bond she chose to use for good, not something forced upon her by secrets older than she could fathom.

Yet the memory refused to leave. She could almost see that woman again, the softness of her expression, the gentle placement of her hands on the boy's shoulders. Alysia recalled the moment in the library when Kael told her illusions were more than conjurations. They could hold entire echoes of the past. Seeing that child-Kael made her realize illusions could serve as windows into histories no one else remembered.

Her eyes stung. She blinked fiercely, refusing to cry. She had no proof, no tangible piece of that memory to show anyone. Just images carved into her mind the way the spiral was carved onto her hand. Was there a record of that event in the academy archives? Did her grandmother ever speak of an ancient ritual involving a child of illusions? Each unknown tightened the vise on her chest.

She inhaled until the tension eased slightly. Then she moved to her desk, rummaging until she found a small piece of scrap parchment and a half-used chalk stick. Her fingers shook, but she forced them to draw. She sketched the rough shape of the woman's face: the slope of her cheekbones, the narrow nose, the braided hair draped over one shoulder. She left the eyes for last, uncertain if she could capture them. When at last she attempted it, she accidentally pressed too hard, snapping the chalk in two. A frustrated sigh escaped her. She set the broken chalk aside, then rubbed her temple. Maybe this was foolish. A half-drawn face would not grant her the answers she craved.

Instead, she wrote three words across the parchment in rushed script: illusions, chosen, anchor. She did not know why those three words felt important, but they rang in her memory. A faint echo from the vision, or perhaps a guess at what was truly happening. Grueling exhaustion settled in her limbs as she stared at the brand glowing on her palm. Despite her fear, she felt a tiny flicker of wonder. She had glimpsed Kael's past, something he might not remember himself. The child in that memory had looked trusting and afraid in equal measure. He was offered to illusions, but for what purpose?

Alysia set the parchment aside, blowing out a sharp breath. Her mind whirled, grappling with one last revelation from the vision. Kael had been chosen not by happenstance or error, but by a magic that recognized him as special. And if that woman with familiar eyes was truly connected to Alysia's bloodline, it suggested that Alysia's summoning mishap in the library had never been accidental. Maybe, in some twisted design or prophecy, it was always meant to happen.

Her chest tightened, and she lifted her gaze to the narrow window. The moon hung outside, pale and watchful. She felt the brand's gentle warmth flicker on her palm, as if it sought to confirm her thoughts. A subtle whisper ghosted through her mind, tugging at a truth she could no longer ignore. Kael was never simply summoned. He was selected by illusions that reached far beyond her normal scope of magic. And that meant he was bound to her, or she to him, long before she uttered that first incantation.

She pressed a trembling hand to her mouth. The dorm room weighed on her, pressing her toward a realization that rattled her soul. She closed her eyes, letting the final echo of the vision settle in her memory. The child, so small, stepping into illusions without fully understanding why. The woman's calm, bittersweet smile. The sense that powerful forces had quietly shifted, forging a link between Kael and the Thorne line.

Quietly, Alysia murmured into the stillness, "You were chosen, Kael. By magic. And maybe…" Her breath shook. She let the words linger, finishing them in her heart. And maybe chosen by me.

The brand pulsed in soft answer, and she knew there was no going back.

THIRTY-ONE

THE MIDNIGHT GATE

Alysia moved quietly through the damp corridor, every footstep echoing against the stone. The glow of her forbidden brand pulsed beneath the bandage around her palm, drawing her forward with insistent little tugs. She had not planned on another reckless excursion into the catacombs, much less in the dead of night, but dread curled in her stomach, impossible to ignore. If Kael truly was in danger, then she could not stand idle in her dorm room like a frightened child.

Salt-tinged air drifted through occasional cracks in the walls. The Sea of Echoes lay not far beyond these chambers, hidden by sprawling labyrinths of tunnel and stone. She had learned to navigate these twisting corridors recently, though her heart still pounded whenever a torch sputtered or cast jumping shadows. Tonight, the flicker of her own conjured light guided her more reliably than the torch brackets. Her magic produced a pale, wavering orb that hovered a stride ahead, illuminating the cramped path.

She stopped at a narrow archway where a faint hum vibrated through the air. The hair on her neck prickled. Dimly, she heard chanting. Cloaked shapes danced in her vision, behind her eyelids whenever she blinked. She felt the brand's heat intensify, like a heartbeat pulsing faster with every fresh wave of tension.

The corridor ended at a massive, rune-etched door. Something metallic hissed along the edges, as if ward-based energies were gradually weakening. She ran trembling fingers over the runes. In class, she had studied the intricacies of layered wards, but these inscriptions were older, wilder. She found no immediate sense of logic in them. Her brand, on the other hand, responded all too eagerly.

She inhaled, recalling how Robin had warned her that diving into the catacombs alone might be exactly what a manipulator wanted. With her free hand, she tugged at the small pouch containing her warding chalk and whispered a rudimentary stabilizing incantation. The brand flared in protest. The synergy she wanted to create felt precarious, as if the brand had its own opinions on how to proceed.

The door rumbled. She pressed her palm to it, letting the runes in her mind align with the living pattern in her flesh. Her brand burned hotter, and a bright red sigil glowed through the bandage. Crimson light spread across the surface of the door, and for an instant, the entire hallway lit up. The door gave a weary groan, then parted with a thunderous crack.

Alysia braced herself. Cold air rushed out from the open chamber, brushing her face in an unsettling caress. She turned her conjured orb of light into the darkness, forcing her feet to move forward. The brand guided her now, a relentless siren call that demanded she keep going.

She emerged into a wide, circular vault known by rumor as the Gate chamber. She had visited a smaller portion of these catacombs before, but this area felt older than the rest. Ancient pillars ringed a raised dais in the center, carved with loops reminiscent of illusions. Atop the dais stood an arch that crackled with faint arcs of red-gold energy. A wave of dizziness washed over her, as if the air had turned heavier. Her sigil flared in time with the arch's pulses, each throb hitting her nerves like a drumbeat.

Ill-lit braziers flickered around the perimeter, their flames tinted in strange hues of violet and dark amber. Cloaked figures circled the dais, joining hands in a silent ritual. At the far end of the ring, a slight figure, tall and graceful, broke away from the rest. Her hood slipped back to reveal the sharp lines of her face. Alysia's stomach twisted. It was Lyric Meridan, Kael's sister.

Alysia's eyes darted around, searching for Kael. He was not among the circle. She swallowed the knot in her throat, letting her conjured orb float higher to reveal more of the dais. No sign of him anywhere. The brand's heat made her grit her teeth. Anxiety chewed at every rational thought.

She advanced. "Where is he?" she demanded. Her voice reverberated, sending faint echoes along the chamber walls. The cloaked figures did not speak, did not so much as shift their stance, but she sensed their combined magic prickling her senses.

Lyric stepped closer. Her posture radiated careful control, as if she balanced on the edge of sympathy and something darker. "You should not be here alone, Alysia," Lyric murmured, quiet enough that the other robed figures could not overhear. "We decided to summon you, but you have arrived sooner than anticipated."

"Summon me?" Alysia struggled to keep her tone steady. "I received no direct message. Only an urge from this brand." She lifted her bandaged hand, though the glow was obvious even through the fabric. "You said Kael was in danger if we did not act. Where is he? And what have you all done with these wards?"

Lyric looked at the shimmering arch. "He is not here. But the Gate is."

Alysia's pulse hammered. She glanced at the dais more closely. The arch was carved from smooth black stone, set with small, half-embedded runic shards that glowed faintly. She recognized the shape from scattered references in the academy's older texts: a gate rumored to bridge illusions and reality. Or so the legends claimed. She never dreamed she would stand in front of the real thing, especially not under the watchful eyes of robed strangers.

She took another step, forcing her legs to remain steady. "What Gate is this? And how does it relate to Kael?" Her voice shook despite her best efforts. The brand throbbing in her palm made it hard to think. One of the cloaked figures spoke, their voice distorted by some concealing spell. "The Gate that merges illusions with the mortal realm," the figure said in a low monotone. "We have awakened it. Your brand resonates with the energy that fuels it."

Another figure chimed in. "It was supposed to be used the night you conjured the boy. Kael was never meant to appear by chance."

Alysia's entire body tensed. "What do you mean I was never meant—" She cut off, reeling as realization sparked. She thought her earlier incantation in the library had simply gone awry. She had told herself that the bizarre summoning was a mishap she must shoulder alone. But if these robed individuals believed otherwise, it meant something else overshadowed everything she knew. The brand on her skin pulsed sharply, as if to confirm that a piece of the truth had just emerged from the shadows.

She stared at Lyric, whose eyes shone with a sort of quiet sorrow. "Where is Kael, Lyric?" Alysia repeated, her voice breaking on the last syllable. "You said he was in danger. You told me to come here. Was that a lie? Or is this entire arrangement some twisted attempt to manipulate me again?"

Lyric's gaze flickered to the Gate. "We needed you to see it for yourself. Kael holds illusions that transcend what normal wards can contain. This Gate has everything to do with why he was chosen." "He's not a prisoner, if that is what you fear. The infiltration is deeper than one captive boy. And our goal is not to harm him."

"Speak plainly," Alysia snapped. Her brand ached like a fresh wound. She forced down the sting of tears. The images from her earlier vision, Kael as a child, offered up by a woman with eyes like hers, crowded her mind.

Lyric searched Alysia's face, then motioned for the robed figures to lower their hands. They stilled, though the arch continued humming with dull waves of light. "I can't speak all truths here with so many ears listening," Lyric said softly. "But believe me, Kael's path was put in motion before we ever arrived at Velgrace. The infiltration seized upon that path and twisted it for their own goals. If you keep following the brand's pull, you will discover every piece of the puzzle you never wanted to see."

Alysia's lip curled in frustration. "I would rather confront a painful truth than remain blind, especially if it means saving him."

A ripple of reaction moved through the circle. Some cloaked figures shifted. Others nodded as if they had expected that answer. The brand flared in response, and Alysia felt the Gate's energy intensify, throbbing in tandem with her pulse.

Lyric stepped back, raising her voice for all to hear. "Begin the next phase of readiness," she ordered. "Make sure the illusions remain stable. We cannot risk a collapse now."

As the cloaked figures obeyed, Alysia tried to glean more details from the magic. The dais's runes seemed to coil around the edges of the arch, forming incomplete lines that needed something else to unite them, perhaps part of a final incantation. She studied the shapes. It reminded her of the brand's spiral pattern. The parallel made her skin itch.

"Why would you build a Gate in secrecy?" she asked, her voice thin. "Velgrace has always confiscated anything that might open unchecked passage for illusions. Headmistress Quen would never—"

Lyric's expression tightened. "The headmistress does not know. None of the official staff do. Our circle formed to find answers that Velgrace officialdom refused to acknowledge. When a relic or a brand can unravel illusions from the inside, you can either bury it, or you can learn how to wield it. We chose knowledge."

Alysia recalled the night she burned her hand with that forbidden scroll Lyric had given her. The memory still stung with betrayal. Yet she saw no open malevolence in Lyric's face. Only a desperate determination, mirrored by the silent watchers around them.

One robed figure, presumably a mage, raised a hand. An arc of illusions glimmered along the dais, forming a translucent net that shimmered across the Gate. The net flickered purple and gold before settling into a steady shape. It almost looked like a door within the larger arch, waiting for a spark to finalize it.

Alysia's heart thumped. "Finish what, precisely?" she asked, stepping toward the dais. "You keep talking about illusions and how Kael's presence was never random. But you're ignoring the question that matters most. Where is he right now? We came so close to losing him before. I won't let you dangle cryptic half-truths when his life might be at stake."

Lyric inclined her head slightly. "Kael is beyond the next threshold, dealing with illusions that only he can subdue. You do not realize how close you came to forging a bond with him that day in the library, the day of your so called mishap. But miscasting that incantation changed everything. The ritual was meant to bind the Meridan anchor, Kael, to the Thorne conduit, you," Lyric explained, her voice sharp with ancient frustration. "Their combined synergy was the key to unlocking the Gate safely. Instead, your spell misfired. It did not forge the bond, it ripped him through the veil. You summoned the lock, but you left the key behind."

Alysia's skin prickled at the word echo. It conjured the memory of watery illusions she had seen in her dreams, Kael's figure flickering but unreachable. She advanced another careful step. The net of illusions shimmered an arm's length away, and she could feel the tang of static energy on her face. "Centuries of planning," she echoed, her voice cracking. "That can't be real. Nobody plans events across centuries, not even Velgrace's founders."

"If you understood the Meridan lineage, you'd see it is entirely possible," Lyric murmured. Her eyes snapped to the brand on Alysia's hand. "Your summoning tried to reawaken an old route meant for illusions far more powerful than what we see in simple parlor tricks. Instead, you brought Kael here alone. Now that your brand has matured, the Gate calls to you."

Alysia pressed her bandaged palm against her thigh, trying to ground herself. The color from the illusions made the air shimmer. The robed circle around the dais intensified their chanting, soft but resonant. It tugged at her insides like a hollow echo, as though part of her recognized the melody.

She felt that same creeping sense of dread she had experienced in every dream since first tasting the brand's power. Perhaps the infiltration was only a fraction of something far larger. Perhaps her entire life had been arranged around a single, masterful design. Her mind whirled. The brand's flame licked at her palm, and the Gate's arcs spat sparks into the stale air.

"Stop," she whispered, stepping backward. Her breath caught in her throat. "I don't want to see more illusions tonight. I only want Kael. I want him safe, and I want us to stand on our own terms."

A faint, sad smile tugged at Lyric's lips. She looked at one final robed figure, who let out a long sigh. Then she raised her gaze to Alysia. "I once thought the same. I believed we could control our destinies without acknowledging the old spells. But some magic is older, hungrier than mortal will. Either we accept it or we become its prey."

Her words settled like a warning. Alysia's eyes darted to the dais, the net of illusions, and back to Lyric. "If you want me to accept that Kael's entire existence here was part of some grand scheme, then prove it. Show me a path to him."

Lyric did not move for a moment. Then she lifted her hand to the dais, her fingertips brushing the illusions along the arch. A low hum coursed through the chamber, and the circle of robed figures parted to let her pass. She stepped onto the raised platform, beckoning Alysia with a solemn, almost reluctant gesture.

The brand on Alysia's hand throbbed, compelling her forward. With each step, the tension in the air coiled tighter. The chanting wove in and out like a living melody, pressing against her eardrums. She climbed onto the dais, her boots scuffing over runes older than any wards she had studied. She stopped just short of the illusions, her breath catching at the back of her throat.

The arcs of energy parted slightly, leaving a narrow opening. She could not see into the Gate, only the magic that seemed to stretch beyond mortal space. She touched her bandage, tempted to rip it away so the brand could feed her clarity. But fear won out. She kept the wrapping in place.

Lyric stood beside her, close enough that Alysia smelled the faint metallic tang of conjurations. Lyric's voice dropped to an almost tender note. "You were never meant to summon him," she said, quite clearly. "You were meant to finish the spell."

Alysia felt her world tilt under her feet. She stared at the open Gate, all its illusions, and the chanting circle. She felt the brand pounding like a second heartbeat. Every suspicion, every fear, crashed into her. She remembered the corridor of illusions from her earliest vision, the figure in the distance, the sense of an older destiny forging her steps. If Kael had not been the final element of that spell, who or what truly was?

Her throat constricted. The red glow of the moon filtered into the chamber through a crack high overhead, bathing everything in a faint, bloody light. She tasted iron on her tongue, perhaps from biting her lip, or perhaps from the illusions around them. Lyric regarded her, her eyes half-lidded, as if bracing for an outburst.

Alysia whispered, "What spell?" But she scarcely recognized her own voice. Danger shivered against her skin. Had her entire life been shaped by someone else's incantation?

Lyric's gaze swept across the dais. She said nothing more, only let the Gate's energy speak for her. Alysia's stomach churned. If finishing this ancient working meant unraveling every truth she clung to, then she was on the cusp of betrayal and revelations alike.

She could not stop trembling. Her brand flared painfully. The chanting soared to a crescendo around the dais, muffling every rational thought. Dimly, she realized the illusions were reaching for her, beckoning her forward as if to complete a circle left open for centuries. Her heart thundered in her chest. She was certain that if she were to step inside that arch, something irreparable would happen.

Lyric slid her gaze back to Alysia and finished with quiet finality, "You were meant to finish the spell."

Alysia's world tilted on its axis. What spell? What truth had been warped for so long that her entire life now stood on false foundations?

CHAPTER

THIRTY-TWO

CHARM REVERSAL

Alysia's heart pounded as she faced the Gate that rose in the center of the underground chamber. Hooded figures ringed the dais in a silent circle, their cloaks shifting with every pulse of arcane energy. The hiss of magic hung in the stagnant air, heavy with an almost metallic scent. Wind should not exist in the catacombs, yet a strange current ruffled her hair. She tasted salt on her lip and realized she was sweating.

She could not ignore the Gate's incessant hum. Twisting arcs of crimson light flickered along the black stone arch, making the runic shards embedded in it flash erratically. It was a worn relic, older than the academy's known wards. She had read scraps about it in half-burnt documents, enough to guess its destructive potential. Now, the illusions and wards linking her brand to this monstrous portal confirmed one truth: the rogue mages intended to harness her personal sigil as a key to open whatever dreadful realm lay beyond.

"Steady," Alysia told herself, glancing at her bandaged palm. The spiral mark beneath that wrapping throbbed, resonating with the Gate's pulses. "This is what they wanted from you from the beginning. Don't lose focus now."

Three robed figures emerged from behind the dais, their faces hidden in the low torchlight. They glided forward with synchronized steps, chanting under their breaths. One figure's hood slid back, revealing the angular cheekbones of a woman Alysia faintly recognized from older references, someone who might have been an instructor years ago. That woman stretched a hand toward Alysia, her nails shining with the faint glow of illusions dancing across the dais.

"The Gate craves your brand," the woman said softly, her deep voice carrying through. "Its wards cannot fully awaken without a living sigil. You will serve as our catalyst."

Alysia's throat tightened. Every instinct demanded she recoil. Yet the scalding heat under her bandage refused to let her retreat. She felt tendrils of power probe at her brand, slithering through her defenses like serpents. Threads of illusions looped around her wrist, winding upward with a mesmerizing glow.

"You can fight, or you can embrace it," another robed mage murmured. "If you assist us, we can show you the future you crave."

Alysia clenched her jaw. Their promises reeked of manipulation. She thought of all the illusions unleashed by these conspirators: stolen ward-stones, half-burnt tokens, endless infiltration attempts. They had cornered her here by invoking Kael's safety and by stirring her own hunger for knowledge. She fought a wave of anger. Yes, she wanted to understand the brand, but not at the cost of delivering Velgrace into the hands of traitors.

She lifted her gaze to the Gate's flickering arch. Energy licked the walls, brightening the catacomb's shadows with crimson slashes. A violent crackle erupted at the top, and she jumped back, her heartbeat racing. Stones from the vaulted ceiling threatened to shake loose, rattling dust along the edges.

"Do it," one of the robed men urged, thrusting his palm out. Magic coiled around his hand and slithered toward her.

Alysia's eyes darted to the illusions forming a ring around the dais. If she let their magic bind her, they would drain her brand's power. The entire Gate might surge to full strength, unleashing something far worse than illusions. She swallowed a rising knot of dread and forced her voice to remain level.

"You're toying with an ancient relic you barely control," she said, stepping carefully across the stone floor. "You have no idea how many lives you risk losing."

An echoing laugh rose from the circle. One figure jerked her hood aside, revealing a twisted smile. "What is spilled today pales compared to the heights we will reach when your sigil powers the Gate. Creation is always born from chaos. Stand still, child."

Her pulse hammered. The brand on her palm burned bright, and she felt the tether to the Gate intensify. She realized her time to act was shrinking by the second. Already, the illusions tugged at her arms as if drawing her forward in slow increments. The robed circle began chanting in unison. With every syllable, the chamber's temperature spiked until sweat rolled down Alysia's neck and trickled along her temple.

She thought of Kael, his grey eyes full of secrets, and the fleeting moments of honesty they had shared. He was absent now, missing from this circle of conspirators. Perhaps that was a blessing, but she would have given anything for his illusions to reinforce her wards. She tasted bitterness, recalling how Lyric had hinted at grand designs centuries in the making. Designs that might have demanded Alysia's brand and Kael's illusions. It was maddening. She had so little time to puzzle out who had orchestrated everything. Right now, her only goal was to stop the rogue faction from completing this twisted ceremony.

The Gate flared, spitting arcs of red-gold light across the dais. A surge of heat exploded at its center. The cloaked mages around it raised their arms, channeling the energy toward Alysia's trembling hand.

"Stop," she gasped, trying to yank her wrist away. Illusory coils slid like snakes around her forearm. They bit into her flesh despite having no real physical form. The line between illusions and reality blurred under the chamber's smoldering lights. Each robed figure fed power into the Gate, and she felt the magic converge on her brand as if it were the final missing piece.

Her brand flared so bright she saw spots behind her

eyelids. A crackling field of energy rippled behind her eyes, distorting her vision. She tried to recall a warding incantation strong enough to sever illusions, but the robed figures had done something cunning. They fused their collective magic with her brand's resonance, linking the Gate to her essence. She sensed the portal's thirst, thrilled and ravenous, like it was about to consume her from within.

A spike of sharp pain lanced up her arm. She cried out, stumbling a step. The cloaked mages pressed closer, forming a boundary of contorted silhouettes. The entire dais spun in her peripheral vision.

Runes carved into the Gate flared, one after another, as if devouring the power they forced through her. The illusions turned from a faint glow to a searing blaze. She felt the brand's violent energy rising through her bloodstream.

No one came to help. Lyric stood at the edge, her hood drawn. She wore an expression torn between fascination and regret. Alysia pleaded with her eyes, but Lyric did nothing. Her posture was rigid, as though she had done all she could before stepping aside.

A bright pillar of light flashed at the Gate's center, impossible, mesmerizing. The chanting swelled, and a wave of scorching air blasted across the dais. The circle of conspirators staggered but continued, fueled by a harsh fervor. Red arcs of electricity snaked along the walls, scorching the stones into dark streaks.

Alysia gritted her teeth, ignoring the sting in her palm. She had studied wards for years, but these illusions were different. They fused with her brand's forbidden nature.

She felt a scraping in her bones. The Gate poured raw magic down her spine, as if it sought to rip her open from the inside. She pressed her trembling lips together while the circle chanted faster. The strings of illusions glowed white-hot.

She gasped, certain she was seconds away from losing consciousness. Then, a small spark flared somewhere deep in her mind. She remembered an old scribble in her mother's half-finished notes, something about reversing illusions through a contradictory charm. It had never been tested. She had always turned the page, uncertain if it was real or a mistake. Now, desperation spurred her to recall the lines.

A new surge of pain raggedly emptied her lungs, and she tasted copper on her tongue. The magic forced her to her knees. Waves of heat struck her, yet that spark in her memory did not fade.

Her mother's whispered instructions drifted through her thoughts. The reversal charm was incomplete in most records. It was forbidden because it defied the usual layering of wards. If used improperly, it could devour the caster's life force along with the illusions. But in that moment, with sweat pouring down her brow and the Gate's thunderous magic threatening to tear her apart, Alysia realized she had no safer option.

She steadied her breath. Her voice quivered as she formed the words in her head. Each syllable carried a faint echo of the brand's burn. If she got this wrong, she would destroy herself. If she did nothing, she would still fail. The robed figures extended their arms once more, illusions blossoming into harsh ribbons of light around her. She squeezed her eyes shut and focused on the reversing incantation.

"Unmake," she managed to whisper, gathering the barest threads of her warding skill. She let the brand's pain guide her. "Untether."

The chamber shuddered. She pulled every shred of energy from her brand and wove it into the words. A chaos of illusions hammered at her. Her heart thundered, and her chest felt too tight to breathe. She forced her shaking hands outward, shaping a circle in the air.

"Unbind," she rasped, giving her final breath to the incantation. "Reversal."

The word tore from her lips, tasting of blood and starlight.

She felt the brand's magic invert, surging out of her with staggering force. The illusions latched around her arms crashed backward, as though flung by an unseen wave. A brilliant flare erupted from her chest, and the robed mages recoiled. Their chanting broke into frightened gasps, their circle unraveling.

The Gate groaned. The stone quaked underfoot as the portal's arcs writhed in protest. Arcs of red light sputtered and snapped, spitting sparks across the dais. Alysia inhaled sharply, clutching the churning power inside her. It wanted to escape, and she let it.

An incandescent pulse burst from her body. It rushed outward in every direction, blasting the robed figures off their feet. Bodies slammed into the walls, hoods flung aside, illusions ripped from their owners. She heard shouts of alarm, the clatter of staff tips, the clang of a fallen brazier. The dais cracked at the center, and the Gate's runes flickered as though extinguished by a sudden wind.

Alysia's arms trembled, but she did not stop. The reversal charm roared through her limbs. Glowing lines spiderwebbed across her skin, following the shape of the brand. Air crackled around her, forming a cyclone of shimmering energy. Hot tears slid down her cheeks, though she hardly felt them. Surging adrenaline blinded her to the pain.

She opened her eyes to see the robed conspirators sprawled across the floor in shock. Some tried to crawl back. One figure, his breath ragged, lifted a trembling hand as if to cast a retaliatory illusion. The attempt fizzled in the molten haze, overshadowed by the brilliance raging from Alysia's shape.

Her own strength astonished her. She had never conjured anything so potent. She glimpsed her reflection in a chunk of polished black stone near the dais and gasped. A raw, cherry-red luminescence haloed her entire body. It was the color of her brand, her pain, now forged into a weapon. The magic wasn't just around her; it was her. The Gate behind her flailed with half-formed illusions, but the shimmering arcs no longer latched onto her brand. She sensed that the portal was on the brink of collapse.

She took an unsteady step forward. The chanting had ceased entirely. She felt the chamber settle into the air like a stunned exhalation. Slowly, she raised her bandaged hand. Strips of the bandage peeled away in the gale, revealing the throbbing spiral beneath. It glowed with an intensity that set her nerves aflame, but the pain no longer felt overwhelming. In that moment, it felt like power.

Alysia swallowed hard, meeting the startled gaze of the nearest conspirator. He pressed himself against the cracked wall and shook his head, as though unable to process what he had just witnessed. Another robed mage scrambled for a staff, yet made no move to attack. Each of them looked to her, truly seeing her for the first time.

She let the reversed illusions burn away, purging the chamber of their hold on her. The Gate's final arcs sputtered in a dying gasp. Tiny fractures spread along the black stone arch, leaving the embedded runes to flicker like a candle flame about to be snuffed out.

For a long moment, no one spoke. Alysia stood in the center of the dais, surrounded by haze and drifting sparks. Her breath came in ragged pulls. She felt the brand's heat radiate along her ribs and collarbones, pulsing with each beat of her racing heart.

She was not helpless. She was not a mere receptacle for others' ambitions or a naive student trifling with spells beyond her mastery. She felt a resonance inside her that extended beyond any text or leftover note from her grandmother's library. This was her magic, her choice.

She glanced upward. Fragments of dust and debris still cascaded from the vaulted ceiling. The braziers lay overturned, their flames snuffed by the blast of her charm reversal. Across the chamber, robed figures struggled to stand, none daring to approach her. She sensed their fear. She also sensed their awe.

The brand's glow faded from blinding red to a subdued ember. She let out a shaky exhale. Her ears rang, and she tasted blood in her mouth from an earlier bite of her lip. She turned slowly, searching the shadows beyond the dais. Lyric had vanished, or perhaps she lurked in some hidden hallway, but Alysia saw no sign of her. Only the conspirators remained, scattered and stunned.

Her vision swam from the exertion of the spell. She pressed her hand against her chest, steadying herself. The illusions that once threatened to trap her had now dispersed, leaving scorching lines in the stone. Still she stood tall at the epicenter, bruised yet unbroken. Her pulse thundered in her ears, shattering the silence.

Quiet footsteps echoed against the far wall as one figure tried to flee. Alysia watched him disappear into a dark corridor, his cloak flapping in the gusts that still circled the dais. She would not chase him. She was not ready to face more conflict. At least not in that instant. The immediate threat was contained. The Gate's power flickered like a spent candle, powerless without the synergy they had attempted to force through her sigil.

A crack from above made her tense, but only a shard of rock tumbled down, clattering off the dais. The adrenaline coursing through her veins provided enough clarity to sense no further collapses were imminent. She took a breath. The air tasted stale, yet strangely lighter than before.

She walked down the dais's lone step, each footfall

measured. Leftover magic fizzled along her arms, shimmering faintly before settling into her brand. Her entire body shook, not from fear, but from the raw surge coursing through her. She closed her eyes and tried to calm her pounding heart, uncertain if she could hold this power again without consequences.

Another robed mage, dazed, leaned against a damp column, his eyes wide with reverence or terror. She might have spoken to him, demanded answers, but her head still reeled. Words failed her. She could almost sense the puzzle pieces snapping into place: the infiltration so determined to harness her brand, the Gate awakening from its centuries-long slumber, and the illusions that nearly devoured her. All of it had collapsed with a single, instinctive spell of reversal.

Alysia inhaled one final time, blinking away sweat and dust. For all her training, she had never imagined she possessed that kind of strength. She stared at her open palm, the angry red spiral glistening softly. She had tapped the brand's forbidden magic and reshaped it before the conspirators could. She wanted to protest that it was impossible, that she only practiced standard wards. Yet the evidence glowing on her skin told another story. She was not just an unfortunate student carrying a cursed mark. She had become something larger than that label.

Movement flickered at the outskirts of the chamber, but she did not flinch. Her outburst felt charged with cautious reverence. Even the walls seemed to tremble in the aftermath of such magnitude.

A single drop of sweat trailed down her chin, and she

let it fall without wiping it away. She felt exquisitely alive, brimming with power she barely understood. The Gate had not consumed her. Instead, her reversal had repelled it. There, in the gloom of the catacombs, she realized at last what lay dormant within her. She was not an empty vessel. She was not a mere catalyst for others to exploit.

She was more than a conduit. She was a force.

THIRTY-THREE

DEAL OR DESTINY

Dazed and reeling, Alysia stood amidst the wreckage left behind by the ritual. The cavern floor was littered with the twisted remains of braziers and broken ward sigils that had once looped around the dais. Smoke curled from the singed grooves in the stone, and the acidic smell of charred magic clung to the stale air. Her body ached with an aftershock of raw power. She had summoned a reversal spell potent enough to shatter the Gate's energy, and nearly her own limits.

Her bandaged palm trembled at her side. Beneath the scraps of linen, the forbidden brand still burned like a living ember, resonating with the lingering illusions in this chamber. She lifted her eyes to where the Gate had partially collapsed. Its obsidian arches crackled with weak arcs of energy, flickering remnants of what had been a formidable portal moments ago.

Figures in dark robes struggled to their knees among the rubble. Many had been thrown across the chamber by her spell, their illusions torn to shreds. Some pressed shaking hands against the floor, wide-eyed and speechless. Others gripped their staffs with trembling fingers, too stunned to fight back. One such staff had rolled near her boot, still humming faintly with leftover magic. She resisted the urge to kick it aside. A single push might trigger more chaos.

Cold footsteps clicked on the stone. Alysia's gaze snapped to a tall, hooded figure who glided forward with unexpected calm. At first, she braced for hostility, a spell or a strike. Her pulse throbbed in her throat, and she clenched her bandaged hand into a fist. Yet the robed leader did not raise their arms in aggression. Instead, the figure drew back the wide hood, revealing angular features and a measured expression. This was the same individual who had chanted ominous verses earlier, urging the Gate to devour her brand's power. Now their eyes looked upon her with something akin to respect, even admiration.

The leader's voice echoed. "You wielded the reversal charm," they said, their tone low. "And you lived. Few mortals could do the same."

She breathed hard, forcing herself to stand upright despite the dizzy spin at the edges of her vision. The illusions still hung in the air like a fading echo, tinted red from the Gate's dark energy. "I did what was necessary."

The faintest curve touched the leader's lips. "Necessary is not enough to fully explain a feat like that." They considered her for a moment, then took a step closer. Alysia noted their cloak was singed at the hem. Strange burn marks patterned the fabric, reminding her that her reversal had not been gentle. It had blasted them all. Even so, the leader seemed unafraid.

She caught herself glancing around for Kael. That impulse squeezed her heart. He was not here. She had charged into this trap alone, guided by Lyric's manipulations and desperate rumors that Kael might be in danger. She swallowed panic, fighting the desperate question: Where is he? She had come here for him, because every lead, every warning, pointed to the chance that this circle of conspirators would harm him next. Instead, they had tried to harness her brand. She forced her jaw tight. If she let fear show, the robed leader might use that against her.

A flicker of movement near the dais made her tense. Lyric emerged from behind a toppled column, her face grimy with dust. She brushed off bits of rubble clinging to her cloak. The fleeting flash of worry in Lyric's eyes vanished the instant their gazes met. Alysia recalled the moment not so long ago when Lyric had coaxed her into these catacombs under the pretense of saving Kael. Yet in the end, it had seemed more like a test. The brand's pain still spiked with betrayal. Now, Lyric stood on the dais as if measuring how Alysia would handle this confrontation.

The leader tilted their head toward Alysia, ignoring Lyric for the moment. "You have seized a power that answers to you alone," they said softly. "It resonates with illusions older than most wards. The Gate recognized your potential. We recognized it as well."

Alysia swallowed. She sensed the the scattered robed figures behind them. They peered at her as if witnessing an ascendant star, fear tangling with something more reverent. Her pulse hammered. She wanted to deny any connection to these illusions, but she could not forget how the brand had burned like a molten sun when it flared forth to break the Gate's hold.

"You have felt the Academy's judgment," the leader said, their voice a silken whisper. "They see a broken lineage. A reckless girl. We see a queen. Join us, Alysia Thorne. Help us shatter the wards of these old men, and we will build a new world where your power is not feared, but worshipped."

Something caught in Alysia's throat. She recalled the many nights when she huddled over old warding tomes, possessed by a hunger to prove herself. She had tasted the thrill of raw magic in those hidden hours, conjuring illusions at dawn where no one would see or judge her. Yet the glittering seduction of the leader's words made her skin crawl. They twisted her past struggles into justification for reckless ruin.

She forced a steady breath. "I fought for Velgrace's safety. I fight for Kael's safety too." Saying his name steadied her, even if it hurt to realize he was not here. "This power you speak of, maybe I can tap it, but only to protect. Not to join your agenda."

The leader sighed. They glanced at the Gate's sputtering remains, where arcs of dying red light still flickered. "Protection alone is never enough. You see how illusions bend to your will. This reversal you conjured toppled wards that stood for centuries."

"I reversed the illusions you forced on me," she said,

her voice rising. "I broke the Gate's hold because you tried to feed it my brand's magic. That is no invitation to collaborate."

Disappointment flickered in the leader's gaze, but they did not seem shocked by her defiance. "Then perhaps you will consider a middle path," they offered. "Join us only when you recognize that your brand can do more than shield. If you harness illusions without limit, you could shape entire realms. You could bring Kael back to your side at last."

A jolt of fear spiked through her. Did they know more about Kael's disappearance than they admitted? She clenched her fists to keep from shaking. "I will not be bargained with."

"She will not," Lyric spoke from the dais. Her voice cut with airy calm, yet underlying tension quivered beneath it. She glared at the group of robed mages who had tried to rally Alysia. "She is unaware of how deep the infiltration goes. Once she sees reason, she may realize you speak something close to truth."

The leader granted Lyric a sidelong glance, then focused again on Alysia. "You are free to refuse, but the outcome remains the same. The illusions you reversed exist inside you now. That brand ties you to the Gate's energy. Eventually, you will crave more of it." Their expression turned cunning. "When that hunger grows, seek us."

Alysia's heartbeat thundered. Every fiber in her body wanted to reject that possibility. She would not become like them, consumed by illusions, unmoored from caution.

She recalled how the reversal had felt, blazing through her veins, unstoppable and exhilarating. It had frightened her almost as much as it had freed her. Even now, the echo of that power pulsed behind her eyes.

She steadied her breath. "No," she said quietly. "I have seen what illusions do when they spiral out of control. They devour trust, they feed on destruction." Her mind flew back to Kael's pained face the night illusions nearly overwhelmed him in the Obscura Wing, and the roiling chaos in the catacombs earlier. "Your path is not mine."

Silence greeted her statement. The robed circle watched, and a spark of curiosity darted across several faces. One of them uttered a bitter hiss, as if disappointed. Another looked ready to protest, but the leader lifted a hand to quiet them. The sound of dripping water from some distant pipe echoed above all else.

Then the leader asked the final question, each syllable poised on a dagger's edge. "You must decide. Will you walk away from this power? You saw how the Gate responded to your brand. You could be unstoppable. Choose carefully."

Alysia lifted her chin. Her heart pounded, but she maintained her stance. "I choose Kael," she answered, her voice low yet unwavering. The moment she spoke his name again, she pictured his rueful grin, the softness in his gaze when they last spoke without fear. She would not trade that for illusions or the promise of dominion. "No matter what illusions or conspiracies you offer, I choose him."

Her choice hung in the air like a drawn blade. The

brand pounded in her palm. She felt the final threads of the Gate's energy sputtering around them, uncertain, perhaps sensing her defiance. Then, as though in quiet approval of her stand, the arcs of red light faded in small flickers.

Lyric descended from the dais in two quick steps. "This is foolish," she said, her eyes narrowed. The side of her face bore a bruise, likely from the blast. Her lips curved at an angle between frustration and regret. "You refuse all of this for Kael? You cannot begin to understand the price you will pay."

Alysia whirled to face her, anger knotting in her chest. She thought of all the times Lyric had manipulated events, weaving Alysia's brand into conspiracies that threatened the entire academy. "You claimed you warned me because Kael was in danger," Alysia said. "Yet you never truly helped me find him. All you did was arrange this show of illusions at my expense."

Lyric flinched, as though stung by the accusation. Then she masked it with a cold smirk. "You needed to see how easy it is to break illusions or channel them. Perhaps you needed to see that your brand is not just a burden but a weapon." A short pause lifted the tension in her shoulders. "You have more potential than you realize."

The leader, standing at Alysia's side, watched them both in silence, curious who might dominate this confrontation. The robed onlookers shifted anxiously. Alysia refused to waver. She squared her stance.

She met the leader's gaze, her own burning with the last embers of the reversal spell. "The power you offer is a cage," she said, her voice clear and steady. "It feeds on fear and promises dominance. I will not be your queen. I will not be your catalyst. I choose a magic that protects, not conquers. I choose him."

Lyric's expression flickered. Her knuckles whitened against the folds of her cloak. A moment of raw emotion cracked her composure, as if something in her had hoped for a different outcome. Then her mouth hardened, and she jabbed a finger in Alysia's direction. "Next time," she said, "we will ask him to die instead."

The cruelty of that statement knocked the air from Alysia's lungs. She could only stare. Her heart hammered louder than any echo in the catacombs. Anger flashed up her spine, urging her to lash out. Yet she saw no use in denying Lyric's threat. This was more than a petty argument. They might truly sacrifice Kael if it served their aims. They held illusions as both threat and lure.

Then, behind Lyric, the Gate gave a final shudder. Stones trembled and parted, releasing one last hiss of red-gold sparks. The arcs collapsed in on themselves with eerie grace. It looked almost graceful, like the reflection of a dying star, the last of its brilliance folding inward. A shock of cold air swept across the dais, and the robed figures all stiffened, as though dreading the Gate's final breath. They had tried to awaken that ancient power, to channel illusions from an older realm. Now it was failing.

Alysia felt the brand in her palm jerk, an echo of that older magic slipping away.

A faint glow traveled up her forearm, flickered across her shoulder, and vanished. Perhaps the Gate's parting pulse was acknowledging her as a rightful key. Perhaps it was simply a dying spark. In either case, the red-gold arcs vanished into a spray of ember-like motes, leaving only the ring of scorched stone in the dais's center.

Her throat felt painfully tight. She looked from the leader to Lyric, waiting for a final incantation, a last desperate strike. Yet no one moved to attack. There was a grudging respect for the power she had unleashed.

She took a shaky step backward. She wanted to demand Kael's location, to tear the answers from Lyric's lips. But the brand pulsed too fiercely, and her muscles threatened to buckle under the strain of the reversal. She had poured almost everything she had into that charm. If the conspirators decided to strike now, she felt uncertain she could avoid a second cataclysmic surge.

The robed leader studied her, then inclined their head in what might have been a salute or a quiet vow. They beckoned the other robed figures into a disjointed line. Some limped. A few glowered. Yet all of them obeyed. Alysia stood at the heart of the scorched dais, her eyes narrowed, unwilling to stand down even though her limbs shook. She sensed they were no longer poised to drag her back into the Gate. The echo of her spell had chased away the madness of the ritual.

Lyric watched with narrowed eyes as the conspirators gathered. Soot clung to her hair, and the bruise on her cheek seemed to darken. Her parted lips betrayed something like reluctance before she forced them shut. The weight of her threat still lingered in the air. Alysia had no illusions that Lyric's anger would fade quietly.

In the distance, a piece of the dais railing collapsed with a sharp crack. Dust rose in a silent cloud. The circle of conspirators retreated toward the chamber's outer archways, some leaning on each other for support. Their leader lingered a moment longer, meeting Alysia's gaze with an inscrutable glint. Then they disappeared into the shadows, leaving behind only their echoing footsteps.

Alysia felt her lungs finally expand, a ragged breath shuddering past her lips. She turned to Lyric, searching for any final motion that might signal attack. Lyric's stare was hard enough to cut diamond. The brand in Alysia's palm flared with heated pain, and she realized her own nails had dug into the bandage, nearly tearing the cloth.

For a breath, neither of them spoke. Lyric's face twisted with a cold, sharp fury. "You chose him over this? Over a chance to control your own destiny?" She laughed, a sound like breaking glass. "Fine. Have your precious anchor. But the Gate still needs a sacrifice. Next time, it will take him instead."

The Gate shimmered once and vanished, leaving only ash and unanswered questions.

THIRTY-FOUR

LAST STAND

Alysia burst up the final steps of the hidden stairwell and out into the open courtyard, her lungs burning. Her vision swam from the abrupt shift from torchlit catacombs to the brilliance of midday sun. Each ragged breath filled her with the acrid tang of smoke. Every alarm ward in Velgrace Academy seemed to ring at once, shrill pulses echoing through the stone corridors above ground. The courtyard's mosaic floor trembled beneath her boots, and she felt the weight of active magic press against her ribs.

She had sensed the disturbance even before leaving the catacombs. The tension in the wards stung at the spiral mark on her palm, letting her know the Academy itself responded to an external threat. Now, the reality of the danger surrounded her with frantic shouts, instructors snapping orders at one another, and students sprinting from hallway to hallway. Scorching sigils flashed in the air around the perimeter as watchers tried to reinforce protective lines, but the signs of strain were clear from the cracks of energy webbing across the wards.

She rubbed her bandaged palm, unsettled by how the brand still thrummed, as though echoing the turmoil of the Academy's wards. She spotted bright illusions flickering over Bastion Hall's ramparts. An entire squad of older students struggled to contain a crack in the barrier there. Ribbons of magic snaked across the sky, like an oncoming storm.

"Reinforce from the west side!" an instructor shouted from a vantage point. Another signaled that the entire southwestern tower needed additional wards. The heat of so many overlapping spells coated the air with a crackling tension, sizzling along Alysia's nerves. Casting anything right now would require caution. She felt the brand twinge with every pulse of the wards.

She spotted a cluster of younger students cowering near a crumbling pillar. Smoke drifted from some unknown source, but she had no time to investigate the cause. All around her, illusions flared in chaotic bursts, half-formed images dancing at the edges of her sight. The illusions had a sharp, uncoordinated feel that suggested a remote attack. A memory of Lyric's words churned in her thoughts. Someone had threatened to strike at Velgrace, and they were making good on that promise.

Alysia forced her steps toward the outer courtyard gates, where a hodgepodge of makeshift defenses had been raised. She passed a line of faculty members chanting measured spells, their voices threading into a single defensive chorus, but the wards wavered, flickering in and out of stability. If the wards gave way, illusions could surge through the Academy's corridors, turning every hallway into a potential trap.

Gripping the edge of a toppled statue for balance, Alysia scanned the chaos. Her heart hammered when she realized Kael was nowhere in sight. She remembered his absence underground and how she had dreaded the possibility of him being in danger. Now, it seemed the danger had come to all of them. Instead, she clung to the hope that he had made it aboveground before she did. The clamor of clashing magic pressed in on her mind, making it difficult to track a single presence.

She caught sight of Robin in the distance, recognizable by the shock of short, tousled hair and the flurry of illusions zipping from her hands. Robin was shepherding a group of first-years to safer ground beyond a partial ward station. Alysia lifted a hand in greeting, but Robin did not see her. Time ran too short for personal reassurances. Students, their power flaring in their hands, hurled spells at intangible shapes hovering just outside the Academy walls.

The shapes weren't just shadows; they were reflections of fear. Alysia saw illusions of crumbling towers, of friends falling, of the sea rising to swallow the cliffs whole. They were psychic weapons, designed to break the defenders' spirits before the wards even fell.

Their features warped in and out of being, like living shadows that prodded at Velgrace's wards.

A bright flash from the next courtyard over sent Alysia's pulse into panic. She flinched, half expecting the wards to collapse. Dust and debris surged upward, forcing her to shield her face. When the rumble subsided, she straightened and ignored the grit in her eyes. Bastion Hall's ramparts held, but the illusions had thumped them again, leaving scorch marks along the outer stones. The brand on her palm flared.

Steeling herself, she forced her legs into motion, racing toward the southwestern corner of the Academy. If Kael were anywhere, he would be at the heart of the action. He always placed himself where illusions were thickest. That was where she needed to be, no matter the risk.

She jogged down a corridor lined with broken wards, leaping over fallen debris. Through an arched window, she glimpsed the Sea of Echoes roiling far below. A red glow stained the horizon, as though illusions bled across the waves. Everything about the scene made her think of an orchestrated assault, shaped by cunning minds. She heard an instructor bark, "Focus your wards, group up!" from behind her, but she kept going.

Sparks of other spells erupted along the corridor. She ducked a stray illusion that buzzed overhead and shattered against the wall in a flash of crimson. The walls rattled. She grit her teeth. If the infiltration extended any deeper, the Academy's entire structure might face collapse. They had to stop this while the wards still functioned.

Panting, she threw open the heavy doors leading to the southwestern battlements. She emerged onto an elevated walkway, blinking against the sudden dust. A narrow tower stood at the walkway's end, ringed by blazing illusions. The wards crackled, sending arcs of energy into the sky in desperate attempts to seal the gap. In the midst of it stood Kael.

He faced outward, his hair whipped by wild gusts of magic. His stance was braced, as though he fought off illusions invisible to the naked eye. Flickers of bright silver lanced from his fingertips, illusions twisting and churning in complex shapes around him. His worn compendium lay at his feet, its pages flapping in the wind. Every line of his body spoke of fierce concentration.

Alysia's chest constricted with pure relief. "Kael!" she shouted over the roar of the wards.

He turned, half startled, though his illusions did not waver. Their gazes locked for an instant. She saw exhaustion in his eyes, the same kind of bone-deep weariness she felt in her own limbs, and also a fierce determination that radiated in the air around him.

Behind her, an explosion rocked the walkway. She nearly lost her footing as the tower quaked. Magic slammed into the wards overhead, producing a thunderous boom that made her ears ring. She stumbled forward, her arms raised to shield her head from the falling shards of a broken parapet. Stones crashed in a cloud of mortar dust. She coughed, blinking through the haze, straining to see Kael through the debris.

A strong, calloused hand grabbed her wrist. She gasped at the sudden touch, feeling a familiar surge of illusion energy brush her skin. It was Kael, pulling her clear of another collapsing portion of the tower walkway. They staggered together into a small alcove where the wind died down. The dust parted just enough for her to see his face.

"Alysia," he said, his voice raw from shouting or inhaling grit. Her heart pounded at the way he said her name. Urgency underscored every syllable.

She fought to catch her breath. "What is happening? I felt the wards shaking in the catacombs."

"No time," he replied, glancing over his shoulder. The illusions in the air thickened again, ghostly shapes pressing at Velgrace's outer defenses. "They are wearing down the wards from every angle. Something is amplifying them."

She nodded, her mind racing. An unspoken thought passed between them about the ancient illusions awakened below.

At the far edge of the walkway, a group of older students attempted a synchronized warding circle. Their chanting stuttered when the illusions crashed against the barrier. Alysia's chest knotted. She and Kael could not fight all these illusions alone, but perhaps they could reinforce the wards. Together.

She spun to face the southwestern vantage point. The exposed courtyard below thronged with panicked novices trying to reinforce the perimeter. She clenched her fists. The brand on her palm blazed with renewed fervor, almost as if it recognized that illusions threatened to tear the Academy asunder. The memory of the catacomb's Gate loomed at the back of her mind, but she forced herself to focus on the present.

"Let's head for the defensive line," she said, her voice

firm despite her racing pulse. "We might steady the wards there if we combine illusions and wards together."

He gave a curt nod. Neither of them spoke about the tension that had pervaded their relationship in recent days. They had no time for explanations or apologies. All that mattered was that they stood side by side now. That was enough.

They dashed along the makeshift rampart, dodging columns of broken stone and bursts of rogue illusions. Desperate faces flashed by in blurs of motion. She recognized some of the frantic watchers as the same upperclassmen who had once mistrusted Kael. Now, no one had the luxury of suspicion. Survival bound them all.

Finally, they reached the main defensive line, a half-collapsed barricade ringed by complex wards. Elder faculty members knelt inside a wide chalk circle. Their chanting sounded ragged, as though they had been at it for hours. A few staff turned with relief when they saw Alysia, their postures hinting that they expected her to help.

She exchanged a brief look with Kael. He stepped closer. "On my count," he muttered, his eyes focused on the trembling wards overhead. Illusions struck the barrier in relentless waves, each hit sending jagged cracks across the golden shield of protective magic.

Alysia exhaled unsteadily, raising a trembling hand. Through the dust, she could sense the raw presence of Kael's illusions. Her brand pulsed in response. Fine lines of power tugged along her veins. She cradled that energy, letting it build behind her sternum. They had done smaller versions of this synergy before, combining ward-weaving with illusions, but never under such high stakes.

Without a word, she and Kael reached for each other. Their hands clasped, palm to palm, her bandaged one pressed against his calloused skin. She felt the spark of his magic surge through her fingertips.

An inward jolt rippled through her core. She drew upon the brand, not just her wards. She felt its forbidden power answer her, a searing heat that surged up her arm. Kael's illusions met it, not as separate magic, but as the other half of a whole. Silver and scarlet, chaos and structure, they fused into a single, blinding torrent of power. It wasn't a spell they cast; it was a piece of their combined souls they hurled into the sky. The circle of older faculty fell silent. They watched the pair with awe, their voices stalling in mid-chant.

Alysia's heart pounded. Her blood thundered in her ears, and for a moment, her vision blurred. The synergy felt raw, sharper than any impetus she had known. She sensed Kael's illusions hum with an urgent clarity, channeling into her wards like water pouring into carefully carved channels. Her brand flared with heat. She concentrated on shaping the combined magic, picturing it as a living shield that could mesh with the wards overhead.

A shriek of twisted illusions attacked from above. The gold-tinged barrier flickered, straining under the assault, but Alysia and Kael poured their unity into it. She felt illusions in her mind, guided by the discipline of her wards. Kael's illusions found anchors in the glyphs and runes etched onto her soul, while her ward-layers encased every flickering ounce of his power, locking it into a single shape.

Their magic coalesced in a blinding surge, brilliant enough to force every onlooker to shield their eyes. A roar like booming thunder shook the air as illusions clashed against the synergy they created. A tremor rumbled through the courtyard. Alysia's knees threatened to buckle under the force of it, but Kael's hand remained clasped in hers, steadying her.

The illusions bent, pressing forward like shapeless fiends. Energy hissed through the wards, screeching in protest. A shudder ran down Alysia's spine. She bit down on her lip, unwavering. Slowly, their synergy stitched itself to the wards, merging in lines of silver and scarlet. She leaned into Kael's warmth, letting his illusions fuse with the final layers of her warding incantation.

A final surge of power flared upward from their interlocked hands. It shot skyward in a blazing column of light. The illusions that had hammered the Academy's defenses reeled back, their forms disintegrating into inert sparks. An expanding wave of brightness swept across the courtyard, pushing the dark shapes outward until they vanished against the horizon in a haze of dissolving magic.

When the glare dimmed, Alysia realized she stood in stunned silence with Kael, their fingers still interlaced. The world around them wavered with drifting dust and leftover sparks of expelled illusions. The wards overhead faintly glimmered in a gentle gold hue, stabilized at last.

Instructors and older students stared in awe, while novices peered around barricades in disbelief.

Exhausted faculty rose to their feet, murmuring to each other while others reached out with warding spells to double-check that the illusions were truly gone. Alysia tasted salt on her lips. She had no idea if this restoration would last, but for now, they had pushed back the threat. The wards remained intact, and Velgrace still stood.

She glanced at the brand on her palm. It had grown warm, pulsing in time with her heartbeat, but the pain and searing heat were gone. In its place lingered a sense of harmonized power, shared with the illusions Kael wielded so deftly.

No one clamored for immediate explanations or demanded a final resolution. The courtyard lay bathed in dusty half-light, and the watchers respectfully stepped back, as if sensing that Alysia and Kael needed a moment.

He looked at her. Lines of fatigue creased his face, his dark lashes flecked with debris, but he managed a smile that made her heart lurch. She parted her lips to say something, anything, but words seemed distant. The next sound she heard was her own breath, shaky and raw.

Her heart hammered so fiercely she feared others might hear. In that trembling pause, she felt the weight of her own choice settle inside her. Choosing to fight at his side was more than a momentary alliance. She felt the significance burn in the back of her mind. She had chosen him, against all the suspicions and warnings, because no one else understood the synergy of illusions and wards like he did. No one else made her feel this vivid, this alive.

They both exhaled at the same time, a ragged release of tension stretched between them, something shifted.

Alysia felt him raise their joined hands. His breath was warm on her cheek, every inch of space charged with unsaid words. She closed her eyes, letting the echoes of power run through her. There was no chaos or condemnation in that instant. The Academy had quieted, instructors too stunned or too busy confirming the wards' stability to interrupt.

Kael leaned closer. For just a moment, she recalled the times they almost crossed the boundary from uneasy partners to something more. All those fleeting glances and half-spoken confessions that never found their moment. Now, with the wards calmed, with illusions banished from the sky, there was only the silent aftermath and the sound of their hearts pounding in tandem.

She felt his presence like a steady current that anchored her. The brand on her palm no longer burned with fear. Instead, it glowed with delicate warmth, reflecting the synergy they had forged. She lifted her gaze to meet Kael's. He said her name softly, but the single word carried all the gratitude and longing of a person who stood at the edge of an unknown future.

They stood in the aftermath of the most formidable illusions she had ever faced, their arms trembling from exertion, their hearts pounding from the risk of total collapse, and still they gravitated to each other. In that stolen second, she felt the heat of his hand splay across her back, and her own hand curved along his jaw. The taste of dust and salt clung to her lips, but none of that mattered. Their magic hummed, wrapping them in a fragile barrier of shared power.

The moment before their foreheads touched, she thought she heard footsteps or distant voices, but the world had receded. In the quiet that lingered, she felt the raw surge of relief and connection that had been building since the day she first summoned him into her life. Then their foreheads pressed together gently, and all she could sense was their combined breath and the unspoken promise carried in that contact.

No illusions marred the moment, and no wards barred them from sharing the aftermath of a battle they had fought side by side. Their magic had fused with the Academy's defenses, giving Velgrace the chance to stand another day. For a breath, neither of them moved.

Then, as though the entire courtyard recognized the significance of that unity, the world around them stilled. Hearts collided in the silence that followed.

THIRTY-FIVE

WHAT WAS NEVER MEANT

Alysia's lungs still burned from the last desperate incantation. The courtyard lay in splinters around her; fragments of shattered ward crystals embedded in stone. Every breath carried the acrid tang of singed magic that lingered in the aftermath of the battle. Staggering forward, she pressed one trembling hand to her chest and tried to slow her heart. Only moments ago, the courtyard was a maelstrom of illusions set loose by conjurers who had nearly broken Velgrace's wards. Now all that remained were scattered coughs and the shifting of debris.

She heard a low groan to her left. There, half-buried under fallen masonry, a third-year student rubbed her bruised shoulder and rose with unsteady legs. Alysia hurried to help, ignoring the fresh sting in her own muscles. Her bandaged palm grew unbearably warm, echoing the brand etched into her skin, the spiral mark that still thrummed with residual power. She helped the young woman stand, but her thoughts drifted to Kael. She needed to see him. With half her mind on the student's well-being, she scanned the wreckage for that familiar figure.

Robin's voice cut through the gloom. "Alysia!" her cousin shouted, weaving around a toppled stone column. Robin's hair was a sweaty tangle, and a thin line of blood trickled from a scrape on her forehead, but she still wore that lopsided grin. "You good?"

Alysia exhaled, relief mixing with the fear that still pulsed through her. "I'm all right. The illusions?" Her gaze darted around them.

"Dispersed," Robin said. She kicked aside a broken plank from a piece of scaffolding. "Looks like your synergy with Kael did most of the heavy lifting. That blast near the end, well, it was spectacular." Her grin widened, though there was fatigue in her eyes. "Not that I'm surprised."

Her cousin's casual praise made Alysia's cheeks feel warm, though she suspected it was just adrenaline wearing off. Over Robin's shoulder, she glimpsed several staff members huddling near an improvised triage station. Headmistress Quen was there, imposing even covered in soot. The older woman calmly oversaw the healing efforts, her regulation robes singed at the hem. At intervals, faculty and advanced students passed out potions amid anxious murmurs. The entire academy seemed suspended in uneasy relief.

A surge of panic clawed at Alysia's chest when she realized she still had not spotted Kael among the scattered forms. She pressed a hand over her brand, ignoring the mild burn. "Robin, do you know where—?"

"South side of the courtyard," Robin interjected, picking up on Alysia's unspoken question. Her face softened. "I saw him earlier. He was with Warden Evara Morn, trying to stabilize the final wards. He looked... strong. But rattled. Like he was searching for you, too."

Alysia nodded, a knot unwinding in her chest. "Thanks," she said, her voice tight.

She found him slumped against a half-collapsed pillar near Bastion Hall's outer walkway. His usually unruly hair clung to his brow, damp from sweat. A jagged cut on his cheek still oozed blood, though he appeared unaware. Kael's chest rose and fell shakily, as if every breath cost him precious energy. Relief flooded Alysia so powerfully that her knees weakened. She hastened to his side.

He glanced up, his eyes flashing between weariness and unmistakable relief. "You're safe?" His voice was coarse with strain.

Alysia pressed her fingers beneath his chin, turning his face gently so she could check the extent of the wound. "Thanks to you," she said softly. The brand flared under the bandage, and she saw him wince, perhaps because his illusions were still keyed to her wards in some invisible tether. "We need to get that cut looked at. Come on."

Despite her urging, he pushed back against the pillar to stand. "I'm fine," he rasped, though pain furrowed his brow. His gaze flickered toward her bandaged palm. "That mark... you overdid it, didn't you?"

She let out a breathy, humorless laugh. "You have a talent for stating the obvious." There was no anger behind her words. Only the lingering worry that the synergy had taken too much from them both. But they were alive, and that counted as victory enough for now.

They took a moment to regain footing, leaning on each other for balance. All around them, the academy staff worked methodically, checking on collapsed wards and scattered illusions. Students who had weathered the onslaught tested protective spells near the scarred court-yard arches. Broken fragments of ward stones glimmered dully at the edges of shattered mosaic tiles. The entire place looked on the verge of collapse, not physically, but in spirit.

Standing together in that grim ruin, Alysia recalled the adrenaline that had coursed through her when she and Kael united their powers. She remembered how, for a single heartbeat, the wards overhead turned brilliant gold, illuminated by illusions streaked with silver. For a breath, they had collectively burned so bright it felt unstoppable. Yet the cost was visible in every bruise and broken stone.

She turned to Kael, searching his face. "We should help the others secure the perimeter," she began, her voice catching slightly. "Seems like the illusions are mostly gone, but there's still residual magic around."

His expression was guarded, but not hostile. "In a moment." He studied her carefully. He looked as if a thousand thoughts pressed at the back of his mind, none of them easy. But he simply nodded. "We'll help them. Then we'll talk."

She mirrored his nod, uncertain what he wanted to say. The fear of prolonging that conversation clashed with the anticipation of it. She was too aware of the closeness between them, still wearing the memory of how his illusions had melded with her wards so intimately, how it felt to hold him in the surging chaos. She swallowed, nodded again, and set off to do what she could.

They separated briefly, each assisting small clusters of students and watchers. Alysia tested the stability of damaged wards near the courtyard gates, layering new protective spirals over cracks in the barrier. She rested a calming hand on the underclassmen, who flinched at each stray shimmer of illusion.

Meanwhile, Kael helped Warden Evara Morn pile rubble away from the triage station, using illusions to steady precarious stones. Now and then, Alysia caught a glimpse of his profile across the courtyard. Each time, her pulse fluttered in a strange mixture of relief and longing.

Eventually, the worst of the disarray was contained. The wards rose again in a shaky patchwork, enough to keep out any immediate danger. With the night sky turning from sooty darkness to the faintest gray, staff members guided the exhausted throngs of students indoors. Lantern light blinked from overturned sconces, revealing dust motes as the courtyard emptied.

Alysia wondered if her legs would buckle as she spotted Kael striding toward her through the haze. He still bore the cut on his cheek, half-wiped blood dried along his jaw, and his illusions crackled faintly around him. She swallowed her nerves and stepped to meet him.

His gaze moved to her bandaged hand, noticing how rigidly she held it at her side. "Let me see," he said. When she hesitated, he took her hand gently, unwrapping a bit of the linen to view the glowing spiral brand. The edges were angry and red, as though it had been seared anew.

He exhaled, a quiet, shaky sound. "I'm sorry if I pushed too hard."

"You didn't," she said. "We both pushed. And it saved lives."

His fingers lingered, radiating warmth against her raw skin. Their synergy might have waned for now, but an echo of that closeness remained. She felt it in the subtle, maddening hum that hovered whenever his aura neared hers. Despite the lingering exhaustion, her cheeks grew hot again.

She gently pulled her hand back. "We should get that gash looked at too," she murmured, reaching up to brush her thumb near the dried blood on his cheek.

A muscle in his jaw tightened. "Later."

In the near-empty courtyard, lit by broken torches and the first hints of dawn, silence pressed around them. Alysia's mind spun with questions she could not voice. What had happened to that raw magic they unleashed? Had they only delayed some larger threat? The brand on her palm burned with secrets she was not certain she wanted uncovered.

Kael crossed his arms, the illusions around him flickering. "There was a moment," he said, his voice tight, "when I couldn't tell where my magic ended and yours began. We were so...connected."

The recollection tightened Alysia's throat. She remembered the rush of color and tremor, how exhilarating it felt to channel illusions that responded to her wards as if they were one living entity. "I felt it too," she admitted softly. "It was terrifying. And—" She did not finish the sentence aloud. She had trouble putting into words the thrill that lingered, even now, in her chest.

He lowered his gaze, a small, humorless laugh escaping him. "It's always like that," he said. "Illusions want to connect. They feed on emotion, on the shape of your heart's desire." He turned his gaze to the bruised pillars. "This time, though, it was more than that. It was the brand. It was you."

They stood there, letting the night sky's last glimmers fade away. Hints of sunrise touched the highest spire of Velgrace Academy. In the distance, someone called for help with clearing the last of the fallen stones, but the staff's voices sounded distant and muffled. For this moment, the world narrowed around them alone.

Alysia's heart thundered. She felt an urge to reach out to him, to anchor him to the reality that they had won for now. Perhaps anchor herself, too. Instead, she folded her arms. "What are we supposed to do with that?" she asked, her voice trembling slightly. "We don't have any easy answers. All I know is that I—"

She stopped. The words hovered inside her chest. She was not sure she could put them into the open air without losing her composure. Kael watched her, something storming in his gray eyes. She recognized it as the same protective concern he wore whenever illusions threatened to overwhelm him. But now, his illusions were calm, leaving only the man who wrestled with them.

Finally, he let out a slow breath. "Sometimes, no

answer is the only place to start," he said. "But I won't force you to be part of anything you don't want. If using illusions together terrifies you, or if the brand demands too much, I get it."

Alysia's pulse pounded at his uncertainty. She felt, in that moment, how easy it would be to push him away for fear of that unknown. Yet she also remembered the times they had steadied each other, when wards threatened to collapse, or illusions coiled too tightly in Kael's mind. She gazed at the courtyard around them. The shards on the ground, the charred edges of the once-pristine mosaic, the acrid stench of undone illusions. They had survived it all by refusing to face it alone.

She tucked a loose strand of hair behind her ear, the wind tugging at the rest. "I'm scared," she admitted, her voice shaking despite her attempts at composure. "But I'm done running from it. From... us."

His gaze rested on hers, searching. A faint, hopeful light crossed his features. "Then we figure it out," he whispered. Slowly, he lifted his hand, brushing the backs of his fingers along her cheek. It was a touch so soft that her breath caught in her throat. "Together."

She inhaled just enough to speak. "Together."

A sudden scrape of boots interrupted them. Robin approached, balancing an armful of heavy canvas sacks filled with leftover ward anchors. Sweat beaded along her forehead, her eyes keen. She studied them both for a moment, and Alysia saw curiosity dance behind that mischievous grin. Yet Robin simply cleared her throat and said, "Headmistress Quen wants a final damage report. I think she's in the triage area."

Kael straightened, dropping his hand. Alysia cleared her throat, baffled by how her heart still pounded. For once, she was glad to see her cousin, though the abrupt intrusion reminded her they were not the only ones who had endured a harrowing night. There was cleanup to do, wards to reset, injuries to treat. "We'll be right there," she told Robin.

Her cousin shot her a small, knowing smile, then hurried off toward the triage zone. Kael and Alysia exchanged a look, something that told her they stood on the edge of a fragile new understanding. She took a careful step in that direction and felt him fall into stride beside her. Her chest felt lighter than it had all night.

They spent the next stretch of time aiding the staff. Whenever their paths crossed, Alysia felt that familiar brush of possibility between them. A fragment of synergy sparked each time their eyes met, reminding her that illusions and wards were no longer the only forces at play in her life anymore. She could not deny how the fear and the excitement churned in equal measure.

Soon, the early sunlight bathed the ruined courtyard. Apprentices and older students now bustled around, clearing debris and coercing spells to fix the worst cracks. Tired relief settled over everyone. Most of the illusions had faded into drifting sparks, leaving only the whisper of undone magic. Alysia found a brief reprieve by a toppled statue, closing her eyes and tilting her face to the warmth of daylight. Weary as she was, she welcomed the new dawn.

When she opened her eyes, Kael stood a few paces away, silent, as though moved by the same cautious hope. But there was a tension in him she had not noticed before. Gently, he gestured for her to step closer, away from passing faculty. Something in his face hinted at worry but also resolve.

They walked together to the quietest corner of the courtyard, away from prying eyes. Dust fell at their feet, and the wind carried the voices of those laboring behind them. Here, near a collapsed arch, they were mostly alone. She parted her lips to speak, but he did first.

"Before we head inside," he said quietly, "there's something I have to tell you. It's about a vision I had. It's... complicated." His voice cracked on the last word, as though the weight of it was too much.

Her pulse quickened. Kael was not prone to confiding these thoughts easily, especially not random visions. The brand on her palm stung again, and she gritted her teeth. "I'm listening," she said, her heart hammering in her ribcage.

He nodded, then turned to survey the courtyard. Broken, scarred, yet still standing. Like them. A fine tremor ran through his shoulders. She stepped nearer, wanting to offer him comfort. He swallowed, steeling himself.

They stood in the wreckage of the courtyard. Kael turned to Alysia, his expression raw. "In the vision, the woman who offered me to the magic looked like you, Alysia. Exactly like you. And she whispered that my purpose was not to control illusions but to be an anchor." He finally met her eyes, his own shimmering with a terrible, ancient sorrow. "An anchor for a Thorne ward-weaver. She said I had to protect you even if it cost me everything."

Alysia's breath caught. Fate had brought them together, but choice would keep them there or pull them apart.

"No," she said, her voice fierce and low. "I don't accept that. We make our own choices. No ghost, no vision, and no prophecy gets to decide your fate. I won't allow it."

THIRTY-SIX

THE FINAL CHARM

Alysia could almost feel her pulse pounding in her throat as she lifted her gaze to meet Kael's. He stood only a few steps away, his breath shallow, his eyes dark with the same uncertainty that churned in her mind. The courtyard around them was quiet now. The fallen stones and half-scorched banners told the story of chaos that had erupted earlier. Dust still floated like drifting motes in the feeble light, turning the air hazy. It smelled of burnt sigils and lingering fear.

She drew in a slow breath, trying to steady herself. He had just confessed visions of a woman who looked exactly like her, foretelling a destiny where he served as her anchor at the cost of his own life. The admission had rattled her. Fate had yanked them together so many times that doubt felt more reliable than hope. Yet her heart refused to yield. If Kael believed he was meant to sacrifice himself, then she would defy that path with all the magic she had.

"Stop looking at me like I've already died," he muttered, his voice tighter than she had ever heard it. The illusions that usually rippled around his fingers were conspicuously absent. He did not conjure a single flicker of color, as though the raw honesty of his vision had drained him of that playful spark.

"You're not dying," she replied. Her voice was low, urgency threaded through every syllable. "I refuse to let some prophecy lock you into that fate."

Kael exhaled in a ragged sigh. "Nothing is fixed, right? We're always told our choices shape the outcome. I only wish I knew how to steer us away from the end that haunts me."

She took a tentative step closer. The stones underfoot shifted with a dull scrape, but she ignored it, closing the distance between them until she could hear his breath. "Then let's decide," she said softly. "We're not just participants in some ancient script. We guide our own magic."

He gazed at her, a thousand emotions warring behind his eyes. She understood the guilt he carried for illusions that once threatened everyone they held dear. She knew the fear of continuing a bloodline rumored to be cursed. But she also saw determination. Slowly, he raised one trembling hand toward her face. She swallowed hard, letting him brush his fingertips across her cheek.

"I can't promise to protect you from everything," he admitted. "Maybe I can't even protect myself. There's so much we still don't understand. The illusions I carry, the ones I've fought so hard to control, feel like they're unraveling inside me."

Alysia's throat constricted with sympathy. "You don't have to do it alone."

His answering smile carried a glimmer of warmth. Yet the moment stretched tenuous and fraught. She reminded herself to breathe. The brand on her palm, her family's spiral mark, tingled faintly, an echo of the synergy she shared with Kael. He might fear his illusions, and she might wrestle with the wards that demanded more from her than she ever expected. But working together had always kept them afloat before.

They turned when loose stones rattled at the edge of the courtyard. The haze parted, revealing Robin picking her way across the rubble. Her short hair stuck out in all directions, and there was a smudge of ash on her cheek that she had not bothered to wipe away. Her expression was uncharacteristically grim.

"Alysia," Robin said, her voice tight. "Whatever you're going to do next...do it fast." She extended her arm toward the southwestern corner, from which a faint shimmer of illusions flickered like a warning beacon. "The wards are still stable, but something big is moving in. Faculty wards won't hold if it strikes a second time."

Alysia's heart thumped. She glanced at Kael. The same realization dawned in his eyes. The threat that terrorized Velgrace earlier had not fully abated. They had driven off some illusions, but not all. A final surge beckoned. Before Alysia could respond, the ground shook, and a plume of dust flew from the far arches. Shouts echoed from somewhere near Bastion Hall.

Kael silently stepped away, already conjuring a faint

illusions at his fingertips. The colors had returned, silver edges tinted with flecks of deeper purple. She caught the micro-flinch at the corner of his mouth. Using illusions no longer felt effortless. He was exhausted. So was she. But there was no time for rest.

Robin jerked her head toward the chaos. "They're calling for us," she said. "Warden Morn's crew can't handle illusions of this magnitude alone."

Alysia did not hesitate. She and Kael ran, their feet pounding the fractured courtyard stones. Robin fell in behind them, illusions of her own snapping at her fingertips, though she was slower after all the day's strain. Bits of conversation flew by in a blur: an instructor barking orders, novices scattering in panic, the hiss of wards barely holding. As they rounded a fractured column, a wave of crackling magic flared across the open archway. A monstrous illusion, like a twisted silhouette formed of flickering charcoal and silver light, reared up, swiping at the academy wards with a sweeping, claw-like extension. Each blow sent a tremor through the wards overhead, hairline cracks spidering outward.

"Hold the barrier!" Warden Morn bellowed at her group of older students, but fear stained their faces. A scorching flash erupted as the illusion hammered the wards again, forcing the watchers to their knees.

Alysia's breath came in ragged gasps. These illusions felt different, colder, more purposeful, as if guided by an unseen puppet master. Her brand throbbed, responding to the intensity of the attack. Kael ground his teeth. She saw the faint flicker of pain across his features.

"I can weave a containment ward," Alysia said, half-gasping. "But it needs an illusion anchor. Something to hold the shape in place."

Kael tied off a quick defensive wave, narrowing his eyes at the monstrous silhouette. "Then let's do exactly that. I'll shape the illusions, you fuse them with your wards." He glanced sideways at her. "But be ready. This could break me if I lose control."

She set her jaw. "We won't let that happen."

They stepped forward, ignoring the crash of falling stones and the protesting shriek of overextended wards. With practiced efficiency, they clasped hands, the brand on Alysia's palm coming alive at the contact. Magic rippled outward from where their fingers intertwined. She felt Kael's illusions as a potent, shimmering current that threaded through every fiber of her being. She formed the ward in her mind, focusing on the runic shapes that could contain something so colossal. Each line of the ward was etched with her own heartbeat, steady and deliberate.

"Combine," she breathed, letting her power saturate the spaces between them. Kael's illusions responded, forming a shell of shifting brilliance that encased her ward incantation. Together, they hurled the synergy at the monstrous silhouette. The explosion of color was nearly blinding. The watchers yelped and shielded their eyes as radiant gold collided with writhing silver illusions. Searing heat swept across the courtyard.

For a moment, Alysia believed they had succeeded. The giant silhouette gave a convulsive shudder, a warped screech echoing through the open air. Then it detonated into a burst of black arcs, condensing into a smaller shape that darted straight for Kael. He stiffened, illusions flickering as that dark energy stabbed into his chest like a living arrow. She screamed in alarm, but the moment stretched too fast. The darkness sank into him, vanishing beneath his skin in a heartbeat.

His face contorted. He clutched at his ribcage, illusions surging madly around him, out of sync. Alysia lunged closer, ignoring the crackling arcs that sparked off his aura. If the infiltration of darkness anchored itself in him, it could devour him from within. Her mind raced. She had no reference for how to forcibly remove an illusion that had bonded like that.

Warden Morn's voice rose somewhere behind them, but all Alysia heard was Kael's ragged breathing and the violent hum of illusions. She cupped a trembling hand against his cheek, though sparks singed her fingertips. Her brand glowed in protest. The illusions hissed in her ears.

"Listen to me," she whispered. "Fight it. Don't let it take you."

Kael's eyes flickered. He exhaled in short, shallow pants. "I'm... trying."

Robin skidded to Alysia's side, her face lined with dread. "We saw this before," she muttered. "It's draining his illusions. If that shadow burrows any deeper, it will tear him apart." Her eyes darted around, searching. They'd faced massive illusions, sabotage, and infiltration attempts before, but nothing that joined with Kael so directly. "Alysia," Robin said quietly, "do you have any ward that can sever that link?"

Alysia's thoughts spiraled, frustration knotting in her chest. No standard ward existed for forcibly extracting a parasitic illusion. She had memorized dozens of runes for dispelling illusions, but the darkness inside Kael was tangling with his own magic to create a single entity. If she tried to rip it out randomly, she might tear a piece of his essence away.

Kael's knees buckled. She and Robin caught him under the arms before he hit the ground. A surge of raw power pulsed outward, forcing Robin to stagger back, illusions crackling around her. Alysia braced Kael's weight with her shoulder, ignoring the sparks that singed the edges of her cloak. His illusions sputtered around them, forming chaotic bursts of silver embers that scattered on the breeze. His eyes searched hers.

Words flitted through her mind like ghosts: the prophecy Kael had mentioned, the anchor, the possibility that he was meant to vanish for her sake. Yet every part of her rebelled at letting that happen. They had come too far. She tightened her grip on his forearm, making sure he knew she refused to let him go.

An idea began to form, a final, desperate idea. If illusions and wards could merge, perhaps she could craft a final charm: an incantation that would hold him together in spite of the darkness. But it would require a deeper bond than anything they had attempted. Her brand flared as if cautioning her. Messing with spells that deeply could reshape them both.

Robin must have glimpsed the determination in

Alysia's face, because she started to protest. "Alysia, wait—"

Alysia shook her head. "He can't last like this. If we do nothing, he'll collapse."

Robin's mouth pressed into a tense line, but she stepped aside, glancing around to guard them from any stray illusions. "Fine. But hurry," she said. "The wards outside are still vulnerable."

Alysia placed both hands on Kael's cheeks, forcing him to make eye contact. The chaos in his eyes burned with anguish. His breath rasped. There was no time to explain. She closed her eyes, summoning the memory of their synergy, the one they had shared when the brand and his illusions intertwined for the first time. She spoke an incantation she had only theorized, blending a ward's anchor point with a conjuration of illusions. If it worked, it could sanctify his body against that parasitic darkness. If it failed, the resulting rupture could kill them both.

Heat flared between their bodies. She bit down on a cry of pain as her bandaged palm pressed against his forearm. It felt as though molten light poured from her chest into his, searching for the source of the corruption. She heard him gasp. The illusions rippling around them collided with the ward layers forming in her mind. She channeled more power and pulled not just from her magic but from her very life force, from the core of the brand. She forged a ward of pure light and pushed it into his chest, a piece of her own soul meant to burn away the shadow that had claimed him.

Everything around them seemed to fade, even the courtyard's destruction, even Robin's anxious presence.

For an agonizing span of seconds, their combined magic hovered at the brink. Then Kael groaned, a guttural sound torn from his soul. A violent shudder seized him, and tendrils of black vapor bled out from his body. A tangle of gold and silver enveloped the darkness, snapping it free from his chest. The illusions shot outward, dissolving into shards of lifeless shadow that the wards devoured. Alysia felt a blinding pain tear across her senses, as though part of her own energy had ripped away.

She staggered, nearly collapsing against him. But Kael's arms wrapped around her middle, holding her upright. For a moment, they breathed in sync, raw magic still sparking at the edges of their auras. Her vision blurred from strain, but she forced it to focus on his face.

He swallowed, his voice rough. "You, what did you do?"

She managed a faint, shaky smile. "I tried my best to keep you here."

He exhaled, relief etched in the lines around his eyes. Yet something about his expression was strange, as if the illusions within him were no longer settled. She saw guilt shift in his features. Softly, he touched her jaw, and she felt his hand tremble.

Somewhere nearby, the watchers cheered. They had no idea what she and Kael had risked, only that the monstrous illusion was gone. The wards overhead, which had trembled like a tattered shield, stabilized into a consistent glow. Robin backed away, her hand pressed over her mouth. The triumph in her eyes mingled with uneasy anticipation. They had saved Kael this time, but something still felt unfinished.

Kael tilted his head, his eyes flicking to Alysia's lips before searching her face. "I feel...different," he whispered.

She nodded in agreement, her heart fluttering. Another wave of exhaustion threatened to hit her. "You're safe," she whispered, hoping to convince both of them.

His illusions, so often weaving color around him unconsciously, dimmed as though the final synergy had spent them. They drifted in a quiet moment that felt like it existed apart from reality. The broken courtyard, the defeated watchers, every pressing threat, they vanished into the background. Alysia realized with a start how close they were. She could feel the warmth of his breath across her cheek.

She parted her lips to speak, but before she formed the words, he leaned in. The kiss happened without fanfare. No triumphant roar, no whispered incantation. It was a kiss of quiet, desperate affirmation. It tasted of ash, salt, and relief. It wasn't a question, but an answer. A choice. In that moment, she wasn't the scared student or the fated conduit. She was his, and he was hers, and that was the only magic that mattered.

Her heart pounded so loudly that she heard nothing else. She pressed closer, her lips parted against his, trying to convey every promise she could not speak. For a moment, everything stilled. The brand on her palm throbbed, but not in pain, rather as a resonance of shared magic. He felt it, too, because his arms drew her closer in a silent vow that made her chest twist with longing.

Then a crackle of energy sparked along his skin, a soft flash of golden light that made her blink. Warm ribbons of magic seemed to lift off his body as though he were unraveling. Alarm lit her veins. She pulled back, but his grip slackened incrementally, and she watched in horrified disbelief as glowing threads of illusion peeled away from him. It looked like someone gently tugging at the edges of his being, unspooling the lines that bound him to reality.

Alysia gasped, her mind reeling. She threw her arms around him, desperate to keep him solid in her embrace. But the golden aura only flared brighter, turning Kael's form translucent around the edges. "Kael!" she cried, her voice breaking.

"No, no, stay with me."

He touched her cheek with one shimmering hand that was already losing definition. Through the speck of gold, she barely made out his tortured gaze. His lips parted, his voice raw against the inevitable pull of magic.

"You were never supposed to choose me," he whispered.

She felt him dissolve in her arms, the last traces of warmth disappearing. Her hands slipped through empty air. She fell forward onto the dusty flagstones, her breath catching on a sob she could not hold back. Where Kael had stood, a faint shimmer lingered like dust caught in a stray sunbeam. Then that light vanished.

Stunned silence enveloped the courtyard. Alysia stared at the empty space where he had been, her hands still shaped as if holding him. A single golden mote of light, the last echo of his magic, drifted down and dissolved before it reached the ground.

He was gone.

A sob tore from her throat, raw and broken. Robin was there, her hand on Alysia's shoulder, but the comfort felt a universe away. Then something pulsed with warmth against her skin. She looked down. In her trembling palm, where Kael's last touch had been, lay the coral amulet from his neck. It hummed with the faint, fading rhythm of his heartbeat.

Alysia closed her fist around it, the sob catching in her chest. The warmth of the amulet was a promise. The brand on her other hand was a weapon. She would get him back. She stood, the ruins of the courtyard fading into a blur. Her grief was a cold, hard thing, but beneath it, something else took root, a resolve as firm as the cliffs of Velgrace.

They had taken him.

Now she would take them apart.

THE STORY CONTINUES

The story continues book two, *TIDES OF FATE,* coming
soon to Amazon

EXCERPT FROM TIDES OF FATE

CHAPTER ONE

Alysia stood at the edge of the courtyard's rubble, the early morning sky stained by the dull promise of sunrise. The stone tiles beneath her boots still held the faint soot from the recent battle. Yet all she could feel was emptiness in the place where Kael had stood. Three days had crawled by since his abrupt vanishing, and each dawn hurt more than the one before. Her vision blurred, but she refused to let despair claim her.

She clutched a small sigil crystal in her palm, the only remnant of him. Its once-lustrous glow had receded to faint glimmer, but it pulsed gently whenever she called his name in her thoughts. As she paced the courtyard, she heard whispers around her. Murmurs of classmates who believed that Kael had simply fled. Some insisted his illusions had always been dangerous, questioning why.

Alysia would care what had become of him. Others spread rumors about a possible rogue infiltration that ended in Kael's abrupt escape. They all rang hollow in her ears.

Robin approached from the shattered archway, stepping past a collapsed pillar with a quiet sigh. A few healing potions clinked at her hip, trophies from nights spent tending wounded novices. She glanced at Alysia's closed hand.

"You're still out here? You barely slept," Robin said. Her voice was gentle, a stark contrast to her usual teasing.

Alysia lowered her gaze. "I keep thinking I'll find some trace of him if I look long enough." She uncurled her fingers to show Robin the crystal. A pale shimmer ran through it, so faint anyone else might have missed it. "But there's nothing. Just emptiness."

Robin set a comforting hand on Alysia's arm. Her gaze darted across the courtyard, as if mindful of eavesdroppers. At this deserted hour, only a couple of upperclassmen stood watch by the broken wards. "You know the truth," Robin said. "He didn't run. That was no illusion meltdown." Alysia nodded. She remembered the moment Kael dissolved in her arms, the feeling of invisible magic tearing him away. The brand on her palm still burned with the memory, even after the bandages came off. "He was taken," she said. "Something else pulled him or forced him away."

Robin exhaled. "Some of the faculty think differently. Headmistress Quen has been in private meetings all night, and the staff is..."

"Accusing him of treachery?" Alysia's voice hardened.

"Of course. They were always wary, waiting for him to prove their suspicions."

Robin's shoulders tensed. "Not everyone. Magister Belros Dain says no illusions left that kind of residue. Evara Morn is... uncertain. But the rumor mill is vicious. Especially after everything that just happened."

Alysia closed her hand around the crystal. Its faint pulse steadied her. "He never would have left willingly," she whispered. "You saw how he fought to protect this place before."

Sympathy softened Robin's expression. "Quen might need more convincing. She and the others worry about a new infiltration, or a threat from the deeper realms. Whatever the cause, they can't act on guesswork."

"Let them worry." Alysia's throat tightened. She shoved the sigil crystal into the pocket of her robe. "I don't need their permission to find Kael."

Robin's eyes widened, but a hint of approval lit her face. "You have a plan?"

"Not yet," Alysia admitted. "I only know that every time I try to cast a searching ward, it fails. As though something, a barrier, blocks me from detecting him. It feels like shoving magic into a murky void. I get no sense of distance or direction."

Robin lifted her chin in thought. "Have you spoken to Magister Dain about advanced illusions that hide someone's aura? Maybe there's a counter-charm."

Alysia frowned. "He offered to help yesterday, but his leads turned up nothing. We found references to older illusions that can displace living forms, but none matched what happened to Kael. There was no stable gateway or portal. He just... vanished."

She recalled it vividly. The gold around Kael's outline, the feverish heat that rushed between them seconds before the air stole him away. Even now, the memory made her blood pound in her ears. The brand on her palm had flared in painful protest, as though it had tried to anchor him.

They walked, stepping over scorched fragments of ward stones. The handful of watchers near the courtyard entrance pretended not to stare, but Alysia recognized the restless curiosity in their eyes. She couldn't bear their pity. She turned away, guiding Robin through a side corridor that was partially blocked by fallen rubble. A faint light trickled in from broken shutters.

The corridor led them toward a lesser-used wing that connected to the library. The calm there gave Alysia a moment to breathe. She paused at a cracked window that overlooked the ocean. The Sea of Echoes beyond the cliffs roiled, reflecting the color of leaden clouds. Tendrils of morning sun tried to break through.

"He told me once the sea was where he felt closest to his illusions," Alysia said softly. "As if everything in him was drawn to that water."

Robin's gaze followed hers to the surging waves. "Do you think that's where he was taken?"

"I don't know." Alysia pressed her fingertips, still ringed with dried chalk from her last ward attempt, against the glass. "But I sense something about the water. I can't explain it."

She remembered Kael's lineage and how illusions had always responded to the ocean's pull. She remembered the uneasy alliance with merfolk, how the undersea realm thrummed with a distinct magical current. For the first time since Kael vanished, that realization gave her hope.

Robin cleared her throat. "We can search the hidden caverns below the cliffs. The tide's been treacherous lately, but I can try illusions to keep the water parted for a little while. If we find anything, any clue, I'll let you know."

Alysia offered a faint smile. "Thank you. The staff probably won't sanction an underwater expedition right now. That doesn't mean we have to wait."

They left the corridor and slipped into the library's side entrance. A silent hallway greeted them, lined with shelves of ancient scrolls. Glass lanterns burned overhead, illuminating dust motes. In the far corner, two novices sat reading. Neither lifted their head as Alysia and Robin passed.

Alysia knew this was the place to deepen her search if she planned to act without official oversight. She led Robin to a desk stacked with texts. The titles formed a mismatched array of illusions, wards, merfolk lore, and old expedition logs referencing the coastal caverns. Hours passed in a quiet flurry as they tried to pinpoint any phenomenon that could yank a person from reality without leaving a stable portal behind.

At midday, Alysia's eyes ached. She pinned notes on a scrap of parchment with references to ephemeral illusions and living auras caught in half-real energies. It all seemed too vague. Nothing matched how Kael had dissolved into pure, golden sparks.

Earlier that morning she had unearthed a half-destroyed manual wedged behind a row of sea-weathered ledgers. Its brittle pages spoke of a "Shatterspell," a spell of unmaking crafted to sever a parasitic illusion from its host. The instructions ended abruptly, charred lines trailing off beneath hurried warnings that the technique was unfinished and perilous. Her brand flared as her fingers brushed the ink. For a heartbeat, an image slammed into her mind, crushing pressure, the taste of salt and shadow, and Kael's eyes wide with a terror that was not entirely his own.

Alysia copied what she could and tucked the fragments away, unsure if she dared attempt them but sensing they might prove vital in the future.

Robin dropped a final book shut with a soft thud. "No leads," she muttered, sliding it away in frustration. "We're missing something, maybe from the undersea realms. None of these references mention subtle illusions that powerful."

Alysia sat upright, heart pounding with sudden resolve. "Then we focus on the merfolk angle. There must be some older record of illusions bridging the surface to the depths. We have an alliance with them, no matter how strained. I'll ask if any merfolk delegates remain on campus."

Robin nodded, hauling a neat stack of logs to the corner. "I'll see if any leftover watchers near the docks spotted unusual magic. Maybe someone glimpsed a shimmer that night."

They stood, pushing their chairs back, but Alysia paused. The brand on her palm throbbed faintly. She pressed her hand against her chest, trying to quell an ache that felt both magical and heartbreakingly personal. Though her body felt drained, her mind roiled with desperation to find Kael's trail.

Robin waited by the library's arch, noticing her hesitation. "You're not alone, Lyss," she said quietly. "We'll fix this."

Alysia forced a tired nod. Together, they left.

But once Robin was gone, Alysia doubled back to the secluded alcove behind the stacks. From her grandmother's folio she retrieved a cramped set of notes on a locator spell meant to bridge impossible distances. The script warned that any misstep could fracture a mage's mind. Determination overrode caution as she etched the complicated sigils and whispered the clandestine words.

The air thickened. A lance of pain stabbed behind her eyes as the runes spiraled out of control. A crack rang through her thoughts, and then the spell blew apart in a sharp psychic jolt. She staggered, one hand clutching her head while the other smeared blood from her nose across the table. For a heartbeat, the world spun, and silence roared in her ears.

When the agony ebbed, she dragged in a shuddering breath. Failure tasted bitter, but it only fueled her resolve. No backlash would stop her from tracking Kael. She tucked the folio away, jaw set, and wiped the last of the blood from her face.

Later that afternoon, Alysia roamed toward the triage station to check on injured classmates. One or two retreated at her approach, fear etched in their expressions. She felt a sharp pang. Apparently, when Kael vanished, that fear had only grown. Rumors soared that Alysia was cursed, that the Thorne brand had devoured him, or that she had performed a forbidden ritual. The weight of it made her chest tighten.

Still, she pressed on, stopping only when Warden Evara Morn intercepted her. Morn wore worn training leathers, her forearms bandaged from the night of the illusions. She studied Alysia's face with an unreadable expression.

"A word?" the warden asked simply.

Alysia braced herself. "Of course."

They moved into a side courtyard, less destroyed than the main square. Weary apprentices restocked supplies from crates stacked under an overhang. Morn lowered her voice. "I know the gossip. And I know you claim Kael didn't flee."

"He didn't," Alysia said, meeting the older woman's gaze.

"A few of us believe that might be true," Morn replied. She scanned the area, making sure no one else listened. "Illusions that are strong enough to remove someone entirely are rare, but possible. If you have any evidence that an external force took him, I want to see it."

Alysia inhaled sharply. At last, a glimmer of official support. She withdrew the sigil crystal from her pocket. Its faint glow caught Morn's eye. "It's linked to Kael's aura," Alysia said. "It never died. I've never seen a synergy crystal remain active once its owner is gone. Maybe that means he's... somewhere else."

Morn's expression shifted from skepticism to measured understanding. She reached out but didn't actually touch the crystal. "All right," she murmured. "I'll keep the corridors clear if you want to search the lower vaults for more leads. But do it quietly. The staff is fracturing over this debacle. If they suspect you're stirring illusions..."

"I understand," Alysia said.

They parted, and she exhaled with determination. The warden's subtle support might buy her enough time to follow the single clue she had. The merfolk.

By late evening, she retreated to her dorm. She had spent the intervening hours briefing Robin on Morn's discreet assistance, sending Robin to gather illusions supplies for a nighttime foray into the vaults if needed. But exhaustion gnawed at Alysia's nerves. She still wore the same soot-stained cloak from earlier. The second she lay on her narrow bed, a wave of fatigue pulled her under.

Her dreams were a mix of confusion. Whispers of illusions, frantic images of Kael standing at the edge of a vast underwater city. The vision rippled, replaced by phantom shapes that lunged at her from currents. At the center of the chaos, Kael stretched out his hand toward her, eyes imploring, but no sound emerged.

Then a sudden pulse of pale light flared in the dreamscape, and the sigil crystal in her hand glowed luminous, brighter than it ever had since the moment Kael vanished. An echoing voice drifted through the haze, words hissing like a distant tide, "Follow the current."

She bolted awake, heart hammering. A film of sweat covered her skin despite the chilled air. She groped for the crystal by her pillow, and its glow persisted, releasing one more pulse of that command. The moment felt more vivid than any normal dream. The brand on her palm blazed with renewed intensity.

Alysia pressed both palms to her face, breath catching in a tremor. She remembered the ocean's dark horizon from earlier. Follow the current. She had no illusions about what that might mean. Kael's illusions were bound to the sea, to the realm beneath. She recalled the uneasy diplomacy with merfolk. She recalled Kael saying once those illusions drifted between worlds, just like undersea tides.

She shoved aside the blankets. Her entire body shook with adrenaline. Robin, sprawled on a spare cot near the desk, jerked upright at the sudden movement. "What?" Robin mumbled, blinking in confusion.

"I saw him," Alysia whispered, voice trembling. "Not clearly. But I saw Kael." Her pulse pounded in her ears. "He looked trapped, or lost, underwater. And I heard an instruction. 'Follow the current.'"

Robin shot to her feet, pushing tangled hair out of her eyes. "Tell me everything. Slowly."

Alysia cradled the crystal against her chest, describing the dream's fractured images. Through it all, the phrase repeated in her mind. "It wasn't just a dream," she finished. "It felt like... a real connection."

Robin's features darkened with worry. "That's enough for me. If Kael is somewhere beyond the surface, we need to focus our search underwater. The staff can cast doubt all they want, but this is the second sign we've had pointing to the merfolk realm."

Alysia nodded, breathing fast. The final dregs of fear fell away, replaced by a fierce determination. For days, she had wandered on the brink of despair, haunted by the emptiness of Kael's absence. But now she had at least one tangible path forward.

Robin dragged a trunk open, rummaging for traveling supplies. Potions, flash-lamps that could glow beneath water for a short time, extra rune-carved shells used for breathing spells. "We'll gather more resources in the morning," Robin said in a strained voice, mindful of other dorm residents. "You'll want to check with Morn or any merfolk delegates left on campus. If we can talk them into letting us into their domain..."

Alysia listened, already planning out the conversation in her head. The merfolk might be reluctant to help if they believed Kael had triggered a dangerous magic. But Alysia wouldn't let that stop her.

She sank onto the edge of her bed, the crystal warm in her hand, reminding her that her fight wasn't over. The single phrase from her dream reverberated through her thoughts. Follow the current.

She locked her gaze with Robin's, who balanced potions and a worn map in her arms. An unspoken accord passed between them. They would find Kael, no matter how deep they had to go.

Alysia's heart pounded with equal parts dread and hope. She felt the brand on her palm tingle, as if echoing the vow. Somehow, the Sea of Echoes shimmered in her mind, as though calling to them with invisible tides.

Before either of them could speak again, the crystal's glow flared so sharply that its light filled the dorm room in a brilliant flash. Alysia jolted, and Robin gasped, nearly dropping the potions. She closed her fingers over the crystal protectively, and for an instant, she heard Kael's voice in her memory. She couldn't catch any clear words, only the lingering warmth of him.

The flash settled, leaving her breath ragged. She realized the path ahead was more dangerous than any they had walked. Yet an unshakable certainty took root in her chest. This was the next step. If illusions had stolen Kael away, illusions or wards would bring him back.

She exchanged a final glance with Robin, whose face shone with determination. Neither needed to speak further. They had preparations to make, truths to uncover, and a realm beneath the waves to confront. The war wasn't over, and Kael wasn't gone.

OTHER FLORID ROMANCE BOOKS

To be notified of new releases and special promotions from Florid Romance, please join our email list:

https://floridromance.lmbpn.com/about/sign-up-for-our-newsletter/

For a complete list of books published by Florid Romance please visit our website:

https://floridromance.lmbpn.com/

BOOKS BY RIVER TATUM

The Dating Diary
One is too Many BF's (Book 1)
Two Many Choices (Book 2)
Three is a Crowd (Book 3)
Four is a Disaster (Book 4)

The Dreamweaver's Pact
Whispering Dreams (Book 1)
Shattered Nightmares (Book 2)
Dawn Awakening (Book 3)

The Elemental Chronicles
Fire and Water (Book 1)
Earth and Sky (Book 2)
Chaos and Harmony (Book 3)

The Cursed Worm Court
The Healer and The Dragon (Book 1)

The Dragon's Bargain (Book 2)
Vows and Wings of Flame (Book 3)

Marked By Magic
Spellcasters (Book 1)
Tides of Fate (Book 2)

BOOKS BY MICHAEL ANDERLE

CONNECT WITH MICHAEL ANDERLE

Website: http://lmbpn.com

Email List: https://michael.beehiiv.com/

https://www.facebook.com/LMBPNPublishing

https://twitter.com/MichaelAnderle

https://www.instagram.com/lmbpn_publishing/

https://www.bookbub.com/authors/michael-anderle

www.ingramcontent.com/pod-product-compliance
Lightning Source LLC
Chambersburg PA
CBHW030337010826
48973CB00004B/1043